Virginia Smith was born in London in 1968. She grew up in Essex, studied in Liverpool, and now lives in Southampton, where she works part-time in a library. Her poetry and short stories have appeared in various magazines and journals. *The Ropemaker's Daughter* is her first published novel.

The Ropemaker's Daughter

VIRGINIA SMITH

First published 2002 by Diva Books,
an imprint of Millivres Prowler Limited, part of the Millivres Prowler Group,
Worldwide House, 116-134 Bayham Street, London NW1 0BA
www.divamag.co.uk

A catalogue record for this book is available from the British Library

ISBN 1 873741 70 7

Printed and bound in Finland by WS Bookwell

Distributed in the UK and Europe by Airlift Book Company,
8 The Arena, Mollison Avenue,
Enfield, Middlesex EN3 7NJ
Telephone: 020 8804 0400
Distributed in North America by Consortium,
1045 Westgate Drive, St Paul, MN 55114-1065
Telephone: 1 800 283 3572
Distributed in Australia by Bulldog Books,
PO Box 300, Beaconsfield, NSW 2014

Acknowledgements

My thanks go to Alison MacLeod and John Saunders, at University College, Chichester, for their early advice and encouragement on this book, and to Chandler's Ford Writers Group for the same things, only later.

I'd also like to thank Helen Sandler, Kathleen Bryson and Gillian Rodgerson, at Diva Books, for their insight; and my wonderful agent, Jane Conway-Gordon, for her continuing faith in me.

My thanks go too to my friends and family, who've stuck around over the last few years and not buggered off on a fag break when I needed them most, especially Bridget Outridge, Maggie McLean, Phil Heard, Yo Tozer-Loft, Laura Ciftci, Oliver Turner, Jacqui Searle, Chris and Graham Cox, Heather Lee-Robichaud, Katherine McKenzie, Mary Pearson, Helen and Darren Cadman, Rebecca Perrott, Imogen Hill and, of course, Eliot (who put up with a lot in the writing of this book).

Last but not least, I'd like to thank Diana Moffat and Michelle Webber for the Caesars, extra spicy, and the unforgettable dancing at Hugo's.

This is for my dad

One

It wasn't always like this. Way back, when it began, I was in control, cool and clever, feeling the tight fizz of success burning in my body, bubbling from my fingertips. And it was easy after all, that first time; the hot flush of touch, the moment of self-forgetting.

I used to go to London for the day back then; travel into the city on a sweaty underground train, and then wander around the National Gallery, pretending to look at the pictures. I wasn't actually there for the pictures, of course. I was there to follow artistic-looking people along crowded corridors, to breathe the tang of leftover cigarette smoke on their clothes, slither myself into the leathery shadow of their jackets. I'd sit alongside them in the cafeteria and listen to their conversations, to the way they talked to each other, and it was as if they had invented a whole world for themselves; a world illuminated by artistry and intellect and imagination. I *longed* to be like them, to transform myself into someone with something important to think about. In reality, I had nothing to think about. I was still living at home, still at school, wearing my dark hair long like a child and eating what my mother cooked.

Sooner or later at the National, I'd begin to grow impatient with what I couldn't have, with who I couldn't be, and then I would want to let it all go, sink myself back into the sweet grey of what was true. It was easier to believe in. I'd let the truth lull me all the way home on the train, until I was safe inside my mother's house, with 'A' level re-vision to do and a late film to watch on TV. I'd draw the curtains tight closed, no light from outside, the cat would curl in my lap, and that was all there was. The rest was only ever going to be fabrication, and I knew the difference. I knew what was real.

But there was one day, back then, when something different hap-pened. I can remember standing on the platform at Embankment stat-ion and struggling to unscrew the tight cap from a bottle of Coke that I'd bought at a nearby kiosk. I wasn't having much success. I was just about to give up and stuff the bottle back into my leather rucksack, when someone touched my arm, very lightly, so lightly in fact that I thought at first they'd done it by accident and didn't even look up. But then someone spoke, quite close to my ear, and turning, I saw a very small, very dark man looking at me expectantly, his white teeth showing slightly in a smile.

"Can I... er...?" He made an unscrewing gesture with his hands. "You are having problem?"

His accent was strange – not English – the ends of his words linger-ing as he spoke them, each new sound nestling against the one before.

I stepped away, startled for a moment by his friendliness. People on the underground aren't usually friendly, but this man didn't look threatening. There was a sports bag down by his feet, and the sleeves of his grey shirt were rolled up over sinewy brown arms, and his smile wasn't one of those meaningful twitchy ones with something else un-derneath. He was just smiling, casual, wanting to help out, so I handed him the bottle and he unscrewed the cap in one easy twist.

"Thanks," I said quietly, and he slipped it back into my hands and watched me lift it to my lips – a bright tickle of bubbles against my teeth.

I wanted to say something else, something friendly, but my voice was swallowed suddenly by the clatter and rush of an approaching train. The little man continued to smile, his hair ruffling up onto his forehead and down again in a musty breeze.

I sipped distractedly at my Coke, then slipped the half empty bottle into my bag. The little man didn't speak to me again, although now and then, I caught the sound of him humming to himself under his breath. I wasn't familiar with the sound he was making, but it was a nice sound, lively and exotic, as if there might be castanets and balalaikas in the background. Each time he glanced back along the platform, he would make sure to catch my eye and smile, and each time, I smiled back.

When the District Line train eventually arrived, I stepped on board and settled myself into a corner seat at the end of a long orange row, started to feel around inside my bag for my book, when suddenly, the little man from the platform was standing in front of me and gesturing to the seat next to mine.

"May I sit?" His eyebrows were slightly raised, and he was already sitting himself down by my side, crossing his legs and turning to look at me.

"You have friendly face," he said, bouncing his crossed leg up and down a little and looking pleased with himself. "Friendly face. Yes."

I stared hard at his up-and-down foot in its raggedy white trainer, concentrating hard on the frayed laces and not knowing what to say in reply, but then he dipped his dark head towards me confidentially and smiled at me with his teeth.

"My name is Hameed." And up close, I could see that his teeth were even whiter than before, glinting at me beneath the spangled lights of the carriage. His brown face was all crumpled up like it needed ironing, and his white teeth were grinning like they'd never stop. I found myself staring at them, transfixed for a moment, and smiling back in spite of myself.

"And *your* name?" he enquired, almost shyly I thought at first, although when my eyes managed to break free from his smile, I could see by the rest of his face that it wasn't shyness at all; more a kind of belated gallantry. His backing off a little and giving me a chance to manoeuvre, a chance to escape, meant it would have been easy after

3

all to turn my head away from this stranger, bury my nose in my book and let him sit there smiling all the way home with no one to talk to, but I didn't.

Instead I cleared my throat and said quietly, "Rebecca."

"Rebecca..." and my name sounded so *nice* when he said it. He seemed to roll it around in his mouth for a while, lingering over the 'R' and sounding out each little 'c' so that I ended up sounding like someone different, like someone *completely* different. "That is a lovely name. Where does it come from?"

I shrugged, shook my head. "I don't know. I've never thought about it really."

"Aaah, you should. It is important to know what your name means, what root you come from." He sat back in his seat and folded his fingers across his stomach. "My name, it comes from the desert."

"Really?"

"Yes. I come from Morocco. My family, they live there still, but I move here to live with my cousin in Ley-ton-stone." He said the word carefully, enunciating each of the syllables, as if to make sure he was talking about the right place. "I come here to study," and he smiled a little ruefully, tilted his head to one side. "And of course, to make better my English."

"Your English is very good."

"You think so?"

"I do."

His face brightened. "I am pleased you think so. I like English. I like England."

"Isn't it cold for you, after Morocco?"

"No, no. I like cold. I like rain. I love to play the football in rain. That is where I am going now." He pointed to the sports bag nestling like a cat at his feet. "I am going to leisure centre at Dagen-*h*am East, to play the football."

"In the rain?"

He nodded; a big nod, friendly. "If there *is* rain."

And I could feel myself warming to him, inexplicably; growing comfortable. "Oh, there's bound to be. You *are* in England after all."

"Aaah, yes. *Very* different to Morocco."

I closed my book tight shut and slipped it back into my bag, and then I looked at him, looked into his face properly like I hadn't before.

"Tell me," I said at last, diffident, still a little uncertain, but unscrewing the cap from my bottle of Coke and offering it to him. "What's Morocco like?"

And he told me, told me all his history in a smile, his words spilling soft like water in a channel that stretched the entire length of the carriage. People didn't seem to notice that their shoes were filling up with water, with the rhythm of Hameed's words. They carried on reading their newspapers and staring at their reflections in the windows as if nothing new were happening. But I listened, felt my heart floating out to somewhere it had never been. He whispered me a desert, where the sands were icing-sugar smooth and camels strolled the day away and licked their lips at nothing in the noonday heat. Behind his eyes, green palms were swaying, their long leaves pointing like fingers, far away to the Kasbah and the bustling souk; market noise where swathes of coloured cloth billowed out to meet my grey suburban senses, swirl them soft, make them into something new. I listened hard to all he said, to all his smile wanted to tell me. I drank in the sky and the whisper and the pin-prick pictures that he poured into the air, but suddenly he was grabbing his bag and standing to leave.

"Dagen-*h*am East!" he cried, his face anguished, his fingers reaching out to clasp my own. "I must leave you…"

And it sounded special, for him to say that. Not *I've got to get off* or *This is my stop*, but *I must leave you*, like he had no choice, like it was the last thing in the world he wanted to do.

"I thank you for listening… Rebecca." He lifted my hand from my lap and brought it to his lips for a moment, just like in the films, right there in front of all those people. "Perhaps we meet again." And then he was gone, smiling, subsumed into the hazy platform crowd.

All the way home, I felt the bristling touch of sand between my toes, as if I'd been where his words had tried to take me, but when the train pulled into my station and I fell into step with the throng of people elbowing out through the ticket barriers and heading for the bus, I knew I hadn't been anywhere, because here I was, on home ground again, and nothing had changed, *nothing* was different.

I trudged up the hill towards the bus stop, with my head down, feeling the sudden sting of rain against my cheeks, and I thought of Hameed in his raggedy old trainers, running across a football pitch in Dagenham East, lifting his face to the sky, tasting the English rain, and the thought made me smile, made me glad. The fact that he had chosen *me*, chosen to tell his story to *me*, made me glad; so glad, in fact, that I was able to lift my head a little and straighten up, proud to show my *friendly face* to the hunched-up group murmuring beneath the bus shelter.

As I approached, I caught sight of someone I recognised. A boy I'd known at junior school, a boy I'd been crazy about (as far as it was possible for a ten-year-old girl to be crazy about anything that wasn't featured in *Just Seventeen* magazine or in an episode of *Beverly Hills 90210*). I remembered his name though. Gary Light; let-there-be-light in Rebecca's dark world – a golden swirl of hair like a girl's and the nicest hands, long tapering fingers, *piano fingers*, as my mother would have called them, except that my mother never knew that I liked Gary Light, and, of course, neither did he. In fact, he didn't know I existed.

Today though, fired by something I couldn't quite name, infused with a strange confidence, I was determined that he *should* know that I existed, and, oddly too, that he should be *glad* I did.

He was at the head of the queue, and when I reached him, I smiled broadly and stepped right in front of him, so he couldn't avoid me.

"Hello. I thought I recognised you."

He peered at me through the rain, furrowing his eyebrows a little.

"How've you been?" I leant against the bus shelter window in a chummy sort of a way and tried to ignore the fact that he obviously hadn't the faintest idea who I was.

"I haven't seen you for..." I shook my head. "Well, must be seven years, I reckon."

He opened his mouth to speak, closed it again, and smiled a very small, puzzled smile.

"What've you been doing since junior school? What senior school did you go to?"

He seemed to mellow a little. "Kingsgate," and then he paused, looking at me hard. "And you?"

"Oh, I'm at St. David's. Nearly finished now though."

"Right."

An uncomfortable silence grew, during which we both squinted into the distance, looking for the bus.

"I haven't been there much this term though," I said gravely. "I've been, er... well, I've been abroad mostly."

"Abroad?"

"Yeah. I've been visiting my boyfriend, in Morocco."

"Morocco? That must've been pretty cool."

"It was." I could feel my heart beating fast, exultant, because look, Gary Light *was* pleased to see me. He was listening now, absorbed and curious, and even though I knew he didn't remember me from school, it didn't matter, because now I was a new person for him, interesting and exotic. I was someone he *would* remember. "We visited Tangier and then travelled out into the desert."

"Yeah?"

"Uh huh. We spent, ooh... at least six weeks trekking across the country, on camels."

"On camels!" His face was incredulous.

"Oh yes, and the moon at night was huge, like a lantern, almost like you could reach out and touch it."

This was exactly what Hameed had told me. I'd liked hearing it then, when he'd said it, and I liked it even more now that it was *mine* to tell. Gary Light was smiling.

"I went to junior school with you, right?"

"Yep." Catching sight of my bus approaching, I slipped my ruck-sack from my shoulder and pulled out my purse. "You used to yank my hair in Miss Whitehand's music lessons."

"Did I?" He had the grace to look embarrassed for a moment.

"And you'd never choose me for your rounders team either." I had to raise my voice a little, as the rumbling bus eased in beside us. I stepped back to let some of the people behind me get on first.

"This isn't my bus," he explained, moving towards me.

"Guess I'll be seeing you then."

"That'd be good. It's been nice talking to you, er... I'm sorry, but I can't seem to remember your name."

I climbed onto the bus and glanced back over my shoulder. "Rebecca," I prompted. "Rebecca Ward."

Gary Light's mouth opened in surprise, and as the automatic doors hushed to a close between us, I waved, just with my fingers, coquet-tish, playful, and he waved back, and gave me a huge smile.

I grinned to myself all the way home, rejoicing inside like I never had before, because it had been *so* easy, so easy to lie, to make him be-lieve that I really *had* been to Morocco. A few stolen phrases, a couple of camels thrown in for good measure, and he had believed me. More than that, better than that – he had *liked* me because of it and had wanted to talk to me. I'd always thought it impossible to become someone new, to change my colours, but it had happened, just for a moment; caterpillar into butterfly, stretching my wings in the blue, riding warm currents of air, and it didn't even seem to matter that those currents of air were lies. Nobody need know that they were lies, after all. Nobody would be hurt by them.

That was how it began, all that time ago. I never intended to do it again. It was just going to be that once, with Gary Light, but the taste of it had been *so* seductive, an opiate sweetness, poppy-red. I couldn't give it up, couldn't resist it. That was how it began, all that time ago. That was how it began. *This* is how it will end.

Two

I met a man last Thursday, a new man, a day of change, like that first day with Hameed, except that this time, *I* am not in control. *He* is.

Less than a week ago I met him, but already my world has shrunk to fit the spaces in his speech, the tiny circles of sunlight reflected in the lenses of the little glasses he wears. His eyes were smiling when we met, and although there was something else there too, something behind the smile, I didn't back away. I moved forward to greet it.

I look for smiles, because people who smile at you before they know you tend to be slightly gullible, seeking approval, willing to tell all if it means friendship, willing to listen and to believe; the perfect invitation for a storyteller like me, and *he* was smiling as he brought his books to the counter that day, ambling towards the counter; casual, disarming. I made him keep eye contact with me. I made it happen, or thought I did.

I work at the university, in the library, breathing in the long-grown must of corridors, angles of learning, pages pale-ochre with age. It's the ideal place for me, a hiding place – a place for my changing face to close and blend, to lose itself in a haze of hurrying students. I am only a few years older than they and can dress to make myself a square in the mosaic. Nobody thinks I am anything out of the ordinary, and of course I'm not, until I choose to be. I sit quietly, file stock cards until my fingertips burn, play computer keys as if they are the keys of a piano. An Ashkenazy of the fiction, that's me. I'm good with fiction.

That day, that Thursday, I was bored and restless. I'd been on counter duty all morning, but nobody interesting had come to have their books issued. A slack day for me, no potential; but then I spotted someone moving quickly through the crowd, and as he approached, I felt the old excitement begin to gather. I opened my mouth a little to the taste of it, and waited.

He was borrowing a stack of books on North American poetry – Walt Whitman mostly, some Robert Lowell, Sylvia Plath. I stamped them slowly; making sure the return date was dead straight on every label, as if I took pride in my work. I wanted him to think that I did, that it mattered to me, because people will trust a librarian, especially a conscientious one. There's nothing safer after all, nothing less threatening than a librarian who loves her work.

All the while, his pale fingers rested on the edge of the counter, both hands, his body leaning in behind them, and each time I raised my eyes from my work, he was looking at me and smiling.

I didn't smile back at first, kept my head low, but when I'd stamped all his books and he was reaching for them, I opened the last of them and began flicking through its pages.

"Do you like Sylvia Plath?" I asked him, stopping randomly at a long poem and pretending to read.

"Very much." And his voice wasn't at all what I'd expected. It seemed to have no depth, no resonance: a strangely piping tone. It was soft. Its cadence was soft, like a whisper, curling up at the corners, and it took me by surprise.

I glanced up from the book, still not smiling, not giving anything away, and asked mildly, "What do you like about her?"

He opened his bag and began dropping the volumes inside it.

"I like the fact that she doesn't care what she says, or who she offends." Lifting the Plath book from my hands, he closed it with a snap. "I like how unconcerned she is about who she hurts."

Inclining my head a little, I folded my hands together on the counter in a sage-like manner. "Odd thing to like."

He leant towards me then, and I caught the cool tang of wine on his breath, and something else beneath it; aftershave, a vaguely familiar scent – sweet like laburnum, like the mottled taste of fern. He zipped closed his bag and lifting it onto his shoulder, asked, "Why do *you* like her?"

I shook my head. "I don't."

"No?" He looked sceptical.

"I think she's mediocre."

He glanced over his shoulder at the gathering queue of students shuffling behind him, and nodded pleasantly to the girl who was next in the queue. For a moment I thought he'd forgotten all about me, but then he turned back.

"So you don't like her?"

I shook my head again, decisive, watched him run his fingers back through his hair; coarse hair, thick, iron-dark, but streaked with lighter strands, as if the sun were moving through it in the places where his fingers moved. He looked at me steadily, sure of himself.

"If you don't like her," he whispered, dipping his head towards me as if with a secret, "why do you carry a copy of *Ariel* with you everywhere you go?"

I sat back on my stool, and took a breath sharp into my lungs. "What?"

He leant his elbow on the counter for a moment, rested his chin on his upturned palm as if he meant to stay, and leaning even further in, he winked at me. "Nothing's sacred any more is it? Nothing's a secret these days." Straightening up suddenly, he began to move away, "I'll be seeing you, Rebecca." And he was gone, swallowed up in the hustle of the crowd, spirited away to somewhere else, with my name and a secret that I couldn't fathom. How did he know my name? How did he know that I carried a copy of Sylvia Plath's *Ariel* in my bag? *How* did he know that? Who had told him? No one had told him, because no one else knew.

11

I stamped the next person's books distractedly, twice missed the date label altogether and stamped 16th October 2000 on the text itself.

"Hey!" An irritated-looking girl with spirally blonde hair was standing in front of me, pointing a long finger at my carelessness. "Watch what you're doing."

"Sorry." I piled up her books as neatly as I could and eased them across to her.

She gathered them against her chest, but didn't move away. Instead, she sighed and her face softened a little. Lifting a stick of chewing gum from her jacket pocket, she unwrapped it and popped it into her mouth.

"Don't let him get to you," she advised, beginning to chew, her tone conspiratorial now and sisterly.

"Pardon?"

"That guy you were talking to. Adam." She gestured into the crowd, waving her free hand in the direction that the man in glasses had taken. "Don't let him get to you. I don't know what he said to you, but he has a way of winding people up, does it *all* the time." Lifting her books from the counter, she tucked them under her arm and began to back away. "He gets off on it, you know. Just ignore him." Her mouth caught hold of a smile for a moment, then let it go. She waved to me. "See ya." Then she was gone too.

Too many things were happening at once. I tried hard to concentrate on what I was doing, but it was no good. Just before lunch, I asked to be relieved and hurried away to the ladies, where I locked myself into a cubicle and leant heavily back against the door.

Adam. How did he know my name? Well, that wasn't difficult. He'd heard one of my colleagues use it, of course he had; someone talking to me on the counter, or calling me for coffee, or he'd seen it written on the timetable. Simple. I relaxed against the door, letting my shoulder blades push back against its weight. I could feel the grainy contours of the chipboard through the thin cotton of my top. But how did he know about the Sylvia Plath book? I'd always felt a little embarrassed about carrying a copy of *Ariel* around with me, as if I couldn't do without it – a security blanket of sorts. I certainly didn't make a habit of telling people that it was in my bag. So how did *he* know it was there? And then I remembered. Of *course*. One lunchtime last week, I'd gone outside to eat my sandwiches beneath the trees. It was the first of those unseasonably warm days we'd been having and the air was very still, sweet with the first tang of autumn. A few seagulls had come flapping in from the docks and were stalking across the grass like they owned the place, dancing behind the little groups of people scattered across the green, then ducking their yellow beaks into bags and taking off with sandwiches, half-eaten chocolate bars. Indignant students were everywhere, chasing after stolen goods, angry at first, then leaning forward on their knees, out of breath and beginning to laugh. Everywhere it seemed, people were laughing.

I lay down flat on the grass and shielded my eyes against the white of the sun, and the ground was warm beneath my body; electric blanket warm. It seemed to give a little, accommodating my shape. I leant across to my bag and, ferreting around inside it, my fingers closed on the spine of a book. *Ariel*. Taking the book out of my bag, I opened it up and began to read, and that's when he must have seen me. With sunlight and words in my eyes, I saw nothing, felt only the light chill of shadows passing across the grass. He must have been one of those shadows, must have recognised me from the library and then looked at the book I was reading. Of course. That had to be it.

Still a little uneasy, but feeling calmer, I hurried back down to the counter, gathered together my belongings and wandered outside to eat my lunch. Finding a vacant tree for myself, I sat down beneath it, leant my head back against the nubbled bark and closed my eyes.

How gratifying it is to think you've unravelled something, to feel yourself superior in slotting a piece of jigsaw into place. I sat under the tree that day, that Thursday, less than a week ago, and let the warmth of the sun sink right through to my bones, listening to the confidential whispers of couples as they passed, sinking myself into ease, and by the time I arrived back at the library counter for my afternoon shift, I was vaguely aglow with sunlight and satisfaction, complacent again, all smiles. In no time at all, I had engaged a French student in comical conversation over a pile of sports science textbooks, asking him what exactly sports science entailed, and if he was enjoying his studies? Could he tell me a little more about it perhaps, as I was *very* interested? Of course he could. He'd be glad to. How about meeting up after work? The French café on East Street maybe? Perfect. See you at six... It nearly always followed this same pattern. At first they were a little shy, reticent, but as soon as I made eye contact and started asking some questions, as soon as they saw that I was interested and that I *meant* it, they breathed out, relaxed. All the reserve that usually hangs between strangers suddenly breaking apart like candy floss and drifting off towards the ceiling, until there we were, facing each other and smiling like old friends.

This time, it was going to be even easier than usual because a week or so earlier, I had met a man who had told me a long and tragic tale about an old girlfriend of his who'd had a nervous breakdown after a failed love affair with a Frenchman in the Pyrenees. I'd squeezed every detail out of him; the girlfriend's history, what it was like living in France, how she'd been treated by the locals, because I recognised what potential there was for myself in a story like that, and tonight of course, it *would* be my story. *I* would be the girlfriend, traumatised by my past suffering, but bearing my troubles with grace and self-possession, vulnerable, deeply in need of love and attention. I couldn't have asked for a better lie to feed on.

He was there before me, the Frenchman, dapper in a pale green shirt and a pair of chinos. He reminded me of Hameed. I remember thinking how much he looked like Hameed. He stood up to greet me as I approached the table he'd chosen for us, and reached out to take my hand. At first I thought he was going to stoop and kiss it, but he didn't. Instead, he shook it a little awkwardly and gestured for me to sit down.

"I thought you had perhaps changed your mind," he said, craning his neck a little to catch the waiter's attention.

I eased my arms out of my denim jacket and folded it gently over the back of my seat. "No. I never break dates. Do you?"

He shook his head solemnly and handed a menu to me just as the waiter arrived by my side, a small stub of pencil poised above his pad.

"Er..." I scanned the exhaustive list of baguettes and savoury croissants. "Just a cappuccino, please."

He nodded at his pad a little impatiently and, without writing anything down, hurried away towards the kitchen.

"Nothing to eat?" asked the Frenchman, slightly pained. "No wine?" He lifted his own glass towards me.

"Not just yet, thanks." And I leant slowly forward then, elbows planted close together on the table. "So anyway," smiling at him, focused and intimate. "How is it you come to be in England?"

He shrugged his shoulders. "The colleges were more better here." He even spoke like Hameed. "The sports facilities..." He hesitated, started again. "My father, he wanted me to have the best education I could, and that was here, in England, not at home."

"Sounds like *my* father." I glanced meaningfully down at the table.

"Oh? In what way like your father?"

"Oh, you know." I hedged for a moment, as if considering whether or not to share a confidence, and then I sighed, lifted my eyes to meet his. "He wanted me to have the best education, too. Ironic really, because he sent me to France to find it!"

The Frenchman looked pleased. "Really? So you have lived in France."

I nodded, reaching into my bag for a pack of cigarettes and a small red lighter.

"But where in France? Perhaps near to *my* family."

"A little village called Najac. I was at a kind of... well, a kind of finishing school, I guess." I placed the cigarettes and the lighter next to me on the table. I don't smoke, but they always look good, I think; sexy. I folded my arms.

"I do not think I know Najac."

"It's near a town called Figeac, in the Pyrenees."

"The Pyrenees. Not my part of France, then. I come from Paris."

"Aaah, I see." A stroke of luck.

"How long did you live there?"

I sat back in my chair, began to chew my bottom lip. "Not long."

"You were not happy?"

"I *was* happy, at first."

The waiter paused at our table for a moment after he had set my cappuccino down, waiting to see if we wanted anything else, but I was centred now, rapt, the old power cupped inside me; the pearl inside the oyster. I waved him away.

"You did not stay happy?" The Frenchman took a sip of wine, the corners of his mouth turning down.

"No, I didn't" – a pause for maximum effect, a tiny sob in the voice – "There was a man, from the village. He let me down very badly, lied to me. I had to come home. I've been ill, you see, very ill because of it, and I'm not well yet, and I..."

He looked up abruptly from his glass, stricken. "I am *so* sorry," and he reached across the table, taking firm hold of my hand, and he *did* look sorry. Oh my God! More than that – horrified almost, aghast. I thought I saw tears in his eyes.

"Er..." And I was confused for a moment, taken unawares, because I knew that my fake sadness, as authentic as I would try to make it, wasn't going to match his *actual* sadness, not by a long shot. He was *actually* sad for me, not just being polite, not just patting my hand and saying *there, there* in the distracted way that most of them did. No, this man was genuinely, embarrassingly sad, and that was when I felt it, just then, as he was squeezing my hand, tears in his eyes, meaning it.

That was when I felt it; the first real pang of guilt I'd ever felt. I was ashamed. I tried to shake it away, mumbled something about the doctors being very hopeful for my new medication, and took a huge gulp of my coffee.

He sat staring at me, his mouth opening and closing like a fish.

"It's all right," I assured him. "Really."

He shook his head, incredulous. "But how *can* it be all right?"

And of course, he was right. It couldn't be. If it had actually happened to anyone, it couldn't be all right, and then I remembered of course, that it *had* happened to someone, the girl from whom I'd stolen the story, and I had to take another gulp of coffee to stop myself from confessing the whole thing right there.

It was as I swallowed, my lips burning against the steaming froth in my cup, that I heard a voice behind me.

"Well, *fancy* meeting you here."

I turned around to see who it was, hoping that it would be one of my colleagues from the library, someone who would pull up a chair and sit down with us, lull the conversation into normality. But it wasn't one of my colleagues from the library. It was Adam.

"May I join you?" But there was no time to say no. He had already commandeered a seat from the next table and was shuffling in close.

The Frenchman looked at me expectantly, but I didn't know what to say. I could feel Adam's elbow taut against my own.

I leant forward a little; and spoke to the Frenchman in a whisper. "Would you like to go on somewhere else? A pub or something?"

But Adam was leaning forward, too. "Well, I don't think you're being very courteous, Rebecca."

I glanced back at him, and found that his eyes, up close, were familiar, very dark and familiar in a way that the eyes in a portrait are sometimes familiar; as if you have met the person before, even though you can't have done because they're Mary Queen of Scots or Disraeli or someone. Either way, I was sure I hadn't met him before; not before this morning, anyway.

I fixed him with a look of casual irritation. "Look, if you don't mind, this is a private conversation."

"My favourite kind."

The Frenchman breathed a small laugh. "You two are friends, I see. You joke with each other. Perhaps I should go."

"No." I caught hold of his hand. "There's no need for you to go. We're *not* friends. I don't even know who he is."

Adam sat back in his chair and folded his arms. "Oh now, come *on*, pretending we don't know each other, indeed."

"We don't." I could feel my cheeks beginning to burn. "Why don't you just go?"

He shook his head slowly, turned to the Frenchman. "So then, Pierre..."

"Jean-Paul. My name is Jean-Paul."

And it was the first time I'd heard his name. I hadn't even bothered to ask him his name.

"Whatever." Adam reached for my cup and took a sip from it. "What's Rebecca been telling you about herself, then? Anything interesting?"

Jean-Paul shrugged, and glanced a little nervously at me. "We have been getting to know each other, that is all."

"Really? And what have you found out about her?"

"Why don't you just leave us alone?" I tried again, but my voice this time was trembling, and I was bewildered to find that his hand was resting on my thigh beneath the table. "What do you *want*?"

He turned to me and gave a theatrical sigh. "I just want Pierre to tell me what you've been talking about, that's all."

"Look," Jean-Paul was standing up and pulling on his jacket. "I don't know what is being done here, or who you are, but you are making fun of me, I think..."

"No, no. Not at all. I'm not making fun of you, just being friendly. Please, sit down."

Jean-Paul hovered. "I do not think you are being friendly."

"No?"

"No. I think you are laughing." He turned his gaze on me. "Both of you."

I shook my head at him, tried to stand, but Adam's grip tightened on my leg.

"I am sorry for what bad things happened to you, Rebecca, but..."

"What's this?" Adam's grip tightened. I could feel his fingernails, sharp.

Jean-Paul pursed his lips, narrowed his eyes at Adam. "I think you know."

"Not at all. Please, do tell."

"You know. I know you know." Jean-Paul dug roughly in his jacket pocket and dropped a handful of change onto the table. "The man she loved," he said quickly. "The one she met when she was living in France."

"Man?" Adam sounded puzzled. "In France?" He shook his head. "I think not." Lifting his hand from my leg, he turned to face me. "Rebecca Ward is an only child, born and raised in scenic, downtown Romford, Essex. She's never lived abroad, as far as I know, and believe me, I *do* know. She's a real little homebird, aren't you, sweetheart?"

I couldn't answer him, couldn't make myself look away from him, but out of the corner of my eye, I saw Jean-Paul bump his way out from behind the table and hurry towards the door.

Adam blinked slowly, then lifted my coffee cup from the table and drank all of what was left. Peering into the empty cup, he smiled.

"Let me pay for this, eh?"

Taking a small brown wallet from his pocket, he pulled out a crisp five-pound note and rested it in the saucer. Then he stood up, sauntered casually to the open door and walked through it, whistling.

I sat for a long time, watching the five-pound note beginning to curl brown in the dregs of spilled coffee. After a while, I lifted it clear of the saucer and smoothed it flat on the table, running my fist backwards and forwards, over and over again.

Three

Wednesday lunchtime, and the sky has that grainy look of rain about to fall. I'm outside again, sitting cross-legged beneath a tree, waiting. I know he will come. Sometimes, you cannot help but know that things will happen. You feel their inevitability like a heartbeat, a constant. All this past week, I have been looking for him. An old man who bumped by me on the street, a young man ahead of me in the queue at Sainsbury's, even the boy who delivered my paper this morning; they were all him, or about to *be* him.

Outside on the grass, I keep the screen of my lashes low and watch, but all the feet that seem about to approach me hurry by. Somewhere to get to. I take my sandwiches out of my bag but don't unwrap them. Instead, I turn slightly to look over my shoulder. There is something going on over by the science block and, for a moment, my old-time love of melodrama gets the better of me. I crane my neck to see.

"Are you gonna eat those?"

The voice above me is vaguely familiar, soft, oddly piping on the grass-stained air, but I turn back only slowly, keeping my head down. My eyes circle a route across the grass, come to rest on a pair of black shoes, right in front of me, but they're not men's shoes as I'd expected. Looking up quickly, I see a mass of spirally blonde hair and a slightly puzzled mouth smiling down at me.

"Only, if you're not, you *could* donate them to a worthy cause."

I take a breath. "Sorry?"

"Got a nerve, haven't I?" The girl dips her chin slightly, looking pleased with herself. "People are always telling me." She drops down onto the grass by my side. "But what the hell. If you don't ask, you don't get. Right?"

"Guess not."

"So. *Are* you?"

"Am I what?"

"Going to eat those?"

"Oh... No." I pass them to her distractedly. "Be my guest."

Grinning, she unwraps the sandwiches quickly and begins to eat.

"We met, the other day. Do you remember me?"

"Yes, I do."

"You stamped my books in the library."

"Yes."

She chews lazily, half-smiling, then, swallowing hard, says, "I bet I know what you're thinking."

"Really?" I look away from her, struggling for composure, scanning the grounds, the perimeter fence. What if he's watching? That's what I'm thinking. What if he's out there, right now, watching me?

The girl clears her throat, brown eyes opening wide. "I bet you're thinking, 'who the fuck *is* this psycho?' Right? That's what you're thinking?"

I shake my head, try to smile. "Not quite."

"Aren't you? God, *I* would be." She hesitates, puts a half-eaten sandwich down on her lap and wipes her palms clean on the faded thighs of her jeans. "My name's Paige." She holds out her hand for me to shake.

Nodding, I take hold of her fingers for a moment. They are very cold, slender, decked out with silver rings. I feel the pin-prick tingle of metal against my skin. I introduce myself a little awkwardly.

"I'm Rebecca."

"Mmm. I know," she says. "I saw Adam in the pub yesterday and he told me *all* about you."

"What!"

Wiping her mouth on the back of her hand, she looks at me steadily.

"Just stuff, you know. It's no big deal, is it?" She flicks her hair back from her face like someone in a shampoo commercial, but it falls gently forward again, and she has to flick it back a second time. "What's the problem?"

I am close to taking hold of her arm. "What did he tell you?"

"About you being his ex."

"His *what*?"

She shakes her head. "Look, sorry. I didn't know it was such a sensitive subject. I didn't think you'd mind me mentioning it, seeing as it was you who finished it, and…"

"Finished it?" My voice is louder than I mean it to be and it makes Paige jump.

She purses her lips and glances away from me. "Okay. Look. I think I probably ought to go, because I've obviously said the wrong thing and I didn't mean to get in your face, or anything. I just thought I'd come over and talk to you, but…" She begins to stand.

"No. Wait." I take a deep breath. "I'm sorry. Please. I didn't mean to be rude to you. It's just…" But I don't have time to finish my sentence. A shadow falls across us.

"Well, hello there. My two *favourite* ladies in the same place at the same time." And suddenly Adam is standing over us, grinning down – cool as a cucumber and delighted. "Must be destiny," he says, clapping his hands together.

Paige lifts what's left of my lunch back into my lap and stands up, brushing the grass from her jeans and swinging her bag onto her shoulder.

"You're a fucking liability," she says to Adam, prodding him lightly in the chest.

"Am I?" He turns to look at me. "Surely not?"

"You're always getting me into trouble."

Adam winks at her, leans in so that his mouth is touching her hair. "Chance'd be a fine thing," he whispers.

But she shakes her head, not smiling, and stalks away without a backward glance.

He shrugs his shoulders, says confidingly, "She's very highly strung," and then he crouches down beside me on the grass. I can feel his heat, smell the citrus tang of his leather jacket. He reaches out a hand and lets his fingers nestle against my arm. "But enough about Paige. I was wondering when I'd be seeing *you* again. We've got a lot of catching up to do, haven't we?" I try to jerk my arm away, but his fingers close tight. "You're not thinking of leaving?"

I close my eyes for a moment, gathering strength, listening hard for the everyday sound of student voices close by.

Adam's grip on my arm relaxes a little as he sits himself down, and I take the opportunity to wrench it free. I turn to look at him. "Who are you?"

He wags his head at me, incredulous. "Why are you being like this? *Why* are you pretending we don't know each other?"

"Because we don't."

"Rebecca." His tone is disappointed. "How can you say that? What about all the good times we shared?"

"What good times? I don't *know* you." I begin to gather my belongings together, clumsily, desperate now to escape, to run for cover, but again Adam catches hold of my arm.

"Are you telling me that you really don't remember me? Don't remember Adam? Adam Cole?"

I stop fumbling with my bag; sit back, the air punched out of my lungs for a moment.

"Adam Cole? I remember Adam Cole, of course I do, but you're not him. You're not Adam."

"How can you *say* that?"

"Because you're not."

"Rebecca..." And I swear that there are tears in his eyes, tears in his eyes at my not remembering him, and yet he's smiling, too, behind it all. His dark eyes are laughing at me, and the longer I look at him, the more familiar he becomes. Not Adam. Not my old boyfriend Adam Cole, but someone else, someone whose face and gestures are already in my head from another time. I struggle to place him, thinking hard, all the way back, as far as I can, but something's not right. The picture falls away into pieces every time I reach for it, so that all I can say again, weakly, is:

"You're not Adam."

"Who says I'm not?" And suddenly his smiling face slams shut. "If I'm not Adam, how would I know about the night we spent in St. Ives, our last holiday together, when we left the window open and that bat flew in from the sea? How would I know that? How would I know about the man we met when we climbed Helvellyn, how he came out of the mist to take us safely down the mountain and when we asked him his name, he told us it was James Bond and we wouldn't believe him until he showed us his driving licence? How would I know about the time you lost your grandmother's ring; how we searched every antique shop in London until we found an identical one to replace it, so she'd never know the difference?"

He shuffles closer, his hands pressing down hard on my thighs, keeping me there, although now I couldn't leave even if I wanted to, because Adam, this man who is *not* Adam, is telling me things that only Adam could know. His strange voice is sweet with my secrets. He leans towards me and rests his cheek against mine, nuzzles his cheek against me like a child, and his skin is a child's skin; soft, strangely smooth against my own.

"How would I know, Rebecca?" he whispers. "How would I know what you like, what moves you... *here*," and he takes his hand from my thigh and presses it to my heart, holding it there. Then he eases back, watching me, the tips of his fingers grazing my breast. "Only Adam would know these things, wouldn't he?"

My voice, when it comes, is hollow, uncertain. "But you're not Adam."

He leans back on his hands and laughs out loud, letting his head fall back so that I can see the white tips of his teeth.

"I am as much *Adam*," he says at last, "as you are *Rebecca*."

"What do you mean? I don't understand what you mean."

"Yes you do."

"Why are you doing this?" I say again, helplessly, feeling the sudden splash of rain on my bare arms. "Who are you?"

Adam lifts his face to the gathering rain, and when he looks at me again, his cheeks are streaked wet; crooked tracks of water that look like tears.

"You can't play with the truth and expect to get away with it forever. Don't you know that?"

He stands up, begins to back away, says softly, "Your sins have found you out, Rebecca." And then he touches his fingers to his lips, blows me a kiss, and I watch as the grey air takes him, and swallows his shadow whole.

Sometimes the darkness drops like a veil, so that all you can see is a sheen of silk, nothing certain behind it. I've been awake all night, or so it feels; footsteps gathering inside my head, my pasts, real and imagined, tap-tapping at the glass, making me remember, *trying* to make me remember, but it's no good. My nightmares won't tell me what is real. I must make a choice, take control. The truth has never been my friend. It won't come of its own accord. I must go out and find it.

So, I have rung into work with a migraine, with another lie, and am sitting now on the lunchtime train to London Waterloo. A plastic cup of coffee has grown cold on the table in front of me and my book rests unopened in my lap. *Ariel*. Adam, the *real* Adam, the Adam I am setting out to find, knew about *Ariel*, knew what it meant to me. I used to quote it to him, recite long poems that made him yawn and pretend to fall asleep. Adam.

That time in St. Ives, the same holiday when the bat flew into our seaside room and sent me screaming into the night, Adam and I spent long days stretched like cats in the sunshine, trailing black tails of seaweed along the empty beaches. I remember very clearly the bright air of Cornwall, the dark pubs with their candlelight – stark white walls covered with pictures of fishermen hauling squirming nets ashore.

Walking along the coast path from Zennor to St. Ives, we stopped to rest at a place called Pen Dennys Point, sat hugging our knees in tight, watching the sea far below us changing from green to blue as it swallowed ravelled tablets of rock. All along the cliff edge, there were poppies growing, battalions of poppies, scarlet-red, and I stood up to point at them, to breathe in the pollen-haze puff from their mouths.

I started reciting my favourite Plath poem, in a loud and meaningful voice, but Adam only drooped his head onto his folded arms, his blond hair falling forward.

"God knows why you like Sylvia Plath," he sighed, looking up at me. "She's so fucking depressing."

"She's not."

"Yes, she is. I can still remember what they used to say about her at school." He narrowed his eyes, groping for the exact phrase. "Oh yeah; *Poetry to slash your wrists by*."

I opened my mouth, affronted. "Not all her stuff's like that."

"No?"

"No. It's clever, ingenious; like she's lots of different people in her writing, constantly re-inventing herself."

"Hmm."

Kneeling down in the grass by his side, I took hold of his hand and hugged it to my chest in a dramatic manner.

"You'd like her if you knew her better. You'd like her tender poetry, I bet."

"Tender? Who are you trying to kid, Bex? She didn't *write* any tender poetry. All that stuff in *Ariel*; it's all really raw and violent. It's all concentration camps and men in raincoats who strangle rabbits for a living."

I moved a little closer, shaking my head at him disappointedly. "How long have we been going out now, Adam?"

"Ten months." He peered at me, apprehensive. "Why?"

"We've been going out all that time, with me trying my best to initiate you into the complexities of modern poetry, and you *still* think of Sylvia Plath as depressing?"

He shrugged his shoulders, leant back on his hands. "She *is*."

I began, in a whisper, to recite another Plath poem, – a love poem this time. I leant in close, kissing him on the mouth, nudging softly at his lips with the tip of my tongue, easing him down with my weight into the soft, brown earth. I didn't finish reciting the poem of course. I didn't need to. We stayed on the cliffs until nightfall.

It goes further back than that with Adam, much further back. I'd met him at university, oddly attracted by his shyness, his diffidence. Sidling down alongside him in the refectory one lunchtime, and unloading my tray with a smile, I proceeded to unravel him a tale about my recent fake year spent in Australia, my adventures, my disappointments, how I'd watched a man's soul sucked right out of his body by an Aborigine with an evil pointing-bone.

He listened with his mouth slightly open, vaguely dazed, but stuck there and not wanting to leave, it seemed. All the while, a thin curve of milk sat like a moustache on his upper lip, until I took a breath and leant across to wipe it clean with my fingertips, very softly, as if he were a child.

"You had..." I pointed to my own mouth in explanation, "some milk, or something."

He blushed. I remember him blushing. I remember the rush of tenderness I felt for him, and something else, like falling through a trap door – a split second of wanting it to be real. Just this *one* time, for there to be no boundaries, no lies.

"My name's Adam Cole," he said at last, in a small voice.

"Cole? Like in Nat King?"

"Uh huh."

"He was American wasn't he?"

He looked puzzled. "Um, yeah, he was."

I leant quickly forward, unable to resist the opportunity. It was too tempting.

"Did I mention to you that I was born in America?"

And so it began, and all my stories came crowding from their corners to seduce him. For a while it worked. He was kind to me, fond of me, and at times, I was *almost* able to be myself, or what I thought myself to be – hard to know by then, after years spent being other people. Some days, it *was* nearly all the truth that I told him, but that is such a hard way to live, and precarious, and tedious, and that's why I had to finish it. Love is honest. I'm not. So, I told him I'd met someone else and that I was moving away. To this day, I can still see his face when I told him, still see that room in his mother's house with its pictures: its dim, innocent images floating at the edges of my vision, and his face, Adam's face, filling up with sadness, breaking over into words of disbelief and confusion.

"But I thought this was as real for you as it was for me," he'd said.

And I'd lied and said no, that it had never been real for me, when of course, my time with him had been pretty much the *only* real thing in my life for as long as I could remember.

Sometimes, even now, I wonder what would have happened if I'd told him the truth, told him how things were with me, how I lived my life. I wonder if he could have forgiven me, if we could have been happy, sated, but I doubt it. You have to be brave to be happy. You have to put yourself at great risk, and that's something I can't do. Mostly, then, I've tried not to think about him. I ran away from his mother's house that day and have never gone back, not even in my head, but today, I must.

The London train arrives at Waterloo late, so I have to race to make my connection. I am heading out into rural Essex, watching factories and tower blocks give way to stubbly fields of green, and it's like one of those weird segments of film; the gradual opening of a flower speeded up, so that the whole process takes only a matter of seconds – petals oozing into colour and sudden breadth, except that this time, it's all in reverse. A year ago, I left Adam, escaped from him on a fast train. Now, I am coming back slowly, crawling through wind-blown villages, familiar towns. My heart is heavy with a hoard of memories by the time the train at last shunts to a halt at Brentwood station. I tug my bag from the overhead rack and step down onto the platform.

Somehow, I thought I might have forgotten my way, that absence might have made my footsteps ponder a different route, but it hasn't. Adam's mother lives close to the station, in a tall red brick Edwardian house at the foot of a hill that leads into town. Hardly a town at all; one street full of family-run shops – a small Marks & Spencer store, a pre-fabricated library. We always said that Brentwood reminded us of those ghost towns in old Western films, that there should have been a ball of tumbleweed gusting along the High Street, and a riderless horse or two nosing into shop doorways. Nothing ever happened here. That's what I remember most; how nothing ever happened, and how, oddly, *that* was the reason we liked it.

It is mid-afternoon, and I find the house I'm looking for. Shuffling like a schoolgirl on the doorstep, I take a deep breath and press the doorbell once, lightly. A long time seems to pass before I hear any movement in the hallway. I measure slow seconds in the beats of my heart. Then, suddenly, so that I'm not quite ready, the front door eases open, and I peer into the half-light inside.

"Mrs Cole?"

A small lady is swaying slightly in the frame of the door, and I wonder for a moment if Adam's mother has moved out, but then a tremulous voice replies, "Yes?" and she leans forward into the light.

"Mrs Cole?" I say again. "*Irene?*" – not believing, because I don't re-member Adam's mother looking like this. She was darker haired, I'm sure, and taller, and her face was different, not pinched and anxious like this woman's face.

I shake my head, stepping back to look along the row of adjoining houses. "I'm sorry. I think I must have the wrong address."

But she puts her hand to her mouth, very quickly, covers her mouth in surprise, or something close to surprise.

"Rebecca?" She speaks my name as if it is a secret, repeats it, sways heavily against the doorframe so that I instinctively reach out to steady her. "Don't touch me," she snaps. "Don't." She shakes her head, slapping my hands away. "How dare you," her soft voice rising. "Why have you come here? What do you want?"

"I've come to see Adam, I wanted to..."

"Mum." A man's voice filters through from inside the house. "Mum, who is it?" And suddenly there is someone else in the hallway, a small man, his sandy hair slightly curly like a boy's, although he is not a boy, any more.

"Will?"

Adam's younger brother stares down at me, unsmiling. "God," he says after a moment. "Rebecca."

"Tell her to go," demands his mother. "Tell her to go, Will." And she comes towards me a little, her pale hands flailing at the air.

Will catches hold of her hands and brings them together, as if in prayer, between his own.

"It's okay, Mum," he says gently, nodding, making her look away from me. "It's okay. Let's go inside, eh? Let's go back into the living room," and he steers her back along the hallway and through a door to the left. I can hear her shrill voice muffled through the walls.

"Make her go away, Will," she is saying. "Make her go."

I stand on the doorstep feeling disconcerted. I guess I should have known not to expect a particularly warm welcome from the family of an ex-boyfriend, but I certainly didn't expect such venom from a woman who used to like me. She and I were friends. She taught me how to make bread, I remember. One winter's afternoon, when Adam and Will had gone to football training, she and I stayed home in the warm kitchen with its shiny old stove, an orangey light shining from the lamps, high shelves lined with bottles and jars, and she taught me how to make bread. We laughed at how bad I was, how my dough mix looked like wallpaper paste. We laughed. She liked me.

Will looks very tired by the time he returns to the front door. He runs his fingers through his hair distractedly and beckons me inside.

"Quiet, though," he warns in a whisper. "I don't want her to know you're still here."

I follow him through into the kitchen and he closes the door behind us.

"Sit down." He gestures to a chair, clears away a pile of newspapers from the wooden dining table. "Can I get you anything? Tea?"

I shake my head, looking around at the dishevelled room, the dusty stove and shelves.

"Will?" I flop down into a chair. "What the hell's going on? What's wrong with your mum?"

Will puts a finger to his lips and lifts his head to listen.

"Sorry," he says, sitting down opposite me. "I thought I heard her call. She's usually okay with the TV, but..."

"Will?"

He closes his eyes for a moment. "Sure I can't get you anything?"

"Please. Just tell me what's going on? Is your mum ill? Are you here on your own with her? Where's Adam?"

Will sits back in his chair. "I thought you knew about Adam. I thought that's why you'd come."

"Knew *what* about Adam?"

He leans forward, elbows on the table, starts picking intently at the knots of wood with a fingernail.

"Somehow, I kind of expected you," he says gently. "Don't know why. I just thought, yeah, now she'll come, now that it's too late, she'll come." And he raises his head, lifts his eyes to meet mine. "Strange, don't you think? That I should expect you, after all this time." He takes a breath, seems to retreat a little inside himself. "Adam's dead, you know, Rebecca. He killed himself on Christmas Day."

Four

The breath catches in my throat; something hard – a stone, a handful of gravel, slipping into the pocket of my chest. I look away, out into the walled garden.

"Dead?" My voice is a whisper. "But..."

Will stands up and wanders over to the window with his hands dug deep into the pockets of his jeans.

"Mum kind of blames you, I guess. She thinks he did it because you left him." He hesitates. "After Dad died, she lost it, you know? Same thing's happened now. Life's too big for her again."

He takes a deep breath and holds it, leaning forward a little so that his forehead bumps softly against the windowpane.

I swallow hard, but the hot ache in my throat won't go away. "I don't know what to say, Will," I try, lamely. "I'm so sorry. Really, I'm..."

"Save it," he says, without turning.

"Isn't there anything I can do?"

I want to put my arms around him, standing there, small as a child, his elbows tucked in tight against his ribs like he's holding himself together.

When he turns around to look at me, his face is set hard. "No. There's nothing you can do. I'll stay here and look after Mum, 'til she's better."

"But what about uni? Weren't you going away to study? Weren't you going to medical school?"

"I was, but things have changed, wouldn't you say? My plans have changed."

"What about your sister? What about Kate? Couldn't she help?"

Will smiles ruefully. "Kate's gone." He lifts his chair back under the table, careful not to scrape it on the tiled floor. "She left before the funeral. She's back in London, or *was* anyway. That's where her last letter came from. We haven't heard from her for a while."

"Why did she go?"

"She had her reasons."

"But you need her here."

He shakes his head hard. "It's none of your business what I need." And then he straightens up and says flatly, "Look, I think you should just leave, really. My brother's dead. My sister's gone. My mother's... well, you've seen what's happened to my mother." He brushes some imaginary crumbs clear from the surface of the table. His hands are trembling. "Now you've caught up with all our news, or whatever it is you came here to do, I really think you ought to go, don't you? I'm sorry, but we don't want you here, Rebecca. Why would we want you here?"

He doesn't say it anger. His tone is gentle, weary, but I know that he means it. I can see in his face that he *absolutely* means it, so I nod my head quickly and struggle to stand.

"I'm sorry. I'll come back another time."

I scramble my way out from behind the table and knock over my chair in the process. I reach to straighten it, but suddenly someone comes clattering through the kitchen door and before I can move aside, a single blow to my shoulder sends me reeling backwards.

"Mum, stop. Come on." Will rushes towards his mother and gathers her up in his arms.

"It's your fault," she sobs into his chest, freeing one of her arms from his embrace and reaching towards me. "You did it to him, *you*!"

Dragging myself up off the floor, I can only watch, tears burning hot behind my eyes, my mouth opening and closing on words that don't come, and wouldn't make a difference even if they *did* come.

Will glares at me across the kitchen, mouths, "Just go," and I do, stumbling out along the hallway and into the stark afternoon air.

I hurry away from the house, my bag slipping from my shoulder, so that I have to keep stopping to tug it back into place. My feet are carrying me fast, eager for escape, so eager, in fact, that I have walked some distance before I realise that I'm heading completely in the wrong direction. I stop and turn, look back along the road; its tall trees bending slightly towards me in the green air. I don't want to walk past the house again. I don't want Adam's mother to have to see me again, but I can't remember another route back to the station. Truth is, there isn't a route to the station which doesn't take me straight past the house, so I haul my bag back onto my shoulder and start walking again, slowly this time, my footsteps suddenly heavy. I carry on walking the wrong way, because I know that this route will take me into town and I can hide out there until it gets dark, try to get this whole thing somehow clear in my head, then skulk back to the station like a criminal and catch a late train to London.

The High Street isn't as I remembered it. There are a lot more people around, for a start; young mothers pushing buggies with coloured balloons tied to their handles, rickety old ladies peering into shop windows, their grey heads bobbing like faded full stops. And the shops have changed, too. Many of the family businesses are gone. In their place are Pizza Huts and New Look stores, building societies, mobile phone shops. It is only a year since I was here last, and yet everything is different. Not just the way things look, but the way the air feels, its texture, the way the pavement seems to move beneath my feet like one of those airport conveyer belts.

I begin to grow oddly unsteady and stop walking; I lean for a moment against a bus shelter. A little way ahead is a bakery, and this, at least, *is* as I remember. Adam and I used to come here for a coffee sometimes, sit in the little café at the back of the shop and make up lurid life stories for the well-to-do Essex ladies ordering their unsliced wholemeal loaves at the counter.

When I sit down at a table in the back of the shop today, a small waitress hurries across to me, wiping her hands on the front of her pink uniform as she approaches. Before she even reaches my table, I see her face open up in surprise, and she points at me.

"Hiya love," she says. "We haven't seen you in ages."

I can't believe that she remembers me after all this time.

"Where's that young man of yours, then? Have you left him up the street with all the shopping?"

I shake my head, look away from her.

"He's... I don't..." But it's no good. I don't know what to say, and suddenly, things seem to be caught in mid-air. There is only a shrinking wall of space and a still point a few feet from my face, one still point where Adam's smile moves; his mouth open and smiling, his hair falling forward into his eyes. He is reaching across the table to touch the back of my hand, moving the tips of his fingers against the network of small bones, counting them, naming them with his touch. I swear that I can feel the pressure of his fingers, even now, and I know that somewhere I am saying his name; a low sound in my mouth which somehow *becomes* his name as the air takes it and claims it. His smile swims in front of my eyes, slipping in and out of focus, wanting to tell me something, but drifting away now, receding. Someone else's face takes its place. Someone else's voice is speaking.

"She needs a cup of tea, if you ask me. Strong, sweet tea."

I catch a blur of pink uniform moving at the edge of my vision, then Will's face suddenly close to mine, leaning in so that I shrink back, startled.

"Rebecca?" He is out of breath, hunched forward with his hands on his thighs. I notice that he has no shoes on his feet. His white socks are grey from the street. "Rebecca?" he says again, more gently, and taking deeper breaths now, steadying himself against the calm air of the bakery, its soft sounds.

He slips into the seat opposite. I can smell baking bread, nutmeg, the salty tang of pastry as the waitress comes back quickly with a cup of tea and sets it down in front of me.

"Now you drink that down," she advises. "It's bound to make you feel better."

She hovers for a moment, looking conspiratorially at Will, but he isn't looking at her. He's looking at me, somehow waiting for me, so she wanders away. I hear her greet a new customer at the counter in a loud voice, cheerful, but then she lowers her voice, and I just *know* that they are talking about me. I glance over my shoulder, certain that they will be looking in my direction, pointing at me, but they're both leaning down into the window display. The customer is pointing at some Chelsea buns.

"No one's *looking*," says Will in a derisory tone, although, when I turn back to him, he isn't making fun of me, and he doesn't look angry or anything. He just looks sad.

I take a deep breath, ask quietly, "What are you doing here, Will? How did you know where I'd be?"

He sits back in his chair and stretches his legs beneath the table. His feet tangle against mine for a moment.

"You and Adam always used to come here, didn't you? It was one of your places." He looks away from me, pauses, adds gently, "I didn't want to leave things. I wanted to talk to you about Adam."

"I don't understand. I thought you *didn't* want to talk about him?"

I sip at my tea, its sweetness diffusing, and watch Will's eyes narrow slightly. His face has changed in the last year. It has harder edges now, new angles. His cheekbones seem to stand out pale beneath the dark sheen of his skin.

"Let me put it another way." He thinks for a moment. "I wanted to make *you* talk about Adam. I want to know why you came back to see him."

"It's hard to explain."

"*Try*," he says, and his voice is exacting.

Suddenly, we are over the edge of something and falling fast. He is drawing back from me.

"It doesn't matter." I wave it away, try to respond lightly. "It doesn't matter now. If I'd *known* about Adam, God! I wouldn't have come."

"Ain't that the truth! You wouldn't have come anywhere *near* us. It's not quite your style, is it, this kind of thing?"

I feel a prickle of exasperation. "That's not what I meant. I wouldn't have come because I wouldn't have wanted to upset your mum."

He smiles with just the corners of his mouth, says wearily, "Yeah, yeah."

"No, *really*."

But Will looks away from me as if I am a stupid child and begins tapping his foot against the leg of the table.

"Will?" I lean forward a little. "I want you to believe me. I know what you must think of me, but I wouldn't want to hurt your mum, or you. You know I wouldn't."

"But it was okay to hurt Adam."

"I didn't even mean to do that. Relationships end all the time. It wasn't anyone's fault."

He shakes his head. "It's *always* someone's fault."

"Look. I was honest with Adam about how I felt."

"Honest?" He leans towards me across the table, says in a measured tone, "You wouldn't know the meaning of the word."

I try to force down a sip of tea, try to hide myself behind the cup. "What are you talking about?"

"You know what I'm talking about. Don't pretend. Don't still pretend *now*." Leaning further forward, he takes hold of my wrist, squeezes for a moment: not enough to hurt, but enough to stop me slipping free of his grasp. "Adam told me that he loved you in spite of your lies, but I didn't. If there's one thing I can't bear, it's a liar, but Adam, he thought it was all..." He lets go of my wrist and breathes a small laugh, a hard round sound into the air. "Endearing. He thought it was endearing that you made up all those stories about yourself. He thought it was because you loved him, that you were trying to impress him, but I was never sure. I thought maybe you just wanted to fuck with him, control him."

"I did love him," but my voice is a weak thing, uncertain, and my words seem to dissolve like water spilled in the desert, because Will begins tapping his foot against the leg of the table again.

"You don't lie to someone you love," he says flatly.

"You don't understand."

"No, you're right. I *don't* understand, and I don't particularly want to. That's not what this is about. I just want to know why you've come back. Come on, Rebecca. What is it *this* time? Must be a good one to have come all this way."

I lower my eyes. "Please don't."

"No. I mean it. I'd *really* like to know what's important enough to have brought you back here."

I open my mouth to speak, but no words come, only the sting of tears, only the shape of a sadness I don't recognise. Its weight seems to move through me, a creeping languor in my limbs and in my hands, a dull ache in my fingertips, and Will's face fills the space of my vision, Will's anger like a shield with the sun on it. I cannot see for the bright light of how angry he is.

"You think I told lies to hurt him, to control him," I say at last, clumsily, my voice stumbling on ahead of me. "But I didn't, Will, I swear. At least, I didn't *think* that's what I was doing. Don't you see? It was all just to make him love me. I had to lie to make him love me. I was never going to be enough for him. I never have been enough, but with my stories, I *am*."

"Rebecca..." He backs off, his clear face baffled and dark.

"Look," I lift my fingers, touch the air. "I never set out to hurt him. I mean, it wasn't *meant* to hurt him; it was never meant to hurt anyone, and if you've never believed anything I've said until now, just please try to believe this. Adam was right about my lies, okay. They *were* supposed to endear me to him, give him someone interesting and special and *exciting* to love. That was always the point. That's *been* the point my whole fucking life, but it wasn't supposed to hurt anyone. It was never supposed to do that. Honest it wasn't."

Will is quiet for a long moment. He has stopped tapping his foot against the table. He looks away from me, towards the open door, and for an instant I think he is about to stand up and leave. He seems to shift in his seat, his muscles tensing for escape, but then he takes a breath.

"I don't get any of this," he says. "I don't get how you didn't see that Adam wasn't taken in by your lies. He didn't believe them. He didn't want them. He just wanted *you*." His tired gaze drifts around the tables like a paper plane. He shakes his head. "Didn't you know him at all?"

The grey light of the bakery makes my eyes hurt. I strain to see through it, squinting back down the months as if down a tunnel into daylight, and I almost catch hold of the colour I am looking for, the shapes that will fit into the spaces that are opening up all around me. I almost touch the edge of Adam; a blond boy on a cliff, his body ablaze with poppies, but he buckles away from me. At the last moment, he buckles away from me, and drops like a rock into blackness.

"No," I say. "I didn't know him at all."

Will watches me, runs a hand back through his hair and holds it away from his face. His hair is like Adam's hair. I think this as I watch him. His hair is like Adam's hair, only curlier, but soft like Adam's is. That's why he has to hold it back, otherwise it slips all the time into his eyes, like Adam's does... did. I swallow hard. We used to say that Will looked like Little Lord Fauntleroy, with his golden curls, his lion-cub face. He doesn't now.

"I'm sorry I came, Will. I shouldn't have come."

I nudge away my half-finished cup of tea and try to stand up, but my stomach is suddenly tight, and something hurts like a splinter of wood or the tip of a blade beneath my ribs, and I have to sit down again.

"You look like him," I say, as if I've only just realised. "You didn't used to." I bend forward, hug my arms as gently as I can into the sides of my body, "But you do now."

"I know."

"Did you really hate me for my lies back then?"

"No. Not *hate*. Of course not hate. Mostly, we just felt sorry for you."

"We? You mean you and Adam?"

"I mean all of us."

I lean slowly back into my seat. "You *all* knew I was making stuff up? The whole family knew?"

"Of course. What did you think?" He shakes his head. "Rebecca, I'm sorry to have to break this to you, but you are a *terrible* liar."

"What d'you mean?"

Will lifts his eyebrows. "Oh, come *on*. Your life was an impossibility. You were what, twenty-three, yeah, and you'd done *everything* and been *everywhere*. Whatever anyone was talking about, you always had something to add to it. There seemed to be nothing outside your experience, and in the end, it was just too difficult to believe in." He leans towards me. "We *wanted* to believe you, but you always took it just that little bit *too* far. You made yourself unbelievable."

I cannot help but smile. "How ridiculous is this, Will. Oh my *God*!" I lean forward and cover my face with my hands, and somewhere deep inside, I can feel laughter bubbling – a fluid thing moving through me, a breaking down. "Why didn't anyone ever say anything to me?"

Will shrugs. "We didn't want to embarrass you, and besides," he glances away from me, "mostly, we *liked* you. We got used to you. We thought you were a bit eccentric, but there didn't seem any harm in your stories back then. It's now, when I look back..." He hesitates, clears his throat, says defeatedly, "You were pretty much one of the family I suppose, and you make allowances for family, don't you?"

"One of the family?"

"Yes. That was why it was so hard, your leaving him. He thought you'd come to stay, you see, and so did we."

"No wonder you hated me."

"It was never hate, Bex, and it isn't now, not even with Mum, really. She doesn't hate you. She just hates that he's dead."

"I don't blame her for blaming me."

Will looks down at the table for a moment and spreads his fingers over its pale surface.

"Look. There was a lot of stuff going on with Adam. I'm not saying that your leaving didn't affect him, because it did, but it wasn't the only thing that affected him."

"How did he die?" I have said the words without knowing whether or not I want to hear the answer, but Will replies straight away.

"He threw himself off a cliff." And then he almost smiles, catches it back, and his eyes fill up with tears. He tries to blink them away. "Can you believe it? Can you believe that he did that? He said he was going to Cornwall, back to St. Ives, for Christmas. He said he'd been there with you, that it was the last place you'd visited together, and the next thing, the *police* are on the doorstep."

I reach across the table and cover his hands with my own, but he eases them away.

"Did he leave a note or anything?"

"Yes. It was in his pocket when they found him. It just said *goodbye*, just that one word. Nothing else." He looks down at his hands. "D'you want to see it?"

"You carry it with you?"

He nods. "Always."

My stomach lurches, but I say quietly, "Okay," because something in Will's face, something in the weighted down, broken down look of him, tells me that he has to show this note to someone.

I don't know how I will react to seeing Adam's handwriting in a suicide note, but when Will hands me the rumpled square of paper and I unfold it, I find that the word goodbye is type-written, not hand-written. It's in block capitals – small black letters adrift on a sea of white. I look at it hard, and my eyes fill with tears, that this was all Adam could find to say, that this was all he could bring himself to leave behind him.

"All the things they say, Bex, about regretting what hasn't been said, what can't *ever* be said." Will is staring at me. "It's all true. Did you know that?"

I nod quickly, wanting to convey the warmth and sympathy that I feel inside, but Will turns his head away.

"Mum won't even use his name any more. She refers to him as 'my late son'. *My late son*, for God's sake, like he's held up in traffic, or something." He starts to say something else, but his words seem to crumple at the edges and the air drains them away. His face is grey, a map of tiny creases. He swallows, lifts his eyes to meet mine. "Why have you come?" he asks again. "Why have you come back?"

"It doesn't seem important now, why I've come."

But he watches me, dips his chin a little, waiting.

"Really," I assure him, meaning it, "it doesn't matter. How *can* it matter now?" I sit up straight in my seat and try to catch the eye of the waitress. "Have you left your mum on her own? Will she be okay?"

"Yeah, she'll be okay. I took her round to Beryl's, our neighbour, then I followed you here as quick as I could."

I begin to gather my belongings together, say brightly, too brightly, "We should go."

He hesitates. "Should we?"

"It's no good, Will. I can't... I mean, the stuff I came to talk about seems so stupid and insignificant now. It's probably just me making something out of nothing anyway." I try to smile at him, and then I stand up. "You know what a drama queen I am."

"Are you still?"

I think for a moment. "Yep, pretty much."

"You're *still* telling your stories?"

"Yes."

He shakes his head at me slowly. "You can't go on doing it for the rest of your life, Rebecca. It *has to stop.*"

"I'm beginning to see that."

Will eases himself out from behind the table and reaches forward, seems about to take hold of my hands in his, but hesitates, and slips them into the pockets of his jeans instead.

"You know, since Kate went, I haven't really had anyone to talk to, and I feel like it's all banked up somewhere inside me and I can't let it out because of Mum, and sometimes, all I want to do is just talk to somebody about him, just say his name and talk about the stuff we used to do, and make the whole thing feel ordinary again. Does that make sense to you?"

"Of course it does. I can't believe you're having to deal with all of this on your own. You should have help. Can't you get Kate to come back from London for a while?"

He shakes his head, lifts my jacket from the back of my chair and holds it behind me, slips it gently up over my arms and onto my shoulders.

"She doesn't want to. I've asked, but she says it's still too raw for her here, after everything that's happened. She misses him so much. She couldn't even bring herself to come to the funeral, for God's sake; said it would kill her to come. I don't want to *make* her come back, and besides, I'm not even sure where to find her. She was living with some friends from uni, but when I rang her London number at the weekend, a bloke answered, and said she'd gone away and he didn't know when she was coming back. I think she just needs some space, to get her shit together, you know? It's funny, though, 'cos some friends of Mum's were on holiday in the New Forest last week and one of them said they thought they saw her in a pub in Lyndhurst."

"Lyndhurst? That's quite near me. I live in Southampton now."

"Perhaps you should go and have a look for her, then, give her a hard time from me." He takes a couple of pound coins out of his pocket and puts them on the table. "A bit of a guilt trip might do her good and bring her home. God knows I could do with the help." He moves ahead of me on to the street, the late afternoon sky falling indigo all around us. "Will you come back to the house for a while? Mum'll be asleep by now." He glances at me out of the corner of his eye. "We could just chat for a bit."

"I don't know, Will. Maybe I should just go, eh?"

"It's up to you."

"D'you really want me to come back?"

He hesitates, looks down at his toes, curls them slightly. "Yes. I do. God knows why I should, but..." He shrugs.

I follow him home.

Back at the house, Will pours me a glass of port out of a dusty green bottle, and then he pours himself one, and we sit side by side at the kitchen table, drinking in the half-light and talking about Adam – the old Adam, the one that I remember and the one that Will has lost in the stark light of what has happened. Then Will stands and opens one of the kitchen drawers, coming back to the table with a pack of photographs.

"I want you to have a look at all the flowers people sent to the funeral." He takes out a wad of photos and begins to flick through them fast. "I think if he'd known how people felt about him, it would have made a difference. Sometimes, you see a hearse go by on the street and the coffin's inside with no flowers on it. It's just bare, bare wood, and you think to yourself that the person inside it must have had no friends, no family, no one who valued them, but look at these." He hands me a photo, a riot of colour. "Look at all the flowers Adam had. Look how loved *he* was."

I've always found it a morbid thing to do, to look at pictures of funeral flowers as if they're a set of holiday snaps, but Will seems so intent and so unutterably sad suddenly, that I take the photo from him, run my fingertips across the floral tributes, and trace the word

Son spelt out in white carnations. I take the next photo and the next and the next, and each one makes me more miserable than the one before.

The last photo is of the coffin being carried into the crematorium in the rain, laden with wreaths, weighted down with flowers and silence. The family are following, their heads bowed, Will's arm tight around his mother's shoulder. Their grief is impossible to look at, unbearably private, so I let my eyes skim instead across the gravel path beneath their feet, the shine of the pall-bearer's shoes, the people in the background. And it is then that I see him. I lift the photo closer; take in his leather jacket, his gold-rimmed glasses, dark hair thick and sleek-black in the rainy air. My heart throbs like a bruise inside my chest, but I keep my voice steady when I point with my finger and ask:

"Who's that, Will?"

Will squints. "Don't know."

"You don't recognise him?"

He looks away, disinterested. "He looks vaguely familiar, probably just an old mate of Adam's or something. There were lots of people there I didn't know. But that's what I mean, see?" He looks into my face and his eyes are bright blue and determined. "He was a popular guy." And he stands up then, turns away from me, reaches for a second bottle of port from a high shelf. "He had good friends from all over, Adam did." He splashes the port into his empty glass and knocks it back, shuts his eyes, keeps them shut for a moment.

Before I slide the photo out of the pack and into my pocket, I look at it again. All the bystanders are turned towards the coffin, their eyes lifted, their bodies leaning ever so slightly into the channel of grief that spills from the pallbearers' shoulders. Only one person *isn't* looking at the coffin. Only one person is looking straight into the camera. The rain dapples tiny flecks of wet onto the lenses of his glasses, so that it looks like he might be crying, but he's not.

Five

Will walks me all the way back to the station, but we don't say much to each other. I don't say any of the things that I *could* say. I don't tell Will about the man pretending to be Adam. I don't tell him that that man was at Adam's funeral. I keep it locked tight inside, a secret like a shard of glass, a confusion so absolute that I couldn't find the words for it even if I tried.

Will steps on something sharp and loses his balance. He bumps softly against me.

"I don't see how Stone Age people managed without footwear," he says, recovering himself and moving ahead of me.

"Years of practice, probably." I take a long breath, steadying, following his shadow. "Your average Neanderthal man had feet like a stegosaurus, apparently." My voice is frayed at the edges, but he doesn't seem to notice.

"Attractive."

"I don't think your average Neanderthal woman was too fussed, to be honest. As long as she had someone to bring home the bacon."

Will turns to face me, begins walking backwards a few feet in front of me. "Or the mammoth, in this case," and his voice is smiling.

His features are growing hazy in the darkness now, his hair catching a glare of yellow from streetlamps as we move beneath them, but I keep hold of the edges of his smile, because he is the Will I used to know when he smiles, and that's who I want him to be. I want him to be Adam's little brother again, sitting at his mother's kitchen table talking about girls and football, and drinking orange juice straight from the carton. Somehow, it is too soon for him to be someone else.

When we reach the station, I think he will say goodbye and go home, but he doesn't. He comes right down onto the platform with me.

I search inside my bag for a pen and a piece of paper.

"Will, look, if you need somewhere to go. If you ever want to get away or anything, you know you can come and see me, okay?" I scribble my address and telephone number on the back of an old cinema ticket and hand it to him, but he doesn't take it. "I know this must be weird for you, and I'm probably the *last* person you'd think of coming to see but..."

"It isn't that."

"Isn't it?"

He reaches forward reluctantly and takes the ticket from me. "All this time, it's been about Mum, about her loss and about how she's dealing with it. No one's given a shit about me, really, and it's bizarre, I guess, that the first person to care about what I'm feeling should be you, of all people." He folds the ticket and slips it into his pocket, then takes a breath, looks at me for a long moment.

In the distance, I can hear a train approaching. I don't know what else to say to him. I take a step towards him and close my arms around his shoulders. He feels so small in my embrace, his body shadowy with grief and hesitance. He tenses against me, seems to lean away, but as the train eases in beside us, I feel him beginning to relax and, at the last moment, he links his arms lightly around my waist and squeezes.

"Come and see me, Will," I say against his hair, "whenever," drawing slowly away from him and turning to open the carriage door. "Give me a chance to make up for being such a bitch, eh?"

"You were a never a bitch, exactly."

I climb aboard the train and ease down the window, reach my hand towards him. He takes it.

"Do you forgive me, Will?" But my voice is air, without substance, because how *can* he forgive me? Why should he? I don't deserve his forgiveness.

He shrugs his shoulders, offers a small, doubtful smile, and then he turns and begins to walk away.

I lift the window closed, and drop heavily into a seat. I feel very tired suddenly, the engine rumbling loud in my ears. We move slowly down the platform, its little lights blinking at me anxiously in the darkness, and, suddenly, there is Will, sitting halfway up the steps that lead to the street. He is hunched forward, looking intently at the cinema ticket in his hand.

I try not to think about Adam. It is too hard to think about him. Instead, I think about Kate, trying to remember what she looks like. If she is living in the South now, then maybe I could make some kind of recompense to Will and his mum if I were to try to see her when I get back home. I could put an ad in the local paper or something, asking her to contact me, and if we met, perhaps I could persuade her to go back to Brentwood. Perhaps I could find a way to make things better after all. And maybe, just maybe, she might have some idea who the man pretending to be Adam really is. I could show her the photo, and see if she recognises him.

All the way into London and all the way down to the coast, I lean my head back on the headrest and freefall into the past. Thing is, I only remember meeting Kate a couple of times. She was away at university for most of the year that Adam and I spent together, and even the occasions when we *did* meet, she seemed somehow barely there; curled up in an armchair reading a book, or breezing past me out of the door on her way to an amateur dramatics rehearsal or to the gym. Yes. That's something I *do* remember clearly, that she was one of those sport-obsessed, ultra-fit women who always made me feel as if I looked like Mussolini on one of his less attractive days. She was taller than I was, taller than Adam too, with long elastic limbs, narrow hips, lots of tawny-coloured hair. I never thought of her as beautiful exactly, but she was striking.

I never really knew what she thought of *me*, but there was one time, early on, when Adam and I had been out to the pub and had come back to his mum's house slightly drunk. We'd stumbled into the living room, giggling, and there was Kate, in a pair of tartan pyjamas, sitting very upright in a chair with her arms crossed and her legs folded beneath her – a disgruntled Buddha, awaiting our return.

Adam covered his mouth with his hand for a moment. I remember him doing that, trying to stifle his amusement, because she looked so cross with us, and then he tiptoed towards her and leant down to kiss her quickly on the lips.

"Sorry Sis. Haven't been waiting up for us, have you?"

She unfolded her arms and reached towards the coffee table, picking up a small glass of what looked like whisky and bringing it to her lips.

"Of course not," she said coolly, taking a tiny sip and putting the glass back down again. Then she looked at him hard and added, "I'm sure you're old enough to look after yourself, aren't you?"

Adam chuckled. "And ugly enough, or were you too polite to say that?"

She shrugged and looked at me, her eyes narrowing ever so slightly. "Aren't you going to offer Rebecca a coffee?"

"I am. I definitely am." Adam took a big breath and turned a little too quickly towards the kitchen. "Ooh, spinny head," he croaked, steadying himself against the doorframe, then straightening up in a purposeful manner and setting off again. I watched him disappear into the kitchen and heard him begin to sing the first few bars of 'Annie's Song'.

"He always sings that when he's drunk," I said to Kate, perching myself on the arm of the sofa. "He loves John Denver."

"Don't you think I know that? Don't you think I know *everything* about him?" She reached for her glass again. "I've known him a helluva lot longer than you have, you know."

"I know." I could feel myself beginning to shrivel beneath the heat of her hostility. "I didn't mean to suggest..."

"And what exactly *do* you mean to do?"

"I'm sorry?"

"Are you?" She took a sip from her glass, and then another, all the while peering at me over the rim, but it was odd, because there was a smile in her eyes, as if she was about to laugh, as if the whole thing were a big joke, and any moment now she'd reach forward and slap my thigh in a chummy manner and offer me a swig of Glenfiddich. She didn't, though.

I could hear Adam clattering about in the kitchen, singing his song, and then he called, "D'you want a coffee too, Kate?"

She sat forward and called back, "No thanks, love," in a light, singsong voice. "I'm just off to bed." And then she stood up and put her glass down on the coffee table.

I thought that was it, she was going. I was relieved that she was, but just as she moved past me towards the door, she paused and laid her hand on my shoulder. It was an unexpected gesture and I flinched, but she leant quickly down and said very gently, close to my ear, so that I could feel her breath, hot like a child's:

"Don't mind me, will you? I hardly ever mean any of what I say." And when I looked up into her face, she was smiling at me really nicely, her eyes all warm and welcoming, and I smiled back, pleased, thinking that it had just been the drink and maybe a little possessiveness over Adam that had made her so odd with me.

"That's okay," I assured her, a conciliatory little laugh in my voice. "I hardly mean any of what I say, either."

"I know," she said, still smiling, but not quite the same smile.

There was a knock at the front door then and Kate went to answer it. A man's voice drifted into the hallway. I heard her kiss him hello, but Adam came into the living room with my coffee at that point. I only caught sight of the matt black of a leather jacket and the curve of an arm, before the door closed and Adam set my mug down on the coffee table. I didn't ask him who the visitor was because I wasn't interested enough. All that interested me then, was why Kate had behaved so strangely with me. I told him what had happened, but he just leant his head against my shoulder and yawned, and said not to take any notice of her, because she was always a bit off with his girlfriends, and that it was nothing personal.

I wonder about that now, the ragged Hampshire countryside sliding by me, and every space of dark taking on the shape of Kate's rage that night. If she was angry with me back then, just for being with him, then how must she feel about me now if she blames me for his suicide? Am I to blame? I know that in some way, I must be, because we all have to take responsibility for how we have treated people, even if the worst we have been is careless. Careless somehow doesn't seem as bad as malicious or selfish or mean, but perhaps it's worse, because it means indifference, a vacuum of feeling. I thought I cared for Adam, I really did; but I couldn't have, otherwise I'd not have run out on him. I'd have stayed. But then, I always run. It's easiest. I'm only sorry this time for what I have left in my wake. I never meant it. God knows, I never meant it.

Back in Southampton, I catch a cab home. It is a windy night, loud with movement and hemmed in by huge banks of cloud. I feel very small, and deeply uneasy.

I live in a flat in a rambling old Victorian house on the far side of the Common; lofty chimney stacks, tumbling gables, spiky ridges, crests and finials. I love it. I love how many lives have been played out within its walls. All those whispers, like the running pattern of leaves around the cornice of my room, a breathing garland of flowers, a soft-sung charm against the outside world, but as the cab pulls up outside my gate tonight, I'm not listening for whispers. I'm listening only for quiet.

I hurry to pay the driver, giving him more money than I need to, but not caring, just wanting to be inside. As I run up the path, however, the huge front door swings open and my downstairs neighbour, Olive, towers like Pallas Athene in a kaftan on the doorstep. She is an elderly lady, with a nest of white hair and a voice like Joyce Grenfell – full of import, and slightly husky from years of cheap sherry and hymn singing.

"Betty," she cries as I reach the door, a tumbler of rusty-coloured liquid perched precariously in her hand. "I've been waiting for you."

She always calls me 'Betty'. I introduced myself as 'Becky' when I moved in, but she must have misheard and I've never bothered to put her straight. Besides, I quite like having another name to go by.

"Hello Olive." My voice is weary, dusty with travel.

She steps aside to let me into the hallway and pushes closed the door behind us.

"There was a *man*," she says, her eyes bright as a kitten's, "*here*, asking for *you*."

This doesn't usually happen. The men I meet, I never give them my address. It's never part of the deal, but I am not surprised that I have had a visitor.

"When was he here?"

"This afternoon."

"Did he leave a message?"

"No. He left you a letter, though, popped it through your door. I watched him do it."

"Thanks for letting me know, Olive."

I turn away and begin to climb the stairs, holding on tight to the brown carved banister as I go. Just as I reach the top, she calls after me in a jaunty tone:

"A gentleman visitor, no less! Perhaps things are looking up for you, dear." And she raises her half empty glass to me, holding it there in the air a moment, so that a ring of tiny lights dance across its surface. Their glare makes my eyes hurt.

I take my key from my bag and slide it into the lock, but don't turn it. Instead, I take a deep breath and then exhale very gently, very slowly, feeling my lungs beginning to empty of sound and circling air.

Beneath my feet, the patterned floor seems to undulate a little, its tiny brown and silver herring-bone blocks rippling like sand under a shallow tide.

Control. I'm not sure if I say the word out loud or not, but I repeat it, and keep repeating it as I turn the key and step into darkness. Control. Because that's what it has always been about for me. If I am in control, then I am safe. I am unassailable. If I lose control…

And that is when I remember it, although I have never really forgotten it, of course. Long before what I tell myself is the beginning, before the days of the National Gallery and Hameed and Gary Light, there is an afternoon, bright summer and innocent as grass. I am small – five years old. I can see my hands like little starfish swimming through blue air. I am standing in the back garden of my parents' house, looking up at my dad who is at the top of a ladder, painting the upstairs window frames. My mum is busy in the kitchen, and I can hear the sound of running water. I am holding in my hands a painting I've just finished, a blur of orange and green. I want to show it to my dad, so I call to him, and as he turns to look down, he somehow loses his balance and I watch, as he topples backwards and comes falling, landing hard on the concrete patio. I run away. I know I should stay. I know I should call for my mum, call for someone, but I don't. I run away, all the way down our street and out on to the main road, and I keep running until I reach a little row of shops, and then the library. I come here sometimes with my mum. I like the cool air inside and the smell of polish, so I push open the doors and walk past the ladies at the counter, and I sit down at a table in the children's section, and start to look at a book with lots of pictures of animals in it.

After a little while, one of the ladies comes over to me and crouches down by my side. Her knees click like someone snapping an elastic band.

"Are you waiting for your mummy?" she asks softly.

I nod.

"Is she in the shops?"

I nod again. "She told me to wait for her here."

The lady smiles. "There's a good girl, then." She hesitates. "What's your name?"

I wait, a lie settling on my lips like honey. "Helen," I say. "My name's Helen." Helen is the name of my best friend at school. She has shiny black hair and a dog called Barney.

"Well, you just carry on with your book then, Helen," says the lady, beginning to stand. "I'm sure Mummy will be here soon."

And I do. I carry on with my book. I try not to think about my dad lying on the patio. I try not to think about him being hurt. Every time I start to think about him, I stop myself, trace my fingertips instead across pictures of zebras and lions, dolphins, gorillas, and, for a while, I have shiny black hair and a dog called Barney, and I haven't made my dad fall off his ladder. It's someone else who's done that.

They find me in the end, of course, my mum and our nice neighbour Auntie Maisie. My mum has tears in her eyes behind her glasses, and her cheeks are pink. She holds me tight against her chest. Auntie Maisie tells me everything's all right and that my dad is okay, and then she takes the animal book to the counter and gets it stamped out on her card so that I can take it home with me.

As we walk past the library ladies towards the door, the nice one who spoke to me before calls, "Bye bye, Helen."

And my mum and Auntie Maisie look at each other.

I liked it. I liked how it felt to be able slip so easily away from hurt. We don't get to do that very often, do we? But I bet we *would*, if we could find a way to do it without losing face. That's all I did that day. I slipped away from hurt. I found a way to make myself safe.

There were other times. I know there must have been other times, after that time and before Hameed, but they are absent now from the picture I see when I look back. It is neat and clean, rounded off at the edges. I am a good girl. And yet I remember the feeling clearly, that first lie unfurling its little limbs inside me, taking shape – one small person inside another. When you're a child, it is such an empowering thing to be able to fool an adult. Nothing is beyond you then. You are in charge, safe. At the heart of all of my lies and all of my duplicity, all these years, maybe I have only ever been trying to make myself safe. I can't do it any more.

I reach to switch on the light, and there on the mat is a white envelope. My name is typed in anonymous block capitals on the front of it, and it isn't stuck down. The flap isn't even folded under. When I look inside, there is no note, only a cassette tape. I close the door behind me, go straight to the stereo and slide the tape inside. I recognise the song at once; those first few bars – little starfish swimming through blue air, a guitar that sounds like running water, and then a voice filled, it has always seemed, with tears and with falling – 'Annie's Song'.

Six

I go looking for him. What else can I do? There has to be a way to regain some semblance of safety here, and maybe if I find *him*, find him before he finds *me*, I will feel differently. I won't wake every morning with tears in my eyes and my heart stopped dead with dismay. I won't see myself reflected in a glass and not recognise the face that stares back: pale as childhood, murky as guilt.

Sometimes, the only way to combat danger is to stalk it down, catch it unawares, and this is what I must do. Will said that someone had seen Kate in a pub in Lyndhurst, so who's to say I couldn't find her if I tried, and who's to say she won't be able to solve this mystery for me? If I show her the photo from the funeral, she might know who the man is, help me to find him, and that's what I *want* to do, find him – see him sitting with a group of friends, a glass lifted to his lips, his face slackened a little at the edges with sociable ease. I will watch him sip very slowly, and before he has had time to swallow, I will move into his line of vision, smiling, full of good humour. I will fill his view as he has filled mine.

Not quite as easy as that, of course. I try every pub in Lyndhurst, then drive on towards Brockenhurst and try every pub there, but nothing; only late season tourists and locals who watch as I pace earnestly amongst tables, looking as if I've mislaid something, I suppose, or some*one*.

In one pub, an elderly man leaning at the bar reaches towards me as I pass and puts his hand on my arm. He has a kind face – a nice grandpa with a pint of stout. His eyebrows are furrowed.

"You all right, Miss?" he asks. "You look a bit lost."

"No, I'm fine, thanks."

Lost. I look lost. I think about that as I climb back into my car and drive on into the forest. For the first time in as long as I can remember, I actually look as I feel. Lost. I sit at a level crossing, watching a seemingly endless freight train trundle by, and I begin to grow anxious. What if I *don't* find Kate? What if I don't find out who this Adam really is and what he wants with me? Dusk is gathering about me; a long, sloping light, and tall trees crowd in, heavy with leaves that shine bright yellow. I wind down my window and take a deep breath. The air is still thick with colour, but the dark is coming closer now; it's mid-October, the end of every warm day laced with cold. I let my shoulders drop, try to relax my muscles.

My car is an old black Volkswagen Golf, slowly falling apart. The top of my gear stick is missing. It fell off a week or so ago, and now there is just a sharp piece of metal edged with old rubber. I like the feel of it against my palm when I change gear; an icicle, a clarity of feeling. I close my hand around it now as the crossing gates begin to lift. I press my palm down hard and feel a shard of pain. My fingertips tingle hot as I drive, and when I look at my hand, a bright circle of blood is spreading like a little sunset across my skin. I lick it clean – an intimation of iron; iron in my blood, iron in my soul. I sit up straight in my seat, bristling with resolve, staring ahead at the fading road, and it is then that I see another pub coming into view. It is painted pink, a dark pink, bordello pink, and there is a huge wooden wheel mounted on the outside wall that faces the road. From the sign hanging outside, I see that it is called the Hobbit. I've heard the name before. Some of the students who use the library come here.

I turn off the road into the car park, lock my car, and hurry across the gravel forecourt to the open door, but it is unexpectedly dark inside. I bump against a chair as I enter, blinking into the adulterated light.

Someone calls: "Mind yourself, love…" in a hearty voice, and there is a small swell of laughter.

I feel my cheeks beginning to flush, as I move quickly towards the bar. I haven't had a drink in any of the pubs I've been to so far, but I mean to have one now. I order a double Jack Daniels and Coke from a barman who looks like Harry Secombe, and drink it down quickly, letting my eyes grow accustomed to the gloom.

This is a small pub, its oak beams stained with years of tobacco smoke, and its floors uneven, so that everything looks a little lopsided. The people approaching the bar seem to be walking uphill. Most of the tables are to the right of the front door, there is only a huge wooden fire laden with thick logs to the left, and all around the walls there are glass cabinets filled with stuffed animals: ferrets, badgers, pheasants, weasels, even a small crocodile. Above some of the cabinets, there are shelves lined with different sized jars and bottles. I move a little closer and stand on tiptoe to see what's inside them. Some are filled with brightly coloured beads and marbles, others with pickled gherkins and white onions floating like little moons, but when I make my way along the shelf to the very last jar, I realise, with a little intake of breath, that it contains what looks uncannily like a huge penis. I look a little closer, wondering if that double Jack Daniels on an empty stomach was such a good idea after all.

The barman is clearing a table behind me. I catch his eye.

"Excuse me," I point to the jar, "but is this a…"

"Certainly is." He straightens up, looks at me gravely. "It belonged to the bloke who had this job before me."

Suddenly I am aware of someone breezing in by my side and hooking their arm through mine. I turn and see, with a mixture of relief and confusion, that it is Paige, the girl from the library, the girl who knows Adam.

She wags her finger at the barman, and grinning at him, says, "He lost it for taking the piss out of his customers, so I hear."

Her cheeks are flushed, her words blurred.

The barman smiles back at her and shrugs. "Won't catch me doing *that*, then."

"Very wise." She leans towards him and nudges an empty pint glass against his chest. "Stick another one in there for us, Reg, will ya? I'm just off to powder my nose." She says *powder my nose* in an aristocratic, Lady Bracknell kind of voice and it makes Reg laugh out loud. She laughs too, a nice sound, deep and engaging, and then she lets go of my arm and weaves an elaborate route through the crowded tables to the far side of the bar.

"It's equine," says Reg after she's gone.

"Sorry?"

He points to the jar and moves past me with Paige's glass in his hand. "It belonged to a stud stallion called Oberon."

"King of the fairies."

"The very same." He smiles at me, nodding. "Would you like another drink?"

"Thanks, just a mineral water, and I'll pay for whatever Paige is having."

"Okey dokey." He begins to fill her glass with Caffrey's, the dark liquid even darker in this light, thick as molasses. "How do you and Paige know each other? Are you a friend of hers from college?"

"Kind of." I think for a moment. "Well, a friend of a friend really. You might know him."

"Yeah? Who's that then?"

"Adam." But Reg purses his lips, thinking. "He's quite tall, dark-haired, little round glasses."

"Nah, sorry." He opens a bottle of mineral water and slides it across to me. "Doesn't ring any bells. Good bloke, is he?"

I pour the water into a tall glass, watching little bubbles burst like tiny explosions, and not knowing exactly how to reply. How do I know what kind of man he is? I don't. I only know that he is not the man he is pretending to be, but that isn't much to know. I shrug my shoulders, watching as Reg lifts Paige's pint very carefully on to the bar. I hand him a five-pound note.

"Paige knows him better than I do. She'd have a better idea what he's like, I guess."

"Paige knows everybody, doesn't she?" Reg punches some numbers into the till and turns back to me with a small handful of change. "There's a story in these parts. You may have heard it. Two people from opposite sides of the world find themselves ship-wrecked on a desert island. Neither of them knows the other, but they both know Paige Mackenzie."

And at that she comes dancing towards us, reaching for her pint.

"Cheers, Reg. Will you put it on me slate, mate?" She winks at him theatrically.

"No need, madam. Your friend here has taken care of business."

She straightens, looks at me, and her face softens. She puts her hand on my arm.

"Thanks, Rebecca. That's really kind of you."

Her voice is filled with surprise, but gentle. She doesn't seem so drunk suddenly.

"Look, I'm sorry about what happened last time we met," she says quickly, glancing down into her glass. "I shouldn't have gone off on one like that. I'm pleased to have seen you tonight, really, because I wanted to apologise. Will you come through and join us?" She points towards an archway, above which is written 'The Gun Room'. "It's a bit quieter through there. I'm just with a couple of friends."

"I wasn't going to stay, really."

"Just while you finish your drink."

She looks at me hopefully, and I begin to think maybe this could be an opportunity to find out more about Adam. At the same time, though, I'm tired and the thought of making small talk with strangers makes me tireder still. The days are gone when I relished the blank canvas of new acquaintance, when I could tangle a web out of conversation and have people fall in love with whatever self I conjured. It seems like another life now, and if Will is right, if I *am* a terrible liar, then it was no kind of life at all.

But here is Paige, smiling at me like she means it, and I haven't the strength to resist her.

"Just 'til I finish my drink, then."

She nods and leads me through into the gun room.

They turn out to be quite nice, Paige's friends; a dark-haired, small-boned girl called Fiona, with big dangly earrings and a Geordie accent, and a man called Phil who looks like an ad for *Mountaineering Monthly*. He has tight, curly blond hair and is very tanned and sinewy. He smiles at me when I sit down beside him on an old wooden settle, opposite Paige and Fiona. His smile is *so* big in fact, that it seems to take over his whole face. His eyes crinkle up and disappear at regular intervals.

I don't say much at first. I just listen to their conversation. They're talking about a foreign holiday from which Fiona has just returned.

"I thought it would be all sangria and sex," she says, lifting her eyes to the ceiling. "But no such luck. The closest I got to an orgasmic experience was a ride on a slightly trembly camel."

Paige and Phil laugh, and Paige glances at me across the table, and lifts her glass to her mouth. When she lowers it, there is a little moustache of foam skirting her upper lip, and my heart seems to fill my chest for a moment when I see it, because I can see Adam too, that first day in the refectory. I can see myself reaching across to wipe away that little curve of milk. I can see him blushing. I can see him falling fast through a darkness that is filled with my name.

I have to look away from Paige, but immediately she places her hand over mine on the table. Her fingers are long and slender; cold from the glass she's been holding.

"Are you all right, Rebecca?" I hear her say, but then Phil and Fiona begin to titter, and when I look up, Fiona is whispering into Paige's ear, pointing to her mouth and then to her glass.

Paige grins and crosses her eyes at me. She makes me smile in spite of myself, but before she can wipe the foam away, Phil lifts himself in his seat and leans across the table so that their faces are close.

"Caffrey's, is it?" he asks softly.

And I watch, in surprise and absolute fascination, as he kisses her, his open mouth moving hard against hers. Her head is pressed back against the wood of the settle, her hair moving like static across its surface, but she doesn't pull away from him. Instead, her body assumes an attitude of passivity, of watchfulness – a kind of stepping aside. She has her eyes closed, but only just.

Through the little gap between their bodies, I can see that Fiona is looking cross. By the time they break apart and Phil slips himself back into his seat with a sigh, Fiona's cheeks are a peachy-pink and her lips stretch like wire across her teeth.

"So, Rebecca," she says brightly, as if nothing's happened, "what do you do for a living, then?"

I take a sip of mineral water and clear my throat. All three of them are looking at me now. Paige lifts her hair away from her face and coils it loosely behind her head for a moment, then lets it go. She looks sleepy.

"We met in the uni library, didn't we?" she chips in helpfully. "Rebecca stamped my books with a workmanlike precision."

"Something like that." My tone is oddly clipped. I don't mean it to be, but I feel adrift, instinctively thrashing around for a story with which to compel them, these strangers: something other than the truth. I still long to be someone other than the truth will allow, and I could do it. Even now, I *know* I could do it. The tools of invention are still in my hands. No matter what Will said, I am a *good* liar. I take a deep breath and hold it, a bubble of air, with my heart beating fast, and Paige meets my gaze. She looks at me, puzzled, inclines her head. I think how pretty she is. I think how kind she is being to me. I keep my eyes on her when I say the words.

"I've worked in the library for about a year."

"And before that?" Fiona's earrings swing softly when she speaks.

"I worked at another library, while I was at university, in Essex."

And there it is, my truth: a flat stone at the bottom of a pool.

"One of the tweed skirt and horn-rimmed specs brigade then, eh?" says Phil, and Paige shoots him a warning glance.

"What?" he says innocently, lifting his hands. "It's just a joke, Mackenzie." He shakes his head and takes a big gulp from his glass.

"It's all right. I'm not one of them, anyway. They don't accept just anyone these days. Before they'll even consider you for membership, you have to have three things." I count them off on my fingers. "A subscription to *People's Friend* magazine, a lemon Acrilan cardigan, and a reasonably lavish thatch of facial hair."

Fiona gives a high-pitched hoot of laughter, and Phil has to put his hand over his mouth to stop his lager from escaping. Paige lets her head fall back against the settle. She is smiling at me.

"You know, you look like those singers," she says. "The Corrs sisters, all three of them. Has anyone ever told you that?"

"No."

"Are you Irish?"

"No." I clear my throat, off-guard now and not liking it. I take a sip of mineral water and then say to her, as casually as I can, but quickly, "Do Phil and Fiona know your friend Adam as well?"

Her smile falters. "I don't think so."

"Who?" Phil wipes the back of his hand across his mouth. "Who's that?"

"I don't think you know him. Just some bloke I met in the Swan one night."

"What night?"

"Few weeks ago. I don't really remember." She lifts her glass a little unevenly and takes a few sips in quick succession.

Fiona leans in. "Would *I* know him, this mystery man? Have you been holding out on us, missy?"

Paige shakes her head. "He's not a mystery man. I just don't think you know him. Okay?" And then she makes a big show of looking at her watch. "Shit, look at the time." She starts reaching for her jacket. "I've got loads to do tomorrow. I better go." She stands up, hesitates. "Don't s'pose you're driving are you, Rebecca? You couldn't give me a lift?" She looks at me intently for a moment, her eyes opening wide. I find that I can see my whole self, reflected in the black of her pupils. I am amazed at how tiny I have become. "I'm only down the road in Sway," she says, "but walking in the dark's a bit lethal round here. There are wild boars on the loose."

I can't tell if this is a joke or not, but I stand up anyway. "That's fine, sure. I can drop you." I turn to Phil and Fiona. "Do either of you need..."

But Phil waves me away as he would a mildly irritating insect.

"Don't you worry about us," he says, looking at Fiona, who looks back at him, bleary as a bloodhound suddenly. "We're used to making our own way home."

Paige leans down and kisses them both on the cheek, but they don't reciprocate. They don't even look up at her. She turns to me with an expression that I can't quite read – impatience maybe, weariness. She shrugs her shoulders.

As we leave the gun room and head for the door, she suddenly takes my arm, says quietly, "Thanks for taking me home. Phil and Fiona are great and everything, but they can get a bit... wearying, after a while, especially when they're doing their drama queen double-act." She leans into me close as we step out into the darkness, yawns a big yawn, adds blurrily, "And besides, I wanted us to have a proper chat. We're gonna get on, you and I. I can feel it in my water. You're my kind of person, I think."

"And what kind of person's that?"

"Oh, you know," she says. "Dead straight, just happy to be yourself."

Seven

The forest dark has edges to it. I am driving inside a shape that might close in tight at any moment, or open up as sudden as a breath expelled: unfamiliar roads, banks of bracken, trees tall enough to flirt with the stars.

Snuggled down in her seat, Paige points out the way.

"It's not far," she says. "Stay on this road for a mile or so, and you'll see a turning for Sway on the left."

I nod, although she isn't looking at me. Her chin is down on her chest and her arms are folded tight.

I want to ask her about Adam, but instead I say, "Are you and Phil an item, then?"

She breathes a small laugh into the air. "Not exactly."

Pulling herself up a little in her seat, she switches on the interior light. Inside the car, everything turns to the colour of butter.

She begins to feel around in the pocket of her jacket. "D'you mind if I smoke?"

I shake my head.

Flicking open a packet of Marlboro Lights, she eases one cigarette out with her lips. "Phil and *Fiona* are an item, kind of." Lighting the cigarette, she inhales and turns to look at me. I can feel her eyes on me. Then she leans towards me, her seat belt stretching taut. "I guess you could say," she whispers it, "all three of us are an item."

I glance at her, waiting for it to be a joke. "A threesome?"

She draws deep on her cigarette, blows a grey stripe of smoke towards the windscreen. "I guess you could *say*." And then she laughs. "Have I shocked you?"

"No."

"I have, haven't I?"

"No." I start to smile. "Well..."

With her cigarette drooping from one side of her mouth like an old-time gangster, she slaps her hands down on her thighs. "That's the best part of it," she says gleefully. "Shocking people."

I shake my head. "You mean, all three of you..." I lift both hands from the steering wheel for a moment, groping the air, remember that I'm driving and put them back again. "You know..."

"Fuck?"

Something catches like a fish hook in my throat.

"I don't know why people get so hung up about sex," she says. "I don't know why the idea of multiple partners freaks people out. Why should it? Isn't it just about pushing the boundaries, making life a bit bigger for yourself? As long as no one gets hurt, as long as everyone knows the ground rules and sticks to them. What's the big deal, huh?"

She turns to look at me. "Take Phil and Fiona, right? Their relationship was knackered when I met them. They'd been together three years, and they were just shit-bored, basically. They'd wake up every morning knowing that nothing was going to surprise them, no jack-in-the-box kicks, no big events, nothing. Dead in the water, and then I met them, or they met me and, well..." She winds down the window and flicks a smudge of ash into the dark. "It made them look at each other in a different way. If someone outside the relationship could find them sexually arresting, then maybe they *were*. It gave them confidence. They have a kind of arrangement now where they take only what they need from each other, don't crowd each other out with unreasonable expectations. It works. See what I mean?"

I open my mouth to answer, but she tumbles on like an avalanche.

"I was reading this biography of Eleanor Roosevelt the other day, and apparently, she said that life was meant to be lived, and curiosity had to be kept alive, and that you should never, for whatever reason, turn your back on life. I agree with her, completely. I'm doing my doctorate on Native American art of the Pacific North West Coast, mostly totem poles and masks, and I've come across some tribes who use sex as a healing art. They offer their bodies to each other as a kind of gratuity, not randomly but freely, you know? I like that. I'd like to live like that, I think, but it's difficult to do in Southampton."

She stops suddenly, swallows, flicks her cigarette out of the window. "Your turn's coming up," she says.

"Pardon me?" My heart skips like a pebble across a stream.

"Your turn." She gestures to the road. "To Sway."

I see the sign up ahead suddenly, and make a slightly wild turn on to the narrower side-road. Paige looks at me quizzically, sniffs.

We drive a while in silence, until, very gradually, something begins to dawn on me: the irony of it. I, who have longed all my life for intrigue and excitement, who have conjured stories to colour the grey, summoned a whole cast of characters to walk the tightrope with me, now find myself driving through the pitch black with a bisexual totem pole devotee, on the trail of a man who has stolen the identity of my dead ex-lover. I couldn't have done it better if I'd written it myself.

I take a look at Paige out of the corner of my eye. I can feel my face beginning to smile, but suddenly she snaps up straight in her seat and shouts, "Brake! Brake!"

Quick as I can, I turn back to the road, only to see what looks like a brown paper bag fluttering ahead of us on the tarmac. Too late, I realise that it isn't a paper bag. It's a rabbit. I slam my foot down hard on the brake and throw the car sideways, but Paige and I both feel the sickening little thud that follows. We come to a halt and the car stalls. The air is white noise.

"Shit!" She fumbles with her door and stumbles quickly out into the glare of headlights. I watch her dip down, her hair filled with tiny filaments of light.

I lean towards the open passenger door. "Is it all right, Paige?" But my voice is broken into pieces. I don't recognise it. "Did it get away?"

She stands up, shakes her head. "No."

I open my door and step gingerly out on to the road, walk around to the front of the car. I don't look down. "Is it dead?"

She puts her hands on her hips, takes a breath. "No."

And then I *do* look down, and a hot wave of nausea buckles me forward. I put both hands over my mouth. The rabbit is lying awkwardly just behind my tyre, its back legs pressed flat to the road, but the front half of its body still intact and twitching in spasms, like some hideous glove puppet. Its eyes are wide open and bright black with dread.

Paige crouches down. "It won't live long," she says. "The shock'll kill it before anything else does."

"Can't we take it to a vet?" I can feel something pressing like a fist against my breastbone. I take a huge gulp of air.

"I don't think we can."

"But we can't just leave it here like this."

Paige stands up and turns to look at me, her face grey as dust. "We won't leave it like this." Taking hold of my hand, she squeezes it. "I want you to get back in the car now, Rebecca."

"Why? What are you going to do?"

Paige bites her lip, lets a tiny sigh float like a moth into the air. "Just get back in the car, okay?"

"I want to know what you're going to do."

"Rebecca..." She reaches for me again, but I take a step backwards. She looks at me, soft as she can. "You *know* what I'm going to do."

I shake my head, turn, walk a few quick paces into the night. I can feel the dazzle of yellow from the car's headlights hot at my back; a searchlight, laying me open, finding me out. My stomach throbs, ochre-dark and thick with confusion. I cannot bear the sound of it. I cover my ears with my hands and turn around, and there is Paige, kneeling down by the car. I watch her fingers moving, circling the rabbit's neck, jerking fast, up and to the side. She lowers its body to the ground, her blonde hair trailing close to the road. She must be able to smell its blood. She must have its blood on her hands.

I begin to walk back, quickly, but all the time she doesn't seem to be getting any closer. I don't understand how this can be, when I'm walking so fast, but then I look down at my feet and find that I'm not walking at all. I'm on my knees in the road. I feel a sudden spur of panic, and something else, too; a rush of air gathering speed, a tidal wave, a giant wall of water sweeping towards me like the hand of God.

I lurch forward onto the tarmac, and a sound comes out of my body that I've never heard before; visceral, hollow – a rat in a trap, a vixen unearthed, a boy falling fast through the night. I start to cry – huge, breathless sobs that make me retch into the darkness. I try to inhale, but I'm drowning in my body's water. I can feel my heart bumping hard against my ribcage, but suddenly I can feel something else, too, a steadying sound, an equanimity, and I can hear Paige's voice.

"Rebecca," she says gently. "Look at me."

I try to do as she asks, but I can't.

"Look at me," she says again, and she takes my chin in her hand and brushes my hair back from my face. She makes eye contact with me and holds it. "Try to take some deep breaths. Okay? Breathe in slowly..." and she measures a breath into her lungs to show me. "And then out, slowly."

I try to copy her, but my body is shaking. I don't understand it and that makes it worse. The panic starts all over again; something with wings beating hard in my throat.

"Rebecca." Paige takes my face in both her hands, says very carefully, "Try to breathe."

And this time I do, as slow as I am able, looking into her face, watching *her* breathe and doing the same, as if I am learning it for the first time. Gradually, my heart begins to slow. I can feel the tiny muscles in my face slackening.

I search around inside and find my voice. "I'm sorry. I'm so sorry."
But Paige puts a finger to my lips, says gently, "Shhh. It's okay."

She slips her arm around me and helps me to stand. I feel like an old lady. I watched an old lady fall over in the street once, and someone rush across to help her up. I remember how her legs kept crumpling away beneath her, and there was nothing she could do about it. I remember how embarrassed she looked.

I lean against Paige like that old lady, and we make our way back to the car. There's no sign of the rabbit. I don't know what Paige has done with it and I don't ask. She moves me round to the passenger side.

"I'll drive the rest of the way," she says, helping me inside. I more or less fall into the seat. "Just sit quiet, all right?"

I nod weakly and she hurries around the front of the car and hops in beside me.

Curling myself up against the door, I try to get warm, but there's a cool breeze churning around my ears. I feel sick, opened up.

Paige puts her hand on my leg and pats it softly as if I am her child. "You'll be okay. Don't worry," she says, and starts to drive.

She takes me to her house, a red brick cottage on a corner, surrounded by small trees, like fists bunched in the dark. The main thing I notice are the windows, which are all different shapes and sizes. I concentrate hard on this fact, although I don't know why. She tells me, as she opens the front door, that it isn't *her* house exactly, but that it belongs to her grandmother.

"Don't worry, though," she says. "The old girl's stuck in hospital at the moment, having her hip replaced. We won't be disturbing her."

I follow her down a narrow hallway and into a little living room. The ceiling is low. She switches on a couple of lamps and gestures for me to sit. I lower myself into a very soft armchair, and watch while she draws the curtains. She has to lean across me to reach, and I catch how she smells – sandalwood and soap and smoke.

"I'll get us a drink." She disappears, and the quiet closes like a net. "D'you like Scotch?" she calls. "Gran's been keeping this bottle of single malt for medicinal purposes for years. I think tonight would qualify, don't you?" And she reappears in the doorway with a bottle and two tumblers.

She kneels at my feet, unscrews the cap with her teeth and spits it softly into my lap, to make me smile. She is trying to make me smile. I think this as I watch her pour Scotch into the glasses and hand one of them to me. I want to smile at her, but my heart is heavy still.

"What shall we drink to?" she asks.

"I don't know."

She thinks a moment, then brightens. "Confusion to the enemy!" she says with a wink, clinking her glass against mine.

"But who's the enemy?"

"Anyone who's not in this room, of course."

And then I *do* smile, and we each take a sip, and I feel the room tilt gently at the edges of my vision and my stomach fill with fire.

Paige stands up and goes over to a little stereo in the far corner. She flicks through a stack of CDs, finds the one she wants and slips it inside. A voice, burnished bronze and slick with tears, lilts into the room, and Paige sways softly to the sound of it.

"Nina Simone," she whispers. "I can always feel her right *here*, you know?" And she places her hand over her heart.

Closing her eyes, she takes another sip from her glass, swallows, makes a little 'Mmm' sound at the back of her throat.

I watch her and I listen to the music. I drink quickly, and my body begins to melt away from me. I like how it feels. I like how Paige looks. She doesn't seem to have any edges any more. She is an accumulation of colours.

Still with her eyes closed, still swaying ever so gently, she says, "It wasn't just about the rabbit, was it?" And then she opens her eyes and moves towards me. "Do you want to talk about it?"

Kneeling at my feet, she leans forward, folds her arms on my knees. "We don't have to, but I'd like to help you, if I can."

"Why would you like to help me?"

She rests her chin on her arms, takes a breath.

"Because once in a blue moon, Rebecca, you meet someone who you connect with straight away. There's just this thing, this radiance that happens, a kind of recognition, and it's such a rarity, such a thing to be cherished, that you don't want to lose hold of it or piss it away like it meant nothing. You want to talk it into staying."

And I don't know if it's the Scotch or the music or the forest dark that we have shared, but I find myself reaching forward and touching her hair with the tips of my fingers.

"You've been so kind to me, Paige, but..." I look away from her. "Tonight, I don't *know* what happened." She lifts her head. "I'm not sure that I can explain it."

I take another sip from my glass, hesitant, wanting to slip out from under her gaze, but she holds me in place with it, poised, waiting, and gradually, something in me begins to relent, and I know that I have to tell her the truth.

"Someone died." I say it quickly. "And I think, I mean... I don't know, but I think, I might be somehow to blame."

She nods gravely. "I see." And then she reaches for the bottle and refills my glass. "This someone who died, are they connected with Adam?"

And my chest grows suddenly tight at the sound of his name. I can feel blood lifting to my cheeks.

Paige must see it, because she says straight away, "It's okay. We don't have to talk about him if you don't want to."

We both sip softly at our Scotch then, the moment diffusing, and I *do* want to tell her – unravel it all into the air and have her make it better, as I somehow know she would, but the words are tied up tight as the grave inside me.

In the end, all I can say, vaguely, is, "It's a long story."

Paige smiles. "Let's save it for another day, then."

And, for a while, we just sit, listening to Nina Simone, drinking single malt, and my body grows loose-limbed and sultry, and the night draws on like a slow dance.

Suddenly though, Paige grows animated.

"I have an idea," she says, standing. "Hang on here a sec." She leaves the room, returning after a moment with a tray in her hands. She sets it down on the carpet. "I'm learning the art of Mehndi," she says. "Henna body painting. Have you heard of it?"

I nod. "Like tattooing?"

"Kind of, I guess, but it's got a lot more to do with ritual and magic, and its very ancient. It's been used for thousands of years in India and the Middle East." She begins to unload items from the tray. "A friend of mine is opening a Mehndi studio down in Christchurch and she asked me if I'd like to get involved, so I've been looking into it, and practising." Dipping her head towards me, she says meaningfully, "The henna plant has the power to protect. It wards off the evil eye, guards against black magic, harmful genies..."

"Is that so?"

"Most *definitely*. It's a feminine art, practised by women on women; a meditation, a kind of spiritual experience, and it's never done carelessly, or lightly..." she wags a finger at me, and then lifts a little ceramic bowl filled with water onto the coffee table by my side "... but always with an eye to the gods."

Dipping a piece of cotton wool into the water, she presses it gently against the side of the bowl.

"Give me your hand," she says.

"Is this going to hurt?"

"No. Trust me."

So I do. I give her my hand and she holds it in hers, and trails the cotton wool across my palm and along each of my fingers in turn, presses against the joints; little circular movements that tickle like the feet of a sparrow against my skin. She is making clean her canvas, and the water is as cool as the night.

After a while, she dries my palm with a towel, dips the tips of her fingers into a smaller bowl on the tray.

"What's that?" My voice is a whisper. I feel like we're sharing a secret.

"Eucalyptus oil. It absorbs the henna and seals it."

She massages my palm, her face filled with concentration, her fingers moving from the centre; out to the tips of my fingers, then back again. My skin feels soft and exhausted beneath her touch.

She looks up into my face. "I'm going to draw a lotus flower for you," she says, and the air prickles with eucalyptus and desire. I try to blink them away.

"A lotus flower."

"Yes." She picks up a little plastic bottle filled with something dark; tobacco-brown, luminous, and she presses the tip to the centre of my palm, begins to draw.

"This," she says, "will bring you good fortune and many blessings. It's the sacred flower of the Hindu gods."

I watch her, and my heart swells, something hot and liquid shifting its weight inside me. This is a new thing, this tenderness, and I do not fully understand it. I have tried, all along, to hold friends at bay. I have turned away from intimacy, because it has never suited my purpose; even my lovers, even Adam – my dear, sweet Adam – I was never true to them, because the truth was an aberration to me. So how is it that Paige has caught me beneath all my defences? How is it that she has reduced me to this actuality? I want to wrench my hand free of hers and run, but I don't.

Instead, I say, "Tell me a story."

"What kind of story?"

I let my head fall back against the cushions, glance up at the ceiling and around the room. "Tell me something nice about this house."

She takes a little cotton swab from a pack on the tray and dabs at the edge of my palm.

"My grandparents lived here when they first got married." She hesitates, thinks a moment. "The story goes back further than that though, I guess."

Adjusting her position on the carpet, she turns my hand to the light and inspects it. I can see a flower taking shape. Its petals are tiny tongues.

"They met during the war. My grandfather was a chaplain to the Hampshire Regiment, and my grandma was a Canadian nurse stationed at a field hospital in Naples." She pauses, reaches for her glass and takes a sip, holding it in her mouth a moment before swallowing. Leaning a little to the side, she stretches the muscles in the small of her back. "The story goes that they were both seven thousand feet up in the Apennines. My grandfather was helping to recover the wounded from the battlefield and my grandma was receiving them. Supposedly, when my grandfather was told that forty men were lying wounded on the other side of the River Gari, near a place called Cassino, and no assault boats were available to bring them back, he immediately stripped off his clothes, tied a signal cable around his waist and swam through the water, which was being raked by machine gun and mortar fire! God knows how he survived, but he did, and when he got to the other side, he hauled a doctor back across with a supply of splints and dressings, swam back *again* to look for a boat, found one, amazingly, all tangled up in ropes mid-stream, and managed to untangle it and drag it to the opposite bank, where it was used to evacuate the wounded." She takes a breath and looks up into my face, smiles a big, proud smile. "He was a bit of a dude, my grandpa."

"To put it mildly."

"Thing is, you see, my grandma saw all of this. She was up on the hill with the orderlies, and she watched him, watched the whole thing, and she knew, straight off."

I lean towards her. Her breath settles like a butterfly on my palm. "Knew what, exactly?"

"That there would never be anyone else like him in the world."

Lifting my hand into the light, she shows me the flower that has taken root there.

"See," she says. "This means that you will be forever favoured, marked as a daughter of the light."

I bring my hand close to my mouth and breathe in the scent of eucalyptus. My fingertips tingle, and the lamplight is lemon-coloured and rests kindly on Paige's face. She sits back, smiles, and discreetly, very quietly, the lotus flower blossoms.

Eight

It is early morning, threaded with mist: forest ponies peering at me from the roadside, their dark heads heavy with sleep and the sound of birds. Trees weep leaves into the path of my car.

I hadn't wanted to stay the night at Paige's house. It had felt like an intrusion, but single malt and the tug of sleep meant that I had no choice. She offered me her bed, then her grandma's bed, then a narrow little coffin-shaped bed in the box room, but, like Goldilocks in reverse, I declined them all. For some reason that I still can't fathom, I insisted on sleeping downstairs in the armchair. Now, every muscle in my body creaks and a hangover the size of Mid-Glamorgan is hoving into view.

I left Paige a note, propped up against a teapot in the kitchen. It said, *thank you for last night*. That was all it said. I'd wanted suddenly to say everything to her, but everything had a shape and sharp edges and a strange scent that I couldn't quite fit in a note, so I just said *thank you for last night* instead, and hoped that she'd guess the rest.

It doesn't take me long to work out the route back to Southampton. I just follow signs for the motorway and in less than thirty minutes, I find myself driving alongside the Common towards home. Everywhere, the air is filled with an uncanny quiet.

When I step into my flat and look at the clock, it reads 7.15am. Paige won't even be awake yet. It is Saturday after all, a day of leisure.

I try to picture her asleep in the room she showed to me last night. She will be snuggled down inside the duvet, her pale hair spilling like water across the pillow. She'll be surrounded on all sides by books and pictures, photographs of college friends and family, big green leafy plants, silence.

There's a huge coloured mask hanging above her bed. I thought it was African at first, but she said no – North American. It's called Eagle Human; a tiny little grinning man with big red lips and flaring nostrils peering over the forehead of a green eagle. The eagle's beak is shaped like a fang, but its expression is benevolent, long-suffering. The little man's hands are tightly grasping the eagle's ears, set for a journey, or so it looks. Paige told me that in tribal tradition, the eagle is a spiritual bird, invoked in times of torment, and that is what the mask is supposed to depict; the moment of rescue, the voyage to safety.

I liked the story. I liked how she told it, although by then, my body had begun to float free of me, and the green eagle actually seemed to be heading out of the room in gentle flight. I leant against the doorframe, smiling like a fool, and she carried on talking, as if it were the most important thing in the world, to talk to *me*.

Now, back inside my own flat, I am cold and tired and last night is taking on an insubstantiality: the pub, the rabbit, henna painting, Nina Simone – far away and quickly receding. I can't quite explain it, but it rests on a sense of things being out of time, mistaken, pictures from someone else's storybook. That was never *me* surely, that ridiculous woman by the roadside, crying like a child. What *was* I thinking? So, I hit a rabbit. Big deal. People must do it all the time in the forest, and although she was kind to me, Paige, there need not be any transformation attached to kindness. It doesn't change anything. I understand what people mean now by *the cold light of day*, because that's what it feels like. I can see everything clearly, unfuddled by drink, music, sympathy. I'd gone to the forest to find out about Adam, but I'd failed. Next time, I might not, and that's all I want to think about.

I make a huge pot of strong black coffee and sit on the sofa sipping at it, watching children's television with the sound turned up high, gathering myself together like the scattered pieces of a jigsaw. After a while, I am a whole picture again, and one that I recognise. This pleases me. I take a deep breath in and exhale very slowly, letting last night flutter out into the white light of today. I make myself some toast with lots of butter, and eat it hungrily, leaning against the refrigerator, and then I turn on the central heating and listen to the water bubbling like music through the pipes.

For a while, I just sit quietly in the living room, trying to think about nothing very much, watching the light changing colour at the window, flicking through old magazines, and a kind of peacefulness settles, diffuses, sinks into my bones like treacle. I run myself a bath. Someone once said that there's nothing like a hot bath to make you feel like yourself again, and that's exactly what it does. By the time I step out on to the bathroom mat and rub myself dry with a huge fluffy towel, I am as purposeful as possible and start striding like a viking about the flat, tidying everything away, throwing great wads of dirty clothes into the washing machine, watering plants in an ecological frenzy.

I pull on a grey vest top and a pair of khaki dungarees and begin to scrub at the tiles that surround my fireplace. I've been meaning to do it for ages, and now is the time, I've decided, and it's *so* satisfying. I start to understand the allure of physical activity. A pleasant sweat breaks out on my forehead; travail, drudgery. I feel noble, at one with the world of work.

Gradually, the little yellow flowers that have been clouded over with crap since I moved in begin to emerge, their petals surprisingly explicit and vivid. I can almost taste them – butterscotch and sunshine and finesse. The man in the DIY shop told me that to remove really deep smoke and oil stains, I should apply a mud poultice, and I bought the ingredients from him in a moment of innocent abandon: paint whiting, hydrogen peroxide. I *love* the sound of chemicals. They make me feel so important, like I know what I'm doing.

Pulling a pair of pink Marigolds on to my hands, I mingle the chemicals gently in a bucket and then apply them with the tips of my fingers and a ball of cotton wool, and everything begins to acquire a kind of perpetuity: petals, green stalks like a tangle of hands, a ceramic snowlight-white. I feel like one of those pilgrim few, uncovering an ecclesiastical mosaic, inch by inch, with a little brush, diligent and selfless. It feels good, removed somehow from Adam and Paige and perplexity.

It is in this mood of sudden fervour that I register the sound of someone knocking at my door. I hurry to answer it, thinking that it might be Olive complaining about the volume of the TV, but, bugger me, if it isn't Paige standing on my doorstep.

"Flippin' Nora," she says, rocking back on her heels. "What have you been up to?"

"What d'you mean?"

"Your face!" She reaches towards me but, instinctively, I duck away. "You're covered in paint, or something."

I wipe the back of my hand across my cheek and step aside as she breezes straight past me into the flat.

"It's a mud poultice," I say, a certain degree of satisfaction in my voice. "I'm cleaning the fireplace."

She crouches down to inspect my work, then turns towards me with a smile.

"A late Victorian burnished cast iron with a rococo filigree," she says. "*Very* attractive."

I feel my mouth fall open.

Paige gives a little laugh. "My mum's an interior designer."

She holds out her hands. There's something in them.

"Here, I made you some pumpkin bread."

"Some what?"

"It should still be warm."

Standing up, she slips off her leather jacket and drops it like a discarded skin on to the sofa, and then she wanders around the room, looking at my pictures.

"Lived here long?" She slides a finger along the mantelpiece.

"Yes... No..." The bread feels like a small head in my hands, luke-warm and pliable as pleasure. "A year or so. Look... Paige," I set my little bundle down on the coffee table and pull off my gloves with a rubbery twang, "what are you doing here exactly, and more to the point, how did you know where I lived?"

She turns around and inclines her head like a border collie. "You told me last night."

"Did I?"

"Don't you remember? We were talking about those Andrew Wyeth books you've got, and you said you'd lend them to me and you gave me your address."

"I don't remember a conversation about Andrew Wyeth."

She nods and narrows her eyes a little, peering past me at some-thing that has taken her interest on the wall behind.

"That's one of his, isn't it?"

I turn to look and she comes and stands by my side.

"Er, yeah it is, I think."

"What's it called?"

"Night Sleeper."

"Night Sleeper. That's nice. I don't think I've ever seen it before." She glances at me, her eyes flickering away from mine and then back. "When did he paint it?"

"Not sure."

I move closer to the picture and look at it properly, something I haven't done for a long time, and I realise that I can't even remember now why I have it. A woman at work lent it to me when I first moved in, but I rarely look at it.

It shows a dog, a Labrador, pale yellow and fast asleep in a window, its head resting on a long canvas bag that is covered with blue and white stripes. Outside the window, there is a stone barn ablaze with moonlight, distinct. The murky light inside the room and the re-splendence outside it seem to settle and coalesce in the little figure of the dreaming dog. It is, I realise with a start, a very beautiful painting.

Paige comes up close behind me.

"What's going on in it?" she asks. "Do you know?"

"I do, actually." And I'm caught off-guard for a moment by how pleased I feel that I can tell her what this picture's about. I feel like a child with the right answer, my hand thrust like a spire into the air to catch the teacher's attention, except that I already *have* Paige's attention, and somehow, that makes it even better. I don't know why it should.

"I read an interview with Wyeth in a book at the library, and he talked about this picture, about where it came from." I swallow back the edge of excitement in my voice. "He said that he woke up one night and came downstairs to get a drink and found his dog, *this* dog, Nell, asleep in the window and when he looked at her, she didn't seem to be his dog any more. Asleep, deeply asleep, she looked completely different. He barely recognised her. The expression on her face had changed her into another dog altogether, so he painted her, to keep the look, you know, to preserve it."

Paige shifts a little behind me and I turn to meet her gaze. Her face is sharp as a cube and full of interest.

"A transformation, then?"

"So it seems."

She slides round to stand in front of me, her face close to mine and animated.

"I kind of know what he means," she says, and her dark eyes widen. "Sometimes, when I've taken someone home and we've fallen asleep, like, you know... after..." She shrugs, almost an apology, but not quite. "Then, I've woken up and they've been there in the bed, of course, but they've looked nothing like I thought they looked. I mean, sometimes, they've been strangers anyway, yeah, but asleep, they've looked even stranger than a stranger – does that make sense? Like something has fallen away from them, pretence maybe, something, and there's just a face in the bed, kind of naked, unfamiliar." She looks at me hard. "D'you know what I mean?"

I look at her and then I look at the picture, and I want to say, yes, of course I know what she means, but I don't. I've never spent a whole night in someone else's bed, or had them spend a whole night in mine. Sex has only ever been an exchange for me, short-lived, a confirmation of how clever I am. I tell a lie and it is attractive enough to seduce, and that's it. The sex itself has always been incidental to the plot.

Only with Adam, maybe, did I catch the edge of something else. One time I remember, near the beginning, we were in his room, at his mother's house in Brentwood, and it was dark, but he'd lit some candles, vanilla candles. Everywhere, the air smelled like ice cream. It made me smile, and *he* made me smile; his face so close to mine that I couldn't focus, his body covering my body. We were laughing, about something, or nothing, I don't remember which, but I remember the *sound* of my laughter, mingling with his – a kind of music, sudden as a shriek of strings, a song of bells. It took my breath away, to be that happy, that un-self-conscious, and making love to him that night, I was quiet, composed; something in me silenced and brought to book. I hadn't any words left for him, because I didn't need any. Only once in a lifetime does that happen, surely, and, oh my God, it had happened to *me*, and I was absolutely confounded by it, and aghast. I moved to the spare room as soon as he'd fallen asleep.

Paige waits, her fingers laced in front of her stomach, until I say, cheerily, "Yes. I know what you mean."

She nods, punches me playfully in the shoulder. "Shall I fix us some lunch? That pumpkin bread goes really well with an omelette and a glass of wine."

So, I put a bottle of Sancerre into the refrigerator to cool and Paige rummages around in my cupboards until she finds the ingredients she's looking for. She seems incredibly at home in my kitchen, almost as if she's been here before. Her fingers tap an inadvertent tune on pots and pans, jars, utensils. I like the sound of it.

"You won't ever have tasted an omelette as good as the one you are about to taste now," she says. "I'm about to give you..." she hesitates, lifts her hands into the air a little, closes her eyes, then opens one and peers at me "... an entirely *orgasmic* experience."

"Is that so?"

"You don't believe me, but you'll see."

She breaks three eggs quickly into a bowl, adds a tablespoon of grated Parmesan cheese and a little black pepper, and beats the mixture together as if her life depended upon it.

I watch her hard at work, and begin to wonder how it is that she has dropped into my life so easily and set up camp there. A few days ago, I didn't even know she existed, and now here she is, intimate and friendly, with one of my tea towels draped over her shoulder, and my name on her lips as if it has always lived there. I don't normally like surprises, but as hard as I may try not to, I can't *help* liking this one.

She chats away, about her grandma in hospital, her PhD, her part-time job at a pub in town, and then, adding a thick spoonful of cream to the pan, she says lightly, "It was at the pub that I first met Adam, actually."

I look away from her. Having wanted, all along, to ask her about him, I now find that the sound of his name clenches my stomach into a fist.

"It was about a month ago."

She concentrates hard on her omelette, tipping the pan towards her until the yellow mixture nearly spills.

"He made some joke about needing to raid the charity box on the bar to be able to afford a pint, and I said something stupid back about where did he think I got all my tips from."

The mixture begins to bubble. Paige turns down the heat and flicks her hair back from her face. Her cheeks are slightly flushed. When she lifts her head to look at me, there is, unmistakably, an apology in her eyes; a child caught out in a misdemeanour.

She shrugs. "I liked him at first. He was funny, and he didn't seem to care what he said to people. I mean, there's loads of wankers out at weekends, all getting hammered or stoned, or both. All talking crap, you know? He wasn't like that. You could have a proper conversation with him, and if anyone was hassling me, he'd kind of step in with some clever put-down to make them look thick, or piss them off enough that they'd go away."

She slices the omelette in two with a wooden spatula and slides the halves on to separate plates.

"After a while though, things changed. He wouldn't only wind up people who deserved it, he'd have a go at anybody; come on all friendly and then turn on them, just like that." She snaps her thumb and forefinger together. "I didn't get it, and I told him I didn't, but he just thought it was hilarious. And then I was behind him in the queue at the library that day when he started on you."

Turning towards me, she puts a hand on my arm and squeezes.

"I didn't know what it was about, Rebecca, but I could see he'd made you feel bad and I didn't like it."

Keeping her hand where it is, she takes a step closer, until our faces are level. I can see little flecks of green in the brown of her irises, like the trails of tiny comets.

"The next night, he came into the pub, all smiles as usual, and I told him off for how he'd been with you, and that's when he said that I had no right to judge him because you were his ex-girlfriend and you'd dumped him and it was only fair that he should get his own back, give you a taste of your own medicine."

I swallow hard. "A taste of my own medicine. What d'you think he meant?"

She cups my cheek in her hand, eases a loose strand of hair back behind my ear.

"I don't know, sweetheart."

Her fingers are warm with a borrowed heat from the stove, and gentle, but her voice, when it comes again, is wary.

"Are you sure *you* don't know what he means?"

I look at her hard. "I'm not his ex-girlfriend."

"Then what exactly *are* you?"

And I don't know how to answer her, because what on earth *am* I to this man, this stranger? I know what I am to the real Adam, but this isn't the real Adam.

I close my hands together over my breastbone and feel my heart beating fast, thudding hard against my palms like a bird against glass, and I look at Paige and an awful thought falls like a blow.

"When did you last see him?"

"That night," she says, and she looks puzzled. "He hasn't been in since."

"Are you sure?"

"Yeah, I'm sure."

I narrow my eyes at her. "Did he send you here, Paige?"

She exhales then, from her nose, a small laugh, and her face opens up in disbelief.

"Are you serious? What d'you think this is, Rebecca? What, you think I'm some kind of fucking stalker or something?" She points a finger at me, jabs it in the air. "Is that what you think?"

"No... Maybe. Look... I don't know."

I move towards her, but she takes a big step back, and her face slams shut. Behind her, the window is filled with leaves and a sky as white as fury.

"I'm sorry, Paige, but I don't really *know* you, do I? I don't know what agenda you might have here."

"Why do I have to have an agenda?" She straightens up, says in a high voice, "Didn't you get any of what I was saying to you last night, about how people connect sometimes? Didn't you get that I was talking about you and me?"

The kitchen seems suddenly filled with too much light and too much air. It hurts my head to breathe them in.

"I did, but..."

"Then what's all this shit about?"

My arms drop to my sides and I feel my shoulders sag. "When you were talking about Adam just then, I guess I got paranoid. I thought maybe you and he were..."

Paige steps forward, lifts the omelette pan from the stove and drops it with a clatter into the sink, and then she turns and looks at me dead straight. The surface of my skin seems to contract, until I am all bone.

"Do you honestly think," she says, each word a breath, "that I would let anyone manipulate me like that?"

And I shake my head straight away. "No."

"Or that I would deliberately set out to get close to someone so that I could hurt them?"

"No."

"Then don't ever say anything like that to me again."

"I won't." I keep shaking my head as if to emphasise the point. "I won't," and then I creep towards her a little, "I'm sorry."

She looks down at her feet and shakes her head, says quietly, "So you should be."

Moving closer still, I reach out and take her hand, hold onto it tight between both of mine.

"Things have been crazy here. I'm just not thinking straight. You wouldn't believe..." But something in my throat turns hard suddenly; silver-white and shiny as panic.

Paige looks up very slowly, sighs, says so softly it almost breaks my heart, "Will you *please* just tell me the truth."

And I do.

Nine

Paige sits on my sofa, with her legs curled under her body, and I tell her everything. We forget about the omelette. Instead, we drink the wine and Paige picks holes in the pumpkin bread, and I watch her face as she tries to fathom the tale that I'm telling. I go right back to the beginning; my dad falling off the ladder, Hameed and Gary Light, the shape of the stories in between, then Adam, Kate, Will, and, last of all, the other Adam, the one *she* knows, the one who has brought us to this inexplicable point of connection.

All the while, she sits quietly, slipping tiny pieces of pumpkin bread into her mouth, chewing thoughtfully, sipping at her wine. Her face doesn't keep pace with what I'm saying. It folds itself into an expression of bemused concern and stays there. I find myself growing gradually heady on fact, breathless with the truth. It sits uneasily in my lap, like a ventriloquist's dummy, constantly ready to contradict itself. I don't let it.

When at last I'm done, I drain my glass dry and wait for what Paige will say, but, for a while, she doesn't say anything at all, just crumples herself up a little more and stares at the carpet. Her hair falls forward like a veil, and the afternoon stretches wide and white around us.

Now that it's over, now that someone knows it *all*, I find myself beginning to breathe easy. There isn't that rock hard thing in my lungs any more – a rattle of ingenuity, a ball of bad sound. There is

91

just the white afternoon burning the back of my throat with release and repose.

Paige lifts her head.

"So you think Kate might know who this Adam really is?"

"Maybe. I have a photo of him, from the funeral. She might recognise him."

"But how are you going to find her?"

"I haven't worked that one out yet."

She shakes her head. "You think this guy, this Adam, is somehow out to get you, then, and all the weird stuff that's been happening to you recently is a kind of, what... punishment, for your lies, over the years?"

"Yes, I do. He said to me, *Your sins have found you out, Rebecca*. What else could he have been talking about but my lies?"

"But who the fuck *is* he? Why would he have such a grudge against you?"

"I don't know."

"He has to be connected with Adam, the real Adam, to know so much about you."

"Yep, but I can't think of any of Adam's friends who would..."

And then I remember.

"Oh God. There was this *one* bloke, but..." I shake it away.

Paige leans forward, intrigued. "What bloke?"

"It was all really embarrassing, and stupid."

"What was?"

I take a breath, let it out with a sigh inside it.

"Not long before Adam and I split up, his friend, Simon, turned up at this party we were at, in London. He'd been away travelling for months and had just got back, and he was just..." I lift my eyes to the ceiling, my palms to the air.

Paige dips her head from side to side. "He was just *what*? Sex-on-a-stick? Dull as shit? An axe-murderer? What?"

"Lovely. He was just *lovely*. He said that Adam had written him all

these letters about me, and that he'd been longing to meet me, and...
God! He was *soooooo* interesting and charismatic, and *full* of stories.
He'd travelled everywhere; paddled down the Amazon in a coracle,
climbed the pyramids, had tea with the Dalai Lama..."

"Blimey! I didn't think the Dalai Lama had tea with *anyone*."

"Well, he did with Simon, and I could see why. There was just
something about him." I smile in remembering. "He looked truly
awful, though. He had this huge great Druidy beard and dreadlocks
and really *bad* clothes, but, I dunno..."

"Yes you do." Paige raises her eyebrows, prods a finger at me. "You
fancied the knickers off him."

"I did."

She laughs. "What happened?"

"I got *completely* shit-faced and tried to snog him in the downstairs
loo, and he told me no, because he was Adam's mate *and* he had a girlfriend, and then he left me there, feeling like a right dog."

"A woman spurned." Paige rolls her tongue around the 'r' sound
and puckers her lips a little. "What did you do?"

"I told Adam that it was Simon who'd made a pass at *me*." I shake
my head, disbelieving. "Christ! I was *such* a manipulative bitch back
then, and *mean*." I look at Paige. "That was a really mean thing to do,
wasn't it?"

She nods. "What did Adam say?"

"He confronted Simon apparently, and they had this big fight. It
was awful, and I knew I'd caused it." I slink down onto the floor, mor-
tified. "Adam wouldn't believe Simon when he said it was *me* who'd
come on to *him*. I don't think they spoke again after that."

"What, not ever?"

"I don't think so. I did try to tell Adam the truth when we split up,
but by then he wasn't interested."

"You drove a wedge between *blood* brothers!"

I cover my face with my hands. "Oh gawd, don't say that. I'd never
have done it if I hadn't been drunk."

"That's no excuse."

"What's worse is that the girlfriend Simon mentioned was only bloody Kate, of all people."

"No way."

"Yeah, *way!*" I let my head fall back against the sofa. "They hadn't been seeing each other for long, but once Adam told Kate what had happened at the party, she wouldn't talk to Simon either. She finished with him."

"Talk about tangled web!"

"I *know*. Believe me. I feel really shit about it, even now."

"What happened to him?"

"I've no idea. Adam and I split up a month after that."

"A loose cannon, then?"

"I doubt it. He was a vegetarian, and a pacifist, and a Buddhist, for fuck's sake. I don't think *stalking* would do much for one's essential karma, do you?"

Paige starts to laugh. "Probably not."

"Back to square one."

She nods, pauses, shakes her head. "I just can't believe you managed to maintain such a complicated lifestyle for so long, though. All that elaborate story-telling all the time. Christ, you must have been so lonely."

"Lonely?" The idea is foreign to me. "I don't know."

"But, not having anyone of your own who you could be honest with. I mean..." She sits forward, rests the heels of her hands on her knees. "It must have been so isolating."

"No." My voice is louder than I mean it to be. "You don't understand. It was... my God, it was *absolutely* satisfying, up to a point, if that's not a contradiction in terms."

"*Really?*"

"Yes." I take a breath, hold it. "Think of the best sex you've ever had, and multiply the feeling by ten, a hundred even..." I lift my hands and clap them together. My face is smiling. "Paige, believe me, that kind of power, it's like a drug."

She shakes her head. "I don't get it."

"You're not meant to."

"But I want to."

"Why?"

Reaching for the bottle of Sancerre, she empties the dregs into her glass. "It feels important, somehow, to understand."

"Why would you want to understand? *Why* does it matter to you?"

Paige runs her tongue along her bottom lip, shrugs. "Who knows?"

She falls back into her seat and looks up to the ceiling. "I used to work with a guy ages ago whose name was Grant Bunny, and he hated it, the Bunny part." She chuckles lightly, shakes her head so that her hair tumbles slightly at the edges. Her face is filled with a baffled light, an iridescence. "So," she says, clearing her throat, "he changed it, by deed poll, I think. Last time I met him, he introduced himself as Grant Bailey, and I was like, *what are you on about?*"

Pulling herself up straight, she looks at me from under her eyebrows. "I didn't get that either, but then I kind of *did*, after a while. He needed to make himself feel better by being someone else, and so did you. It's not the end of the world to do that."

"But my life was a lie."

"No it wasn't."

"Yes, it was."

She slips onto the floor and sits on her knees, asks wearily, "Drunken encounters in public conveniences aside, did you love Adam, the *real* Adam?"

I hesitate, swallow hard. "I think so. I mean, I really cared about him. I think I probably did, once."

"Then that wasn't a lie."

"No, but…"

Leaning forward, she places a finger to my lips. "Leave it there," she says.

"He died though, Paige, because of me, maybe."

"No. You shouldn't think like that."

Hauling herself to her feet, she comes to sit beside me on the sofa. Her body seems to fill my space. "People do all sorts of things for all sorts of reasons, and if we were to try to work out our place in their thinking every time, we'd go *barmy* with it." She covers my hands with her own. "Maybe you didn't do the absolute best by him. Maybe you *did* hurt him by leaving, but people leave all the time. People fall out of love *all* the time, and whose responsibility is that, after all? Would you have done a better thing by staying when you didn't mean it?"

I shake my head.

"Well then." She takes a last long gulp from her glass and sets it down precariously on the coffee table. "I rest my case."

And something lifts in an arc above my head – a smoke signal, a coloured flare. I breathe in tight. "It can't be as easy as that."

But Paige turns full tilt to look at me, her eyes shining; marble-heavy and keen as hope. "Why the *fuck* not?" she says.

And I let my face open up into a beam of light. Its edges are sheer and slippery as snow underfoot. I almost fail to recognise it as my own.

"You, madam," says Paige, slipping her arm around my waist. "Need to let yourself off the hook."

"Easier said than done."

"Not... at... all."

She touches the air on each word, watches me as if I might break into pieces and flutter away, and then, before I realise quite what's happening, she moves forward and kisses me on the lips; a quick kiss, light and comical, but then she hesitates with her face close to mine and moves her right hand onto the curve of my shoulder, then into my hair. Her expression, for a moment, is one of cautious optimism.

She smiles at me, moves slowly forward and kisses me again, deeper this time. Her hand tangles tighter in my hair, keeps my mouth moving against hers, and it's the most surprising sensation I can ever remember. I could pull away if I wanted to. I could leap indignantly to my feet and demand that she go, but I don't. I stay there, unutterably fascinated by how her lips feel – so soft that they almost aren't there at all; and how her skin feels – smooth as a child's; and how her hand closes warm around the back of my neck and sends a shock, like static electricity, clear down my spine and into the tips of my fingers.

I let myself sink into it, spellbound, feeling her left hand moving tentatively inside my vest. I'm not wearing a bra, and she cups my naked breast, then lets her fingertips circle the nipple with the lightest of pressures, until it stands out hard. I try to lift my hands to touch her, but they are two stones in my lap; pale as water and burning with ineptitude. Instead, I keep my eyes closed, and feel how our tongues move distractedly, over and under each other, and I wonder how it is that I have never tried to summon this sensation before. I have lived my life outside of every parameter except this one, and I can't for the life of me think why.

Suddenly, there is a knock at the door, and Paige and I break apart.

"Don't answer it," she whispers, her eyes very wide and twinkling with misconduct.

"I have to. It's probably Olive from downstairs. She knows I'm home."

"So?"

"So, she'll keep knocking at the door until I answer it. This woman could aggravate for England, believe me."

Paige nods and settles back into the cushions, says in a martyred kind of a voice, "So be it."

Standing up, I take a breath and press my fingers to my lips for a moment, gather myself, and then I walk to the door and open it, and Olive is nowhere to be seen. In her place is a man I recognise, but his features are misted over with fatigue. He looks as if he has just woken up, or is just about to fall asleep.

"You told me it would be all right to come," he says, setting a brown canvas bag down by his feet. "I had..." he shakes his head, rakes his fingers back through his hair, "I couldn't think of anywhere else to go and I *had* to go somewhere."

He sways slightly in his place, reaches his hand out and steadies himself against the doorframe. "I couldn't stay there any more, Rebecca. I just..." His voice breaks and falls.

"Will... my God, look at you."

I take a step towards him and close my arms around his shoulders, hold him tight, but his whole body is trembling. I squeeze him hard as I can, try to transfer my warmth straight through his skin to his bones, but I can almost hear the weary murmur of blood in his veins, faint as leaves falling.

He makes a soft sound against my neck, falters slightly. "I'm sorry," he says.

"Don't be."

Keeping an arm firm around his waist, I reach for his bag and help him into the flat like a wounded soldier.

Paige is already on her feet and searching for her jacket.

"I'll go," she says quietly, looking at Will and then at me. "If you want me to."

"I think that might be best."

I ease Will down into a seat, where he leans his head back and closes his eyes. He looks so cold, his skin paper-thin and grey as old rain, and he isn't even wearing a coat, just a faded black sweater and a pale pair of jeans.

Crouching down by his knees, I take hold of his hand and rub it gently between my own. Paige comes to stand over me.

"I'm due at the Swan in an hour," she whispers. "Maybe you could come down later and see me?"

I look up into her face. "I don't know. It could be difficult, now."

She nods. "I understand that, but it might be just what he needs. From everything you've told me, this boy has had enough quiet nights at home to last him a lifetime. See what you can do? We should talk."

"Okay."

She winks at me, turns towards the door, but just as she reaches it, I call after her, "Paige."

She swings round, inclines her head.

But I look away from her face and then back, and then away again. "I had something to say, but…" I shrug my shoulders.

She just grins, turns, and pulls the door closed behind her. I can hear her whistling as she runs down the stairs. I can hear her feet tap-tapping on the marble, and I can taste her, even now, sweet as wine and pumpkin bread in my mouth – an unsettling sacrament.

Will sleeps in the armchair for five hours straight and then he wakes up, wide-eyed with embarrassment and wanting a bath.

"I shouldn't have just turned up like this," he says, leaning in the bathroom doorway while I turn on the taps and slosh some revitalising bubble bath around in the water.

"Stop saying that. I invited you, didn't I?"

"Yes, but…"

"No buts. Here…" I hand him a towel and ease myself past him. "Take as long as you need, all right? I'll make us something to eat."

He nods, smiles with one side of his mouth, says, "Thanks, Bex," in a voice which is so much like his brother's that I feel sudden tears burning needle-hot behind my eyes.

I turn around to face him, but I can't say anything. Instead, I just nod my head fast and hurry into the kitchen.

It is dark outside now. The window has become a mirror, snaky with steam and blurred at the edges, and there I am, framed, staring hard into a rectangle of black; smudges of oil from the fire like bruises on my cheeks, my hair vaguely chaotic with touch, my lips parted as if I'm about to say something, except that I'm not. For the first time in a long time, I have nothing to say. There is only the sound of silence singing through my blood, and, for a moment, it is too much for me. I panic, turn the radio on loud and make lots of noise with pots and pans and running water. I sing along to songs, keep switching stations so that there isn't any break in the music. I drown myself out with a shriek of activity, until, suddenly, Will is standing in the doorway, smiling.

"Very tuneful," he says. "Are you planning to take it up professionally?"

"Not exactly." I gesture for him to take a seat at the table. "Is beans on toast all right? I haven't got much in."

"Anything would be all right. It's just nice not to have to cook."

I slide a steaming plate in front of him and he starts to eat immediately, and I swear I've never seen anyone look so pleased by beans on toast.

"In case you were wondering," he says between mouthfuls, "Mum's staying with that neighbour I told you about. I haven't run out on her."

I sit down opposite him with a plate of my own and start to eat. "I didn't think you'd run out on her, Will. I just thought Kate might have come back or something."

"No. We still haven't heard from her. I'm getting a bit worried, to be honest." He pokes a few beans around with his fork. "Mum's in a terrible state. As if it hasn't nearly ruined her to lose one child, now it's like she's lost another one. Kate promised to get in touch for Mum's birthday last week, but she didn't, and that's not like her."

"She hasn't been in contact at *all* recently?"

"Not for a few weeks, but I guess she might just be away with friends or something. I hope she is. I hope she's sunning herself on a beach somewhere and taking it easy. Adam's death was so hard on her, and then there was the inquest, which meant we couldn't have the funeral for a few weeks, and that *really* got to her, not being able to say goodbye, you know? But, even so..." he takes a breath. "I miss her."

"Doesn't she have a mobile phone?"

"Yes, but she left it at home with us. I was gonna give it back to her at the funeral, but she didn't turn up."

"Ah yes." And suddenly, my appetite loops and falls. "The funeral."

"Why d'you say it like that?"

"No reason."

He lowers his eyebrows. "You're still a shit liar, Rebecca."

"Okay. I'll tell you, but you're not going to like it."

He puts down his knife and fork and sits back in his chair. "Try me."

And so, for the second time in the same afternoon, the truth, or what I believe the truth to be, rises like a measure of mercury and spills, and Will takes it all in without flinching, but when I'm done, he looks me straight in the eye and a thin shiver of light seems to shoot between us.

"How can I be sure that this isn't just another one of your stories?"

And, of course, I have no answer for him, nothing to say that could ever convince him that this is the truth, a truth that is intolerable to me, and a burden in a way that my lies never were. I wish it *were* a story, but it isn't.

I lean my elbows on the table. "I guess you can't be sure. You have no reason to trust me, but I need your help, all the same."

"How can *I* help you?"

"You can help me try to work out who this man is, and why he's turned up now, and what he *wants*."

Will looks at me for a long moment, seems to be struggling with something, and then he stands up.

"Where's my bag?"

"It's over by the front door. Why?"

I follow him through into the living room, where he crouches down and rummages around inside the brown holdall. After a moment, he turns to me with a videotape in his hands.

"Do you remember my cousin Pete? He used to play football with Adam and me."

I think back, and yes, there he is. Pete, trotting up the driveway in his football kit, the studs on his boots rattling like a round of applause on the concrete. I liked him. He was tall as a tree, with rusty brown hair and an emphatic smile.

"Yes. He lived in Colchester with his girlfriend, didn't he?"

Will nods and holds the videotape out for me to take. "This is a video of his wedding, last month. I was watching it yesterday, and I brought it with me so you could see how the family are doing."

I take it from him, a little bewildered as to how this fits in, but pleased anyway. "Thanks. It's a nice thought."

Will sighs. "It's something else now, as well."

I turn to look at him. "What do you mean?"

"I know you stole one of my photos."

"Yes. I'm sorry about that, but I can explain."

"You don't need to. It was because *he* was in it, wasn't he?"

I nod, and Will turns on the television, takes the tape from me and slips it into the recorder underneath, then sits down on the sofa. I sit next to him with the remote control in my hands, and we watch the video together without speaking. I forget for a little while who it is that I am looking for. Instead, I lose myself amongst the flowers and the hymns, the sloping sound of easy-going Essex voices, until, suddenly, the camera veers away from the wedding party, standing for photographs in the church doorway, and out into the churchyard itself, where little groups of people are huddled and colourful and smiling under a blue sky.

I see Will, holding Irene's arm. A lady in a big purple hat, like a flying saucer, is talking to Irene, but she doesn't appear to be listening. Will is answering for his mum, filling in the spaces that she is leaving blank with her impervious face and her silence. I feel so sorry for him, comfortless in a suit that is too big and too black, a suit that I recognise at once as Adam's. He wore it to our graduation ceremony; so handsome, stalking across the stage like a panther to collect his certificate, coming back to me with his face alight and his fingers folded tight around the future.

I look away from the screen for a moment and then back. The lady with the hat is still talking, but it isn't really her that I see this time. I look past her, towards the road, where a few gravestones poke up through the grass like broken fingernails, and there, leaning against one of them, smoking a cigarette, is the man I recognise. He is wearing a beige suit with a bright blue shirt underneath, sunglasses and an expression of polite curiosity. His thick hair ruffles slightly in the breeze, makes him look inoffensive, approachable, except that no one *does* approach him. The camera moves past him in an arc, and then moves slowly back, and this time, he is staring straight into the lens, smiling. He flicks his cigarette stub into the air, turns, walks out of the church gates and away into the afternoon.

Will takes the remote control from my hands, presses the stop button and sinks back into the cushions.

"It wasn't until I watched the video yesterday that I remembered I'd seen him at the wedding, *and* the funeral, and then I realised he was the same man you'd pointed out in the flower photo. I didn't think too much of it, but..." Will rubs his eye with the heel of his hand, takes in a deep breath. I hear the air slide like a rush of silk into his lungs. He turns to face me, says very quietly, "It *is* him, isn't it?" I nod. "When did he last contact you?"

"There was a tape through my door when I got back from seeing you last week."

"A tape?"

"'Annie's Song'."

Will shakes his head and touches his forehead with the tips of his fingers. "How would he know about that?" His voice is erratic suddenly. "I mean, that was Adam's song. How would he know?"

"I've no idea." I feel very weary suddenly.

He takes a quick breath, stands up. "What the fuck's going on, Bex? Why is someone out there, saying they're Adam, pretending... it's just obscene, it's..."

"I know."

And he looks around himself for a moment, as if he's put something important down in a safe place but can't remember where, and then he snaps up straight and holds out his hand.

"Let's go," he says.

"Where to?"

He looks at me impatiently. "To find him."

"I wouldn't know where to look for him, Will."

"No, but I bet *he* knows where to look for you."

Ten

I take a quick shower, put on a blue suede dress and a little make-up, and then we leave the flat and drive in circles around Southampton, pausing every now and then outside my favourite pubs so that Will can jump out of the car and run inside to see if he can spot a face in the crowd that he recognises. Each time he returns, shaking his head, and the Saturday night sounds of carnival enter the car with him; a blare of cold air, misplaced and inappropriate.

I watch his hands clasped hard in his lap. He digs his fingernails into the skin that covers the delicate swell of his knuckles, stares straight ahead.

At one point, turning slightly, he asks, "Why doesn't your gear stick have a top?"

And I reply, "I like how it feels without it, the sharpness, against my palm."

And he nods hard like he knows exactly what I mean. It strikes me that he probably does.

When we reach the last of my haunts, the café on East Street, I decide to park the car and accompany Will inside. I need a coffee and my eyes are growing weary from the road. However, as soon as we are sitting at a table and I'm beginning to relax a little, I catch sight of Jean-Paul, the Frenchman from last week. He is sitting with two other people at a table by the bar, and he is looking at me. I can feel his eyes on me, the reprimanding heat of them, though his face is cold; blue light like ice splintering between us, and when I try smiling at him, he looks sharply away and doesn't look back.

"I can't stay here, Will."

"Why not?"

I start to stand up. "I'll explain in the car."

"No." Catching hold of my arm, he eases me back into my seat, asks again, "Why not?"

"There's someone here that I know."

He spins around to look. "You mean, he's here? Where?"

"Not *him*. Someone else."

"Who?"

I look over to the bar where Jean-Paul is laughing now with his friends, his head bowed over a tall glass of beer, his cheeks flushed with amusement. The sound of his laughter springs lightly towards us across the tables and I breathe it in, savour it. I know that I will never make him laugh like that, that he will never sit easy with me in a place like this and trust that my interest in him is honest and good-humoured. All he will remember of me is humiliation and disdain, and I can't bear to think about it.

I look away, but Will is leaning towards me with his menu, poised and expectant.

I try to smile. "It's no one really, just someone I met."

He lifts his hands. "And?"

"And nothing." A clatter of cutlery cuts through me like glass. "I'm just not comfortable, that's all."

"Comfortable!" Will raises his voice high above the noise. "What has your being comfortable got to do with *anything*? That's not why we're here. That's not why we're driving around in the dark, looking for some wanker who's using my brother's name like it meant fuck all to anybody, is it?"

I shake my head. "No, but..."

He slams his hand down flat on the table. "It's always the same with you, isn't it? As long as Rebecca's okay. As long as Rebecca's getting what *she* wants. Well, that's not what life is like, and the sooner you get used to it the better."

He flips his menu up in front of his face and I sink down in my seat with a feeling of intense mortification, and when my coffee comes, I drink it hot and burn my tongue and know for certain that that's *exactly* what I deserve.

By the time we get back to the car, my steps are laboured and the streetlights dazzle disapproval.

Will climbs into the passenger seat and pulls a map of Southampton out of the glove compartment.

"Where to now?" he says. "Where else should we go?"

I shrug. "Paige said he sometimes goes to the Swan."

"Paige?"

For an instant I feel my cheeks prickle. "The girl who was in my flat when you arrived."

"Is she a friend?"

"Kind of."

He shifts slightly in his seat, but doesn't ask me to elaborate, and I'm thankful for it, because I don't know what I would say. Everything is so muddled now, so out of sequence and disorderly. I think of Paige, of her kindness to me, of her intimacy last night and today, and my heart swells hard in my chest, but that's all. I can't fathom an explanation for it, or find a formula to explain away how everything takes on a kind of shine when I think of her name. It is alien to me and incomprehensible. If I can't clarify it for myself, how can I possibly clarify it for anyone else?

Instead, I negotiate the traffic like a rally driver, reckless now and a little desperate for space and sleep, and we end up haphazard and breathless in the Swan car park. I realise how late it has become. People are already spilling out onto the pavement, swaying vaguely into the dark. I like how they look, laced around each other, their bodies marshmallowy and sweet with delectation. They make me smile, but Will is finished with smiling. As soon as we arrive, he flings open the car door and leaps out.

"Are you coming in?"

I look towards the entrance, about to say no, but then I catch sight of someone I recognise. It takes me a moment to place her, and then I remember. Fiona.

I begin to undo my seat belt and open my door, and as I do, I hear someone calling my name.

"Rebecca, over here."

And it's her, of course, Fiona, waving like a maniac. I wave back, half-heartedly, but still she comes tottering towards us on hazardous heels.

"How're you?" She nudges at my shoulder, her face displaced by drink and well-being. "Paige's on her way out. We're going on to Maclaverty's. Wanna come?"

I steady my hand against her arm, stop her swaying.

"I don't think so."

"Aah, go on." She leans in close. Her earring catches cold against my cheek. "It's Ladies' Night, and you know what *that* means." She winks at me unevenly, shouts into the dark, "Penis power!" And then she tumbles suddenly against me and her head drops.

I put my arm around her, take her weight, which isn't very much at all, and say quietly, "Don't you think you should be getting home, Fiona?" But she flings her arm up around my neck and tries to pull herself straight.

It is then that Paige appears. She is wearing a short black dress, tight, with spaghetti straps, one of which has fallen away from her shoulder. Her hair is up and her face is slick and animated.

"Oh my!" she says when she sees us. "What *do* we have here?"

I hate how she sounds – insinuating, painfully distant, but I try to smile at her. "I think Fiona's a bit the worse for wear."

She turns to the man alongside her, a tall, blond man whom I've never seen before, and says brightly, "Never heard it called *that* before."

And then she looks past me at Will and her eyes narrow. She steps forward until she is next to him and then bumps her hip softly against his.

"I see you brought Junior with you," she says, not looking at me. "Think he can take the pace?"

I move towards her and take hold of her arm, saying gently, "Leave him alone, Paige. You're drunk."

But she closes her free hand over mine and pulls me forward, whispers into my ear, "And you're *hot*."

And then she pushes me away hard and her arm flies out white to hail a taxi. One stops almost immediately.

I reach for her again, but she slips free.

"Paige." My voice crumples slightly, but I can't help it. "What's going on?"

But she just opens the cab door and helps Fiona inside, and the man who was with them walks around to the other side and climbs in, and then she turns back to us and inclines her head.

"Aren't you coming?"

I keep eye contact with her and she doesn't waver, drunk as she is and with Fiona tugging at her skirt from behind, she holds me dead still with her gaze until I say, defiantly, "No."

But Will steps in front of me and asks her, "Where are you going again?"

"It's a club on Kingsway, Maclaverty's. You could follow us down." She leans forward, her hands on her knees. "D'you think you're up for it... Junior?"

Will spins around to look at me. "We should go, Rebecca. He might be there."

"He might not."

"We've come this far. What have we got to lose?"

And I ponder this question as I watch Paige over his shoulder; watch her looking away from us, blunted by our indecision, leaning down into the car to kiss Fiona full on the lips. I watch as Fiona's hands flutter hazily into the air, touch Paige's arm, brush against her breast.

I look at Will and I straighten up into a different kind of defiance, wanting, obtusely now, to maximise the moment, to push it as far as it will go and fall with it fast over the edge. I want control again, that old-time temerity to make things happen as *I* desire them. I hope that Adam *is* there, at Maclaverty's. I hope that I find him and that he admits who he is and what he wants. I hope for deliberacy and tears and disaster and for this whole sorry mess to be over. Most of all, I hope, suddenly, mournfully, to shake myself free of Paige and her game playing, because that's obviously all it is. I should have known. She's no better than I am, and maybe that's the thing that's most difficult to take, because I thought she was.

I look at her, kissing Fiona in front of me and not caring, and my world breaks itself unexpectedly into pieces, and I turn and say to Will, "All right. Let's go."

I've been to Maclaverty's before. It's small and noisy, but affable. The drink is cheap, and the music is a mix of old seventies and eighties tracks, with a few club classics thrown in. I came here last with some people from work and we danced the night away to Wham! and Culture Club and the B52s; fifteen again and liking it.

It feels different tonight, significant and a little daunting. For a start, as soon as we've paid our entrance fee and are safe inside, Will clings to me like a limpet and I'm not sure what to do about it. I buy him a couple of beers and he drinks them fast, leaning against a fruit machine, but when I suggest that we split up to look for Adam, he shakes his head.

"No. We should stick together."

"Why?"

He shrugs, drains dry his second bottle of Beck's. "We'll lose each other in the crowd otherwise."

"No we won't."

Tapping his foot to the music, he looks away from me, nonchalant, and then he looks back. His face is cloudy in the half-light. I squint to see what he's thinking.

He sighs, blows gently into his empty bottle until it hums, dangles it between two fingers.

"Look," he says at last, subdued. "Not to sound stupid or anything, but this..." He gestures around the room. "It's kind of new to me. There aren't any clubs in Brentwood, as you know. It's not exactly the rave centre of the universe, is it? I was looking forward to all of this, going away to college. It would have been different then, but now, suddenly, it's just a bit much to take. I feel" – he shrugs – "out of place, I guess, on edge, after Adam and Mum and everything. D'you see what I mean?"

I put my hand on his arm and squeeze hard. "Let me get you another drink?"

He nods. "Maybe just the one." And I'm about to turn back for the bar when someone bumps hard against me from behind and sends me flying into Will's arms.

Fiona is leaning in very close to my face.

"We were wondering what happened to you two," she says, not quite as drunk as before, it seems, but inordinately friendly and delicately stoned.

"You should have come with us in the cab." She draws deep on the joint poised between her fingers, lets her breath out slow. "Paige said she wanted you to."

I smile and try to mean it, because I feel a little sorry for her somehow, on her own. She looks small and very exposed amongst all these people; like someone could crash into her in the middle of a dance and snap her in two. None of this is her fault, so I lean towards her.

"Can I get you a drink, Fiona? I'm just off to the bar."

Concentrating hard on my face, she says, very slowly indeed, "Double vodka and Red Bull, please."

I turn to Will, but he gestures towards Fiona, smiling. "I'll have the same."

I swallow hard. "Are you sure?"

"What d'you mean, am I sure?" He points his empty bottle in the air like an elongated finger. "Course I'm sure."

I turn away. "Fine."

I hear the two of them chuckling behind me, a low sound, private, and it makes me cross to have the circle close and to find myself on the outside, when I've always managed to talk my way to the centre. I don't like how it feels, even for a moment, so I stalk to the bar and elbow my way through, shout at the barman when I don't need to, and end up feeling mean-spirited and stupid. This isn't what I'm used to and I resent it, but worse than that, disturbingly, and for the first time in my life, I don't seem to know how to change it.

By the time I get back to the fruit machine, Will and Fiona are pink with pleasure and Paige is there too, of course, smiling like the Queen Mother, solicitous – a spindly glass of wine hovering close to her lips.

I hand Will his double vodka and Red Bull, and, much to my horror, he downs it in one and stares at me as if his insides have imploded.

"Jesus!" he gasps, grinning, reaching into his pocket and thrusting a five-pound note towards me. "Any more where that came from?"

"Are you sure?" I sound like his mother, but I don't care. "I don't think you should. You've never been much of a drinker."

Paige sighs loud. "For Christ's sake, Rebecca, what're you getting so bent out of shape for?"

I shoot her a glance. "What's it got to do with you?"

She shrugs. "Nothing." She laces her arm around Fiona's shoulder and nuzzles in soft against her neck. "But I can easily get him a drink if you don't want to."

Will dips his head towards me and gives a little laugh, and I look at him and then at Paige, and I draw myself up to my full height, snatch the money and turn back again towards the bar, not listening this time to how they might be laughing at me. Instead, I weave my way around the edge of the dance floor and let the music move through me hot as lava, and when I get to the bar, I lean in with the swell of bodies and let the tide take me; beer and sweat and smoke, and everywhere couples rocking tight – their skin changing colour with random shocks of neon red and green. And I realise, with a tiny breath of helplessness, that I want, very badly, to go home.

I close my eyes, let a cold wave of panic rise and then subside, and when I look again, there is someone filling my view. I take a small step back. Adam. He takes hold of my arm and wrenches me clear of the crowd, says very close to my face, "What did you bring him here for?" I try to struggle free, but he pulls me nearer. "Answer me!"

I shake my head, blood singing in my ears. "Who?"

"You know who. Will. What's Will doing here?"

I look around me, try to tunnel a view through to the fruit machine, but the dancing crowd keeps opening and closing like a mouth.

"He wanted to come," I say at last. "He wanted to find you."

"What?"

I take a breath and lights weave bright in front of my eyes. I don't see Adam's face for a moment, and then I do see it, and he looks... afraid.

I start to pull away from him again, and this time, he relaxes his grip. His arms drop to his sides.

For a moment, we just stand there like that, glaring at each other, and I don't know whether to run away or stay and hold my ground. It seems, oddly, that *he* doesn't know what to do, either.

"Why does Will want to find me?" His voice sounds different, ragged at the edges.

"Because he wants you to stop using his brother's name, and so do I."

A woman on her way to the bar moves between us, and topples slightly sideways into Adam's body. She steadies herself against him, saying, "Sorry, love," in a voice that jangles loud with drink, but she keeps her hands flat on his chest, looks up into his face with a strange expression, surprise almost, like she might be trying to work something out, but can't remember why, and then she moves on unevenly, and the air seethes hot between us, until I say, at last, the thing that I came here to say.

"I don't know who you are or what you want, but if you don't leave me alone, I'm going to call the police, okay?" For a moment, he just stares at me, blank as a fish. "I don't know why you're pretending to be Adam, unless it's just to freak me out, give me a hard time, *a taste of my own medicine*, just like you told Paige, but I recognised you from the funeral and from Pete's wedding, and I reckon you're just some old mate of Adam's, and he told you what a bitch I'd been to him, and you've decided to avenge him somehow. Is that it? Are you supposed to be my nemesis or something? Well look, you can just go straight back to wherever it is you've come from and leave me the fuck alone. I'm sorry about Adam, I really am, but it's over now and we all have to move on, right?"

I say this all in one go, with barely a breath, and I'm so pleased with myself for having done it, so proud of myself for having solved it and said it and sealed it, that, for a moment, I fail to register the fact that Adam, or whatever his real name is, is smiling at me; a tiny smile at first, nudging at the corners of his mouth, vaguely disparaging, but then he leans forward a little and covers his mouth with his hands. His eyes narrow, and then he whips his hands away like a magician, and he is actually laughing at me, really hard, and he goes on laughing, and the people close by, they hear him and start to smile, too. They think I've made the funniest joke ever, and they're grinning at me, nodding. A couple of them even pat Adam on the back in a kind of amused camaraderie.

I feel my body shudder as if against a rush of cold air, and I turn my back on him, very slowly, and start to walk away. It's all I can do, escape, careful as I can; a high-wire act all the way back to the fruit machine, with Adam's laughter resounding in my blood. The music is painfully loud, but I walk as close as I can to the huge speakers, let my stomach throb black with the bass. *Still* I can hear him laughing. In the end, all I can manage is to cover my ears with my hands and stumble my way through, blindly, chaotically, but when I get back to the fruit machine, there's nobody there.

Eleven

It seems a long time that I look for them, a lifetime until I catch sight of Will dancing with Fiona. They pivot at the heart of the crowd, stuck together, moving to the music. 'Mustang Sally' is playing; Wilson Pickett's voice sultry as sin – soft saxophone sound sliding out to seduce the crowd, and each time the chorus comes, Fiona and Will slip their hips together in a circular motion, grinding into each other, slinking down. Will's arm is tight around her waist, but he has a bottle in his free hand and he keeps lifting it to his mouth. Even in this murky light, I can see that he is smiling. I can see that he is having a wonderful time. Fiona grows limp in his arms for a moment, and then grows animated again. A couple of times, she hunches forward and kisses him quickly on the lips, and then a new song starts, a distraction of hands, everyone reassigning their bodies to a different beat. Will and Fiona flip apart and then back again, breaking into a jumbled kind of a jive. I don't know how to disturb them.

Instead, I look for Paige. I keep walking in a circle out from the fruit machine and then doubling back, certain that if I stay close to where we last were, she will eventually find me. I don't look towards the bar at first. I let my gaze evade it each time I scan the room, but I am growing more agitated. I can't help it. I can feel it building in me like a snowdrift, icy with dread, blocking out what little light there is.

If I'm on my own, he'll find me. I know he will. My breath comes short and fast, as if I'm up high, where the air is thin and furious, until, abruptly, I see Paige's face, and everything in me empties towards her. I have never felt so relieved, so *unutterably* happy to see someone.

I start pushing through the confusion of bodies, trying desperately to make eye contact with her, but she isn't looking at me. She is looking at Adam. I stop dead still. A woman dances into me, pushes me out of the way, and there I am, exposed at the edge of the dance floor, and they are facing each other just a few feet away. Adam has a glass in his hand and he is sipping from it, while Paige leans in close with a profusion of words. She looks angry with him, her mouth moving fast, skimming the edges of speech, but then she puts her hand on his arm and her face softens, just for a second, until he shakes her off, slams his glass down on the bar and walks away. She closes her eyes, lets her head drop, and then lifts it slowly and turns. She sees me. Something wavers between us, something going astray like sunlight under water. I don't know what to make of how she is looking at me, because her face is set hard, but her eyes are wide as a child's and penitent. She reaches towards me, but I back away, uncertain, and then I turn and run.

Inside the ladies, where I end up, I wait for a cubicle, and when one becomes free, I step inside and lock the door tight shut. For a moment, I lean forward with my hands either side of the cistern and breathe, as evenly as I can, then I lower the toilet seat and sit down, rocking myself very softly back and forth.

Voices outside clatter, women murmur, taps turn on and off, and each time the outside door opens, I catch a burst of song, a rush of crowded sound. I think of Will and Fiona dancing out there in the darkness, of the extraordinary look on Paige's face when she knew I'd seen her with Adam, of Adam's laughter, and I don't know what to make of *any* of it.

"Rebecca." I recognise her voice at once. "Rebecca. Are you in here?"

I stop breathing, pull my diaphragm in tight under my ribs and steady it there with my fists.

"Rebecca." She begins tapping on adjacent doors. "Look, I know you're in here."

I can see her shadow moving stealthily like fog across a space of white floor, and then she taps on my door.

"Rebecca." Her voice is very soft. "Come on, sweetheart, please. I need to talk to you."

I let my breath out slowly, and she taps again, and then someone opens the outside door and I catch the opening bars of a song that I know: Nina Simone's 'Feeling Good'. The sound of it glides me smoothly forward into lamplight and the tang of single malt and the warm pressure of Paige's fingers on my wrist. I look at the lotus flower on my palm, and last night gathers me up in its arms.

"Rebecca." She says my name in a whisper and it moves through me like liquid. *"Please."*

I can almost feel the heat of her body arching towards me through the wooden partition. If I reach out my hands, it will be like reaching into a flame. I know this, but I do it anyway, because I simply can't bear *not* to do it.

I lean forward and unbolt the door, and for a long moment she just stands there, looking down at me. Her face is pale, and there is something webbed behind her eyes, until she steps into the cubicle with me and closes the door. Then she smiles, crouches down in front of me, and her dress slides up tight over her thighs. If I touched the skin there, I know that it would feel as smooth as fruit beneath my fingers.

She kneels forward on the cold, tiled floor and puts both her hands into my lap.

"I'm sorry about before," she says.

"Which part of before?"

She shrugs. "All of it."

Spreading her hands flat over my thighs, she presses her thumbs forward and then back, leaving little tracks of light in the dark suede of my dress. "I was a bitch."

"Why?"

"I was drunk and I was pissed off with you for not coming to the Swan."

"But I *told* you it would be difficult."

"I know you did."

I lean back until my shoulder blades push against the enamel of the cistern. It chills the tips of my bones white.

"What about all that stuff with Fiona?"

Paige slips her hands out of my lap and into her own. "Yeah," she says, sheepish. "I'm sorry about that. It's just... I don't know, easy, I guess, for me with Fiona. Comfortable. What you saw tonight, well, that's just how we are with each other. I don't think anything of it any more, and I don't think she does either. It's not even sexual these days. It's just intimate; a particular *kind* of intimate, if that makes any sense. She came into the pub tonight, really upset because Phil's dumped her, yet *again*, and we got pissed together, and..." She hesitates, inclines her head, and a wisp of a smile dances across her face. "Did it really bother you, then?"

I take a deep breath in, and it tastes of how Paige smells. I look into her face.

"You know it did."

She nods very softly, says, "Yes." And the column of air trapped between our bodies bristles with complicity.

She lifts herself forward, brings her face close to mine, but at the last moment, I turn my head to the side and say in a careful tone, "I saw you talking to Adam."

"I know you did."

"What did you say to him?"

She sighs against me, and there's an awful weariness in it, a kind of depletion. For a moment, she doesn't answer, just keeps her face close to mine. I can feel her breath against my cheek, held in, and I begin to feel suddenly very small and clumsy in front of her. I struggle to feel easy, controlled, but all I achieve is a queasy vulnerability, and I wish I hadn't asked her about Adam. My bones ache with the possibility of losing her because of him.

"I told him to leave you alone," she says at last.

And I turn back to look. "Is that all?"

"He won't be bothering you again."

"How can you know that, Paige?"

Lifting herself slightly, she slides back until she's leaning against the door. "I just do."

"I need to know how."

"Well then, let's just say that working in a pub, you get to meet all sorts of people, and some of them aren't the kind of people you want to get on the wrong side of, if you get my drift." She lets her head drop back with a little bump against the door, looks up to the ceiling, and her throat is ribboned for a moment with bars of light and dark, like someone's fingers. "I told Adam that if he carried on hassling you, I would call in some of the favours that are owed to me by some of these less *respectable* friends of mine, which makes me sound like one of the Kray brothers, but..."

"You threatened him?" I can't quite believe it. A sudden bubble of exultation fills my throat. "You told him they'd beat him up?"

"I actually told him that if he didn't fornicate off, then the next time he joined in at a karaoke night at the Swan, he'd be singing soprano."

I start to laugh then, I have to, and so does she; a compound sound that chimes like the opening bars of a song, a new song that you fall in love with the first time you hear it.

Paige's face is all light for me now, all colour, so beautiful. I want to touch her. It surprises me just how *badly* I want to touch her, to place my hand over the bare curve of her shoulder and feel the two of us fused there, a low pulse in my fingertips, a chaos of veins and cells and skin intermingling. She smiles at me, and it's there in the air between us – unmistakable, electromagnetic.

"So…" She reaches her hands behind her head and re-adjusts her hair where it has begun to fall. "Hopefully, he's gone for good."

I nod slowly, watching her, softly stunned by how it makes me *feel* to watch her, and then I reach forward, tentatively, stroke my fingers, very lightly, down her cheek and along the line of her jaw. For a second, I can't believe I'm doing it. It seems presumptuous somehow, daring, but she slants her head to one side, nestling into my touch, and then she closes her eyes and catches hold of my hand in hers, presses her lips to my open palm.

"Paige."

She looks up into my face, takes my breath clean away. I swallow hard.

"Why did you talk to Adam for me? Why have you involved yourself in this?"

"Because I care what happens to you."

"Why? Why do you even *like* me?"

She shrugs. "I just do."

"You see, that's what I don't get. You're meeting me at the very worst time of my life. I am at my *absolute* worst at this moment. What is there to like about me?"

She kisses my palm again, says casually, "Nothing, I guess."

"Seriously. I want to know."

"Would you believe any reason I gave you?"

"I might."

"Okay then. I guess, I feel like… I spend all my life surrounded by people who seem to want something from me, or who expect something *of* me, which is partly my fault, because, for a long time, I put myself in situations where that was what I wanted, too. It was absolutely my desire. It made me feel validated, affirmed, somehow, but now, I don't know. Maybe I've changed, or the feeling has, because these days it all just makes me feel crowded out and pressured, and… sad, mostly. But you..." She dips her head towards me. "You don't ask anything of me, which means I can give to you and enjoy it and feel like it was all my own idea. There are no demands here, except those that I place on myself. On top of all that, you're kind to me and funny and... inventive."

I raise my eyebrows at that, but she raises hers right back.

"I find you..." she circles her fingernail delicately along the inside of my elbow "... intriguing."

"Intriguing."

"Yes." Lifting herself towards me a little, she smiles. "Either that, honeybun, or I just want to fuck you."

At that, the outside door crashes open and Fiona's voice spills into our cubicle like a bucket of icy water.

"Paige," she shrieks. "Paige, he's just about to start. Are you coming?"

Paige keeps her eyes on me, calls back, "I'll be out in a minute."

"But he's just about to *start*."

"In a *minute*, Fiona."

There's a moment's hesitation, and then, slyly, "Is Rebecca in there with you?"

Paige places a finger to my lips, shakes her head. "No."

But Fiona makes a dubious huffing sound.

"Shame," she says. "I've been looking for her everywhere. That boy she brought with her, he passed out stone cold in the middle of the macarena."

Someone has propped Will up in a chair near the bar and given him a pint glass filled with orange juice to drink. He is only vaguely awake by the time I find him: green at the edges and gloomy.

"Can we go home?" he croaks when I kneel down by his side. "I really need to go home."

"Course we can." I rub his back for him. "I'll go get our jackets."

I ask the barman to keep an eye on him for me and then I head towards the cloakroom, ascertaining, on the way, that Ladies' Night is now in full swing. Tom Jones' 'You Can Leave Your Hat On' is playing, and a huge crowd of women are laughing and applauding at the edge of the dance floor. Occasionally, an item of men's clothing flies into the air and the women grab for it, screeching like gulls, elbowing each other out of the way.

I pause for a moment, smiling, wanting suddenly to join in, feeling a heady kind of liberation take hold of me by the hair and shake me to my toes. I want to find Paige. I want to put my arms around her waist from behind and hold her against me, feel the breadth of her laughter moving down through her body and into mine. I know she's here somewhere, nearby, and I know she'll be laughing at the man who is dancing, just as I am laughing, just as *everyone* is laughing. The air is thick with frivolity.

We promised to find each other, Paige and I, before we left, but now I have to get back quickly to Will and there's no sign of her. Thankfully, I catch sight of Fiona ahead of me, wriggling her hips to the music, clapping her hands.

"Fiona." I wave flamboyantly, but she doesn't see me, so I push my way through. "Fiona."

"Hey you!" she shouts when I reach her, the colour high in her cheeks. "Fancied a ring-side seat, did you?" She points to the dance floor, giggling. "He's great, isn't he?"

I take hold of her arm. "Have you seen Paige anywhere?"

A sudden whoop goes up from the crowd and something thin and leathery lands at Fiona's feet. It looks for a moment like some small and sinewy reptile, but then I realise; it's a G-string.

Fiona swoops on it and waves it in the air like a trophy. "Mine," she squeals. "Mine."

"*Fiona.*"

She glances at me impatiently, pulls her arm away. "What?"

"Have you seen Paige?"

She twirls the G-string around on the end of her finger, smiling in a way that tells me something's not right, and then she points to the dance floor.

At first, I see only the man, the stripper, naked now, except for a ludicrous Stetson and a pair of cowboy boots. He is the same man who accompanied Paige and Fiona out of the Swan earlier, and he is danc-ing with a woman, a woman in a short black dress with spaghetti straps, a woman who, as we watch, reaches up and unclips her blonde hair so that it falls loose about her shoulders.

She isn't just someone he's pulled out of the crowd. The way they are moving is too intimate, too knowing for that. I even hear one of the women close by say to her friend, "Ooh, I love it when *she* gets up there with him, don't you?"

She, Paige, moving in very close to the man who is dancing, who is pressing one hand to her breast, and the other flat into the small of her back, gliding it down over the swell of her buttocks so that she is clamped to him tight.

For a moment, they dance like that, coupled together like that, but then she eases herself back a little and begins to slide down his body, running her hands up over his chest and then down over his thighs, and then she drops to her knees and the crowd starts to roar, and the music thunders, and I'm thinking, no, don't do it, Paige. You can't do it. Please don't do it, but she does; places her hands on his hips and takes his erect penis into her mouth, just for a second or two, moving her head back and forth to the music, before he reaches down and lifts her, swings her up on to his stomach, holds her there. She wraps her legs around his hips, her arms around his neck, and then she kisses him, long and deep, sinking herself into it like she's sinking into quicksand.

I turn away, and Fiona is looking at me. Her eyes are heavy-lidded now, and incredibly sad.

"What else did you *expect*?" she asks.

But my voice is choked in. "Who is he?"

She glances towards the dance floor.

"Oh, that's Rick," she says. "Paige's husband."

Twelve

Will is sick twice on the way home, and both times, I think *I* might be, too. An awful swell of nausea keeps lifting into my throat, the tang of bile, but I swallow it back and keep my hand tight on Will's leg as we drive.

"Not far now, love," I say it to him over and over. "Not far now."

And by the time we reach the flat and stagger upstairs, he *does* begin to brighten a little.

As I put my key into the lock, he reaches out, touches my arm and asks in a blurry voice, "Woss he there after all?"

I think for a moment, remembering how Adam looked, standing there, laughing into my face, and I shake my head, because what good would it do to tell Will the truth? What good does the truth ever do?

"No," I say. "He wasn't there, but Paige said she'd seen him recently and he told her that he wouldn't be around any more anyway."

"Really? What, juss like that?"

I push open the door and ease him in ahead of me. "Sit yourself down. I'll make some coffee."

He flops into an armchair. "Is he going away or something, then?"

"I guess he must be."

"Thass odd. Don't you think, Bex? Don't you think thass odd?"

"I don't care if it is, as long as he's going."

Will nods, but his face stays groggy and perplexed. "Don't you wanna know who he was exactly, though? What was going *on*, like? I wanna know."

I go into the kitchen, turn on the cold tap and fill the kettle with water, a loud sound that floods my thinking, makes my words come out damp and distracted.

"I do, too, but..." Plugging the kettle into the wall, I flick the switch. "It's like, I think..." But of course, I don't know *what* I think, and suddenly, there are tears in my eyes and Paige dancing towards me through them – someone else's hands on her body, someone else's mouth covering hers. Rick. Her *husband*.

"Bex." Will's face appears round the door. "You all right?"

I nod. "Just tired."

Patting his arm, I move past him into the living room. "Look, can we talk about this in the morning? D'you mind?"

"Nah. I'm pretty beat, too. I won't bother with coffee, juss a little glass of water." But he hesitates and a smile catches at the corners of his mouth. He digs his hands into his pockets. "I had a great time tonight, you know."

"I know you did."

"They're kinda cool, your friends."

I push open my bedroom door. "Get yourself a drink and then come to bed, all right?"

He sways towards me, then back. "What, you mean in *there*, with you?"

"You'll freeze out here, and besides, I *think* I can probably resist you, if I try really hard."

He grins, takes a step, but misses and bumps his shin on the coffee table.

"Shit." Reaching down to rub it, he looks up at me from under his eyebrows; a cheeky face, disarming. "Not sure I'll be able to do much about it if turns out you *can't* resist me."

"I'll try all the same though, yeah?"

But once I'm in the dark on my own, undressed and under the

covers, the cold air swallows my resolve and all I want is to have someone put their arms around me and tell me everything's going to be all right. All I want is for Paige to put her arms around me, but each time I close my eyes, she's there on the dance floor, and it feels like nothing's going to be all right ever again.

I hear Will bumping about for a while in the living room and then he knocks lightly on the door and comes in slow. He might be visiting an elderly relative, or someone in hospital. He's being *that* careful, trying so hard not to make any noise, to take his clothes off quietly, but he keeps losing his balance and toppling into things. By the time he climbs into bed beside me, he is so out of breath, he just lays there like a stunned wildebeest.

I listen to the sound of his breathing, and it soothes me, just to have him here. It feels, in some intrinsic way, like having Adam here, the real Adam; something familiar, something steadfast from before that won't dissolve as soon as I touch it with my fingers. And that's what I want to do.

Turning so that I can see his profile silhouetted in the dark, I move my hand under the covers until I find *his* hand, resting flat on his stomach, and I take it in mine and hold tight.

He turns his face towards me, and his breath smells of toothpaste; a sprig of mint from the garden.

"I thought you were going to resist me."

"I am. I just wanted..." I turn away and onto my back, shaking my head. "I don't know what I wanted exactly."

But Will squeezes my hand and brings it up on to his chest. I can feel his heart beating fast beneath it.

"Don't be sad, Bex."

"I'm not, I'm just..." But there really aren't any words for what I am.

"You know that song that Rolf Harris used to sing?" he says suddenly. "The one about the two little boys and the horse?"

"Yes, I do. God. That was a long time ago."

"Adam used to sing that to me when we were small."

"Did he?"

I feel his head nod on the pillow. "Yep. When I was upset, you know? Some little wanker at playgroup nicked my Action Man one time and pulled his head off, and Adam gave me *his* Action Man and sang that song to me. I don't think he knew all the words or anything, but he knew the bit about there being 'room on his horse for two'."

I snuggle in against Will's shoulder, and try not to let him see that I am crying. I can't help it, because I can picture them so clearly, those two little boys, sitting on the grass; the tiny one with tears in his eyes, and the bigger one singing fragments of a song he didn't know very well to make the tears go away.

Will squeezes my hand tighter, presses his lips to my forehead.

"You're not on your own, you know." His voice is still drunk, but dense now and very deliberate. "I'm here for you, Bex," he says. "I'm here."

And I take him at his word, and reach for him the way someone who is drowning reaches for the swimmer who has come to rescue them. I take him down with me, all the way down, crawl on top of his body and put my arms around his neck, press my hips hard into his.

He is solid as summer grass beneath me, and that's what I want. Not sex, not to feel him inside me, but to feel him like this – his lips pressed to my forehead, his knowledge of me intact, all the cracks still visible, but harder to see now and softer to bear. He knew me when I was just a hiss of lies with a name attached, when my voice was the scrape of fingernails down a blackboard. He could hate me if he wanted to, but his arms are tight around my waist and when I kiss him, he opens his mouth and I push my tongue inside and taste that tang of mint, as distinct as forgiveness.

I don't think about Paige. I fold my body around Will's and we touch each other for a long time; stroke each other's arms, backs, thighs; clutch at each other as if our lives depended upon it, and he cleaves to me just as insistently as I cleave to him, and as gravely.

Only once do I run my hand down over his penis, and it isn't hard, but he breathes out fast when I do that, and then he says, "Sorry," in a kind of gasp.

I shake my head, even though he can't really see me.

"It's all right. *This* is all I want. This is enough."

And he puts his arms around me and draws me down on to his chest, kisses my hair.

The tracks his fingers leave on my skin feel like the clear marks of a pen, like they might be indelible, and that's what I'm looking for; something lasting, something so consistent and exact, that I'll be able to see it every time I look. I think of the lotus flower on my palm, a henna imprint already fading. In a day or two, it will be gone, and I'm glad of it.

Gradually, our breathing slows and our fingers flicker to stillness, until we are lying side by side, holding hands. I listen to Will falling asleep, his body drifting away into the blue, and then I must fall asleep too, because it is the shrill sound of the telephone that wakes me.

It must be near dawn now, because a pale, lilac light is seeping into the room, and the birds have begun to sing outside my window.

I stumble out of bed and into the living room, cold air clouding around my ankles, but just as I reach the telephone, it stops ringing. I'm just about to turn back, when it starts ringing again. I pick it up, say warily, "Hello."

"Are you fucking my little brother, Rebecca?" It's his voice, that strange voice, thin as a reed. "Are you? Bitch."

I turn my body so that I'm standing square between the phone and the room where Will is sleeping, my body a shield.

"No."

"Liar."

"I'm not lying, and he's not your brother. He's nothing to you."

The air sighs between us.

"Isn't he?"

I feel anger burning white-hot in my stomach, a sudden defiance. For a second, it overcomes my fear, and my discretion, and I say through gritted teeth, "Okay. If he *is*, if I'm wrong and you *are* Adam, then why don't you come and see Will? I'm sure he'd be delighted to catch up with a brother who's been dead for ten months."

He is silent.

"Why don't you? Why don't you come and see him?"

I hear him swallow, and then he says quietly, "I might just do that."

The line clicks, goes dead, and I drop down onto the sofa with the receiver still in my hand. Why did I say that? *Why* did I challenge him? Everything races ahead of me for a moment, blood nudging slow through my veins. It takes a huge effort to reach across and pull the telephone wire out of the wall.

"Bex."

Will is standing in the bedroom doorway in his boxer shorts, his hair ruffled up a little on one side.

"Was that the phone?"

He rubs his eyes with his fists, yawns; a little boy at playgroup again. Adam isn't here to make anything better for him any more, but I am, and I know that I would turn myself inside out to keep him from harm.

I stand up unsteadily.

"Wrong number." I'm shivering slightly. "Come on, let's go back to bed."

And I take his hand in mine, and lead him through.

It is late in the morning when I next wake, my body bleary with hunger and disquiet. I leave Will sleeping and go to the kitchen, make myself some coffee and sit at the table with my hands curled tight around the mug. The sound of children's voices and the random barking of dogs filters up from the Common, and for a few moments, the world seems ordinary again.

If this were any other Sunday morning, I'd be making myself breakfast and listening to *The Archers*, reading the papers, driving into the forest to go for a walk. I won't be doing any of those things today. Today, I'll be waiting for Adam.

When I go to look in on Will, he is still fast asleep, so I move through to the bathroom and run myself a bath, and when it's full, I climb in and sink myself down in it and stay there until the water cools.

The flat seems very still around me, hollowed out somehow, vacuous. I look around the bathroom and feel its chill, its lack of anything that singles it out as mine: no pictures on the walls, no fragrant candles, no quirky toiletries or favourite books to read in the bath. It's like a hotel bathroom – functional, sombre. Every room in the place is like this one. I've never really thought about it until now, but it's true. The previous tenants decorated the whole flat before they moved away, and I haven't changed a thing, haven't marked my territory with anything more permanent than a few house plants and some crossword puzzle toilet paper that I picked up at the petrol station because it was all they had left. Even the Andrew Wyeth painting in the living room belongs to someone else.

I take a long breath into my lungs and slip myself slowly under the water, feel it bubbling into my ears like foreign conversation, lapping against my thighs and shoulders as if against the sides of a boat. I can hear my heart beating. I can feel little muscles flexing all over my body. I am absolutely and unmistakably alive in the present moment; solid flesh, intellect, imagination. I am uniquely myself, so why is there nothing *of* me in the place where one would most expect to find it, my home?

Coming up for air, watching the water slip in little rivulets down over my breasts and stomach, I know the answer and it troubles me. All those years I spent taking on other people's personalities, assuming their opinions and their preferences, I left no room for my own. In fact, I didn't even consider what my own might be. It wasn't important to me then, but it is now. If Will can forgive me for what happened to his brother, and if I can forgive myself, then maybe there's still be time for me to...

Someone is knocking at the front door. I stay very still for a moment, and then I hear Will call my name from the bedroom, and the sound of the bed creaking as he begins to get up. What if he answers the door and it's Adam? What then?

Climbing quickly out of the bath, I wrap a towel around myself and hurry through into the living room.

"It's okay, Will," I call. "You stay there. I'll get it."

But when I reach the door, I just stand there, water sinking dark into the carpet beneath my feet. I reach my fingers towards the handle, draw them back. I can hear someone shuffling about in the hallway outside, and then they knock again, harder this time. I take a step away from the door, my fingers to my lips, and then the letter box flips open and Olive's voice comes tiptoeing through it.

"Betty, dear. Sorry to disturb, but I do just need a quick word with you."

My breath comes out in a long, loose sigh, and inside my chest, everything seems to be heaving with cold, but I reach for the door quickly and open it.

"Oh dear," says Olive, staring at me. "I had no idea you were in the bath."

I try to stay polite. "What was it that you wanted, Olive?"

She hesitates, seems to have forgotten, but then she raises a finger and points it at me. There is a key hanging from it.

"My new gentleman friend, Mr Bickerstaff, has asked if I'd like to accompany him on a visit he's making to some cousins in Cheltenham. We'll be away until Wednesday." She gives me a big smile. "I was wondering if you'd mind feeding Pooky for me while I'm gone?"

I lift the key from her finger. "Course not." But my voice buckles tight with tiredness all of a sudden. "Is he still on that vegetarian diet?"

"Ooh, no!" She tilts her head back and opens her mouth to laugh. A single gold tooth winks at me like a match struck in the dark. "I couldn't cope with all the, er... after-effects. Pooky's poop's no picnic, as I'm sure you'll recall."

I nod, try to smile, and Olive folds her arms across the front of her kaftan.

"No, he's back on the Whiskas now. I'll leave some tins out on the side."

"Fine."

Just then, Will calls my name from the bedroom, and Olive raises her eyebrows very high.

"Well, well, *well*." Reaching out her hand, she pats my arm hard. "I really *am* sorry I disturbed you, dear."

I open my mouth to explain, but find that I really don't have the energy, and besides, she's already moving off down the hallway.

"See you Wednesday," she calls, and then she says something I don't quite catch, and I almost have the door closed, when someone sticks their foot between it and the doorframe and pushes it back open.

"Good Lord," says Paige, looking me up and down. "Been taking a bath with the neighbours again?" She glances back along the hallway. "I wouldn't have thought she was your type."

She tries to move past me into the flat, but I stand in her way.

"I don't want you here, Paige." My fingers on the door handle are trembling.

"What d'you mean? Why not?"

"You *know* why."

She purses her lips. "You're cross about last night."

"No shit, Sherlock!"

Tutting very lightly, she wags a finger at me. "Language, language."

But I grab for her wrist and hold it still. "Don't fuck with me, Paige."

"I'm sorry. Okay?"

She looks sharply down at her feet and then back at me, seems about to say something, but changes her mind. I let her wrist fall, and as I do, my stomach seems to contract and blood swims up crimson in front of my eyes. I feel myself beginning to sway.

"Go away. Please. I..." But my voice is just breath now, and suddenly Paige's arms are around me and we are lurching towards the sofa.

She eases me up straight against the cushions, and then helps me to bend forward.

"Keep your head between your knees," she says. "And try to breathe."

A pair of bare feet appears in my line of vision, and I hear Will's voice above me, and then Paige speaks again.

"When did you last eat?" she asks. "Have you had anything today, yet?" I shake my head, and her voice veers away from me. "See what there is in the cupboards then, Will, some soup or something, and make some tea, yeah?"

I watch Will's feet retreat, while Paige rubs her hand very gently up and down my spine, smooths my hair away from my face, and gradually, the world begins to slip back into focus and the throb in my stomach subsides. I wait a moment longer, just to be sure, and then I sit up straight and sink back into the cushions.

"Why haven't you eaten anything, Rebecca?"

"I forgot."

"Bullshit."

I shake my head very slow. "It's none of your *business* what I do."

"Of course it is."

Taking off her black leather jacket, she wraps it around my shoulders, but I push her hands away.

"What are you doing here anyway, Paige? Shouldn't you be at home with Rick?"

She winces slightly, and sits forward with her fingers over her knees. "What exactly did Fiona tell you?"

"The truth, I assume. That you're married."

"That's all she said?"

"What else *is* there to say?"

"A lot, actually." She clears her throat. "You see, Rick and I, we're not…"

But I don't want to hear it. I struggle to my feet, pulling her jacket from my shoulders and dropping it into her lap. "Don't bother, all right? Don't waste your breath on it."

She stands up too, and tries to catch hold of my arm. "For Christ's sake, Rebecca. Will you just let me explain?"

"Why? What's the point? You explained about Fiona and I believed you, and now there's Rick, and you'll make something up and I'll believe you again, but then there'll be something else, some other skeleton in the closet, some other secret. I mean, how many stories have you got? Exactly how many people *are* you, Paige?"

Inclining her head, she almost smiles, then she points her hand towards me and says to no one in particular, "Kettle, I'm Rebecca. You're black!"

I stare at her hard. "Yes, okay. You're right. I lied to people in the past and I'm sorry for it, but I haven't lied to you."

"I know you haven't, and whether you believe me or not, I haven't lied to you, either. I just haven't had time to tell you *all* of the truth, that's all." She takes a step towards me. "I *can* though, tell you the truth, if you'll let me."

I look straight into her eyes. "But how can I *trust* you?"

She shrugs. "Same way I can trust you, I guess." Taking hold of my hand, she draws it to her and places it over her heart. "Because I want to enough."

Thirteen

Paige and Will sit with their elbows on the table and watch, while I devour a bowl of Weetabix, a plate of scrambled eggs on toast, two tangerines and a big glass of chocolate milk. Then Paige makes some fennel tea while I get dressed and Will runs himself a bath. He looks pretty awful; dark circles under his eyes, an ambling confusion in his movements. I suspect that his hangover is very bad indeed.

When I join Paige in the living room, she is sitting on the floor with her legs crossed, smoking a cigarette.

She looks up when I enter, and smiles. "You look much better."

"I feel it."

She gestures towards the coffee table. "Fennel tea, madam?"

"Thanks."

Picking up the mug, I bring it close to my face and breathe in a little curl of steam.

"I *was* going to tell you," she says suddenly, drawing deep on her cigarette. "It's just not something I talk about, or think about really, any more."

"How can you not think about being married? That doesn't make any sense."

Stretching her legs out in front of her, she leans back against the sofa, shakes her head. "It's difficult for me to…" But then she looks up into my face. "Will you sit down? You're making me nervous."

I ease myself into the chair opposite and begin to sip delicately at my tea. It is hot and coppery on my tongue, sour as an old coin.

Paige says nothing for a while. Then she says, "I'm not going to pretend to you that it was a mistake, getting married." She swallows, stubs out her cigarette on the sole of her shoe. "It was what I wanted, at the time."

"When *was* the time?"

"Eighteen months ago. I was studying in London, finishing off my Masters. My mum lives there, in Denmark Hill. I was living with her, on and off, and one of my part-time jobs was in a pub."

"And that's where you met Rick?" My throat snaps closed over the word like a Venus flytrap.

"Yeah, and it was..." She hesitates, reaches for her cigarettes and pulls another one from the pack with the tips of her fingers. "Instantaneous. I knew, right then, with him standing at the bar, as I opened his bottle of Grolsch and handed it to him, that he was the man I was going to marry." She looks away from me, puts the cigarette to her lips and lights it. For a moment the air burns sweet. "I always thought it was a joke, people like my grandma saying that they knew straight off when they'd met *the one*, but it's not, you know. He was it, for me. In some ways, he still is."

"I don't understand, Paige." My voice comes fast. "If Rick's *the one*, your big destiny or whatever, then what the hell have you been doing with me? And what about Fiona, and Phil, and..." A sudden light blazes. "Or is that it? Rick gets off on you being with other people."

"No, no: nothing *like* that. I'm not even with him any more. We're separated. That's what I've been trying to tell you."

A little flicker of ash drops from the end of her cigarette on to her top and she brushes it quickly away.

"I want to tell you." She hesitates, starts again. "I want to make clear to you that I don't regret marrying Rick. When I did it, I loved him and only him and I didn't think that there would ever be any man I would love more. I still don't think there will be any man I will love more. He was *it* for me. In that arena, in the... I hate the word, but I'll use it, het-ero-*sexual* arena, then he was it, but you see..." She looks at me hard. "*It* wasn't enough for me, in itself, and it's my fault that it wasn't, because I guess I always knew what I was really, *who* I was. Back then, though, I wanted to be somebody different, and I wanted to be married to Rick. I thought I could do it, you know – husband, children, the works – but it just didn't go far enough or deep enough for me and I wasn't filled up by it. I'm not talking about sex. The sex was okay, as far as it went. No. I'm talking about something more organic even than that; a kind of surrender, a giving over of yourself to someone else to such a degree, and with such absolute trust, so *nakedly*, that nothing in you is left unanswered. Now, *I* think I can only find that with a woman. I mean, I don't know, but... I didn't find it with a man, any-way. I didn't find it in being married. I wanted to make Rick happier than he'd ever been, I really did, but *I* wasn't happy, and it showed, and I got to be mean-spirited because of it, and started to resent him for something that had never been his fault. That was the worst part." Her eyes fill suddenly with tears, and she looks at the cigarette between her fingers as if she isn't quite sure how it got there.

"That's what I felt worst about, I guess: that I'd drawn someone else so completely and so irrevocably into my own confusion, and be-lieve me, I was *very* confused." Blinking slowly, she glances towards me and then away. "I wasn't sure what I wanted, but I knew I didn't, *couldn't* stay married. Simple as that, and it didn't matter that he was loving and sensitive and strong, everything I needed. I mean, he was the Swiss Army knife of heterosexual men, Bex, but..." She lifts her shoulders, lets them fall. "I had to finish it.

"I let Rick down in the worst way anybody can, I guess, and some-times I'm amazed that he still wants anything to do with me, but he does. We're friends now, *best* friends, and it's better with him and more meaningful than it ever was when we were together, because all that stuff that fucked it up for us is gone. Everything's clean with us now, straight: no pun intended." She lifts her eyebrows. "He knows that I'll never have a relationship with any other man that will come close to the relationship I had with him. He's still *the one* for me, the man for me, but it isn't a man that I need, or want. I know that now, and he knows it, and respects it. He's with someone else now, anyway. He went travelling after we split, met a girl in Peru, and brought her home with him. She's sweet. Not *my* type, really, but..." She grins, but her lips are trembling against her teeth. She puts her cigarette to her mouth again and inhales.

Sliding my mug on to the coffee table, I lean forward and look at Paige closely, trying to see what's behind her eyes.

"How can you say that it wasn't a mistake, then, if it went so badly wrong?"

"Because I loved him and he loved me, and love's never a mistake, surely, is it?" She begins to stand up. "And besides, I don't believe in regret. The bad stuff that happens in a person's life forms them much more significantly than the good stuff, don't you think?"

She touches her fingers to my hair for a moment and then moves past me into the kitchen, calls over her shoulder, "Do you have any alcohol in the house, Rebecca?"

I wait, and then follow her through, stand watching as she opens and closes cupboard doors, peering inside each one like an environmental health inspector.

Moving past her to the cooker, I open the cupboard high above it and lift down a bottle of dark rum. Paige's eyes widen.

"Aah! Jim Lad!" she says, reaching for it. "That'll shiver me timbers, and no mistakin'!"

I find two glasses and hold them out while she pours, but her hands aren't steady and she won't look at me.

Settling the bottle down on to the worktop, she takes one of the glasses from me and lifts it to her lips, but before she can take a sip, I ask her, "What about last night, on the dance floor? Was that about being friends as well?"

She drinks the rum down in one gulp, lifts the bottle and pours herself another measure. "It *was*, actually. I was helping him out."

"You were sucking him off, Paige." My voice is black with disdain, and she straightens against it, her mouth full of rum, eyes darkening. "In front of all those people. My God! How *could* you?"

She swallows, leans back against the worktop. "Do you think I enjoyed it?"

"You looked as if you did."

She shakes her head, and her voice, when it comes, is low and unfamiliar.

"Rick's an actor," she says. "He doesn't get much paid work yet, so he does some dancing, and not all of it the kind of dancing you saw last night. But occasionally, yeah, when he's got a gig at Maclaverty's, I go along and I dance with him and we make a real show of it, and the bouncers turn a blind eye. The women love it, which means the management love it, which means they ask Rick back. It's all very logical." Her face closes hard. "And not in the least bit pleasurable." She pours herself another rum and knocks it back. "I do it because I love him, and because I owe him, and you can think what you like, but that's the truth."

The air in my lungs is raw iron. I've hurt her and I can't bear it. I can't bear for her to be sad because of me, and suddenly, I don't care about Rick or Fiona or any of it. All I care about is *her*.

Lifting my glass to my lips, I drink the rum quickly, and then I move towards her and place my hand over the curve of her shoulder. She glances at it dubiously.

"I'm sorry, Paige. I shouldn't have said that." I shake my head, repentant. "I'm sorry."

She stares at me for a long moment, but I don't know what else to say to her.

It is then that Will appears in the doorway.

"I feel like shit," he says, slumping down into a chair by the table.

Paige moves towards him and gives him a little hug from behind. "How about some fennel tea, Junior?"

He swallows hard. "Not for me, thanks all the same."

"Suit yourself." Straightening up, she looks at her watch and then at me, and her face gives nothing away. "Rick's in a production of *Othello* at Corfe Castle this afternoon," she says lightly. "I told him I'd be there. It's probably going to be awful, just a charity thing, but I wondered whether you'd like to come with me, both of you, that is. You could meet Rick and we could get some food after. There's a nice pub in Corfe. I thought we, maybe..." But her voice trails away uncertainly.

I take a quick step towards her. "I'd love to. I could do with some air. What d'you think, Will?"

"Sure. Whatever."

I take Paige's hand in mine and squeeze. "I'd like to meet Rick. Who's he playing?"

"Desdemona."

"Pardon me?"

"It's a comedy production. All the women are played by men and vice versa."

"How unusual."

"Isn't it just?" She holds my gaze. "We ought to go soon. It starts at two."

"Okay. You round up the horses and I'll pee on the fire then, yeah?"

And she nods, gives me a small smile like a leaf on a breeze, and lets her hand slip out of my hand, very slow.

All the way to Corfe Castle in the car, Paige talks, and I've never heard anyone talk so fast or with such enthusiasm.

"I'm going to tell you my life story," she says, tugging off her jacket and her shoes and flinging them over her shoulder. Then she slides down a little in her seat and settles her feet onto the dashboard. "That way, there'll be no more misunderstandings between us, okay?"

I nod, and Will groans softly from the back seat. I sneak a peak at him in my rear-view mirror. He looks like a refugee from *Night of the Living Dead*.

"You all right, Will?"

"Mmm." But he drops out of sight, crumpling up on the old upholstery and pulling Paige's jacket over his head. "Daylight, bad. Darkness, *gooood*," he croons, and Paige and I look at each other and grin.

She goes back to the start.

"Where all my threads unravel to," she says. "My grandparents."

And she tells again the story of how they met, and how they married a month later, in a tiny chapel high up in the Apennines; mortar fire sounding in the distance and the mountain air choked with burning metal and the emphatic colours of spring.

She tells how they came back to Hampshire after the war, her grandpa resigning his commission in the army and becoming rector to a parish in the New Forest, how they lived in the little village of Sway, happily, for eight years, had a child, a girl they called Anne, but how her grandpa's health gradually began to fail.

"The doctors put it down to him working too hard," she says. "Nervous strain and fatigue." And then she stops and looks hard out of the window. "I don't know, though." She shakes her head, lets it bump against the glass. "I wonder whether sometimes, if someone has experienced things really intensely, like he did during the war, maybe they can never really settle to a normal life again. Maybe something switches over in them to a kind of overdrive and they can never switch it back."

She turns to look at me, her eyebrows low, but then her face relaxes and she puts her hand on my thigh and keeps it there.

"After he died, my grandma decided to go back to Canada, to Prince Edward Island, where her family were. My mum was only three when they left England, so she did all her growing up back on the Island. She met my father there, when she was eighteen – Alastair Mackenzie, one of a long line of Mackenzies, a potato farmer; two hundred acres and a tractor the size of an elephant. That was about all he had going for him when they got married, but I don't think it was his worldly goods she was after. I've seen photos of him when he was young, and, oh my *God*! He was absolutely *gorgeous* – bit like Hugh Grant, minus the floppy hair." Paige grins. "They were happy for a long time, I think, but my mum always wanted to come back to England. She had a real longing for it, but Dad wouldn't consider leaving the farm. I can understand it for both of them, really, which means I can understand why it became impossible in the end. They still loved each other, right the way through, but neither loved the other *enough* to give up what they wanted most in the world. So..." She lifts her shoulders a little and stretches her arm up around the headrest. "When I was nine, Mum and I moved to London and Dad stayed home on the Island. Mum went to college to study interior design, which was something she'd always been interested in, and I went to school and worked on losing my Canadian accent. It's pretty much gone now, don't you think, although, whenever I go home to see my dad, I come back saying *aboot* instead of *about* and rounding off all my sentences with a question mark."

"Do you still think of it as home, then, Prince Edward Island?"

She thinks for a moment. "Yes."

"Even though you've lived a long time here?"

"It's the place I'm happiest in the world, and I guess that *makes* it home, for me." She taps out a little tune on my thigh with her fingers, making my skin tingle. "You should come visit sometime," she says. "You'd like it. The Micmac Indians, who settled there way back, called it *Abegweit*, which means *Land Cradled on the Waves*. It's very beautiful, but not in a big, showy way. Understated, you know? The legend goes that a Micmac god called Glooscap, who roamed the earth as a giant man, fashioned the Island out of clay in the shape of a crescent, filled it with trees and flowers and birds, and transported it on his shoulders to the gulf's edge. I like that. I like the idea of him carrying the Island on his shoulders." She lifts her arm down from the headrest and reaches forward to open the glove compartment. "You haven't got any fags, have you?"

"No, sorry."

She snaps it shut. "Probably just as well. I smoke too much, anyway, drink too much, eat *all* the wrong things. You watch. I'll be a dried up husk of a woman by the time I'm forty." She leans towards me a little, smiling. "You'll end up having to push me about in a bath chair and help me on with my surgical stockings."

"I could do that." I say it quick, and she bumps her shoulder against mine.

"*Could* you now? I'd drive you barmy, you know."

"You already do."

Paige laughs, and something soft in my chest dips down and dissolves at the sound of it. I love that she is laughing because of me. I love that she is here, in my car, with her feet on the dashboard in their Scooby Doo socks. I love the close proximity of her, the smell of her, the way the air seems to break and settle around her like a fall of snow.

"Go on with your story," I urge. "Tell me the end."

"That's about it." She shuffles over so that she can rest her head against my shoulder. "I finished school, went to UCL to study sociology, stayed there for my Masters, married Rick." She hesitates. "And then, I moved down here, for the PhD."

"To Sway?"

"Yes." Paige takes a breath. "Gran had stayed in touch with a lot of people from the village, and when she found out the old rectory was coming up for sale, she put in an offer and got it. She moved back the middle of last year, which was great for me, obviously, and for her." She straightens up, folds her hands together in her lap and looks at them. "She says it makes her feel close to him, Grandpa, I mean. The house has changed a lot. It's been forty years, but she says she can still feel him." She turns to look out of the window. "Sometimes I think I can, too."

"Does that freak you out?"

"Not at all. I like it." She looks at me out of the corner of her eye, her mouth working into a slow smile which feels like it's all for me and no one else. She focuses on me, bounces her hand on to my thigh again. "Apparently, he used to say that nearly everything we encounter boils down to relationships, and all the work people put into their lives is really just them trying to find ways to be loved a little more."

"I think I would have liked your grandpa."

Paige narrows her eyes, and a gust of breeze like an intake of breath whispers through the car windows. She touches my hand on the wheel with the tips of her fingers and says, very softly, "I think he would have liked you, too."

Fourteen

By the time we reach Corfe Castle, the afternoon has turned cold and the sky above us is a mix of ominous indigos and greys.

We leave the car in a little gravel car park next to the gift shop, and climb a path around the castle walls, until we reach the gatehouse entrance. There, a ginger-haired woman in a makeshift booth pokes her head towards us like a pigeon and scowls.

"How many?" she snaps.

"Three," says Paige.

"Did you book?"

Paige shakes her head. "No, but I'm on intimate terms with Desdemona, if that helps."

The woman looks at Paige suspiciously, and then she opens a big book on her lap and scans her finger down a column of names.

"Hmm," she says, after a while. "I *suppose* I could fit you in. You'll have to sit on the grass up by the bastion, though. You can't have deckchairs!"

Paige smiles with all of her teeth and claps her hands together. "That would be just *dandy*," she exclaims. "Thanks *so* much."

She hands the woman a ten-pound note and some change, and moves past her with something that resembles a curtsy.

Will and I follow, heads down, trying not to snigger, but just then Paige halts and spins around, reaches out flamboyantly and places her hand on the woman's arm.

"I do hope," she says softly, patting her arm, "that they gave you a refund."

The woman looks blank. "Who?"

"Why, the charm school, of course!" And then she grabs us both and hauls us, running, onto the grass and up a slope towards the tumbledown castle ramparts. She keeps us running, laughing, up and up and up, until Will's hung-over legs turn to elastic and he crumples to the ground and lies there, panting, opening and closing his eyes at the sky.

Paige and I stand over him with our hands on our hips, looking at each other and catching our breath, and all around us, on every side, grey stone and sky blur like a bad photograph.

Paige points back down the hill and asks, "Can you see Rick?"

I follow the line of her finger to a scatter of deckchairs with people in them, all of whom are looking towards a gold and white gazebo, edged by fake trees and grubby shrubs. Nothing seems to be happening, but a huddle of characters in period dress are milling about near the entrance, tweaking at their costumes, limbering up.

I turn back to Paige. "I'm not sure which one's him, to be honest, but then, I wouldn't recognise him with his clothes on, would I?"

She looks at me doubtfully for a second, not sure if I'm joking, but when I smile and sit myself down next to Will on the grass, she comes to sit close beside me and leans against me hard. We pull our knees in under our chins and watch the actors shuffling towards the gazebo and then away, their long robes and dresses fluttering like fresh washing in the breeze.

After a minute or two like that, Paige takes my hand and holds it in both of hers against her chest, crushing the little bird-bones in my wrist, pressing my hand really tight into her ribs, until I say, quietly, "Adam rang me last night."

"Did he?"

"Yes."

"He said he wouldn't." I can feel her heart knocking tight against my skin. "What did he want?"

I clear my throat. "Not sure."

Down below, the actors are taking their places, and suddenly the sound of Whitney Houston singing 'I Will Always Love You' begins to drift up the hill towards us.

"Oh, great!" sighs Paige, her head dropping deadweight onto her knees. "Sixteenth century Venice to the dulcet tones of bloody *Whit*ney!" She shouts the name, and a couple of people in the deckchairs spin around and squint up at us.

"Not a fan, then?" I whisper it against her hair, and she lifts her head, grinning.

"I guess you could say that."

"I'm surprised. I mean, there's a rumour that she's, you know..." I'm not quite sure how to say what I'm thinking. "One of *you*, right?"

"What d'you mean?"

"You know what I mean. She's gay, isn't she?"

Paige's face stays very still for a moment, and then she puts both her hands to her mouth and breathes out against her fingers, looks away from me. She leans down towards Will.

"If Rebecca and I go for a walk, will you be able to tell us what happens?"

Will peers up at her. "What's the play, again?"

"*Othello*."

"Green-eyed monster and all that crap, yeah?"

"Yeah."

He crosses his arms over his face. "Sure. That's fine. Absolutely. I'll tell you what happens. You go for your walk. That's fine, go for a..." he takes a big breath in and yawns "... walk," but the word skims soft across the surface of sleep and I know that his eyes will close as soon as we are gone, and stay that way until we come back.

"Come on." Paige stalks away up the hill so fast that I have to leap to my feet and run to catch up with her.

"What about Rick and the play, Paige?"

She shoots me a glance. "He won't mind. Come on." And she holds out her hand to me, and I take it and she draws me forward, until we are clambering over broken stones and up a series of uneven steps into what's left of the main keep of the castle. She pauses for a moment, looks back at me, and her face is all shadow.

"Are you tired?"

I shake my head even though I am, and she sets off again, even faster, through a series of ruined chambers, up some more steps, and then some more, and then out into sudden daylight.

"Look," she says, leaning over the battlements. "We can see everything from up here."

My lungs ache from the climb, but I join her, smiling as best I can, and peer over the edge. A long way below are the deckchairs and the gazebo, actors on the stage, and, away to the right, beneath one of the crumbling towers, Will, stretched out like a dead man on the grass.

My voice lifts breathless. "There's Will."

But she turns and sinks down with her back against the nubbled stone. Plucking a long piece of grass, she twists it between her fingers and looks up at me.

"Does it bother you that I prefer women to men?"

I stay standing for a moment, considering the question, wanting to give the right answer.

"No," I say, but I hear the corners of my voice lift a little, and she hears it too, and she frowns.

"*Why* does it bother you?"

"It doesn't, exactly." I shuffle down beside her with my back against the wall. "I really don't mind if *you* prefer women to men, but I guess I mind if *I* do."

"Why?"

"Because it's just not something I've ever thought about for myself, and it's weird for me, and also I'm wondering if it's real, if I'm *really* feeling these things, or if it's just about you, *only* about you, and after you, I'll go back to being attracted to men."

Paige snaps the piece of grass in two. "What do you mean, *after* me?"

And suddenly I'm embarrassed and adrift. I can feel a flush of pink tickling my cheekbones. I look away from her.

"I mean, if all this finishes, I guess."

"Why should it?"

I shrug. "Have you ever had a relationship that *hasn't* finished?"

"So, we are actually *in* a relationship, then?"

I nod, vaguely, but then I shake my head. "I don't know."

"Rebecca." The tone of her voice makes me turn back to look. Her hands are open in her lap.

Keeping her gaze away from me she says, carefully, "It only has to happen *once*, you know, and you have to make space for it to happen, otherwise it never will. Don't you see that?"

"Of course I do, but I just think..."

"That's your problem." She jabs a finger at me. "You think too much. You've spent your life thinking, working out your next move, planning a strategy, and where's it got you? Shagged out and nowhere. For Christ's sake, don't you see? It's not about thought. It's about feeling. It's about giving up control and going with the fucking *flow*."

I feel my head droop a little. "It's not as simple as that for me."

"Oh, of course it is. You just don't know it yet." And then she turns and clambers across me, so that she is sitting with her legs astride mine, her weight across my thighs. She leans forward and says, very close to my face, "It doesn't matter whether we are gay or straight or bisexual, whether we like to have sex with animals or dwarves, or root *vegetables*. None of it matters. All that matters is that we are *honest* about it. Honest about *everything*. Surely you see that? After Adam. After all that's happened to you. You *must* see it now, surely?"

She takes my face in her hands and looks hard into my eyes, like she's trying to root something out, make certain of something.

"Rebecca." And my name shapes itself into a smile on her lips. "Just try to trust what you feel, sweetheart, not what you think. If I am the only woman you've ever been attracted to, then let it be, and let it happen, and if it turns out to be wrong for you, then let *that* happen, too. Just be honest about it."

I nod slowly, let my head drop back against the stone. "You make it sound so effortless, though."

"I don't mean to." She huffs a little laugh against my cheek. "I mean, it isn't, but it's necessary I think, and... transforming." She leans back. "When I was going through all that stuff with Rick, trying to decide what to do and how to be, trying, really, to find a way *not* to leave him, I was also having to do a load of reading for my doctorate. I was researching how some tribes use masks and body art in their ceremonial dances and festivals. There are hundreds of different masks, but the ones that feature most in dance dramas, in spirit dances, are what they call the transformation masks; really elaborate, brightly coloured arrangements with feathers and blood and all sorts of crap. Now, these masks are mostly used to illustrate the transition from one form of life to another, like wolf to man, or raven to man, because tribal myth suggests that it's possible to be more than one living form in a lifetime – *if* you know the spells that can make it happen." She crinkles her nose. "It's an idea I quite like. If I could take on an animal form, I'd be a scorpion, I reckon; frying in the heat, menacing, sexy as fuck." She winks at me, leans forward onto my chest with her arms crossed.

"The transformation mask consists of one mask inside another, and at the high point of the spirit dance, the dancer tugs on strings that pull apart sections of the outer mask to reveal the one inside; *but*, there's this one winter ceremony, very sacred, called the Cedar Time, when a single transformation mask is used, and at the high point of the dance, when the dancer tugs on the strings and the outer mask falls away, there isn't another mask beneath, there's just the dancer, buck naked and blessed by the gods." She grins at me. "Do you see?"

"Buck naked and blessed by the gods?"

"Absolutely."

The exaggerated clatter of a pushchair over the stones heralds the sudden arrival of a family of four with a picnic basket. The man and woman hover in the broken-down doorway, breathing hard and looking perplexed, while two small children go galloping past us without looking.

Paige lifts her weight onto her heels and stands up, holds out both her hands to me.

"Pardon us," she says to the couple. "We were just trying out a little liberation therapy."

The couple look at each other and then back at us and then the woman takes a step forward and calls, "Sophie... Damon?" in a mildly terrified voice, and the two small children come galloping back like terriers and get themselves all tangled up with Paige and me, so that we have to dance around them in a laughable little jig.

"Toodle pip," calls Paige over her shoulder, holding my hand tight in hers and skipping us down over a space of bumpy grass and alongside a wall that is wet with moss. We turn a corner and step up into a circular chamber and a rush of cold air buffets us backwards. We are high up on the castle ramparts, and I feel a thrill of exhilaration slip scarlet to my toes. Through ragged gaps in the wall, I can see the gazebo far below, lamp-lit now and suddenly enchanting.

"This is called the Gloriette Tower," says Paige, spreading her arms wide and turning herself round in a circle. "The royal apartments were in this part of the castle. Henry III loved Corfe, and whenever he came to visit, he'd stay in this top tower room, right here, right where we're standing." She trails her fingers along the wall. "The story goes that he loved the colour green, and even though green paint was incredibly expensive back then and very rare, he insisted on it for all the walls of his chamber."

I put my hands on my hips with a theatrical sigh. "Do you know *everything* about *everything*, Paige Mackenzie?"

She shrugs. "I *do*, actually, and none of it any use to man nor beast, as my grandma would say. Speaking of which, that brings another old biddy to mind."

She trots across to the far side of the chamber, plucks a fistful of grass and then scrambles up so that she can peer through the narrow turret window. She turns and beckons to me, and her smile is roguish, intriguing. I haul myself up alongside her and peer down into the gathering dark. We are facing east now, and there beneath us, outside the castle walls, is a cluster of farm buildings and a grey curve of road leading up to the village.

"Watch this," whispers Paige, taking a thick blade of grass and settling it between her thumbs. It takes her a moment to get it in the right position, but when she does, she brings her clasped hands to her mouth, presses the blade of grass to her lips and blows hard. A shrill sound, a kazoo, the zealous buzzing of a bee, shoots like an arrow into the stillness. All at once, a Jack Russell terrier comes zipping out of the back door of the farmhouse below and starts barking – a high-pitched sound, fervent and furious. After a moment, an old lady appears in the doorway, wiping her hands on a tea towel. She steps out into the garden and looks around, glances up to the castle, seems to be looking right *at* us. Paige grabs me and we duck down, giggling like schoolgirls, hanging onto each other so that we don't slip away from the window. We wait until the Jack Russell stops barking, then peep over the edge again. The old lady has gone, but the little dog is still standing in the garden, sniffing suspiciously at the air, trotting backwards and forwards to make sure he hasn't missed anything.

As soon as he goes back into the house, Paige grins at me, brings the grass to her lips and blows again, and, sure enough, out he comes, skidding to a halt in the flower bed, barking up at the castle again, his little voice hoarse with rage and utterly indignant. The old lady is quicker this time, tottering out onto the grass with her hands on her hips. She and the dog stand looking around them in confusion, and Paige is just about to bring the blade of grass to her lips a third time, when I catch hold of her hand, laughing so hard I can barely speak.

"Not again..." The breath is tight in my lungs and I'm gulping at the air like a long distance swimmer. "I can't take it."

She's laughing too, tears in her eyes.

"All right... All right, but she falls for it every time, believe me. It's a bit mean, though, isn't it?" She opens her hand, drops the grass to the floor and snuggles her chin into her chest. "Poor old bird, eh?"

I start to laugh again, sharp little shrieks that sound as if I'm in pain, which I actually *am* suddenly, as I lose my foothold, tumbling away from the wall and landing in a heap on the castle floor.

Paige scrambles down, still laughing, but trying hard not to. "Oh God! Are you okay?"

"Yeah." I rub at my bruised regions, and Paige plops down beside me and leans back on her hands, and for a long time we just sit side by side, looking up to where the tower roof would once have been. Vague clouds are moving in slow motion across the face of the stars. Their languor makes me drowsy. The afternoon has grown dark around us and I can't see Paige's face clearly any more, but when at last she turns to look at me, she is smiling. The sound of applause ripples towards us from the gazebo.

"Half-time," she says. "We probably ought to be getting back."

"Not just yet."

She inclines her head and then turns and lifts her leg over mine like she did before, except that this time, she leans forward and bears me gently down onto my back. I lift my hands and slip my fingers tight into her hair and she rests her cheek against mine and keeps it there. I can feel her along the length of my body, how she fits, how *her* softness and mine blend and fuse. There are no straight lines here, no austerity in the shape and texture of us, nothing inflexible.

I think of last night, with Will; how his body seemed to set itself against me in a network of muscle and sinew and bone. It was what I wanted then, to be separate; to feel everything transferred to the surface of my skin, but this is *so* different. Paige's leather jacket is open and she's only wearing a T-shirt beneath. Her warmth sinks straight through to my bones, a soft hum of blood, an assimilation. I close my eyes and think of the spirit dance, the Cedar Time. I think of the dancer, at the height of the dance, letting his mask fall away to reveal...

Paige lifts herself and when I open my eyes, she's looking down at me. "Do you think," she asks, "that we might be a little bit in love with each other?"

And I draw her down fast and kiss her lips, smiling into that kiss, hearing the heartbeat of tribal drums coming closer, pushing my tongue between her teeth so that I can taste her deeper, and there's a little sound like a sob in my throat. It surprises me. I've never heard it before.

I can hardly bear to take my mouth from hers, but when I do, I hold her face very close and just look at her, gather her in, greedy suddenly, unscrupulous in my need of her but not knowing what to do about it.

"Whatever happens," she says suddenly, "do not imagine that I will ever forget you or forsake you."

I nod.

"*Whatever* happens," she says again, firmer this time, and then she clambers to her feet and brushes herself down.

"We should go now," she says.

I get up reluctantly. "Yes."

And she walks ahead of me, very slowly, back alongside the mossy wall and across the grass to where the family with the picnic basket disturbed us. They're gone now. The air is eerily calm.

"Hey, look at this," she says, stooping and cupping her hand close to the ground. "I haven't seen one of these in ages."

I crouch down beside her in the grass. Beneath the little roof that her fingers are making, there's a butterfly, pale yellow and grey, opening and closing its wings against the air.

"It's a Clouded Apollo," whispers Paige. "They're really rare in the south."

I look closely. "It's pretty."

"It's ingenious, too. It's the only butterfly that can change its wing colour, and its markings, to match the environment it's in."

"Like a chameleon?"

She nods, and touches her fingertip to one of the butterfly's antenna. It quivers, opening its wings wide like the pages of a book.

"It can choose loads of different shades and markings for itself, and somehow, it *knows* exactly which ones to go for, which I think's amazing." She looks at me, her eyes wide and excited. "*This* is what it looks like naturally, though." And she points. "These are its *actual* markings, and they're the most beautiful of all." She leans closer, whispers to the butterfly, "No need to hide from us, is there, little sweetheart? We think you're perfect as you are."

Suddenly, the butterfly shifts under Paige's hand and lifts into the air, flies between us and up over our heads. We watch it go.

"Cool," says Paige slowly, and then she leans over the parapet. "I wonder if the interval's over. Can you see?"

I lace my arm around her waist and peer down towards the gazebo, then let my eyes wander up the hill, towards the crumbling towers, wondering if Will is awake yet. I can't quite see him at first, because the light from the stage is a shadowy yellow and very weak. I lean further forward, squinting, and then I *do* see him, still lying on the grass, but hunched over on his side now, facing away from us. It takes me less than a second to realise that there is someone standing over him. It takes me even less than that to recognise who. Adam.

I clutch at Paige's arm. "Will." I say it quietly at first, a whisper, but then a huge breath, like a howl of thunder, rushes clear out of my ribcage and I shout, "Will!" and I watch Adam lift his head, very slowly, leisurely as a lizard in the sun. He looks straight at me. I can feel his eyes on me, and then he raises his hand and waves.

Suddenly, I'm running and Paige is close behind me; back into the old keep and down a long flight of steps, down and down and down, over cobblestones and out onto the grass, sprinting across the grass, calling Will's name, over and over. But it's like one of those awful dreams where you're running as fast as you can and not getting anywhere. It seems to take forever to reach him, but I do, at last, dropping down onto my knees and shaking him hard.

"Will." I look around us frantically, swooping my gaze like a searchlight over the people in deckchairs; the actors shuffling back onto the stage. I know Adam must still be here somewhere. "Will."

"Wha-aat?" He opens his eyes and blinks up at me. "What's going on?"

And Paige appears by my side, out of breath, leaning forward with her hands flat on her thighs.

Will opens his mouth in a yawn and sits up. "Talk about rude awakening," he says blearily. "Is the play over?"

I sit back heavily on the grass and Paige and I look at each other.

"Where's he gone?" she says.

Will shakes his head. "Where's *who* gone?"

"He was here." I say it quick so it won't sound so scary. "Adam. He was right here."

"Standing over you," adds Paige. "We saw him from up on the battlements."

Will's eyes widen and the colour drains fast from his cheeks.

"Are you all right, love?" I put both my hands on his forearm, but he tenses.

I look around us again, squinting hard into the twilight, but there's no sign now of Adam.

"What's that?" says Paige suddenly, pointing at Will's coat.

There's a piece of paper sticking out of his pocket, poking out like the point of a handkerchief.

"I don't know," he says dubiously, looking down at it as if it might be about to explode. "It wasn't there before."

Paige and I glance at each other, then back at Will. He takes a breath, pulls the paper from his pocket and unfolds it.

"Oh my God," he says. "It's from Kate."

Fifteen

Dear Will, I'm sorry I haven't called you. I meant to be in touch, but you know how hard everything has been for me. I miss Adam so much. I know you do, too. I'm gradually beginning to feel better, though. I'm sorry for any hurt I've caused. Go home and tell Mum that I'll see her very soon. Go home, Will. I'll meet you there as soon as I can. I love you.

Kate.

Will looks up from the paper, blinking.

"I can't believe it," he says quietly. "After *all* this time." And then he smiles and hands the note to me. "It doesn't feel real, you know? Read it, Bex, read it and tell me it's real, that it's really from *her*."

I scan the paper, the typewritten words, all block capitals. "I don't know. I guess it must be." But my heart is thumping loud in my ears and I'm not sure of anything.

Paige reaches her arms around me from behind and reads over my shoulder. "Good news," she says. "A family reunion."

Will reaches for the note and reads it again, grinning. "She's coming home." His voice lifts, sharp as a kite. "I can't believe she's coming home." He starts to stand up. "I've got to find a phone. I've got to tell Mum."

"Hang on a sec, Will." I don't want to snatch the moment away from him, but something uncertain is needling. "Are you sure this is from Kate?"

He stares down at me. "Of course I am."

"Yes, but…"

"No *buts*, Bex." He reaches out his hands and helps me to my feet. "Come on and help me find a phone."

Paige points towards the entrance. "There's one just outside on the main road."

"Excellent. Have you got any change?"

I take hold of his sleeve. "Wait, though, Will. Maybe you shouldn't ring your mum yet."

"Why not?"

"What if Kate changes her mind and doesn't turn up at home?"

"I'll take the *risk*, for Christ's sake. Now will you please stop pissing on my firework and lend me some money."

Paige and I both burrow in our pockets and give him what coins we have and he turns and runs towards the entrance with his coat flapping open.

Paige sighs behind me. "I do so *lurve* a happy ending, don't you?"

"Is that what this is?"

"Don't you think so? Kate goes home. Will goes home. The family's together again."

I turn to look at her. "I don't know. This note from Kate turns up in Will's pocket just after we see Adam standing over him, so Adam must have put it there, yes?"

Paige takes a step towards me. "I guess so. You were probably right all along about her knowing him. Maybe she was a bit fucked off with you over what happened to her brother or something, and she and this mate of hers, or mate of Adam's, whatever he is, just wanted to give you a scare. I dunno, but it doesn't matter now, does it, not now that she's going home and everything's going to be okay."

"But how do we know it's gonna be okay?"

She shrugs. "She said she was sorry for the hurt she'd caused, didn't she, and that she was feeling better? I think that's a lid on it."

I fold my arms between us, a lilting chill lifting the hair away from my neck and letting it drop. Paige presses her palms over my hip-bones.

"Let it be over," she says, "and it will be."

But I shake my head, uncertain. "How the hell did he know where to find us, anyway?"

"He must have followed us."

"God, that's freaky, though. To think he might be watching us." I look up again to the castle ramparts, the jagged castle walls. "What if this note *isn't* from Kate? What if it's fake?"

"Why would it be? Why would someone want to make Will think his sister's going home if she's not?"

Suddenly, someone is calling Paige's name and we both turn to look. A woman is trotting towards us, her long dress trailing over the grass, black hair streaming out behind her like a spillage of ink.

"I wasn't sure you'd make it," she says when she reaches us, and her voice is surprisingly deep. It makes me peer at her closely, as she leans forward and kisses Paige on the cheek.

Paige keeps hold of the woman's hand. "We wouldn't have missed it for the world."

"You probably should have. It's shite."

"Rick." Paige gestures towards me. "This is Rebecca."

And the woman, who I can now see is quite obviously *not*, shakes my hand and smiles, and says, "It's good to meet you," as if he means it. Then he hitches up his skirts and winces. "This bloody girdle's killing me."

Paige grins. "The things we do for our art, eh?"

"It's got a lot less to do with art than with paying the rent." He turns back to me with a genial little shrug, and his eyes linger, taking me in, surmising.

"Listen," he says. "Why don't you two get off now? You don't have to stay."

Paige and I say, "We don't mind," in unison, and then all three of us grin at each other, and Paige slips her hand into mine.

"No, really." Rick straightens his wig and glances back to the stage. "Nothing interesting happens now, anyway. I die. Othello dies. That's about it. I'd rather meet you in the pub later."

Paige shakes her head. "If you're sure."

"Yeah." He leans forward and kisses her quickly on the lips. "Now scat, go on. I'll see you in the Wolf at six." And then he turns and trots away from us, hanging onto his wig with one hand and re-adjusting his girdle with the other.

"Is this okay with you?" Paige's face is tilted towards me, the light behind her.

"Of course it is."

"We can catch Will on his way back."

"Sure."

But we just stand looking at each other and then looking away. The lights go up on the stage and a skitter of applause falls between us. Paige dips her head as if to meet it, scuffs her shoe back and forth over a tuft of grass.

"What d'you think of Rick then?" she says.

"He seems nice."

She looks up sharp. "He *is* nice, isn't he?" And her voice is pleased. Sliding her arm through mine, she begins to walk us quickly down the hill towards the entrance. "I was hoping you'd like him, that you'd like each other, you know?" She squints towards the gazebo. "He makes a pretty convincing Desdemona, doesn't he?"

"Definitely. I actually thought he was a woman when he first came up."

"Seriously? But he's got such a deep voice, and stubble."

"Yeah, well…" I clear my throat. "I thought he, *she*, was maybe a friend of yours, you know, a *butch* friend of yours." Paige starts to laugh. "What d'you call them? A petrol dyke?"

She laughs even harder. "Do you mean a diesel dyke?"

"That's the one."

"You have got a *lot* to learn, my dear."

"And I suppose you're gonna teach me, are you?"

Paige turns to look at me. "If you'll let me, honeybun. If you'll let me."

And I feel a blush rush hot from my toes to the roots of my hair. I am a walking firebrand. As we pass the people in the deckchairs, I imagine them having to shield their eyes against how bright my body has become, but when I glance, no one is looking at me. Their faces are turned towards the stage.

I hear Rick's voice, a pitch higher and flung out on to the air like a net filled with Desdemona's words.

"*Be assured,*" he is saying. "*If I do vow a friendship, I shall perform it to the last article...*"

And I arch my back a little and look at Paige, and she is looking at me, and I know then that it's real, what we feel for each other; in this moment, with the breeze at our backs and the moon above us, thin as a communion wafer. *Be assured.* I hear it again. *If I do vow a friendship, I shall perform it to the last article...* And the light is like water suddenly, viscous, difficult to breathe, because it has happened, the thing I thought would never happen. I trust and I am trusted; one creature's need and another's response. I say her name and she hears me, and that's all there is, for a moment, until I remember Adam, standing over Will, looking up at me, and the hairs on the back of my neck rise and I shiver, so that Paige asks, "Are you okay, love?"

I nod. "Just cold."

She slips her arms around my waist, one around the back and one around the front, and I press her head against my shoulder and we walk comically like that, a three-legged race to the entrance booth where the ginger-haired woman is peering out at us, aghast. For a second I think she's going to clamber over her counter and manhandle us back to our places, but she lets us pass with nothing more significant than a nod of the head.

We find Will in a telephone booth under the war memorial and lean against it, one on either side, until he's finished, until he steps out, beaming, and then we link our arms through his and walk away from the castle and onto a street that is crooked with cobblestones.

"I didn't get to speak to Mum," he says. "She was having a lie-down, but I spoke to Beryl and told her that I'll be home tomorrow and that Kate's coming home, too, and she's going to tell Mum for me. Mum's not going to *believe* it. I bet you she won't believe it, but it's true, isn't it? Kate's coming home and things will start looking up, won't they? Things can only get better now, *and* my hangover's gone. Shit! I feel *great*."

His pleasure is contagious, and I can't help but let myself sink into it and start to believe. A tiny part of me starts to believe that things *are* going to get better now, that Adam isn't going to be bothering me again, and it's like a window opening onto sunlight.

Will skips his steps suddenly, so that all three of us bump hips and start to laugh, and I think how strange we must look to people passing. I begin to wonder what they make of us, but almost as soon as I do, I realise that I really don't care *what* we look like *or* what they make of us. I don't care what people think, and it's new to me, not caring. I like how it feels.

"You know what I think?" A hoot of laughter bubbles up and out of my mouth. "I think that hangovers are simply God's way of telling us to *stay* drunk."

And they both smile, and Paige says to Will, "I like this girl's thinking, don't you? She's sharp." She leans around him to look at me, winking, and then she looks away and cries, "Ship ahoy!"

We are standing outside a little stone pub built in amongst the houses, so you'd miss it if you didn't know it was there. A pointy-nosed wolf is smiling down at us from the sign.

"He doesn't look very predatory," says Will.

I try to think who the wolf reminds me of. "He looks like Basil Brush."

Paige furrows her eyebrows. "Wasn't Basil Brush a fox, though?"

"He was." Will nods up at the sign sagely. "He was a fox, in a waist-coat, and a tweed cape, *very* rare species."

"What, like men with a sense of humour, you mean?" Paige glow-ers at him for a second, but then she smiles and says, "Boom! Boom!" in a derisory tone, flailing at him with the back of her hand.

She glances away to a little blackboard nailed above the door. "Oh great!" she says. "Hairy Hawker are playing tonight. They're excel-lent." And she moves inside ahead of me. "They're an Irish folk band. You'll like them. I know the guy who plays the bodhran."

"Trust you to know the guy who plays the bodhran." We reach the bar and lean in together. "I don't even know what a bodhran *is*."

Will excuses himself and slips away to the gents, while Paige catches the barman's eye as he's wiping some tables. He smiles at her like he's known her all his life and heads towards us with a tea towel slung jauntily over his shoulder.

"A bodhran?" Paige thinks for a moment. "Well, it's a little drum thing, that you hold, you know?" She tries to show me with her hands, but then she shakes her head and says, "Never mind. You'll see in a bit. What're you having to drink?"

"Oh, just a mineral water, thanks."

She raises an eyebrow at me. "Reckless as ever, eh?"

"I'm driving, and besides, I've got work tomorrow."

"Why don't you just chuck a sicky? We could get drunk and stay here, go back up to the castle and sleep out under the stars?"

"We'd freeze."

She tuts at me. "No sense of adventure."

"Excuse *me*, Mackenzie, but I beg to differ." I pull myself up to my full height. "I'll have you know, I once had sex in the crypt of Winchester Cathedral." Her mouth falls open. "During Evensong." She starts to snigger. "Presided over by the Bishop!"

"No *way*." She puts her hand to her mouth. "You didn't?"

"I did."

"What was it like?"

"Oh, you know; cold, damp, sacrilegious."

"Well, bugger me with a fish fork," she says, grinning. "With stuff like that in your past, why did you *ever* have to make anything up?" And at that, the barman arrives in front of us and Paige drops her elbows on to the bar with a thud. "Mineral water, please, and a large G&T and..." She turns to me. "What d'you think Will would like?"

I shrug. "Hair of the dog?"

Paige raises her eyebrows in complicity, nods, says to the barman, "And a triple brandy and ginger please."

We grin at each other while he sets about preparing our drinks, and then a couple of men squeeze by us with big black instrument cases, and Paige's face opens up in recognition.

"Hey Matt! How ya doin'?" She reaches for the smaller of the two men and he steps back to see who she is, and when he realises, he shakes his shoulders from side to side like he's dancing and lunges forward to hug her.

"I didn't know you'd be here," he says, stepping back. "Are you gonna join us?"

She looks dubious. "I don't think so."

"Aah, go on." His voice is soft Irish, crushed velvet. "You know you can always cook up a storm with that voice of yours. 'She Moved Through the Fayre', yeah? I'll call ya up?"

"I don't know."

He gives her a look as if to say, 'Now come on,' and then moves ahead of us to a little stage set back in a corner, where his friend has already opened his case and is clicking a music stand into shape.

Will sidles in alongside us and Paige lifts his drink down from the bar.

"A toast!" She hands me my mineral water and brings her own glass to her lips. "Confusion to the enemy," she says.

"And who's the enemy, again?"

She looks at me over the rim of her glass, eyes ablaze. "Why, anyone who's not in this *room* of course."

And we drink, and the bar begins to fill around us; a swell of voices made easy with alcohol. There's a fire burning in the hearth, orange and yellow candles crowding in the alcoves and on the window ledges.

We sit down at a table near the stage and order some food. While the band are setting up, we eat mussels straight from the shells, butter dripping hot from our fingertips and huge chunks of bread, bitter with caraway seeds. I hadn't realised how hungry I was, but I eat as if I haven't eaten in days, and the sea-salt tang of the food makes my tongue burn.

Paige orders a bottle of Rioja and another brandy and ginger for Will. He takes a big breath when it arrives and I think he's going to decline, but then he picks up the glass in both hands and splashes the contents into his mouth, screws his eyes tight shut, swallows.

"Good stuff," he says, his voice strained. "I could get used to this."

"Why don't you?" Paige leans towards him. "Why not stay here with us and get drunk *every* day, indulge in some south coast shenanigans." She licks her lips. "You could become our little Essex sex slave."

"I don't think I'd be qualified, somehow."

"No? Aren't Essex men like Essex girls, then?"

"Not this one."

Paige places both her hands on his arm, whispers in a jokey manner, "You're not a virgin, are you, Junior?"

Will's face slackens for a moment, but he holds her gaze.

Draining the last few drops from his glass, he says casually, "Well, if that's what you kids are calling it these days, then *yes*, I am."

"Well, well, well." Paige pours herself a glass of wine and slides down in her seat. "Who'd've thought it?" And then she sits, sipping, regarding Will with a confused mixture of disdain and fascination.

He clears his throat, lifts the bottle of Rioja from the table and tilts it towards me.

"Glass of wine, Bex?"

"Go on, then. Just the one."

I hold my glass out to him and he pours, glancing at me intermittently. His face is fighting off a smile. He's stunned Paige into silence and he likes the fact. He likes that she doesn't know what else to say.

I start to drink my wine slow and it tingles pinpricks of warmth into my cheeks. After a moment, I ask him, "Is it just that you haven't met the right girl?"

"Not exactly."

"Then what?"

He raises his eyebrows a little, as if to say, 'You already know' – but I don't.

"Is it some kind of religious conviction?"

He chuckles at that. "No."

I pour some more wine into Paige's glass and then top up my own. "I don't get it, then. It's not as if you haven't had the opportunity, surely?"

"It's not about opportunity. It's about waiting for what I *want*."

Paige sighs. "And what exactly *do* you want, Junior?"

"I want the genie in the bottle." His face dips forward into an arc of firelight. "I want the feast, the ring of fire. I want long, slow, lost weekends in bed. I want heat and sweat and blood. I want to come so hard and so sharp that it's like a knife between my shoulder blades. I want the thrust and the touch and the inside-out colour of love and the edge of the world and the first time and the last time and the sweet, soft, wet core of it all. That's what I want."

He sits back in his seat and folds his arms across his chest.

"Oh my!" says Paige. "You *have* given this some thought."

And at that, the band starts to play and Paige glances away, clapping her hands and whistling encouragement. "I'll tell you something," she calls over the music, looking Will straight in the eye. "You're gonna be hauling your cookies around forever if you hold out for *that*."

Will and I watch each other for a long moment. If there was a time I looked at him and saw a child, I can't recall it. He is all edges now, the angles of his body sheer as stone. I try to slip his face back amongst all the familiar images of Brentwood, but it's like a piece of jigsaw that won't go. He isn't anybody's little brother any more, and he looks at me defiantly, knowing that I know how much he's changed.

Suddenly, he leans towards me and whispers, "I think we should talk about what happened last night, when we got back from the club."

I shrug. "If you want to."

"Later, yeah?" He lifts his glass to his lips. "I don't want there to be any misunderstandings between us. I want us to be honest with each other."

"Okay." But I have a bad feeling about this situation and I don't know what to do with it. I swallow something back inside, try to look Will in the eye. "Can I ask you something?"

He nods.

"D'you remember Simon, Adam's friend?"

"The one who went out with Kate?"

I swallow again. "Yes. Do you know what happened to him? There was some kind of *misunderstanding* between him and Kate, wasn't there? Did they get back together in the end?"

"Christ, no. I'm not sure what went wrong there, and he and Adam fell out big time, too, which was a shame, 'cos they were *really* good mates." He leans forward, with his chin on his hand. "He hung around in Brentwood for a bit after Kate dumped him, but neither she nor Adam would have anything to do with him."

"What happened to him?"

"He got done for drunk driving one night; drove straight through the window of John Lewis. It was in the local paper."

"Really?"

Will nods. "Ended up in rehab. His parents were loaded, so they got him into a private clinic in London, but he lost his place at uni and everything. He'd won some big PhD scholarship thing, with a thesis he'd written on that American poet. Um..." He clicks his fingers, thinking.

"What's his name? You know the one – the 'Song of Myself' guy with the Grizzly Adams beard..."

"Walt Whitman?"

He nods. "That's the fella. Adam and Kate used to joke with Simon that he must have modelled himself on Walt Whitman. D'you remember how scarily hairy Simon was? God! The bloody Forestry Commission should have done something about him."

I try to smile. "What happened to him after rehab?"

"Don't know."

My throat feels tight and dry. "Was he a good bloke, would you say, when you knew him?"

"I didn't really know him. Adam didn't bring him round much. They always hung out at Simon's, because Simon had his own place. I thought I might get to know him a bit better when he and Kate hooked up, but she kept him to herself, and they didn't last long anyway." He lowers his eyebrows a little. "Why all the questions?"

"I was just wondering about him."

"I didn't even know you and he had met."

I take a sip of wine. "Just the once."

My heart is beating hard in my chest. I look at Paige, but she is looking towards the stage, kicking her leg up and down to the music. I want her to look at me. I want to tell her what Will has told me, but it's no good. She is focused on the performance.

There are three men in the band, all of them hunched seriously over their instruments. Paige's friend, Matt, has a small, flat drum in his hands, and he's beating it with what looks like a wooden spoon. He's singing, too, his voice lifting quickly, tumbling like water. The song is something about a harvest and a maypole and a girl with black ribbons. I've heard it before, but don't know it well enough to sing along with Paige and the others. They all seem to know the chorus. Each time it comes, Paige turns to look at me, winking and singing, tilting her head from side to side. A couple of times, she reaches across the table and prods Will in the chest.

"Come on," she cries, "join in." And after a while, he actually does, his face relaxing. He stretches his legs out in front of him and folds his hands behind his head, confident now, singing loud, liking the feel of himself amongst all these strangers. I try not to think about what Will has said about Simon. I concentrate on the incandescent ebb and flow of the moment. I concentrate on Will, and it makes my heart glad to see the shine of him.

The next song is an instrumental and just as jaunty as the first. Matt is playing a fiddle this time, his fingers a blur of colour on the strings. The other two men are playing tin whistles, and everywhere, people are clapping and whooping and stamping their shoes on the flagstones.

At one point, Paige jumps to her feet and pulls Will to his, and they start dancing a chaotic little jig around the table.

"That's more like it!" She laughs into his face. "Swing yer pants, Junior!"

And my eyes fill with tears as I watch them, the tiny muscles in my cheeks aching from how hard I am smiling. I have to gulp back a little choking sound, something seeping hot lava into my throat, because I just can't believe it. I can't believe this happiness. It is inexplicable to me, an impossibility, and everything falls away in the face of it: everything becomes inconsequential. Nothing matters to me but this.

Paige reaches out her hand to me as she swings past. "We're dancing our way to the bar," she explains. "What're you having?"

"I'm okay with my wine, thanks."

Rolling her eyes to the ceiling, she puckers up her lips and kisses the air. "Cheap date or *what*?" she shrieks, and then they skip unevenly away and disappear into the crowd.

I drain my glass fast, and watch the band change instruments for the next song, and then Matt steps forward to the microphone, a sheen of sweat on his forehead.

"We're going to slow it down for you now," he says, "with a little help from an old friend of ours." He teeters forward on tiptoe, peers into the crowd. "Where is she? Paige Mackenzie? Where you keeping yourself, girl?"

I look towards the bar, but there's no sign of Paige. I don't know whether I should say anything. Matt turns to the other members of the band and shakes his head, but just then I hear her voice, and the barman from before pushes his way through and shouts, "Here she is."

He has hold of Paige by the arm and is tugging her towards the stage. She looks embarrassed, disgruntled, but the crowd begin to applaud, and she smiles to them and waves her hand, pretending to curtsy as she joins Matt at the microphone.

"Thought you were gonna let us down for a second there, pet," he says, putting his arm around her.

She leans in. "Didn't get the chance, did I?"

The crowd titter, and Matt whispers something to Paige and she nods. One of the other men in the band steps forward with a penny whistle and Paige places her right hand on the microphone and clenches her left hand into a fist at her side. She closes her eyes for a moment and then opens them and says, "This song's called 'She Moved Through the Fayre'."

If it's possible to be so surprised that you stop breathing, that your lungs forget what they're supposed to do and your diaphragm hangs inside your ribcage, limp as a broken rubber band, then that's what happens to me when Paige starts to sing. I am amazed by the sound that comes out of her body. It is so clear and so cool, so perfectly pitched, that the air in the bar resonates and fractures and people's faces fall open in astonishment.

She doesn't make any big gestures. The song is very simple and there is just her voice and the delicate echo of the penny whistle, but everything is arrested.

My young love said to me,
"My mother won't mind
And my father won't slight you

For your lack of kind."
And she stepp'd away from me
And this she did say,
"It will not be long love,
'Til our wedding day."

She holds tight to the microphone as she sings, and fastens her gaze on something in the middle distance, some still point that won't confound her, that will keep the cadence clear. She opens and closes her eyes, clenches her fist, then relaxes it, and halfway through the next verse, suddenly, she looks for me and she finds me. I can't read the expression in her eyes. I don't know quite what she wants to convey, but she watches me intently as she sings, and, just for a second, her voice falters.

The people were saying
No two were e'er wed
But one had a sorrow
That never was said...

And she takes a breath, bows her head.

And I smiled as she passed
With her goods and her gear,
And that was the last
That I saw of my dear.

I smile at her when she lifts her head, and I keep smiling, trying hard to reassure her, but she looks straight past me, concentrating on something behind me. When I glance over my shoulder, I realise that Rick is standing a few feet away from our table, leaning against the wall with a pint of beer in his hand. He isn't in costume any more. He's wearing a pair of jeans and a black T-shirt, and he doesn't see me at first, because he is looking at Paige; his face a ripple of dark in the shadow from the candles. After a moment, he must sense that someone is watching him, because he glances across, catching my eye, and something passes between us like a note slipped under a door.

As Paige finishes her song and everyone begins to applaud, Rick raises his glass to me and I raise mine in response. He smiles at me and mouths the words, "Look after her."

I nod, and he turns and disappears into the crowd.

Sixteen

We don't stay on at the pub. As soon as Paige returns to the table, she asks if we can leave. The crowd is calling for her to sing again, but she shakes her head at them, smiling, and scoops up her jacket from the back of her chair so that they know she's really going.

"You don't mind, do you?" she asks, as we make our way towards the door.

"Course I don't."

She walks in front of me with her head down, and there's a weariness about her that I haven't seen before. Her poise is failing. I feel that I ought to have my arms around her in case she falls. She looks so tired suddenly.

We find Will sitting outside on a wooden bench, staring up at the night sky.

Paige ruffles his hair. "What're you looking for, Junior?"

"The Plough." He shakes his head. "Can't see it, though."

"That's because you're looking in the wrong direction." Paige points way over to the left. "See? There it is."

And Will nods slowly, making a little clicking sound out of the corner of his mouth. "Trust me not to know where to find the clearest constellation there is."

Paige starts to walk down the hill towards the castle.

"Don't sweat it, mate," she says, without turning round. "We all

179

look for what we want in the wrong places sometimes."

I feel adrift. I feel like I ought to know what to say to make her feel better, because something has shrunk away from us. All the seams are showing and I don't know how to cover them. Instead, Will and I walk a few paces behind her all the way back to the car, and when we find it, Paige leans heavily back against the door. I try to reach around her to unlock it, but she stays in my way.

"Why didn't Rick stay tonight?" she asks suddenly.

"I don't know."

Will slides himself onto the bonnet. "Who's Rick?"

"He's Paige's husband."

He slides himself off again. "Blimey! I didn't know you had a husband. I thought you were a…"

Paige and I both glare at him, and he takes a small step backwards.

I toss him the car keys. "Get in, Will. We won't be a sec, okay?"

He obeys without a word. I watch him hunch up on the back seat like a child in disgrace.

I put my hands on Paige's shoulders. "What's all this about?"

"You tell me."

"I don't know why he didn't stay, Paige."

"You didn't say anything to him?"

"Like what? What would I say?"

Letting her head drop, she gives a long sigh. "I don't know. I don't know what I'm saying. I just feel so…" she hesitates "… guilty. I just feel so guilty. I pretend that it's all all right, that he and I are friends, and we are, kind of, but God…" Leaning forward, she bumps her head against my shoulder. "Tonight, he's standing there looking so fucking *wounded*."

"That's why you got upset, during the song?"

She lifts her head to look at me.

"When you were singing, that bit about *No two were e'er wed, but one had a sorrow…*"

"*... that never was said.*"

Closing her eyes tight shut, she slips her arms around me, hugs me into her body.

"But you *did* say it, didn't you? You had the courage to tell him the truth. You did the right thing."

"Yes." But her voice sounds bruised and uncertain.

I move her away from me so that I can look into her face. "You're a good person, Paige."

"You don't really know me, Rebecca."

"I know how kind you've been to me."

She smiles with one side of her mouth, a bisected grin, and then she slides her fingers through the belt loops on my jeans and eases my hips forward into hers.

"Ah yes," she whispers. "But I have an ulterior motive there, don't I?"

I feign a sigh. "*Now* she tells me."

Paige nuzzles her mouth against my neck, kisses just below my ear, and a little shock of pink fizzes through my blood, streaks down through my vertebrae. I lift myself up straight, so that Paige relaxes back against the door.

"I'm sorry I'm such an obtuse old bag," she says.

But all I say is, "Shhh," very softly, feeling her hand move up under my top, stroking my spine, from the small of my back to my nape, and down again.

Will taps on the window.

"Are you two gonna be long?" he asks through the glass. "I'm freezing my nuts off in here."

"We're just coming, Junior." She smiles at me, glances at her watch. "Look, it's early yet. Could you drop me off at the hospital? My gran's supposed to be coming out tomorrow, but I'd like to see her tonight if I can. We might just make visiting time if we hurry."

"Sure. Get in."

But I'd forgotten that the word 'hurry' isn't in my car's vocabulary any more. We chug along at forty-five miles an hour, being overtaken by old Skodas and Reliant Robins. Plus, I can't get the heater to work, so all three of us sit bundled down in our seats and watch our breath drift out of our mouths; cobweb-grey and sweet with drink.

Each time I look in the rear-view mirror, Will is staring at me, and he doesn't look pleased. His eyebrows are down low, and as we pass under streetlamps, his face seems to loom eerily towards me.

A couple of times, I turn slightly and say, "You okay back there, Will?" – and he grunts in response and folds his arms tighter around his body.

Paige directs me to Southampton General, and as we park outside the main wing, she unclicks her seat belt and asks, "Don't suppose you'd like to come in and meet her?"

"Would you like me to?"

She nods, and then she turns round in her seat and rests her hand on Will's leg, squeezes.

"How about you, Junior? Fancy dipping your toes in my gene pool for a bit?"

"No. I'll wait here, thanks." His voice is bland as paper. "You won't be long, will you? I want to get an early start home in the morning."

We assure him we'll be back as soon as we can, and then we go in without him, trotting up the stairs to the orthopaedic ward. The bell rings for the end of visiting time just as we walk through the doors.

"Shit!" says Paige quietly. "I thought we'd have more time."

We walk a tiled line between the beds, dodging all the visitors who are on their way out. A couple of nurses scowl at us. One of them looks at us and then at her watch, tapping its face in a meaningful manner, but we press on until we reach a bed in the far corner. There is an old lady sitting up in it, a book open in her lap.

"Hey, Gran," says Paige, leaning forward and kissing her on the cheek. "How're you feeling?"

The old lady's face lifts and shines.

"Paige," she says gently, holding her granddaughter's face in her hands for a moment. "You didn't need to come tonight. You should've stayed home."

"What, and miss my last chance to lust after all these handsome doctors?"

The old lady chuckles softly, shakes her head. She has the whitest hair I've ever seen and the darkest eyes, black as onyx, and her accent is a singsong Canadian; bevelled at the edges.

She looks at me, points at Paige, says, "She doesn't think I know by now that she prefers girls."

Paige inhales with a whistling breath. "Gran!"

But the old lady just smiles and pats the bed for us to sit down.

"Aren't you going to introduce me to your friend?"

"I'm not sure I should. What other secrets of mine are you going to give away?"

"That's the only one I know, more's the pity." Paige's grandma holds out her hand. "My name's Rose."

"Rebecca."

She keeps hold of my fingers in hers and her touch is cool and dry. I can feel the crystalline joints of her knuckles, a blue tangle of veins. She is delicate, breakable, something wrapped in naphthalene.

A nurse pops up at the foot of the bed and says sweetly, "Visiting time's over, I'm afraid."

Paige nods. "We won't be long." She turns to her grandma. "Are you still coming out tomorrow?"

"God willing. They've had me prancing up and down the ward like a young gazelle all week. They think my new hip's taken fine. I just have to wait for the doctor to do his rounds in the afternoon."

"Great. I'll come for you after tea, then?"

Rose nods and lifts her chin. "Will we be seeing you again, Rebecca?"

But before I can answer, Paige reaches out and takes hold of my hand, turns it over, presses her thumb soft into my palm.

"Without a shadow of a tiny doubt," she says quietly.

And Rose closes the book in her lap with a hush of pages and tips me a conspiratorial wink.

We are almost back to the car when Paige remembers something and makes us take a detour to the maternity wing. A friend of hers, Louise, has just had a baby boy and Paige wants to look in on them.

"Won't it be a bit late, though?" I suggest.

She looks at her watch. "Nah. Maternity wards have different visiting hours to everyone else. We'll be okay."

"Won't we be in the way if her husband's there?"

"She doesn't have a husband."

"Oh, I see."

Paige stops walking and turns to look at me. "She isn't gay. I mean, she and I had a bit of a thing way back, but..."

"So she's bi?"

"It's not as clear-cut as that, Bex. Sexuality is a complicated business, you know, shifting sands. It's not a fixed mark, not for everybody, anyway." She shakes her head. "Do you think *all* my friends are gay or bi?"

"Aren't they?"

"No. I *do* have some straight friends, believe it or not."

"Like me, you mean?"

I don't know why I say it. I don't even know if I mean it, but Paige just smiles and lowers her eyes.

"Not *exactly* like you," she says, and starts walking again.

I have to hurry to catch up. "So, this friend, Louise, she'll have to support the baby herself?"

"Yeah."

"What does she do?"

"She's an industrial abseiler."

"Good Lord!" I slip my arm through hers. "Do all your friends have unusual jobs? Rick wears women's clothes or no clothes at all, Matt

184

plays an instrument no one can pronounce, Louise is an..." I struggle for the phrase.

"Industrial abseiler."

"That's the one. What do Phil and Fiona do?"

Paige grins. "Phil designs waterproof clothing for domestic animals and Fiona works with ceramics. She makes tiles, specialises in ones with... erotic designs." She starts to laugh, puts her hand to her mouth. "Images from the Kama Sutra, mostly."

"See what I mean!"

"Okay, okay. But *you* don't have an unusual job. You're a bloody librarian."

"Yeah, well." I see the doors to the maternity wing up ahead and slow my step. "I can be your token boring friend."

Paige turns, and her teeth flash at me, white in the light overhead.

"I hope," she says, "that you'll turn out to be a lot more than that."

I let her go ahead of me through the doors and down a corridor to the nurse's station. There are two side wards, in darkness except for the little yellow spotlights over each bed. The air is quiet and everything smells of fabric softener and school dinners.

Paige comes trotting back.

"It's just one visitor at a time," she whispers.

"That's fine. I'll go back and wait with Will in the car."

She kisses me quickly on the cheek. "I won't be long."

I watch her go into the ward on our left and see her open her arms wide as she approaches the bed nearest the window. The woman in it, Louise, is sitting up with a fog of pillows at her back and a tiny baby curled on her stomach. Paige leans forward and hugs Louise, holding on to her for a long time, and then she lifts the baby very gently into the air and holds him there for a moment, looking up into his face.

I mean to go then, back to the car, back to Will, but something in the way Paige is looking at that baby, something in how intent she is, how unguarded she seems, makes me take a few steps forward, so that I am standing just outside the ward door and can hear what she is saying.

"Who's the best?" she croons softly. "Who's the best boy in the *world*?"

And she sits herself down on the edge of the bed and settles the baby into her arms, her hair falling forward so that I can no longer see her face. Louise inclines her head and touches the baby's hand, and I hear Paige say, "God, he's so small, Lou."

Louise puffs out her cheeks and blows. "Well he didn't *feel* small coming out."

The two women smile at each other, and Paige dips her head lower and brushes the baby's hair with her lips, and then they just sit there, very quietly, and I know that it's time for me to go, that this is *their* moment, not mine.

On my way back to the car, I remember what Paige said to me outside the castle: "You don't really know me, Rebecca."

And I realise that she's right, that there's nearly everything left to learn about her, and my pulse skips as fast as my footsteps at the thought of it; that this is only the start, that the best with her is probably yet to come.

In that short walk back to the car, I let myself think about the future. I count off new resolutions on my fingers, savouring the flavour of a new beginning. I think of Kate's letter and I will myself into believing that it's true, that she's really going home, that the fake Adam, whoever he was, is gone from my life, forever.

By the time I get back to the car and climb inside, I am smiling. Will isn't.

"What's going on?" he asks briskly, leaning forward.

"Paige has just nipped in to see a friend of hers in the maternity wing."

"I don't mean..." He closes his hands around the headrest of the passenger seat and slides himself forward. "I mean with you and Paige?"

"I'm not sure what you're getting at."

"Yes, you are. Are you and she..." He lets out a breath, then starts again. "Look, that girl from last night, Fiona, she said that she was Paige's girlfriend."

I keep my voice as even as I can. "Did she?"

"Yes, she did, but you and Paige, when we were leaving Corfe, you and she were..." He stops dead. "Are you sleeping with her?"

"No."

"Are you thinking about it?"

"I don't know."

"What d'you mean, you don't know? Jesus!"

I turn right round so that I'm facing him, but he's staring straight ahead, his mouth set tight against me.

"Look, Will, I know this is weird, but..."

"*Weird!* You're not kidding. What the fuck are you playing at?"

"I'm not playing at anything."

"You must be. You're not a dyke. You're as straight as I am."

Turning away from him, I press my palm over the raw point of the gear stick, and a little sliver of pain sinks into my skin, steadies my thinking. My voice when it comes is very quiet.

"Truth is, I don't know *what* I am."

"Don't be ridiculous. Of course you do."

"Don't you remember what we talked about when I came to Brentwood? About my lies, about how I'd spent years making everything up?" Closing my hand over the bottom curve of the steering wheel, I turn to look at him. "Come on, Will, it was you who told me what a terrible liar I was and that I should just be myself, remember?"

"But this isn't *you*, Bex." He sits back in his seat in disbelief. "This is just another self you're trying out. Can't you see that? This is just a new lie."

"You're wrong."

"Am I?"

I hesitate. "I think I'm in love with her."

He doesn't say anything for a moment, but the muscles along his jaw line ripple as if someone has passed an electric current through them.

"And the fact that she's a woman, and you're attracted to men, is insignificant, is it?"

"But that's just it. I *was* attracted to men, but..." I shake my head. "Look, I just don't know."

"Bullshit."

"Why? Why is it bullshit for me to question my sexuality? Haven't you, ever?"

He looks at me defiantly. "No, I have not."

"Liar."

I try to smile at him, try to ease the tension, but it's no good. He looks at me like he's never seen me before.

"What *are* you doing, Rebecca?"

Winding down the window, I take a long breath into my lungs, but the air outside is dry and cold, and thick with the stink of old petrol. It makes we want to retch.

"I'm going back inside," and I scramble quickly out of the car, slamming the door behind me.

I hear him call out, "Bex!" but by then I'm running across the forecourt and back through the main doors.

As soon as I'm inside, I go to the drinks machine and buy myself a bottle of water. I drink it down fast, and then I perch on one of the blue plastic seats with my hands folded in my lap. I will wait here for Paige and we'll go back to the car together. I just need to see her, just need to have her put her arms around me, to know that Will is wrong. This isn't a lie. This *can't* be a lie.

I settle back into my seat, relaxing, and it is then that I hear Paige's voice. At first, I can't tell where it's coming from, but when I stand up and follow the sound, it leads me around a corner and along a short corridor towards the outpatients department. I can't hear what Paige is saying, but her voice keeps lifting and lifting and all the 'S' sounds in her speech seem accentuated. I follow the hiss of her voice, passing under a sign saying 'Telephones', and then I come to a large square of carpet, some more plastic chairs, and Paige, with her back to me, a telephone receiver gripped in her hand. She is hunched against the wall, head down, tangling the telephone wire tight around her finger.

"I can't," she says. "I can't do it." She is silent for a moment. "This isn't what we agreed."

I take a step towards her. "Paige."

She turns around slow. The telephone wire snaps free from her finger and spins loose, tapping against her leather jacket like it's trying to get her attention.

"I've got to go," she says into the receiver, holding my gaze. "I'll call you tomorrow."

She hangs up, still looking at me.

"I thought you were waiting in the car."

"I was, but..." I move a little closer. "Who were you talking to?"

She takes a breath. "My mum." And her face falls. "She was supposed to be coming down from London to look after Gran for a few days, but now she says she's too busy. She wants *me* to do it." Shuffling over to one of the chairs, she sits down. "I can't do it, though, Bex. I can't look after an old lady. I don't know anything about old ladies."

I slide down beside her. "I don't think there's much to know. I bet you'd be okay."

"You think?"

"I do. And besides." I put my arm around her shoulder. "I'll help you."

"Really?"

"Sure. It might be a laugh. Your grandma seemed like a groovy old bird."

"She is."

"Well, then. Tomorrow, we just find out from the doctor exactly what we should be doing, and we do it."

"As simple as that?"

I shrug. "Probably."

Paige smiles, nudges her head against my shoulder, rests it there. "Do you still think I'm a good person, Rebecca?"

"The best." I whisper it against her hair. "The *absolute* best."

But she looks up into my face, perplexed. "You're very tolerant of people's failings, aren't you?"

"Probably because I've got so many of my own. Why d'you think I spent all those years pretending to be someone else?"

She slides her hand onto my leg, pushes her fingers over the inside seam of my jeans, pushes further so that her hand is tight between my thighs. Her rings catch the light.

"You're not pretending any more, are you?"

"No, Paige," I reply, meaning it, exulting in it. "I'm not pretending any more."

Seventeen

We drop Paige off in town. She's going to meet Phil and Fiona for last orders. She invites Will and me to join her, but he glowers at us from the back seat.

"I want to catch the earliest train I can tomorrow," he tells her. "The sooner I get back home the better."

She glances at me and raises her eyebrows. I haven't told her about the conversation he and I had while she was visiting Louise. She must wonder what the hell's going on.

"I guess this is *goodbye*, then, Junior," she says, turning in her seat and leaning precariously round to kiss him. Will proffers her his cheek, but Paige turns his face straight and gives him a big smacker on the lips. As she draws away and turns to the front again, I watch Will wipe his mouth with the back of his hand.

Before Paige gets out of the car, she flicks open the glove compartment and begins to rummage about inside.

"What *are* you looking for, Mackenzie?"

"I know it must be in here somewhere."

"What?"

"Aha!"

She surfaces with a little black globe of plastic in her hand; the missing top to my gear stick.

"I don't know why you didn't put this back on straight away. It doesn't take much doing." She clicks the top in place over the exposed metal and presses down hard. "There," she says, flicking it with her finger. "At least now you won't hurt yourself. It was pretty sharp, that spiky bit underneath."

I take a breath, my heart blooming clear through my clothes with love for her, and she scoots across in her seat and kisses me quickly.

"So you'll come to mine after work tomorrow, then?" She keeps her face close. I can see the little shards of green in her eyes again, flecks of fern. "Be prepared to do all sorts of old lady activities."

"Play Scrabble, eat prunes, talk about the war?"

She grins and climbs out of the car, waving flamboyantly through the window as she flings the door closed.

I watch her turn and cross the road, and I don't drive away until she is out of sight. Even then, I'm reluctant to go.

Will leans forward. "What are we waiting for?"

"I just want to make sure she's okay."

"Oh, I'm *sure* she's okay." His voice is all spines. "People like her are always okay."

"What d'you mean?"

"Oh, come on. She's resilient. She could charm her way *into*, or *out of*, anything."

"So?"

"So she's a fraud. It's all show with people like her, everything for effect."

"That's what you used to say about me."

"Yeah, well." He sits back wearily and leans his head against the window. "I guess you're a perfect match then, aren't you?"

I don't rise to the bait. I start the car and drive home placidly, and when we get there, I give Will the keys so he can go in ahead of me. He lets the door swing back in my face, and then stalks around the flat like a caged animal while I fix myself a drink. I stand in the kitchen doorway with a rum and Coke in my hand and hold the glass out to him.

"Would you like this? It might make you feel better."

"I feel fine." Switching on the TV, he sits down on the floor in front of it.

"Okay. If you change your mind, though, I've left the bottle out on the side. I'm just going downstairs to feed my neighbour's cat."

"Whatever."

I gulp the rum and Coke down quickly, scoop Olive's key up from the coffee table and step out onto the landing. For a moment, I just lean my hands on the banister and let my head drop so that I'm looking down into the stairwell. The marble floor seems to emit a breath of mint and water, and the chestnut-coloured wood is cool beneath my fingers. I steady myself against the stillness, take my time going downstairs and letting myself into Olive's spacious flat, and once I'm there, I just sit on the edge of her tasselled sofa and let Pooky walk in purring circles around my legs. He's a tall cat, sleek black and half-Siamese. His eyes are narrow and sleepy. He's looking at me as if he'd like to seduce me.

When I eventually go to the kitchen to feed him, I find that Olive has left about thirty tins of cat food out on the side. I pick two of them out at random and waft them in front of Pooky's face so he can choose.

"What d'you think, Pooks? Rabbit and chicken, or tuna and sweet-corn?" I shake my head and look at the second tin closely. "*Sweetcorn?* Blimey! Whiskas have gone a bit health-conscious, haven't they?"

Pooky looks doubtful, but I open the tin for him anyway and spoon the food into a dish that has 'Mummy's Little Treasure' emblazoned on it in big black letters. He sniffs the mixture, dips his nose into it, starts to eat.

Just then, I hear the door to Olive's flat close with a bang. I know I left it on the latch, so the wind couldn't have blown it shut. When I step into the living room, Will is standing by the sofa with the bottle of rum in his hand.

"Why d'you do it, Bex, eh, mess with people's feelings?" He lifts the bottle to his lips and takes a big gulp. It makes him cough.

"You're going to make yourself sick like that."

He waves the bottle at me. "You haven't answered my question. Why do you do it? What kind of kick does it give you to let people get close to you, just so you can shit on them from a great height?"

I move towards him and try to take the bottle away, but he shakes his head, hugs it to his chest.

"That's not what I mean to do." I let my hands fall to my sides. "I don't mean to hurt anyone."

"Well you *do*. It's what you've always done."

"I'm sorry."

"Like you were sorry about Adam, you mean?" He takes a step towards me. "God, if he knew what you've turned into! If he knew you were with that dyke bitch..."

"He'd tell me to be happy."

Will laughs, but it's a hollow sound, meagre. He takes another gulp from the bottle, and then another, and then he drops it onto the rug and comes towards me fast. Instinctively, I step away, catching my heel on the leg of the coffee table. I tumble backwards, twisting my arm behind me, and suddenly he is leaning over me, his face dark and barbed and unfamiliar. He takes my wrists in his hands and pulls me to my feet, pushing me back until I slam into the bookcase against the wall. I watch one of Olive's Art Deco figurines topple and fall to the floor. It splits straight down the middle and the two halves fall open like mouths.

"Will." I look hard into his face. "Let go of my hands."

He shakes his head, just the once, and then he looks down my body, slow, and when he looks back up, his eyes are filled with tears.

"Will. This isn't *you*." I say it softly. "This isn't what you do."

"Maybe I should *start* doing it. Maybe then I'd get some of the things I want." But his voice is crumbling, and his grip on my wrists begins to loosen. I ease them free. There are red marks like rope burns on my skin.

"Shit!" He dips his head when he sees them, and his forehead bumps softly against mine. He draws in a breath that trembles.

"Are you all right?" I crouch down a little more so that I can look up into his face. "D'you want to go back upstairs?"

He nods without looking at me and turns away with his head bowed. As I pull the door closed behind us, I catch sight of Pooky sniffing at the little pool of rum seeping into Olive's rug.

I follow Will up the stairs. He has left the door wide open, and once we're inside, he goes straight into the bedroom and curls himself up on the bed. I don't know what to do. I make my way to the bathroom and run the cold tap until the water comes out icy, and then I splash my face with it and press a towel against my eyes until all I can see is a swirl of tiny fractals, purple and gold.

I go to the kitchen and make some black coffee, but my hands are trembling as I pour the water and I spill some of it on the worktop and on the floor. I kneel to mop it up with a cloth, and as I do, I realise that little drops are still falling onto the floorboards, little raindrops, salty. I'm crying and I hadn't even noticed. I sit back on my heels. I'd thought that if I could just be honest, just learn to be real, then everything would be all right, but it's my *honesty* that has done this to Will. I should have lied about Paige. He'd been having such a good time. He was so pleased about Kate going home, and now I've ruined it. I've ruined everything.

I stand up unsteadily and wring the cloth out in the sink. The red marks on my wrists stand out sharp against the white enamel, but I know they'll have faded by morning. They don't matter. What I've done to Will *does*. I think of how I'd been so sure I could look after him; protect him from Adam, soothe him through his hangovers, somehow make up for all the wrong I'd done him in the past, *and* for how I'd treated his brother. Now, I've just made everything worse.

I take a big mug of black coffee through to the bedroom and place it on the bedside cabinet next to Will's head.

"Try and drink this," I say quietly, but he doesn't respond.

He has coiled himself beneath the covers, fully clothed, and his eyes are tight shut.

I leave the night lamp switched on, take my clothes off quietly, and climb into bed beside him. He keeps his back to me, taut, and for a long time, we just lie there. His breathing is very shallow. I know he's not asleep.

After a while, I turn on to my side, away from him, and as I do, I feel the bed give and Will says quietly, "I'll pay for the ornament."

I turn back and he is leaning up on his elbow, looking at me.

"You don't need to. We can probably mend it. Olive need never know."

"She'd notice the crack. I'd rather pay for a new one."

"It was Art Deco. Expensive."

"Oh." He looks downcast. "Could we get a fake?"

I lean my head into the pillow and reach under the covers to find his hand. It is curled into a fist, but I unfurl it gently with my fingers.

"I don't think so."

He slides across so that his body is close to mine but not touching.

"I'm sorry."

I press my finger to his lips. "It was *my* fault."

"No, it wasn't."

"Let's not talk about it."

"I think we should."

I shake my head, ease myself in closer. His body tenses.

"Don't be afraid of me, Will, okay? I wouldn't do anything to hurt you. Not ever."

I mean it. My only intention now is to do the *right* thing, but his eyes are white with surprise and he starts to back away from me fast.

"This isn't what you really want," he says flatly. "This isn't you."

"This is whoever you want it to be."

"I want it to be *you*. I want it to be Rebecca."

"Then it is."

I slide my hand around his neck and ease his mouth down on to mine, and he sinks into that kiss in spite of himself. I can taste the rum on his lips, honeyed and black.

I trace the curve of his cheekbone with my fingers as we kiss, and then I shift slightly forward and lift myself onto my knees. Taking

Will's hands in mine, I lift him with me, until we are kneeling, facing each other, our breath close. He reaches for me then, suddenly, pulls me into his body and crushes me against him. The buttons on his shirt press against my naked breasts like fingernails, but I don't feel any pain. I just feel numb.

He buries his face into my neck and kisses along the curve of my collar bone, says against my skin, "Are you sure you want this?"

And I nod, because I *am* sure, sure that this is something I can do to make recompense, to set things right between us, to atone for Adam.

I think of what Paige said about those North American tribes, how they use sex as a healing art, offering their bodies to each other freely, unselfishly, and that's what I want to do, just this once. Paige would understand. She did something like this for Phil and Fiona – gave them back their desire for each other. I can give something to Will. This single act will make up for *everything*. Paige will understand. I waver for a moment, her face swimming at the edges of my vision. I picture myself telling her about this tomorrow. I listen for what she will say, but Will's breath is hot and fierce against my ear. He drowns Paige out.

I help him pull his shirt off over his head, and then lay him down on his back, while I undo his jeans and slide them onto the floor. I slip my hand inside his boxer shorts, and he shuts his eyes, his lips parted like he's tasting the air. He stays there like that, poised and resolute, and when I tell him to, he arches his spine, so that I can ease his boxers down over his hips. He stays very still, while I reach across to the bedside cabinet, pull open the top drawer and take out a condom. I bite the little packet open and then slip the condom onto him, rolling it down slow, so that he opens his eyes, very wide, watching me.

I sit astride him, keeping my back straight, and come down on him just a little way. He breathes out hard when I do, and then he doesn't seem to breathe at all. I move slowly, keeping just the tip of his penis inside me, and then I adjust my weight and drop down, very gently, little by little, until he is all the way inside.

He lifts his arms up over his head and his fists hit the wall. I can feel him trying to spread his legs beneath me. He raises his hips each time to meet my stroke, the dull thud of bone on bone, and when at last he comes, his eyes snap open and he looks right through me.

I lean forward on to his chest and nestle my head against his shoulder.

"Are you all right?"

He nods, and says very quietly, "Thirsty."

"I'll get you a drink."

I don't look at him when I climb off the bed. I go to the bathroom first to clean myself up and then to the kitchen. I hadn't realised that I'd left all the lights on and the curtains open. I have to hurry across the living room in a glare of yellow and white. I imagine late-night dog-walkers down on the Common catching sight of something out of the corners of their eyes, glancing up to my window and opening their mouths in surprise. I once lived opposite a couple who would chase each other naked around the bedroom every night with the lights on, and then sit down on the bed and drink tea out of a little red Thermos. The memory makes me smile, although I was already smiling. I come face to face with myself in the glass door of one of the kitchen cabinets, and there's something new behind my eyes, a composure; sleepy and peaceful. I have preferred someone else's needs to my own. I have set myself aside, and the effect has been... transforming.

In the kitchen, I run the cold tap and fill a glass for Will, and then I slip my mouth under the faucet and drink straight from there. The water is a flare of cold against my teeth, exhilarating.

By the time I get back to the bedroom, Will is fast asleep.

I wake next morning early to the sound of tinkling glass and crockery, and when I get up and make my way through to the kitchen, I find Will hunched over the stove, earnest as an alchemist. He is wearing my old kimono bathrobe with his boxer shorts underneath, and he has set the table with my best placemats and cutlery.

"Damn!" he says when he sees me. "I wanted to surprise you."

"You have."

"No, no..." He flicks a tea towel over his shoulder. "I wanted everything to be ready."

"Can I give you a hand?"

"Absolutely *not*. You just sit yourself down." He eases a chair out for me and leads me to it, like an old lady. "You could probably do with the rest, after all that exertion last night!"

He winks at me, does a sexy little shuffle back to the stove and once he's there, he picks up a wooden spoon and holds it to his mouth like a microphone, sings the first couple of bars of Barry White's 'Can't Get Enough of Your Love, Baby'. He is hopelessly out of tune.

I laugh out loud and lean forward on my elbows to watch him. He is aglow.

"Don't you have a hangover, Will?"

"Nah." He begins to stir some scrambled eggs around in a pan. "I must be getting used to the alcohol intake. Either that, or the sex sorted me out. Nicest hangover cure I can think of."

"Was it what you expected?"

"Not exactly."

"Were you disappointed?"

"Do I *look* disappointed?" He beams at me. "I feel like buying champagne, Bex. I feel like celebrating. I can't tell you..."

"You don't need to."

I sit back in my chair, smug as a bud, humming with complacency, and a stream of autumn sunshine ripples through the window like a benediction.

We eat the scrambled eggs and drink coffee and grapefruit juice, and then I take a shower and get ready for work, while Will packs his things together and checks train times.

I offer to drop him off at the station and on the way, he leans across in his seat and rests his head on my shoulder. It bumps softly up and down as we drive.

"Thanks for last night," he says.

"You're welcome."

"It was great."

I swallow hard. "Yes, it was."

Sitting up straight, he turns to look at me. "I'll get back as soon as I can, okay?"

I smile at him, a little bewildered. "What d'you mean?"

"Well, I reckon Mum'll improve no end now Kate's coming home. She won't need me for much longer." He slips his hand on to my thigh. "I could be back in a couple of weeks, less maybe, although we probably oughtn't to tell Mum for a while, I guess."

"Tell her what?"

"About *us*, of course." He glances out of the window. "She knew Southampton was one of the universities that had offered me a place to study medicine, so I could just tell her I've decided to take it after all. I bet if I wrote to the dean and explained, he'd actually let me start this year instead of next. We're only just into the autumn term, aren't we?" He is looking at me, his eyes open wide. "Bex?"

There is something hard and glassy in my throat. I swallow past it.

"You're coming back to study medicine?"

He wags his head. "I'm coming back to be with *you*, stupid. Studying medicine'll be the excuse. I won't lie to Mum or anything. I just won't mention that you and I are together until I'm sure she'll be okay with it."

"Together?"

The word slithers softly out of my body, takes shape, assumes a meaning, and Will squeezes my thigh hard and kisses me on the cheek.

"I know," he says, smiling. "I can't quite believe it either."

Eighteen

I can't tell Will the truth. I let him kiss me goodbye, climb on the train and wave to me out of the window. I let him go home believing that he and I are *together*, a couple, each other's unlooked-for destiny. It almost breaks my heart to do it, except that my heart feels like a stone inside my chest; granite, implacable.

All day at work, I feel sick. Every time my thoughts veer towards the night before, I try to bury them underneath a pile of shelving, or lose them in small talk with my colleagues, but it's no good. They're there, at the back of everything, leering at me. I'd felt so self-satisfied, so magnanimous in bestowing the gift of myself on poor virginal Will. Now, I just feel stupid and ashamed, all my good intentions turned inside out and revealed in their true light; nothing more than vanity.

I eat lunch on my own in the staff room, and in the afternoon I ask if I can catalogue the periodicals in the basement store. It's a job everyone hates because of the dust and grime, but dust and grime seem to be pretty much the elements that suit me, or so it feels, and the senior librarian is so pleased that someone has offered, she says yes straight away.

I spend four long hours hauling huge piles of magazines from one shelf to another, dating and indexing them one by one, then hauling them back. My arms and shoulders ache, and my hands are black with dirt and ink, but I *do* begin to feel better. It's a penance, to be stuck down there in the bowels of the building, a solitary confinement, and by the time I surface, I'm starting to think that maybe things needn't look so bleak. All I need to do, obviously, is to talk to Paige. She'll know how to mend this. She'll find a way for me to redeem the situation and get myself out of the mess I'm in, without hurting Will.

It's my late night at work, but I manage to leave a few minutes early and on my way to the car, I stop at the Student Union bar and order a large whisky and lemonade, and then another, and then I drive fast through the evening traffic. A couple of times, I jump a red light, but I don't care. I just need to get to Sway and everything will be all right.

As I enter the village, I pass a petrol station and stop briefly to buy Paige a little bouquet of flowers; pink and yellow freesias, tiny white carnations. They have a combination sweetness about them, like a newly opened box of chocolates. I feel like I need to have something to give to Paige, a peace offering. I made such an issue of her dancing with Rick at Maclaverty's, and now I'm about to tell her I've slept with Will! The hypocrisy of it seethes hot as venom through my blood. But it's going to be all right. Everything's going to be all right, and there *is* a silver lining. With all that's happened in the last twenty-four hours, I haven't once thought about Adam. I haven't looked for him. I haven't even expected him. He's gone. He's really *gone*.

I almost smile as I park my car outside Paige's house and trot up the path to the front door. I knock once, my stomach fluttering, full of moths, but no one comes, so I knock again, and this time I hear footsteps approaching. I lift the little bouquet up in front of my face, listening for the sound of the door opening, and when it does, I whip the bouquet away theatrically and... Fiona is standing in the doorway, looking down at me.

"Oh..." My voice bumps up against her, falls flat.

She sighs. "You'd better come in."

I follow her into the narrow hallway and she moves ahead of me slowly.

"Paige is out the back in the conservatory," she says, turning. "She'll be pleased you've come."

I take a breath. "I didn't know you'd be here, Fiona."

"I've been here all day." She doesn't say it like she's trying to make me jealous or anything. She just says it, plain, like I should already have known.

She narrows her eyes. "She wanted someone with her."

"What d'you mean?"

Folding her arms, she looks at me quizzically.

"I take it you've been to the hospital?"

"Not yet." I look at my watch. "We're going in about half an hour. We're bringing Rose home."

"Rebecca." She touches her fingers to my arm. "She's dead. Rose is dead. She died in the early hours of this morning. I thought you knew."

"What are you talking about? She's not dead. I mean..." I look down at the little flowers in my hand, their scent suddenly saccharine and raw. "She can't be. We only saw her last night. She was fine."

"It was very sudden, apparently. A pulmonary embolism. It's a kind of blood clot."

"I know." My head feels very heavy on my shoulders. "I know what it is."

I can remember using it one time to explain the sudden and tragic death of a favourite grandparent when I was small. I can remember sitting in the library and reading up on all the ways people could die without warning, quick as a wink. Pulmonary embolism. That was a good one. I kept it in reserve until the right occasion arose. I swallow hard now, all four of my grandparents parading through my mind, pink and plump and luminescent with good health. How could I have done that? How *could* I have conjured up their premature deaths to suit my own purpose?

"God." I lean against the wall.

"Paige has taken it pretty hard. She's been asleep for most of the afternoon, but she got up and took a bath a while ago. Her mum's coming up from London tomorrow to handle the arrangements."

I nod. "Good."

Fiona lifts a jacket from over the banister and starts to put it on.

"I was due to cover Paige's shift at the Swan because she thought she was bringing Rose home, so I'll do that anyway."

"Okay."

She opens the front door. "See if you can try and get her to eat something, will you?"

I nod, and we stand for a moment looking at each other, shaking our heads gently, disbelieving. It has started to rain.

"It's such a shitty thing to happen," says Fiona, squinting away towards the road. "I don't *get* why things like this happen, do you? She didn't even have a chance to say goodbye."

I don't know what to say. I just shake my head more emphatically, and Fiona pulls her car keys out of her pocket and stares at them.

"Tell her I'll look in on her tomorrow." She glances up at me and then turns and walks briskly down the path.

I close the door and walk back along the corridor to the kitchen. The small conservatory is just beyond it, its glass doors opening onto a courtyard garden filled with flowers. Purple clematis and Virginia creeper climb the brickwork, framing a space of pallid sky, and Paige is sitting inside on an old wooden settle, against the conservatory wall. She's wearing a pair of faded Levi's, torn at the knee, and an old checked shirt. Her feet are bare.

She looks up when she hears me and her face softens.

"Hey you," she says in a whisper. She has a cigarette in her hand and she brings it to her lips, inhales. Her fingers are trembling hard. She looks at the bouquet in my fist, stubs her cigarette out. "Are those for me?"

I nod. "I wanted... I..." But my voice fumbles and falls.

Paige reaches out to me, and I go to her quickly and put my arms around her, hold her as tight as I can.

"I'm so sorry, Paige." I say it over and over again, rocking her gently.

And she keeps saying, "I know, I know," and then she buries her face in the dip beneath my collar bone, and keeps it there. I can smell the warm tang of shampoo in her hair; fruit punch, cranberry juice.

It doesn't seem to be tears now, but *something* is shaking through Paige's body; a chill that I can feel in my hands when I touch her, a trembling swell of movement. I clasp her even tighter, but it doesn't make any difference.

"I went to the Olympic Mountains once," she says suddenly, very clear, "in Washington State. There's this place there called Hurricane Ridge where the wind is so strong, you have to reach your arms out wide and fall into it and it holds you up so you feel like you're flying." And then she says, "Do you believe in heaven?"

"Yes. I do."

She nods softly. "So do I."

After a while, she seems to have fallen asleep, but when I try to ease her head down into the crook of my arm, so she'll be more comfortable, she opens her eyes and they are black and despairing.

"You're not leaving?"

"No. I'm not leaving."

She lifts herself up alongside me on the settle, and then she slides down onto the floor in one movement, like her body is fluid, liquid mercury, and then she teeters forward on her knees towards me.

I kiss her, soft at first, tender because of her hurt, but she slips her hands around my neck and locks her fingers under my hair, and her mouth is hard and anxious. I can feel the tips of her teeth, sharp against my lips.

I give myself up to her. I give up all my control and all my misgivings to what she wants of me in this moment. She is letting her grief be subsumed into desire, and I am her accomplice in it and desperate to please her.

I think of Will last night, how all the control was mine, all the moves old ones, weary routines, but *this* is unknown to me; a virgin territory of my own. This is something outside of all of my experience, so *far* outside, in fact, that I've never even tried to make it up.

I lean into the wind. I stretch my arms out wide inside and fall, and Paige catches me and draws me gently down onto the floor. I can smell the flowers: jasmine, japonica, hazy blue birdgrass, sweet lilies. I can taste Paige; smoke and cinnamon, her face smoothed out, her pupils bright and dilated.

She pulls her shirt off over her head, and then she lifts my arms for me, as if I am her child, and eases *my* top over my head, too. I get tangled in it and we both laugh, and then, for a long time, we just sit looking at each other.

She strokes my breasts with the backs of her fingers, very gentle and slow.

"Louise's baby yesterday," she sighs. "His hair was so soft, I felt like I should only touch it with my lips." She looks into my eyes and then away. "Your skin's amazing."

She dips her head and kisses my breast, just above the dark line of my bra, and I feel the touch of her mouth like a rush of light. It isn't at all what I'd expected. I thought it would be something marshmallowy and vague, something to sink myself into, but instead, it's sharp; ice in a glass, the fine point of a needle. My breath catches thick in my throat.

She reaches her hands behind my back and unhooks my bra, slips it down my arms and over my wrists, onto the floor, and then she unhooks *her* bra too and slips it off, and, for a moment, we are just attentive to the look of each other's bodies, the sheen of each other's skin.

"Are you all right, Bex?"

I nod. "I want to touch you."

"Okay."

"I don't know how to."

She smiles. "Just do what you feel, sweetheart."

"I feel like a teenager."

She reaches for my hands, draws them towards her, presses my palms against her breasts, and her skin is smooth and very warm now; all the heat inside her body seeping up like magma to the surface. She circles my fingers gently over her nipples, and then she closes her eyes and tilts her head back, breathing light with her lips parted.

When she lets go of my hands, I keep them where they are. I keep them moving, and she arches her body towards me.

"Do you want to stop?" She whispers it.

"No."

She leans forward and loops her arms around my neck and down my back. I can smell the foxgloves in the garden, like incense, mingling with how Paige smells, and the Scotch that I drank on the journey spirals up into my temples and out into the tips of my fingers and makes me bold, bolder than I've ever been. I start to undo the buttons on her Levi's, and she starts to undo the buttons on mine, and the space between our bodies is all breath suddenly, and heat, and expectancy.

We struggle free of what's left of our clothes, and then Paige lowers me onto my back and kisses my mouth with such delicacy, such tenderness, like she's trying not to hurt me, that I just can't help it; I start to cry – my tears mingling with hers. She licks my cheeks, then kisses me again, deeper, so that I can taste my body's salt, and then she moves her mouth away from mine, slipping down, circling her tongue over each of my nipples in turn, sucking soft and then hard, until I can't bear it, until I reach my fingers into her hair and draw her back up so that I can see her face, look into her eyes.

"Paige." My voice sounds drugged. "Let me do something for *you*."

But she shakes her head and moves down my body again, little butterfly kisses down my breastbone, tracing her tongue across my belly, and then she slips her arms underneath my thighs and eases them up, so that my feet are flat on the floor. Clasping her hands together in the small of my back, she lifts me slightly, angles me, and then her head dips and I feel her tongue pushing up inside me, filling me, laying me open. I arch my back for her, and she slips out of me, touches the tip of her tongue to my clitoris, tasting it, circling it, and my body soars away from me. I am free-falling through the sweet air, stepping like Columbus onto dry land, an undiscovered country... But suddenly, I feel Paige lurch back and when I look, she is up on her knees with her face in her hands.

"I can't," she is saying – breathless, stricken. "Not like this."

I pull myself up, my head filled with blood, my body feeling bruised and swollen, and I crawl my way towards her. "Like what, love?" I swallow everything back. "Like what?"

She reaches for her shirt, pulls it roughly over her head, and then she just looks at me, so sad, touches my cheek, her fingers soft as smoke.

"I'm not *here*, Bex. I'm not... focused."

The cold air catches me and I shiver hard, cross my arms loosely over my chest.

"I don't understand."

"I don't want to be somewhere else in my head. D'you know what I mean?"

I try to think, but the air is a blur. I can hear the sound of cars passing by on the street outside, their tyres on the rainy tarmac, like someone saying, "Shhh", over and over again.

"I want it to be perfect, and it's not. It can't be, not today, not with Grandma and everything." Her face is close to mine. "Please say you understand?"

I nod, but tears are swelling hard in my throat.

"Why did you...?" I look down at our bodies. "Why did you let it go *this* far?"

"Because it *is* what I want. I *so* want it. Can't you tell how much I want it? I just got... I don't know..."

I start to reach for my clothes, but Paige says, "Don't get dressed. Stay with me. Just come upstairs, and we'll hold each other and we'll sleep, and tomorrow, things will look brighter. I'm sure they will. Please don't make me feel any worse about today than I already do." Her eyes are filled with tears. "I'm sorry, Bex. I just..."

She looks so small, so pale, and her shoulders are hunched forward like she's trying to keep her body safe and secret, like the dark won't come for her if she curls herself into a comma and keeps ever so still.

I turn her hand over in mine and bring her open palm to my lips.

"I'll do whatever you want me to," I tell her, and I mean it.

I put my underwear back on, and then reach my arms around Paige and help her to stand, and she goes ahead of me up the stairs. The house is painfully quiet, and the air feels old and fatigued. It prickles against my bare skin.

Paige goes straight into her grandma's room.

"I need to sleep in here tonight," she says. "I need to feel close to her."

I nod. "I understand. I'm just going to use the bathroom, okay?"

She pulls her shirt off over her head and then she climbs into the high bed and tugs the covers up under her chin. She looks like a poorly child.

"I can't believe she's gone." Her voice is water. "She's never coming back. I'm *never* going to see her again." And she looks at me hard, her eyebrows furrowed. "How can that be true, Bex?"

"What about heaven?"

I feel stupid as soon as I've said it, but Paige actually brightens a little.

"Yes." She breathes out like it's a relief, and then she closes her eyes. "Heaven," she sighs, but so quietly that all I hear is the last syllable: *fun.*

In the bathroom, I run myself a glass of water and gulp it down fast. I look at my body in the mirror and feel a disturbing mix of wonderment at what just happened, and confusion over whether or not it was the right thing to have happened, and, at the same time, a spur of anticipation that it might get to happen again. It's like being in a room filled with people who are all talking at once. You can only catch the edge of one conversation before another supersedes it. One voice, however, sounds out loud above *all* the others. Will's voice, unmistakable; the word *Together*, irrefutable.

I drink another glass of water, and then tiptoe back to the bedroom. Paige is already asleep. I take off my underwear and climb into bed beside her, and as I do, she half-wakes and says my name.

"I'm here, sweetheart." I curl myself around her and she nestles into my body. "I'm here."

She nods into the pillow, makes a tiny sound like a sigh, and then she slides her hand under the covers, across my stomach, until she finds *my* hand. She laces her fingers around mine and says, very softly, so that I almost miss it, "Love you, Bex."

Nineteen

In the morning, Paige and I drive to the café on East Street for breakfast. Paige looks better than she did last night. She has more colour in
her cheeks, and she's wearing tight dark trousers and a lime green and
brown top, which make her look quirky and fun, although I know
she's feeling neither.

We drink tall cappuccinos and eat croissants with apricot jam,
and we don't say much to each other. Mostly we just sit quietly,
looking around us, glancing out of the window at people hurrying
past on their way to work. When we *do* catch each other's eye, we
smile, gently. It's all we need.

"Mum's coming at lunchtime," she says suddenly.

"Right. How long's she staying for, d'you know?"

Paige shakes her head, takes a sip from her cup.

"I guess she'll stay 'til after the funeral. Usually about a week, isn't
it, from when someone... dies?"

She swallows on the word.

"What's she like?"

"Smart."

"What, like well-dressed smart, or intelligent smart?"

"Both."

"Blimey."

She sighs, sits back in her chair. "Are you around tonight? If I ask

Fiona to cover my shift again, can I come to yours?"

"Course you can." Reaching across the table, I place my hand over hers. "You don't think your mum will want you to stay home, though?"

She shrugs. "Doubtful. She's one of these annoyingly competent people. She'll breeze in and take over everything, which is good, because *I* wouldn't know where to start, but..." She shakes her head lightly, as if she's shaking something irritating out of her hair: an insect, a scrap of sound. "She pisses me off."

"It's a rule, isn't it, for us to be pissed off by our parents, and vice versa?"

"I guess."

"She *has* just lost her mother, though, remember. I doubt she'll be quite her usual self."

"Probably not." She looks a little abashed.

"Well look, I get back from work about six. Come any time you like after that."

"Thanks." Turning my hand over in hers, she strokes her fingertips slowly across my palm and back again. "I've got some stuff to do in the department this morning, and then I'll meet Mum's train and take her to Sway."

"Okay."

She looks away from me, out of the window, and her face seems to be struggling with something. Clearing her throat, she glances at me and then fixes her gaze on what's left of her croissant.

"Look, Bex. I want to apologise for last night."

"You have nothing to apologise for."

"Don't I?" She lifts her eyes to mine.

"Of course you don't."

"But I know it must have been a big thing for you, being with a woman, and I ruined it. I fucked it up for you."

"No, you didn't."

She breathes a little laugh into the air. "Why are you always so forgiving?"

"Maybe because there's nothing to forgive."

"Would you forgive me anything?"

"Probably."

She reaches across the table and touches my hair, and I swirl the dregs of my coffee around in my cup and don't look at her. Instead, I ask, "Would you forgive *me* anything?"

"Oh, I should think so. Although if you started wearing pinafore dresses and listening to Julio Iglesias records I might have something to say about it." She dips her head and grins. "And I wouldn't be best pleased if you started screwing around on me. It's the one thing I can't take; infidelity."

I swallow a mouthful of coffee too fast and start to cough.

Paige stands up quickly and pats me on the back until I signal her that I'm okay, and then she crouches down by my chair and slips her arm lightly around my waist.

I take a few deep breaths, and then say, very quickly, "What about Fiona and Phil, though? Weren't you sleeping with them while you were still married to Rick?"

She looks at me strangely for a moment, then shakes her head.

"No. I wasn't. I wasn't unfaithful to Rick. I may be a cheap whore on the odd occasion, and I know I go on about free love, and sex as therapy and all that, but if I'm in a *relationship* with one person, I don't fuck anybody else." She hesitates. "Do you?"

And I want to tell her about Will. I swear to God, I want to just say the words and explain to her how it happened and why, and assure her that it meant nothing to me, but I can't. The truth sparks bright above my head like a sky full of fireworks, but I close my eyes to it and say, "No, of *course* not," like it's unthinkable, and then I look fast at my watch. "I should be getting to work."

"Okay." But she doesn't stand up. She keeps looking at me, her face level with mine. "You're sure you're all right about last night, though?"

"Yes." I lean into her. "I'm sure."

"Because I don't want to mess you up or anything."

"And your tenderness is going to mess me up, is it? You telling me you loved me is gonna mess me up?"

Paige lowers her eyes. "I hope not."

I take her face in my hands and hold it there, and then I kiss her, catching her tongue softly between my teeth, letting it go, and when we break apart, everyone in the café is looking at us. I don't care.

"You know I love you too, right?"

I say it looking into her eyes, and she replies, "I do now," looking into mine.

At lunchtime, I call my mum. I haven't spoken to her in months, and her voice is shrill with surprise when she realises it's me. She carries on eating her lunch while we talk because she's due back at work at the hospital shop soon, but it's good to hear her voice. I know I've neglected my family all these years, kept myself separate and superior. I want to put it right. I want to start again. I ask her if it's okay for me to come home for a weekend soon.

"Ho-me?" She stutters, like it's a word she doesn't quite recognise. "You're coming home for a weekend?"

"If that's okay."

"Well of *course* it's okay."

"Would you mind if I brought someone with me?"

"No. Bring whoever you like." Her voice is smiling. "Is it a boyfriend?"

"Not quite."

"One of your friends, then?"

I hear my mum take a bite of whatever it is that she's eating.

"Yes... No. Well, it's..." and for a second, I can't say it, because my heart is about to burst with incredulity. Am I actually about to tell my mother that I'm gay? It seems remarkable to me, and unlikely. I don't even know if it's true, but what I feel for Paige *is* true, and that's what this call is about.

"Rebecca? You still there?"

"Yes. Sorry." My mouth is as dry as Ghandi's flip-flop. "She's called Paige, the girl I'd like to bring home, but she's more than just *one* of my friends, Mum. I guess she's my..." and I almost want to laugh, but I don't "... *girlfriend*."

I hear a sound which could be my mum swallowing her fork, and then there's silence.

"Oh," she says after a long moment. "I didn't know... I mean..." She clears her throat hard, then lets out a steadying breath. It rushes down the line towards me like an approaching train. "Paige." She tries the name out for size, and then she says, "You just let me know when the two of you are coming. You're both welcome any time, Rebecca."

And, amazingly, I know she means it.

Paige is sitting on my doorstep when I get back to my flat after work. She looks drunk, and very cold. There's a bottle of tequila wedged tight between her knees.

"Hey, babe," she cries when she sees me coming up the path, and she tries to stand, but topples to one side.

"Paige." I steady her. "How much have you drunk?"

"Not nearly enough." She lifts the half-empty bottle and peers at it. "Tequila's such a *good* invention, don't you think?"

"If you say so."

I help her inside and keep my arm around her waist as we climb the stairs. As we move past Olive's door, I remember Pooky and realise that I haven't fed him since Sunday night. Plus, I need to do something about the rum stain on Olive's expensive rug. I make a mental note to come back down when I've made Paige some coffee.

By the time we reach my door, Paige is singing, loudly. She starts with an old Blondie number, but when I deposit her on the sofa, she has moved on to John Denver, which surprises me, because I wouldn't have put her down as a John Denver fan. She seems to know all the words to 'Leaving on a Jet Plane'. She sings it straight through, twice, badly.

I go to the kitchen to switch the kettle on, and somehow, she manages to follow me.

"You're not cross, are you?" She sways gently in the doorway.

"No. Of course I'm not cross. I just worry about you."

"No need." Leaning against the doorframe, she brings the bottle of tequila to her lips, takes a quick swig, asks in a refined voice, "Did you have a spiffing day at work, daaahling?"

"Average." Moving towards her, I place my hands under her elbows, try to steer her back to the living room. "Why don't you just sit and take it easy and I'll make us some coffee."

"Coffee!" She spits the word out in disgust. "I don't want coffee, Bex. I want more tequila." She rubs her eyes. "That's the one negative thing I would say about you. You never have enough alcohol in the house."

"I've never needed it, until now."

"Are you suggesting I'm a halcoholic?"

"Now, as if I would suggest *that*."

"'Cos I'm bloody not, you know. I may have had some... issues..." she burps softly "... with alcohol in the past, but I'm okay now. I'm..." she thinks hard for a minute, stands up as straight as she can "... in control. One hundred percentage. Yes indeed."

"Of course you are, my love."

And I swivel her around quite fast, so that she won't have time to do anything about it, and walk her to the sofa, sit her down.

"You don't understand," she says in a small voice, as I head back to the kitchen. "Drink just takes the edge off for me, that's all, makes me forget about all the things that make me sad."

"Are there that *many* things that make you sad, Paige, that you have to drink this much?"

"Fuck yes!" she says, sharp, and then she glances away from me and her face changes. I watch her take a long breath. "If you only knew, Bex, you wouldn't..." She shakes her head.

"Wouldn't what?"

"Nothing." And she lifts the bottle to her mouth again.

"This is about your grandma, isn't it?"

"Partly."

"And about your mum?"

She shrugs. "Partly." But her voice falls like snow and settles with a hush, confidential, and then suddenly, she seems to brighten, slipping herself to the edge of the sofa and setting the bottle down on the coffee table. "What music have you got? I feel like dancing."

"*Dancing*? You'll be lucky if you can walk, madam!"

She tuts at me. "Have you no *faith*?" And then she stands carefully, walks to the stereo against the wall, and starts flicking through my CDs. "Blimey O'Reilly. Your taste in music's a bit suspect."

I leave her to it. I wait for the kettle to boil, make some coffee, put two mugs and the cafetiere onto a tray and head back to the living room. Paige is just slipping a CD into the machine. I recognise the opening bars straight away. It's an old New Order song called 'Bizarre Love Triangle'. She starts to dance her way towards me unevenly. I put my tray down on the table and fold my arms like a schoolmistress.

"This is a blast from the past. I used to shake my buns to this at youth club discos." She smooches up against me, very hot, presses her stomach against mine, the rest of her body moving gently to the music, her arms lifting and falling in an arc of sound. Her face is close to my own. "Aren't you dancing with me?"

"I think you should drink some coffee first."

Paige lets her head fall back, slips her hands around my waist and pulls me tight, starts to move my body with hers. I keep my arms folded between us for a moment.

"Paige, come on. Sit down before you fall down, eh?"

But she takes no notice. She lets her eyes snake down my body and up again, keeps me moving with her, and in the end, of course, she seduces me into it, and I start to smile in spite of myself. I move my body into hers and we dance as if we are one person. It feels good. I slip my left hand under her hair and my right hand over the curve of her hip, and I let the music take me to where *she* is. The chorus veers towards us, and Paige sidles down, dancing, right to the floor and up again. I don't know how she's doing it, drunk as she is, but it's like she's found an equilibrium in the music, a straight line to follow. She does it over and over again, down to the floor and up, and her face is attentive all the while and bright with delight.

"You're a sexy mover, missis!" She shouts it over the music, but I shake my head at her.

"I'm just copying *you*."

She laughs, pulls me closer, nestles her face into my shoulder, but her body is growing heavy now. I can feel the languor of drink settling inside her limbs, slowing them down. As the song draws to a close, she eases away and lets herself crumple back onto the sofa. She's breathing hard, but smiling up at me like a child who's just been on a roller coaster ride.

I watch her, and something shudders implausibly under my heart, slows it almost to a stop. Something in me is stilled, looking at Paige, loving her, knowing that she loves me. Will was wrong about this being a lie. It's the truest thing I've ever felt, whatever name I put to it, and suddenly, words from a long time ago come into my mind, a line from an old hymn I used to sing at Sunday school when I was small: *Jesus, lover of my soul.* I always used to wonder, back then, whether it meant that Jesus was my soul's lover, active and connected, like a human lover, or that he was the person who loved my soul, cherished it, cupped it in his palms and carried it like a lustre of water in a dry land. Now, looking at Paige, I *know* what the line means. It means both things at once. I know this, because that is what Paige means, for me: both things, a miracle of multiplicity. Again, the fluttering in my chest, a flare of tiny fists. I swallow past them, take a breath, and then I lean forward and rest my palms on Paige's thighs.

"*Now* will you have some coffee?"

She nods, shuffles herself upright, and I lift the cafetiere, fill a mug and hold it out to her. She closes her hands around it, warming her fingers, looking up into my face.

"Thanks, Bex." She takes a long sip, puts the mug down carefully on the carpet and stands up. "I think I need a wazz. Can I use your felicities..." She shakes her head, just the once, grinning. "I mean, *facilities*."

I point the way and watch her walk, a little wearily, to the bathroom and close the door behind her.

"Wow!" she shrieks as soon as she's inside. "Novelty toilet paper! *Coooool!*"

The music is still playing loud, so I get up and turn it down, and it is then that I see the red light is flashing on my answering machine. I have a message waiting. I rewind the tape, press 'play'. It's Will.

"Hey, hot chick," he says in a drawl. "Just wanted to let you know that I got home safe and that all I want to do now is turn around and come back." He laughs lightly. "I want to say thanks, as well. All that stuff I was going on about in the pub in Corfe, about what I wanted sex to be and everything? Well, it was *so* much more than that with you, Rebecca. You *made* it so much more for me. I can't stop thinking about you. I just..."

When I hear the toilet flush, I press the 'stop' button on the machine as fast as I can, and then I stand in front of it like a goalkeeper covering the net. I am facing Paige, smiling, as she comes out of the bathroom. I am leaning forward, beginning to walk towards her as she steps across the room, but at the same time, I am reaching behind me, feeling for the 'erase' button on the machine. My fingers locate it, and I hear a little click, followed by the sound of the tape rewinding, erasing. Thank God! My face keeps smiling, but I feel myself blush and Paige inclines her head, puzzled.

"You okay, Bex?"

I nod, but the air feels thick and cloying.

"You know what?" I say quickly. "I'm supposed to be looking after my neighbour's cat this week, and I haven't fed him since Sunday.

D'you mind if I go down and do it now? It won't take me a minute."

"No, that's fine." She looks sleepy. "I'll sit and watch some TV or something. Maybe later I could cook for us, yeah?"

"That'd be nice."

I move past her to the kitchen, hear her switch on the TV behind me. I root around in the cupboard under the sink to find a cloth and some carpet cleaner, and then I go back into the living room where Paige has taken off her shoes and is sitting cross-legged on the sofa. She looks at the bottle in my hand, gestures to it.

"Do you not like this cat then?"

"Sorry?"

"D'you want to see it on its way?"

I look at her blankly.

She snorts.

"Carpet cleaner! You can't feed a cat carpet cleaner."

"Oh…" I shake my head, laughing; fraudulent, nauseating. "No. This is *for* the carpet. Obviously, I wouldn't feed the cat this." I lift the bottle into the air, an improbable trophy. "We… I… spilt some rum on this really expensive rug that Olive, my neighbour, owns. I need to see if I can get the stain out before she comes back."

Paige nods, but then her eyes narrow.

"Why were you drinking rum in Olive's flat?"

I open my mouth to make something up, because I'm good at making things up, except that this time, I don't want to, and I can't.

"Look." I take a step towards her. "When I come back, there's some stuff I need to talk to you about."

She looks up at me, innocent and tender. "Okay."

"It's nothing really. It's just…" but I have to breathe out, "something, to talk… about."

She nods, glances away from me to the TV. "Okay."

I pick Olive's key up from the coffee table and let it dangle from my finger.

"I'll be back in a sec, then."

She smiles at me then, holds her face towards me like a gift, un-expected, undeserved, and I leave the room quickly, pulling the door behind me, but leaving it ajar.

I trot downstairs and let myself into Olive's quiet flat, and Pooky is there straight away, with a raucous meow, glaring up at me like I'm the worst person in the universe.

"I know, man. I'm sorry."

I kneel down to stroke him, but he turns his back on me and stalks into the kitchen, his tail slicing at the air like a cutlass.

I follow him through and switch on the light, find Sunday's tin of food in the refrigerator and spoon all of what's left into his dish, and he starts to eat, looking up at me intermittently, his narrow eyes dark with reproach.

I run my cloth under the hot tap, go back into the living room and start to sponge at the brown stain which sits, like a map of Africa, at the heart of Olive's Persian rug. Under the curve of the sofa, poking out through the tassels, is one half of the Art Deco figurine. I'd for-gotten all about it. I sit back on my heels and look around me. *How* am I going to explain this to Olive? More importantly, how am I going to explain what happened with Will to Paige?

I try not to think about it for a moment. I keep it at bay, starting again on the stain, this time spraying the creamy carpet cleaner over it as evenly as I can, and then sponging at it hard. It doesn't seem to make *any* difference. In fact, it looks even worse than when I started.

I lean forward and put all my weight behind my hands, press deep, and as I do, I hear footsteps clattering down the stairs, followed by the sound of the front door slamming shut. I lift my head, and Pooky comes sauntering past me, sits himself down by my elbow, and starts to wash.

"What was that, Pooks, eh?"

There are only two other people living in the house; one opposite me and one opposite Olive. I hardly ever see either of them. The man who lives opposite me works nights at Tesco's. I look at my watch. He would have left for work hours ago.

Leaving the cloth and the carpet cleaner where they are, I open Olive's door wide and call up the stairs.

"Paige?"

The TV is still on in my flat, the theme tune to *Hollyoaks* filtering down the stairs. I take a step and call again, "Paige?"

Still nothing. She obviously can't hear me over the noise of the TV, but I want to make sure she's okay, so I run up the stairs two at a time and push open the door.

"Paige? You okay? I heard the... door..."

But she isn't sitting on the sofa. I walk through to the kitchen, then the bedroom, then the bathroom. They're all empty, and her shoes and her jacket are gone.

I stand in the middle of the room, my hands on my hips, looking about me in confusion, and out of the corner of my eye, I catch sight of the red light on my answering machine. It is still flashing.

I go to it quickly and press 'play', but all I hear is a little click before the tape starts to rewind. When it reaches the start, I press 'play' again, and Will's voice tumbles out into the room like a grenade.

"Hey, hot chick! Just wanted to let you know that I got home safe and that all I want to do now is turn around and come back..." I take a shaky step backwards. "I want to say thanks as well. All that stuff I was going on about in the pub in Corfe, about what I wanted sex to be and everything? Well, it was *so* much more than that with you, Rebecca..."

I press the 'stop' button and cover my mouth with my hands. When Paige came out of the bathroom earlier, I must have pressed 'rewind' instead of 'erase', and if the message was at an end when I found it just now, then she has listened to it.

Twenty

I run back downstairs, fling open the front door and step out into the gathering dark.

"Paige?"

But my voice breaks over her name, scatters small. A man passing by glances at me, keeps looking as he walks on.

I hurry down the path and stand on the pavement, looking one way and then the other. There aren't many people on the street. Even the Common is bleak and deserted, cold air grumbling through the trees towards me. There's no sign of Paige.

I go back inside and close the door, leaning my shoulder against it for a moment. Pooky is sitting at the bottom of the stairs, peering at me with interest. I scoop him up and take him back into Olive's flat, deposit him in the kitchen and switch off all the lights, and then I run back upstairs to look for my shoes and jacket. Paige can't have got far. I will take the car and look for her. I will explain everything and she'll come home with me. We'll drink the rest of the tequila between us and we'll play music and dance again, and everything will be all right. I know it will.

I drive down towards town, slowly, all the way to the water, and then I turn around and drive all the way back, along the other side of the Common. Maybe she's decided to cut across it, along the cycle path, or maybe she's gone the other way entirely, towards the university. Truth is, she could have gone anywhere.

I drive to the Swan and run inside. It isn't very busy yet and I spot Fiona immediately, her elbows on the bar, talking to a female customer.

"Fiona!" She looks up as I approach and her face is puzzled. "Has Paige been in?"

"No." She stands up straight and puts one hand on her hip. With the other, she reaches for a glass from the shelf above her head. "She said she was with you tonight."

"She was, but..."

"Rebecca?" Her face is pinched and cross. "What's going on?"

"Look, we had a bit of a misunderstanding, that's all, and she left."

"What kind of misunderstanding?"

"It doesn't matter, but if she comes in, will you *please* tell her to come back to the flat, or to call me?"

Fiona looks down into the empty glass in her hand, and when she looks up again, she's smiling, but it's not a nice smile.

"I *told* her this would happen," she says.

"Told her what would happen?"

"That you'd let her down."

"I haven't."

She looks at me softly, knowingly. "No?"

I shake my head, but there are tears burning shame inside my throat, because I *have* let her down, and the knowledge of it is intolerable to me.

"Will you tell her to call me, Fiona?"

She nods slowly, looks almost sorry for me.

"If she comes in, I'll tell her."

I turn away, but my steps back to the car are laboured, and when I get inside, I rest my forehead on the cool curve of the steering wheel.

Why didn't I tell Paige about Will when I had the chance? Why didn't I trust her with the truth? I may not actually have lied this time, but I haven't exactly been honest, either. I think of Paige, out there somewhere in the dark, drunk, weighed down by grief over her grandma, bruised by my betrayal, and I just can't bear it.

I lift my head and start the car again, drive quickly out of the city this time and west into the forest. She'll have gone home, surely, to Sway. Of course she will. She'll have boarded a bus in town and she'll be on her way home right now. Maybe I'll even get there before her. I could be sitting on her doorstep, waiting for her, just like she was waiting for me earlier. We could start the night over again. We could put it right.

By the time I reach Sway, a heavy rain is falling. I get out of the car and then I get back in again, uncertain. Lights are on in the house, and I can see a figure moving about in the living room, but it isn't Paige. It must be her mum. I wait for half an hour, looking over my shoulder every now and then for the bus, but then I start thinking that Paige could have caught a cab home instead, in which case she could already be inside.

In the end, I get out of the car, lift my jacket over my head like a tent and run up the path. The door swings open to me before I even reach it. There's a tall woman standing in the doorway, her arms folded across her chest, her short hair, dark grey and sleek as a cat's.

"Would you like to tell me," she says slowly, "why you've been sitting outside my house for the last thirty minutes, looking in through my window?"

"I'm sorry. I was waiting for Paige."

"I see." But her long face stays hard. "Well, she isn't here."

"Have you any idea where she might be?"

"She said she was spending the night with a friend. I don't know who."

I nod, drops of water falling in front of my face, making Paige's mum shimmer slightly; a drizzling mirage.

"Do you want to leave a message for her?" Her voice is crisp.

"Yeah, please. Could you ask her to call Rebecca? It's quite important."

She nods, a flicker of interest. "Will she know what it's about?"

"Yes. She'll know what it's about."

"Fine."

She starts to close the door, and I turn back towards the road, but she calls after me.

"If it's *that* important, you could always see if Rick knows where she is. He's her husband." She says the word *husband* with a brisk deliberacy.

Rick. Of *course*. Paige's best friend. If someone's upset, then where do they think of going first? To their best friend. She's certain to be with him.

"Do you have the address?"

Paige's mum leans out of view to her left, keeping the door open with her foot, and then she reappears with a Filofax in her hands. She flicks through it, pauses.

"213 University Road."

"Thanks."

I run back to the car and climb inside, set off again. I don't know how fast I'm driving and I don't care, but the rain is pounding against my windscreen, obscuring my vision, and in the end I have to slow down, because the traffic ahead of me is snaking slow as fatigue. It seems to take hours to get back to Southampton.

When I eventually reach University Road and find the right house, it is in darkness. I knock on the door, once, twice, three times, and then I call Paige's name through the letterbox. There's no response. I sit myself down on the doorstep, in the pouring rain, my head heavy in my hands, because I simply don't know where else to look.

I go home. I switch on all the lights in my flat, almost as if I can turn it into a beacon to draw Paige back safe, and then I sit on the sofa and wait. The half-empty bottle of tequila is on the coffee table in front of me. I snatch it up and start to drink. At first, it is oily and sour, and every mouthful makes me retch, but after a while, I stop tasting it, and it becomes simply a glimmer on my tongue, a discernible warmth that makes me lift my chin as I swallow. I sink back into the cushions; a gesture behind my breastbone, an agitation of hands, drowsiness, sleep.

I wake to the sound of the telephone ringing. The lights in the flat are still switched on, bouncing bright against the weak daylight nudging at the windows. I look at the clock. It's six-thirty in the morning. I've slept all night on the sofa.

I stumble my way to the phone and pick it up.

"Hello." My voice is cotton wool.

"Rebecca? It's Will."

"Oh God, Will." I crumple down onto the floor. "I was going to call you."

"Listen." His voice sounds odd, officious. "I'm at Waterloo Station. I'm just about to get on a train back to Southampton."

"Look, please, *don't* do that, I..."

"I *have* to talk to you." I hear an announcer's voice, brittle in the background. Will speaks over it. "I was tidying Kate's room, for when she comes home, and I found her diary, under her mattress. I was making her bed, and her diary was..." He falters. "Rebecca. There's some stuff in it." His words become fluid. "It's about what happened with..."

The line hisses, goes dead.

"Will?"

It's no good. He's gone. I replace the receiver and crawl across the carpet, back to the sofa. I feel sick and the Battle of Agincourt is underway inside my head: the clash of steel against steel, the beat of the flag-bearer's drum. The bottle of tequila on the coffee table is empty. I peer at it close, but it splits in two, reassembles, splits again.

I go to the bathroom and take a long shower, then stand in the kitchen wrapped in a towel, waiting for the kettle to boil. I make some strong black coffee and drink it down, even though my stomach contracts at every sip. I think about eating some food, but as soon as I do, a thick swell of nausea pulls my diaphragm in tight, and I have to run back to the bathroom and be sick, after which I feel better. All the same, I ring into work and say that I have a migraine. My senior librarian sounds suspicious, but I don't care. I tell her I'll try to make it in to-morrow, and then I sit down on the floor in front of the television and let the lilt and fall of words and faces lull and beguile me.

When the phone starts to ring again, I decide to ignore it. I can't bear the thought of Will coming back. I don't want to talk to him. I don't care about Kate's stupid diary, but the phone rings and rings, and I suddenly think that maybe it could be Paige and not Will, so I crawl back across the carpet and lift the receiver. It slips through my fingers at first, bounces away from me, so that I have to stretch even further to retrieve it.

"Hello." I can hear how irritable I sound.

"I didn't wake you, did I?" Adam. The breath in my lungs turns murky and black. "I wouldn't want to deprive you of your beauty sleep, considering how much you need it, but I thought you might like to know that while you were snoozing like a baby, I was taking a trip, with a friend of yours."

"What do you want?" Every word hurts.

"I want restitution, Rebecca. I want you to admit your guilt and atone for it."

"I don't know what you're talking about."

"Yes, you do. You owe me."

The room opens and closes around me like something at the bot-tom of the ocean.

"What d'you mean?"

"Don't pretend you don't remember."

"Remember what?"

"Your lies."

I grip the phone tighter. "Please, leave me alone."

"Can't do that."

"Why?"

"Because things have to be rectified."

"What things?"

"I'll tell you when you come."

I shake my head. "What are you talking about? Come where?"

"To join Paige and me, of course."

The receiver falls out of my hands, lands with a soft thud, like a bone. By the time I bring it back to my ear, all I can hear is the sound of Adam laughing.

"Have I surprised you?"

"No. You're full of shit and I already knew that. You haven't surprised me, and Paige isn't really with you. What are you trying to pull?"

There's quiet for a moment, a muffled exchange and then... Paige's voice:

"Bex?" I can't breathe. I *literally* can't breathe. "Bex, take no notice of him. He's just fucking with you. I'll take him for a drink and calm him down. I'll..."

A burst of breath, a scuffle, and then a whimpering sound, drawn out and appalling.

"Paige?" Silence. "Paige?"

"No. Only me, I'm afraid."

"What do you want?"

"Only your presence, dear heart."

"Where? Just tell me where and I'll come, but you leave Paige alone. D'you hear me?"

He sighs. "How touching your concern for your friend *is*, but don't you think it's a little late in the day for you to start playing the martyr, pretending to care about someone else? I mean, you've never done it before."

I want to cry, but I hold it back. "Fuck you!"

"Well, it's funny you should mention that. Do you remember the last time we made love?"

"What?"

"You and I, in St. Ives, six weeks before you left me? We'd been to that pub in Zennor. You know the one. Now, what *was* it called...?"

"The Tinner's Arms."

"You *do* remember." His voice is gleeful. "Well, Paige and I are actually here, *at* the Tinner's Arms. Isn't that a coincidence? And soon we're going to take a walk along the cliffs, just like you and I did, and we're going to stop at Pen Dennys Point and wait for you. It was pretty there, d'you remember? D'you remember the poppies, Rebecca?" I open my mouth to answer, but I can't make anything come. "Well, anyway. I hope you can join us. It would be an absolute delight to see you. Take care on the journey. Ciao, baby."

I sit with the receiver in my hand, staring at it, disbelieving. I look at the tequila bottle, waiting for it to split in two again, *willing* it to split in two, but it doesn't. This call was real, not some phoney drink-induced drama. It was *real*.

I haul myself to my feet and hurry to the bedroom, throw on some underwear, a black sweater and a pair of combat trousers, almost falling flat on my face as I pull on a pair of baseball boots and head for the door. I can't seem to get enough oxygen into my body. I'm gasping at the air as I stumble down the stairs, panic-stricken. I can feel the cool marble seeping up through the thin soles of my boots – a staircase of snow, hazardous.

Twenty-one

I stop in town for petrol and then drive out onto the motorway. I'm heading in the opposite direction to most of the morning rush-hour traffic, so at first, I make good time, but once I leave the motorway behind me and head on through rural Dorset and then west into Devon, everything slows. The open road keeps being interrupted by articulated lorries, cattle trucks and caravans. A couple of times, I try overtaking them, but my car won't accelerate fast enough, and I have to fall back in frustration. All I can do is match the pace of the vehicle in front of me, and pray for long stretches of dual carriageway.

I seem to drive for hours, before I finally pass a sign by the side of the road saying 'Welcome to Cornwall'. My body tenses. I can feel adrenaline rushing green into the dips and hollows of my muscles, swirling fast around the soft fruit of my heart.

I drive even faster, reckless now, the curving road ahead of me scattered with fallen leaves – rust-coloured, like old blood. I take every corner with a screech of brakes, the steering wheel sticky in my grasp, and the molecules beneath the surface of my skin seem to bond and break apart, over and over again: a continual fragmentation. The possibility that I know who Adam really is, and that deep down I've known all along, fingers its way inside me like a cancer. How did I not recognise him that first day at the library? How did I not look into his eyes and remember that *other* time I'd looked into his eyes, a year ago – a

London night smoothing itself at the glass, the ramshackle sounds of a party on the other side of the door, his hands pushing me away, soft voice telling me *no*. How did I not know him sooner and save us from this?

It is lunchtime before I reach the tiny village of Zennor. The air here is thin and salty, and the sky is everywhere. I park the car outside the Tinner's Arms and start to walk along the narrow lane that leads to the cliffs and the sea. Already, I can hear the white surf slamming against the rocks, as distinct as cannon fire.

A thought strikes me, and I stop walking. A huddle of cows in the field to my right lift their heavy black heads to look at me. What if they're not here? What if I've driven all the way down here, when he and Paige are really somewhere else? What if it's all some elaborate and nauseating game? But what if it's not? I look up at the sky, a haze of grey, disconsolate. I had no choice but to come, even if it is a game. While he has Paige, I have no choices.

I start walking again, quicker this time, and then I start to run. The lane narrows to a dirt track, edged by nettles and bracken, and then it opens onto the headland; a gasp of white with the green sea inside it.

I move fast along the path, clambering over rocks, climbing inland and then coming sharply down again to the ragged edge of the cliff. The ground is soft and brown; little purple speedwell and coltsfoot springing up like coloured stones beneath my feet. I run and run and run, jumping over rocks, skidding down runnels of wet grass, and all the while, the sea roars and falls at my side like something alive.

Far ahead of me, in the sky, I see a little flurry of seagulls circling, calling to each other. Something has caught their interest. The path here is steep, but I scramble up it as fast as I can, clutching at tufts of spiky grass, feeling the soles of my boots slipping away beneath me, and when I reach the top, and stand, breathing hard, I realise that I am looking down on a scene that I recognise. Pen Dennys Point. And there beneath me, where the path snakes closest to the edge of the cliff, two figures stand, looking out to sea.

For a moment, I don't know what to do. If I call Paige's name, she will hear me, but he has his arm around her waist, and I don't want to startle him. I want to give myself time to be ready for whatever's going to happen, so I take the path down very slowly, keeping my head low, watching them. I'm within fifteen feet of them, when the soft ground beneath my feet shifts suddenly, and I feel myself slip and fall. No sound comes from my mouth to forewarn them, but they must hear the air disturbed, because they both turn, and he smiles.

"You weren't trying to sneak up on us there, were you?"

I stand up unsteadily and move a little closer. Paige's face is ashen. I can hear her breathing, hectic and irregular. He has her held fast.

"We weren't sure you were gonna make it, were we, Paige?"

He looks at her, and she shakes her head. The seagulls above us are rowdy with curiosity.

"What do you want?" My voice sounds like it belongs to a stranger. I swallow, try again. "Whatever it is, let's just get it over with."

"There's no need to hurry, is there? We've got all the time in the world."

He is wearing a long wool jacket and trousers that look too big for him, and in this stark light, his face is dark, his thick hair seedy looking, unkempt.

"Why don't you sit yourself down, hmm?"

"No. I want this finished." My body is trembling, but I grit my teeth, pull my muscles in tight. "I know who you are now."

"Do you?"

"Yes, and I know why you're doing this to me."

He tilts his head to one side. "Really?"

"It's you, isn't it, Simon? I knew I recognised you. You've got rid of your beard and your dreads, but I knew there was *something* about you that I recognised."

"It's taken you long enough to work it out."

"Yes, but I know now. It's been you all along. It was you who put the tape through my letterbox, and it was you who left that note in Will's pocket."

"Ah yes." The corners of his mouth twitch into a grin. "Kate's note."

"Except it wasn't from Kate at all, was it?"

He shakes his head. "Well, no. All my own work, I'm afraid."

"She isn't going home?"

"Christ knows." He shrugs. "She might be."

"You don't even know where she is?"

"Overseas, last I heard."

"Then why did you write the note saying she was going home?"

"Because I wanted Will gone. You shouldn't have involved him. This was only ever supposed to be about you and me, Rebecca. Nobody else."

"Look." I take a breath, hold it. "I know I did a terrible thing, and I know what the consequences of it were. Will told me what happened to you after I lied about you and me at that party. He told me about Kate finishing with you and how Adam didn't want anything to do with you." My words are coming fast now, a stream of sound. I try to slow my breathing, but it's no good. "He told me about your drinking and how you ended up in rehab, and I can see how you might look back and think it was all my fault, and you'd be right, and I'm sorry."

He opens his mouth, and his voice, when it comes, sounds different. It seems to lift into the air, changing shape, curving light towards me.

"You think Kate finished with me because of that, because of you?"

"Didn't she?"

He chuckles to himself then; a scatter of stones. "Of course not. Nobody believed your story. Nobody ever believed you, Rebecca. They knew I was telling the truth about what went on at that party."

"Then why did Kate finish with you?"

He raises his eyebrows. "Can't you guess? Come on now. You're supposed to be the mistress of invention. Try to work it out."

"I can't, and look, for Christ's sake, I don't care. Just tell me what you want from me, and let Paige go!"

"Let Paige go?" His voice is a blade. He glances back at her, starts to laugh, but it's a brittle sound and she winces against it. "Did you hear that? She wants me to let you go." And then he turns back to me and his eyes are tiny points of light, incisive. "Not fucking likely, sweetheart."

He swivels round and reaches for Paige again, and as he does, something in my body changes; a chemical reaction, a fusion of muscle and will. I lunge forward and try to grab Paige's arm. If I can just get hold of her, if I can just draw her away from the edge of the cliff, then we can start to run... But he sees me, and he lifts his arm fast and jerks it back hard into my stomach, makes me lurch forward with my hands on my thighs, retching into the grass, coughing up air that tastes as bitter as poison.

I can hear Simon laughing, and underneath his laughter, something else. Still bent double, I lift my head, and what I see in that moment closes the valves of my heart tight shut. The blood in my veins calcifies. Everything in my body stops dead.

Simon has his arm around Paige's shoulder, but very softly now, intimate. They are leaning into each other's bodies, smiling into each other's faces. Simon lifts his fingers and touches Paige's hair, and they sway together, exultant, and then Paige looks at me and says, in a voice that I do not know, "You didn't seriously think I was interested in *you*, did you?"

I try to stand up straight, but my spine is liquid and my knees are shaking. Suddenly Paige is walking towards me, sauntering, with her hands lifted in something like supplication.

"Why would I be interested in a lying, manipulative, *boring* little slag like you?" She grabs hold of my arm and wrenches me forward so that I fall hard onto my knees. She leans down, her mouth against my hair. "D'you think I enjoyed fucking you, sticking my tongue inside you?"

"Paige." My voice is tiny. "Don't. For God's *sake*..." The seagulls screech above us, turning in wild circles. "You can't mean it."

"Yes I can."

"You told me you loved me."

She opens her mouth, runs her tongue slow along her bottom lip, her grip on my arm getting tighter.

"I lied. Just like you did, to Adam, to everyone."

I can feel a swell of tears burning hot behind my breastbone. "But I believed you."

"That's *your* problem."

"But I love you."

She shakes her head. "That's your problem, too."

Something lifts inside my throat and spills – a sob, unrestrained.

"Was it *all* a lie? Have you been with *him* all along? You're not gay?"

She smiles. "It's not as simple as it looks. I *told* you sexuality wasn't a fixed mark, didn't I?" She flicks my temple with her fingernail, and then she straightens up. "I'm sorry, Rebecca, but it's time you knew the truth, the whole truth." And she flings my arm away from her.

As she does, a box of matches falls out of her pocket and lands on the path. She has to lean right down to retrieve it.

She hesitates, just for a second, her face next to mine.

"When I say run," she whispers, less than a whisper. "*Run!*"

I look up quickly, but she stands, like it's all becoming quite tedious, and strolls back into Simon's arms.

"You see," he says softly, slipping his hand around Paige's waist. "You're not the only one who can tell lies and get away with them. We can all do it. It isn't a gift or a talent. It's just a choice that you make, out of necessity, except you never *needed* to lie, did you? You lied because you enjoyed it. You got off on fucking with people's feelings. But you see, Rebecca, your lying *has to stop*. Someone has to stop it."

I shake my head. "But I'm not like that any more."

"No? What *are* you like?"

"I'm different."

He takes a step towards me. "Are you?"

"Yes."

"But Adam's dead because of you."

I cover my face with my hands. "Yes."

He takes another step towards me. "Are you familiar with the old biblical premise of *an eye for an eye*, Rebecca? "

I pull myself to my feet, hold myself as straight as I can, but the world has begun to slip in and out of focus; sea and sky falling like sheets of glass all around me, and Simon is coming towards me with his arms outstretched, like a friend who's pleased to see me, like a brother receiving me home, and I *almost* want to go to him, to have it over, to atone.

"Simon." My voice folds in on itself. "Simon, I…"

He shakes his head, presses his finger to his lips for quiet, but then I hear a sharp cry and all at once he is face down on the ground in front of me, with Paige struggling on top of him yelling, "Run, Bex… *Run!*"

But I can't. My feet won't move. I am rooted, and Paige is looking at me, her face desperate, uncomprehending.

"Bex…"

But it's no good, and suddenly Simon rolls Paige off into the dirt and starts kicking at her hard, gets her on her back on the ground.

"You *bitch!*" he screams at her, his voice lifting and lifting. "You scheming little *bitch*," over and over, and each time he says the word bitch, he slaps Paige in the face; once, twice, three times.

When I hear the sound of Simon's hand make contact with Paige's cheekbone for the third time, something in my stomach grows hard and black and resolute, and I lunge forward blindly and grab him round the neck, press my forearm into his windpipe and wrench him backwards. I can hear him choking. I can see Paige's face, streaked with blood, aghast. I can smell the mud, lifting sour all around us, and

Simon is struggling against me, his hands flailing into my body. He isn't as strong as I'd expected, but he manages to prise my arm away from his neck and start to turn.

I grab again, hooking my fingers into his hair, pulling as hard as I can, but he breaks away from me and hauls himself forward, spins around on his knees so that he's looking me square in the face; his mouth open, his eyes levelled at me like an animal.

"Is this a fight to the death then, Rebecca? I didn't think you had it in you." And his mouth opens in a thin laugh, as if there's not enough air in his body to keep him in one piece, as if he's held to-gether only by spurious sound.

I slide back onto the grass, shuffle myself backwards, pushing with my heels, and Paige is shaking her head, reaching out her hands to me, saying my name, but Simon simply pulls himself to his feet and dusts himself off. He takes a breath and glances down at Paige.

"I should have known I couldn't trust you," he says. "I should have known you'd let me down."

Paige lifts her face, says quietly, "I couldn't let you do it."

"Shut up." His voice is broken glass. "You just shut your fucking mouth!" And then he looks at me, very calm. "Why is it," he says, "that good people always end up with bad things happening to them, and yet people like you, evil people like you, get what they want, every time, get away with... murder? Why is that? Why wasn't it *you* who ended up going over this cliff?" He gestures towards the sea. "Why was it my Adam, when it should have been you?"

"*Your* Adam?"

I shake my head, but he raises his hand fast, says, "Don't. You just listen for once. For *once* you don't get to do the talking, Rebecca. I do." He breathes deep. "Adam and I were okay until you came. We were perfect until you came. He was *everything* to me; all I needed, all I wanted, and then *you*." He jabs his finger in the air. "He told me it was over, that we couldn't go on like we had been, because *that* time, *our* time, was past for him. That's what he said; that he was beyond it, beyond *me*, now that he had *you*. All he could offer me was friendship. Friendship." He spits the word. "That's when I went overseas, to get away, but I couldn't stay away."

"You were..." I try to pull myself onto my knees, try to move towards him. "Simon. You were *lovers*?"

The bald fact of it slithers out of my body softly and he dips his head to meet it, opens his mouth to the taste of it.

"He never told you?"

"No."

"I guess I was his dirty little secret."

"How long were you..."

"*Fucking* each other?" He sucks the word onto his tongue, settles it there. "It started when we were sixteen."

"But what about Kate? You were seeing Kate."

"She was my way of staying close."

"Did she know – about you and him?"

"I told her. After that party, I told her. I was sick of the lies, but that's when Adam said he didn't want me anywhere near him any more, because I was a liability. He thought I was going to tell you about me and him, and I would have too, if you hadn't dumped him and left." His mouth curls at the corners, but his eyes stay hard. "I thought maybe he and I might have had another chance, with you gone, but he didn't want me."

"I'm sorry."

"Are you?"

"Yes."

"Sorry for lying your way into his bed? Sorry for taking him from me?" His face starts to contract. "The one person I loved beyond anything in this world, and you took him from me like it meant nothing." He looks at Paige then. "And now, somehow, you have taken from me someone I thought I could trust *with my life!*" He struggles back from the edge of tears, falters, tries again. "Paige." And he reaches his fingers to Paige's face. "How *could* you do this?"

She tries to catch hold of his hand, but he snatches it away, holds it to his chest. Still looking into Paige's eyes, he says to me, "Paige and I met while we were in rehab in London, didn't we, pet?" He tilts his head, like he's waiting for an answer. "She was busy getting her sorry ass clean, and so was I, and we hit if off big-time. We looked after each other. It was like we'd known each other forever. That happens sometimes, doesn't it? You meet someone and you feel like you've known them all your life. It's like... a kind of recognition."

He turns to look at me. "When we got out, she was just breaking up with Rick. Her world was falling apart. *I* brought order to it. She was in pieces and it was *me* who put her back together again. My parents' money paid off all her student debts and her solicitor's fees, and I found her somewhere to live after her mum didn't want her, and then, I drew her into this..." And he lifts his hands, palms upward, offers them to me, but starts to move away from us, turning his face to the sea.

"I told her what you'd done and how wrong it was, how wrong your lies were and what they'd caused, the pain that *you'd* caused, and because she owed me, she said she'd help me to teach you a lesson. Whatever I needed her to do, she said she'd do it, because she owed me." He glances over his shoulder. "More lies."

He moves further away, right to the edge of the cliff, and he teeters there, slips off his jacket and stands with the wind from the sea buffeting against him.

Paige and I look at each other, and all I want to do is take her inside my body and keep her there, so that nothing can ever hurt her again. She shifts onto her knees, and then she half lurches, half crawls across to me, tears streaming down her face. She puts her arms around me and we hold onto each other with all the strength left in us. I can smell the warm earth on her clothes, the salt on her skin. I can taste her, sweet as a miracle on the broken air.

"I'm sorry," she whispers. "Sweetheart, believe me. I'm *so* sorry. Those things I said..."

"It's all right." I rock her, tight as a seashell. "Everything's all right."

But when Simon hears what we're saying, he turns and comes striding back to us, standing over us with his fists clenched.

Paige touches his leg. "I couldn't let you do it, Simon. I never thought you'd take it this far. I just couldn't let you do it. It wasn't right. You *know* it wasn't right. Rebecca's not a bad person. She's sorry about Adam and she's..."

But Simon spits on the ground by Paige's hand, and then he backs quickly away to the cliff edge again, and lifts his face to the sky.

"Simon!"

We both move towards him, but he steps back even further, so that his heels are treading the air.

"This isn't *fair*," he cries, and then he looks at me, his eyes ablaze. "*You* never loved Adam, did you, but he chose you, and because he chose you, he died. Where's the logic in that? Where's the *justice* in that? If he'd chosen me..." His face crumples and falls. "You don't know what it's like to lose someone you love as much as I loved him. This misery I feel, this..." He touches his fingers to his heart. "This hard thing that lives in me; I thought if I could find you, make you *pay*, then maybe it would go away. But it's never going to go away. This misery, it has to stop, but I don't know..." He lets his head fall heavy. "I don't know how to make it stop."

And he starts to cry then, silently, desperately, like there isn't any sound in the universe that could bear the dimensions of his grief. His body begins to sway, balance seeping away from him, his hands clawing at his face.

He bows his head, and as he does so, Paige makes a swift move towards him, reaching out her arms, but he startles and buckles away. I don't see him fall. All I see is Paige sinking down onto her stomach in the grass, her arms flailing over the cliff.

"Bex!" Her voice has all the air squeezed out of it.

I scramble across to the cliff edge, the sea crashing over the rocks far beneath us, but Paige has hold of Simon by his left arm, and he is swinging in a tight arc, his white face looking up at us; attentive, mildly surprised.

I lean over as far as I can, reaching to him.

"Take my hand, Simon…" I plead. "Reach up. You can do it. Take my hand!"

He stares at me, inquisitive, his mouth opening over words that I can't hear because of the sound of the waves.

"Simon…" Paige is crying, trembling hard. "For God's sake. I can't hold you on my own. *Please*…"

Simon has had his hand clenched in a fist but he opens it now, his palm lifted to us like he's waiting to catch something. He looks past us at the sky, and when he speaks this time, I hear him.

"It has to stop," he says, and as he says it, his wrist begins to slip free of Paige's grasp. She grabs for him again, desperate, but it's no good. We watch as he falls, his arms stretched wide, the green sea opening its mouth to receive him.

Epilogue

Paige told me a story, from tribal legend. It was called 'The Ropemaker's Daughter' and it concerned a girl, destined to assume her father's trade after his death, weaving cedar rope and flax for use in her village. He taught her all he knew – imparted to her his secrets, bequeathed to her his tools and his superlative expertise, but she abused the gift. Instead of using her weaving skills for the good of her tribe, she used them to fashion for herself playthings, clothing, adornments. The Great Spirits grew angry with her for her vanity, and they sent a raven to the village, who carried her off to his nest in the mountains and kept her there, his prisoner. The ropemaker's daughter regretted her past selfishness, and out of the twigs and bark and feathers that the raven brought to his nest, she began to weave herself a rope, secretly, in the gloomy air. She remembered all she had been taught, and eventually, the day came when the rope she had made was long enough for her to climb down from the nest in the mountains and return to her village, where she never again looked to her own vanity, but resolved to live a good and useful life amongst her people.

Sometimes, I wake from a dream of falling; grey light pressing its fists against my chest, the sheets tangled around my wrists like ropes. Sometimes I wake and take regret onto my tongue like a communion wafer, longing for absolution, for the undoing of all the wrong I've done. But I'm not fool enough to think it's as easy as that, or that there will be an end to it. I don't *want* to forget it. I want my heart to break every time I remember it, and mend, and break again.

Sometimes I wake, thinking of the ropemaker's daughter, and I wonder about forgiveness. Paige says we can make amends in being sorry, and I really want to believe her. Maybe one day I will, but for now, I believe only in her touch, which is almost enough, and the fingerprint mark of the dark, and the benediction of tears.

More new fiction from Diva Books

Smother
Linda Innes

A dark comedy about the harm we cause each other

Mary has an obsession: to prove her devotion to Tanya, no matter
what abuse she gets in return. But why are the two of them locked in
conflict over the very nature of love? And what would it take to push
Mary over the edge? As the story unfolds, memories and events show
how each woman's relationship with her own mother has affected
her adult love affairs. And now, it seems, someone will have to pay.

"A hugely enjoyable debut novel; a passionate journey through a
landscape of damaged relationships. Innes writes beautifully
with a divine eye for detail. This is a powerful new voice,
exploring difficult and important territory, and it's immensely
readable, too" Julia Darling (author, *Crocodile Soup*)

"A damned good read... Dialogue is the usual slangy mix of
insult and humour but it's the narrative that drives this novel,
sketching in terse, punning sentences the outlines of very dark
secrets... Read it and weep" Rainbow Network

RRP £8.95 ISBN 1-873741-61-8 Out now

Maddie and Anna's Big Picture
Jane Marlow

A witty look at the messy 'big picture' of modern relationships

Rents in London are soaring and for Anna, a City lawyer with an eye for figures, buying a flat together has never made more sense. But for her partner Maddie, the transition from idealistic twenty-something artist to thirty-something home-owner is a little more problematic. Wishful thinking doesn't quite match reality, monogamy doesn't quite come up to scratch... It's when love triangles turn into polygons that the girls know something's gotta give.

"Jane Marlow offers a clear and insightful take on the joyful, dirty, messy, sexy, intimate and often profoundly dysfunctional round of modern relationships. Girls and girls, girls and boys, boys and boys, and – blessed relief – not a gay stereotype among them. This is a version of love and lust that is gratifyingly honest in its intricacies, thoughtful in its language – *A Midsummer Night's Dream* **with career, finances and property as the meddling fairies" Stella Duffy**

RRP £8.99 ISBN 1-873741-71-5 May 2002

Diva Books are available from bookshops or direct from Diva's mail order service on the net at www.divamag.co.uk or on freephone 0800 45 45 66 (international: +44 20 8340 8644). Please add P&P (single item £1.75, two or more £3.45, all overseas £5) and quote the following codes: Smother SMO618, Maddie & Anna's Big Picture MAD715, The Ropemaker's Daughter ROP707

niñera de
MONSTRUOS

 Bruño

Título original: *The Grerks at Number 55*,
publicado por primera vez en el Reino Unido
por Hodder Children's Books,
una división de Hachette Children's Books
© Texto: Kes Gray
© Ilustraciones: Stephen Hanson

© Grupo Editorial Bruño, S. L., 2010
 Juan Ignacio Luca de Tena, 15
 28027-Madrid

www.brunolibros.es

Dirección Editorial: Trini Marull
Edición: Cristina González
Traducción: Begoña Oro
Preimpresión: Mar Garrido
Diseño de cubierta e interiores: Equipo Bruño

ISBN: 978-84-216-8290-6
D. legal: M-13485-2011
Impreso en: HUERTAS, Industrias Gráficas, S. A.
Printed in Spain

2.ª edición

niñera de monstruos

LOS GREAK

B Bruño

KES GRAY

—Si los monstruos existen,
¿por qué nunca he visto uno, papá?
—preguntó Nelly.

—Porque nunca salen —contestó
su padre.

—¿Y por qué no salen?

—Porque nunca consiguen canguro
para que se quede cuidando
a sus hijos.

—¡Pues yo seré Nelly, la niñera
de monstruos!
—sonrió Nelly.

En la mesilla de noche de Petronella Morton había cuatro cajones.

Tres eran normales y corrientes, pero el cuarto era muy especial...

Escondía un secreto.

Nelly (Petronella Morton prefería que la llamaran así) se agachó muy decidida frente al cuarto cajón y lo abrió poquito a poco.

Sus ojos tropezaron con un pijama azul y rosa a rayas perfectamente doblado y planchado.

Nelly levantó un poco el pijama, tanteó la pila de cinco camisetas que había debajo y deslizó los dedos justo entre la cuarta y la quinta.

Una chispa iluminó sus ojos en el momento de sacar el secreto de su escondite.

Se lo colocó sobre las piernas, lo contempló un instante y luego lo acarició cariñosamente con la punta de los dedos.

Era una botella de plástico de color verde loro, de esas que se rellenan con agua caliente para no pasar frío en la cama.

Hecha en Taiwán. Rellene con agua sin sobrepasar la línea, aparecía escrito en ella.

Nelly acunó la botella unos segundos... y a continuación la abrió como si fuera un bocadillo.

Sin que nadie de su familia lo supiera, había dado a esa botella un uso completamente distinto del habitual:

La había rajado a lo largo con unas tijeras de manualidades y ahora ocultaba un hueco secreto que solo se descubría al abrirla.

Metió los dedos en el hueco y sacó el objeto del que estaba tan orgullosa.

Era un cuaderno de tamaño folio, con espiral.

La tapa era roja y lisa, pero Nelly le había añadido un título escrito con rotuladores de purpurina, uno dorado y otro plateado.

El título decía, en letras doradas:

El monstruoso
cuaderno secreto
de Nelly,
la niñera de monstruos

LOS GRERK

Y debajo aparecía, en letras plateadas y subrayado dos veces:

¡¡¡NO ABRIR, O SI NO...!!!

Solo Nelly tenía acceso al monstruoso cuaderno secreto de Nelly, la niñera de monstruos. Y no porque ella fuera una chica especialmente reservada. De hecho, solía compartir hasta sus pensamientos más íntimos con su familia (bueno, con todos menos con su hermana Astilbe). Pero había aprendido que algunas de las cosas que veía cuando hacía de cuidadora de monstruos era mejor guardárselas para ella misma. Ya sabes..., cosas viscosas, mugrientas o afiladas que podían llegar a asustar a otras personas o, por lo menos, ponerles la carne de gallina.

Lo que hacía que Nelly fuese alguien tan especial es que cuidaba monstruos.

Ninguno de sus amigos se habría atrevido a hacer de canguro para una familia de monstruos, ni siquiera habrían tenido valor para llamar a su puerta.

Todas las personas que conocía Nelly, incluida su hermana gemela Asti (Astilbe Morton prefería que la llamaran así), creían que los monstruos eran bichos raros y peligrosos que era mejor evitar. Nadie pensaba en ellos como esos vecinos a los que hay que dar la bienvenida cuando vienen a vivir a tu barrio.

En ese sentido, Nelly no era como los demás.

LOS GRERK

Tenía un corazón enorme y unos nervios de acero.

Por suerte para ella, su padre y su madre también eran muy generosos. Desde el primer día la habían apoyado en su idea de hacer de canguro para que los padres monstruos pudieran salir un poco más.

El padre de Nelly estaba convencido de que hacer de cuidadora de monstruos sería «educativo» para su hija, y la madre de Nelly tenía la esperanza de que eso mejorase sus modales en la mesa.

Sí, desde luego, Nelly tenía suerte de tener unos padres como los suyos.

Abrió su cuaderno secreto y hojeó algunas páginas al azar.

En ellas se leían, escritas a mano, cosas como «LOS HOJPOG», «LOS WIZZIL» y «LOS GLOOBLE».

Cuando encontró la primera página vacía, sacó con los dientes la tapa de un rotulador morado de punta fina, escribió el encabezamiento con su mejor letra: «LOS GRERK», y a continuación añadió tres puntos.

Esos tres puntos, los puntos suspensivos, querían decir: «Próximamente, más información».

En la agenda de peluche de Nelly figuraba que esa tarde debía cuidar a un monstruo. Era la primera vez que hacía de canguro para los Grerk, así que tendría que esperar hasta la noche, cuando volviera a casa, para completar la información de su cuaderno.

LOS GRERK

Sabía cómo sonaban los Grerk por teléfono. De hecho, los había confundido con los graznidos chirriantes de los Squiddl. Pero en cuanto a su aspecto, no tenía ni idea...

¿Tendrían escamas, o púas? ¿Serían viscosos, o peludos?

Para Nelly, la mitad de la diversión consistía en intentar adivinar cómo serían, y la otra mitad, en descubrirlo.

Los Grerk, que vivían en el número 55 de su misma calle, le habían pedido a Nelly que hiciera de canguro de seis a ocho de la tarde.

Ya eran las seis menos veinte, así que Nelly metió su cuaderno secreto en el interior de la botella de plástico y volvió a guardarla cuidadosamente en su escondite, en el cuarto cajón de la mesilla.

Ya estaba cerrándolo cuando el picaporte de la puerta de su cuarto empezó a temblar y a moverse de lado a lado.

—¿Por qué te has encerrado? —gritó su hermana desde el otro lado de la puerta.

—¡Para que no entren las Barbies! —respondió Nelly.

LOS GRERK

La mayoría de los días se llevaba regular con su hermana, y el resto de días se llevaba fatal.

—¡O me dejas entrar, o se lo digo a mamá! —chilló Asti.

En vez de hacerle caso, Nelly abrió la puerta del armario de su habitación, sacó su jersey favorito y lo puso sobre la cama.

Era verde con los bordes naranjas, y en la parte de delante ponía «SARDINA» con grandes letras plateadas.

Nadie, ni siquiera la propia Nelly, sabía muy bien por qué ponía «SARDINA» en aquel jersey, pero precisamente por eso le gustaba tanto. Porque era diferente.

Mientras se recogía su pelo negro como el carbón con una goma amarilla fosforito, el picaporte volvió a agitarse con furia.

—¡DÉJAME ENTRAR! —chilló Asti.

Nelly sonrió, abrió la puerta y, al salir, aprovechó para darle un empujón a su hermana.

—Serás friki... —siseó Asti.

—Serás tentáculo viscoso pantanoso... —masculló Nelly.

Asti se puso las manos en las caderas y se quedó mirando cómo Nelly bajaba las escaleras.

Asti no era tan rápida de mente como su hermana, de modo que necesitaba un poco de tiempo para preparar su siguiente insulto.

Las palabras «apestosa», «rarita» y «mugrosa» pululaban por su cerebro, pero para cuando dio con el insulto que quería decir («cochambrófila»), su hermana ya había desaparecido de su vista.

Como de costumbre, Nelly iba diez peldaños por delante de Asti.

Brincó por las escaleras y corrió hacia la cocina con la vaga esperanza de que hubiera algo de comer preparándose para la cena.

Pero, para no variar, lo único que vio sobre la mesa fue un bote de salsa de tomate...

CAPÍTULO 2

n casa de Nelly, el asunto de las comidas nunca había sido sencillo.

Su madre era vegetariana, su padre era carnívoro como un león, su hermana era una tiquismiquis y a Nelly no le gustaban las zanahorias (en realidad —y esto era un secreto—, ni le gustaban ni le dejaban de gustar, pero al ver que toda su familia era tan especialita con las comidas, había decidido tener su propia manía gastronómica).

Nelly entró en la cocina y encontró a su madre apoyada en la encimera y con la mirada perdida, pensando qué podría hacer para cenar que requiriese el mínimo esfuerzo y la menor cantidad de cacharros por fregar.

—Mamá —dijo Nelly—. ¿Sabes ya qué vamos a cenar?

Su madre se quedó mirando los ingredientes que tenía delante y suspiró. Cambió los *nuggets* de pollo por una pescadilla congelada, y la lata de macarrones al queso por tres largos palitos de apio y un aguacate.

—Ojalá te gustaran las zanahorias, Nelly. La vida sería mucho más fácil así —dijo.

—¿Y si pedimos que nos traigan algo? —sugirió Nelly.

—¡Qué gran idea! —exclamó su madre, encantada—. ¡Pediremos una pizza!

—¿Podemos pedirla para las ocho? Volveré a esa hora.

—¡Estupendo, estupendo! —dijo su madre mientras forcejeaba con la pescadilla para que cupiese otra vez en el congelador—. Me tumbaré en el sofá un par de horitas. No me vendrá nada mal. Me pregunto qué echarán en la tele...

—Las típicas tonterías de los sábados por la tarde —dijo el padre de Nelly nada más entrar en la cocina desde el jardín de atrás—. Todos los sábados, la misma basura en la tele.

—¿Por qué te estás chupando el dedo, papá? —le preguntó Nelly.

—*Bola de Nieve* —respondió su padre con cara de dolor.

—¿Ya has vuelto a meter el dedo entre los barrotes de la jaula del conejo? —dijo la madre—. ¡Pero si ya sabes que a *Bola de Nieve* solo le gusta Nelly!

LOS CRERK

Era cierto. El conejo de la familia Morton en realidad era de una sola persona: Nelly.

Era blanco como la nieve y suave como una pluma, y vivía en el cobertizo del patio con derecho a excursión diaria al jardín, cortesía de su jaula portátil.

Parecía el conejito más mono y adorable del mundo, pero tras esa naricilla tan graciosa y esos suaves bigotes acechaba un auténtico asesino con dos afiladísimos dientes capaces de partir en dos una zanahoria de acero puro.

Nelly no sabía por qué *Bola de Nieve* la había elegido como su única amiga en el mundo, pero vaya... Si eso hacía que Asti se pusiera celosa, mejor que mejor.

El padre de Nelly lanzó una mirada lastimera a su mujer y se fue cojeando hacia la cocina (siempre cojeaba cuando quería dar pena).

—¿Y ahora por qué cojeas? —le preguntó la madre—. ¡No me vendrás en serio con que el conejo te ha puesto la zancadilla!

—A lo mejor *Bola de Nieve* lo ha cogido en brazos, le ha dado varias vueltas en el aire... ¡y luego lo ha despachurrado contra el suelo! —se echó a reír Nelly.

Su padre suspiró.

Si lo que buscaba era compasión, estaba claro que se encontraba en el lugar equivocado, a la hora equivocada y con la gente equivocada.

LOS GREEK

Con la llegada de Asti, la balanza se inclinó un poco más a su favor.

—¡Oooh, pobrecito! —exclamó Asti nada más ver la cara de angustia de su padre.

No iba a dejar pasar la oportunidad de ganar unos puntos con él, así que se lanzó corriendo a abrazarlo mientras Nelly gruñía por lo bajo.

—¡Qué horror! ¿Es una herida muy profunda? —preguntó Asti en plan dramático—. ¿Qué te ha pasado?

—*Bola de Nieve* —logró responder su padre, armándose de valor.

—Odio a *ese* conejo —soltó Asti, enfadada—. Deberíamos librarnos de él antes de que asesine a alguien.

Nelly miró a su madre.

Niñera de monstruos

Su madre miró a su padre.

Y todos miraron a Asti.

Para ser una chica con tan poca imaginación, esta vez se había superado.

Asti intentó dar marcha atrás:

—Bueno, no me refiero a que vaya a asesinar-asesinar de verdad. Pero ¿y si muerde a alguien y le contagia la mixomatosis? Entonces ¿qué?

No convenció a nadie.

—¡Vale, me rindo! —suspiró Asti, fulminando a su padre con la mirada—. ¡Pues que sepas que es solo un mordisquito de nada y, además, deberías ponerte de mi parte porque yo me he puesto de la tuya!

Hecha una furia, corrió escaleras arriba a ponerse un poco más de brillo de cereza en los labios.

Nelly miró el reloj.

Tenía que marcharse ya.

—Volveré poco después de las ocho —dijo mientras escribía el número de teléfono de los Grerk en un *post-it* de color rosa y lo pegaba en el espejo de la entrada—. ¿Podéis pedir una *pizza* picante con guindillas ardientes para mí, por favor? ¿Y un poco de pan de ajo para mantener a raya a Asti?

—Deja de meterte con tu hermana —gruñó su madre—. Y no te olvides de dejar apuntado el teléfo...

LOS GRERK

—Lo he pegado donde siempre —dijo Nelly antes de coger su abrigo del perchero y abrir la puerta de entrada.

—¡Ojalá un monstruo asqueroso de doce cabezas te coma entera! —le deseó Asti desde lo alto de la escalera con una risita de lo más tenebrosa.

—Se les pasa el hambre en cuanto les hablo de ti —sonrió Nelly.

Asti se quedó pensativa. Su hermana había vuelto a dejarla en el sitio con una de sus típicas «nellyadas». Antes de que tuviera tiempo siquiera de levantar un pie para patalear, Nelly ya había cerrado la puerta a su espalda y había salido triunfante al jardín.

—¡Cochambrófila! —reaccionó por fin Asti..., demasiado tarde, como siempre.

CAPÍTULO 3

Para Nelly, cuidar monstruos era la oportunidad de ser como su jersey: distinta.

Sobre todo, distinta de su hermana Asti.

La vida puede llegar a ser una auténtica «mismidad» cuando tienes una hermana gemela. Todo el mundo espera que seas la mitad de una misma persona, que lleves la misma ropa, que hagas las mismas cosas, que sientas lo mismo.

Todos sacaban las mismas conclusiones sobre las dos, cuando Nelly no se parecía en absoluto a su hermana Asti (vale, se parecían físicamente, pero en todo lo demás eran como la noche y el día).

Nelly no temía a los monstruos.

Asti, sí.

A Nelly, los monstruos le parecían encantadores.

A Asti, no.

A Nelly no le importaba dar la mano, o la pata, a alguien con siete dedos.

A Asti, sí.

A Nelly le encantaba jugar con cualquier criatura de largos tentáculos colgantes y ventosas en la frente.

A Asti, no.

LOS GRERK

Los monstruos eran la especialidad de Nelly, lo tenía muy claro.

Solo seis meses después de poner su anuncio en el periódico local, la calle Dulce y toda la urbanización Montelimar se habían convertido en su territorio particular como canguro de monstruos.

Y no los cuidaba por dinero. Lo hacía sobre todo por echar una mano, y también por lo emocionante que resultaba.

Porque, cada vez que había cuidado a un monstruito, siempre había acabado metida en una aventura genial, y estaba segura de que aquella tarde no sería diferente.

La calle Dulce, donde vivía Nelly, era muy larga. A primera y última hora del día estaba muy transitada, pero por las tardes se volvía mucho más tranquila.

En general, toda la urbanización Montelimar era muy agradable, especialmente los fines de semana, cuando la gente cambiaba los coches por máquinas cortacésped.

Era una urbanización muy agradable, respetable, segura y también muy limpia y ordenada, dividida en pequeñas parcelas con jardines bordeados por árboles... un poco raros.

Lo de los árboles y su extraña poda había sido objeto de muchas discusiones aquel invierno.

Un frío día de febrero, Nelly había visto cómo un jardinero-cirujano vestido con un chaleco naranja fluorescente cortaba todas las ramas de los árboles con una sierra mecánica.

Por lo visto, eso es lo que significa «podar»: dejar los troncos pelados, sin una sola rama.

Incluso ahora, bien entrada la primavera, camino del número 55 de la calle Dulce, Nelly ponía en duda los resultados de aquella cirugía-jardinera.

Básicamente, los árboles ya no parecían árboles. Sin sus ramas, solo con algún que otro palito muy fino que había brotado del tronco, parecían brochas de afeitar gigantes.

Nelly pensó en ir a protestar a Greenpeace, pero al final decidió que estarían demasiado ocupados salvando ballenas.

niñera de monstruos

Doce brochas de afeitar más adelante, Nelly empezó a fijarse en los números de los portales de la calle. El 55 era un número impar, lo que significaba que, para esta visita monstruosa, no sería necesario cruzar la calle.

Echó un vistazo por encima de los muros de los jardines por los que iba pasando. La primera placa dorada en la que se fijó tenía el número 73.

Aún le quedaban nueve casas para llegar.

«Con escamas, cuatro orejas y dos cabezas. Sí, seguro que así son los Grerk. O puede que tengan tres cabezas...», iba pensando Nelly.

Para ella, ese era uno de los mejores momentos de su trabajo como niñera: intentar adivinar cómo sería la familia de monstruos antes de conocerlos en persona (o, mejor dicho, en monstruo).

Pasó por delante del número 63, el 61, el 59, el 57... Y llegó al 55.

A veces, el color de las puertas de las casas daba una pista sobre sus habitantes. «Cuatro ojos», se dijo Nelly. «¡Las puertas moradas siempre quieren decir que quienes viven ahí dentro tienen cuatro ojos!».

Se detuvo ante la verja del jardín, se ajustó la goma del pelo y se planchó el jersey con las palmas de las manos. Para Nelly era muy importante causar buena impresión.

Como también lo era ser puntual.

Miró el reloj. Las 17 horas, 59 minutos y 47 segundos.

Esperó pacientemente durante tre-
ce *segundos*, avanzó hacia la puerta
principal y apretó con fuerza el timbre
amarillo mostaza, que sonó como una
especie de gorgoteo: *glogloglo-glup*.

«Cuatro ojos, ¡segurísimo!», sonrió
Nelly.

CAPÍTULO 4

Justo cuando separó el dedo del timbre, se oyó un aterrador rugido de lobo que procedía del interior de la casa.

Sin embargo, Nelly esperó tan tranquila.

Un cerrojo se descorrió, una cadena se liberó de su soporte y la puerta morada por fin se abrió, aunque solo una rendija, con un sonoro crujido.

Nelly levantó la vista.

Un ojo rosa del tamaño de una cebolla la miraba desde arriba con gran curiosidad.

Más abajo, Nelly encontró un segundo ojo.

Siguió bajando y bajando y empezó a contar.

Uno, dos, tres..., cuatro ojos rosas en fila, como las luces de un semáforo, situados en una enorme cabeza de color verde repollo que salía, como un gigantesco chupa-chup, de una camisa blanca... ¡con corbata!

Nelly mantuvo la calma y los finos labios de anfibio del monstruo se transformaron en una amplia sonrisa de bienvenida.

LOS GRERK

—¿Eres Nelly, la niñera de monstruos? —preguntó con un agudo chirrido aquella boca llena de dientes.

—¡Sí! —respondió Nelly, dando un saltito hacia atrás al ver asomar por la rendija de la puerta una segunda cabeza con dos lenguas colgantes de color naranja... que iban directas hacia sus rodillas—. Y ustedes deben de ser los Grerk.

De pronto se desató un frenesí de chirridos mientras los cuatro ojos de la parte superior intentaban controlar las dos lenguas de la parte inferior.

Nelly se quedó a cierta distancia, mirando con interés cómo la puerta se cerraba, se volvía a abrir, se volvía a cerrar...

43

Cuando se abrió por tercera vez, lo hizo de par en par...

Había dos monstruos en la entrada. Eran altos, verdes y anfibios, y uno de ellos llevaba en brazos a un monstruito que no paraba de moverse.

—Perdona, Nelly —chirrió el Grerk que aún tenía sus cuatro tentáculos libres—. Espero que nuestro precioso bebé no te haya asustado. Se pone muy nervioso cuando ve gente nueva. Por favor, deja que nos presentemos. Yo me llamo Scroot; esta es mi mujer, Pummice, y este es nuestro pequeñín, Glug.

Nelly dio un paso adelante y le tendió la mano a Scroot, que se la estrechó amablemente entre dos de sus viscosos tentáculos.

LOS GRERK

—Encantada de conocerles —dijo, e interpretó aquellos diez ojos parpadeantes y aquellas dos lenguas colgantes como una invitación a entrar en la casa.

Nelly siguió las puntas de las colas verdes y llenas de escamas de los Grerk mientras serpenteaban por el pasillo, y pasó por delante de una mesa de trabajo llena de rollos de papel pintado morado... y peludo.

Definitivamente, aquel era el pasillo más raro que Nelly había visto en su vida.

Las paredes eran oscuras (y también peludas), el suelo era claro (aunque sin pelo), los zócalos eran rosa fosforito y en el techo había un barullo arremolinado de colores amarillo, verde y marrón.

—¡Cuidado con el cubo! —rechinó Pummice mientras guiaba a Nelly hacia el interior de la casa—. ¡Estamos en plena reforma!

Nelly miró hacia abajo y vio un gran cubo morado lleno hasta los topes de una sustancia viscosa de un tono verde guisante.

—Perdona por el desorden —chirrió Scroot.

—No hay nada que perdonar —dijo Nelly, esquivando el cubo—. Yo también estoy pensando en cambiar un par de cosas de mi habitación.

—Ah, pues si necesitas un poco de papel pintado para la pared, ¡tenemos un montón de rollos de sobra! —sonrió Scroot.

—Me temo que no soy lo bastante fuerte como para pegar un papel tan pesado —dijo Nelly, que sospechaba que un *solo* rollo de aquel papel pesaría tanto como un perro lanudo talla XL.

—Oh, lo único que necesitas es un poco de pegamonstrumento de secado rápido... —empezó a chirriar Pummice señalando hacia el cubo.

—¡... y una *buena brocha!* —completó la frase Scroot.

Nelly sonrió y siguió a los Grerk hasta el salón.

Allí se encontró con otra habitación en completo desorden.

Había latas de pintura amarillo limón con lunares negros apiladas junto a la ventana. Las paredes blancas estaban embadurnadas a trozos con muestras pegajosas de pintura rosa y marrón. Y una gran franja de papel peludo pegado chapuceramente asomaba por detrás de uno de los dos sofás. Bueno, Nelly pensó que se trataba de sofás... Era difícil saberlo, porque todos los muebles del salón estaban envueltos en papel de plata.

—Es para protegerlos —rechinó Pummice.

Cuando Nelly se sentó en uno de los sofás, el papel de aluminio crujió.

Luego se quedó mirando aquellas paredes que esperaban su decoración definitiva.

—No acabamos de decidirnos si ponerlas peludas o viscosas —chirrió Scroot—. Llevamos varios días con la reforma y necesitamos un descanso. ¡Estamos tan contentos de que hayas venido a cuidar a nuestro chiquitín!

—Es un placer —sonrió Nelly.

Pummice se sentó en el otro sofá, le dio un besito en la nariz a Glug y rechinó:

—¿A que es un horrorcito?

Scroot se acomodó junto a su mujer y le pasó tres tentáculos por los hombros.

Nelly volvió a sonreír educadamente y se tomó su tiempo para analizar las características de los tres monstruos que tenía delante.

Allí había algo que no encajaba...

CAPÍTULO 5

lug parecía tan distinto a Pummice y a Scroot que costaba creer que fuera hijo suyo.

Para empezar, tenía dos ojos en vez de cuatro, dos lenguas en vez de una y seis patas en vez de dos. Tenía pinta de cachorrillo con patitas de araña, incluso llevaba un lazo azul en la cabeza. Ah, y no paraba de menear sus cuatro colas.

Sí, las diferencias entre Glug y sus padres eran más que llamativas.

Pummice le dio un achuchón antes de dejarlo en el suelo con mucha delicadeza, y a continuación se cruzó de tentáculos mientras observaba cómo Glug se acercaba a Nelly babeando con sus dos lenguas.

—¡Le gustas! —rechinó—. ¡Nunca le había visto mover tan rápido sus colitas!

Nelly se bajó del sofá y se puso de rodillas en el suelo para recibir a Glug con los brazos abiertos.

Glug era grande para ser un bebé, como del tamaño de una cabra. ¡Y cómo lamía! Nelly cerró los ojos y apretó los labios, pero daba igual hacia dónde girase la cabeza. Siempre había una lengua dispuesta a darle un lametón de bienvenida.

LOS GRERK

No quisiera ser entrometida, pero...
—comentó entre lametazo y lametazo—... Glug no se parece mucho a
ustedes...

Los ocho ojos-cebolla rosas de
Pummice y Scroot parpadearon un
instante..., antes de que sus bocas
de anfibio rompieran a reír escanda-
losamente.

—¡Pues claro que no se parece a nosotros! —soltó Scroot entre chirriantes carcajadas—. Glug no es un Grerk..., ¡es un querro! ¿Los humanos no tenéis querros en vuestras casas, Nelly?

Mientras Glug utilizaba una de sus lenguas como brocha para extenderle saliva por toda la cara, Nelly se dio cuenta de su error y también se echó a reír:

—¡Nosotros tenemos «perros», no «querros»!

Cuando se recuperó de la risa, decidió que ya la habían babeado bastante por hoy, así que apartó un poco a Glug y volvió a sentarse en el sofá envuelto en papel de plata mientras se secaba la cara con la manga del jersey.

LOS GRERK

Al darse cuenta de que la fiesta se había acabado, Glug se fue a buscar a otro que le hiciera caso.

Correteó por el suelo, se subió al regazo de Pummice y se puso boca arriba, a la espera.

—Le encanta que le hagan cosquillas en la barriga, ¿verdad que sí, espantito mío? —rechinó Pummice, aplicándose a la tarea con tres de sus tentáculos.

Nelly sonrió, pero estaba llena de dudas.

Era la primera vez que cuidaba de una mascota de monstruos.

—No creas que Glug es un querro cualquiera, Nelly... —chirrió Scroot—. Su pedigrí es exquisito. ¡Pura raza

55

Peonza de Oro! ¡Con decirte que ha sido Megacampeón de Horribilidad en Gruñidos durante tres años seguidos!

—Y mañana volverás a ganar otra vez en el campeonato, ¿verdad, horrorcín? —rechinó Pummice, regalándole una sesión extra de cosquillas en su panza peluda—. Vamos a comprar a nuestro Glugito bonito un precioso lazo nuevo y un collar bien brillante para la competición de mañana, ¿eh?

Nelly no sabía qué decir.

Tenía claro que una sorpresa acechaba tras cada puerta de la casa de un monstruo, pero nunca se había imaginado cuidando querros.

Pummice cogió a Glug del suelo, lo levantó y se lo pasó a Nelly, que sonrió con cautela.

LOS GRERK

—Debemos irnos ya, Nelly, o si no, nos cerrarán las tiendas —chirrió Scroot—. Tenemos que comprar algo de comida especial para querros con pedigrí exquisito. ¿Te importa que te demos un par de instrucciones antes de irnos?

—Por supuesto que no —dijo Nelly, y siguió obedientemente a Pummice y a Scroot hasta la cocina.

Allí, todo estaba limpio e inmaculado..., aunque los muebles eran rosa y verde chillón a rayas.

Scroot alzó un tentáculo para abrir la puerta de un armario y, con ayuda de sus ventosas, cogió una enorme lata de estofado de mocodrilo.

—Es muy importante que le des la cena a Glug a las siete. Los querros de competición como él siguen una dieta y unos horarios muy estrictos. Recuerda, Nelly, a las siete en punto. Ni antes, ni después.

Nelly se volvió a mirar a Glug, que jadeaba a sus pies.

—Me acordaré —prometió—. ¿Pueden dejarme un abrelatas?

Plummice hundió un tentáculo en un cajón y dejó el abrelatas sobre la lata de estofado de mocodrilo.

Desde que había visto la lata, Glug no había parado de menear sus cuatro colas como loco. Nelly dedujo que le encantaba el estofado de mocodrilo y le dijo sonriendo:

—Más tarde, Glug, más tarde. Venga, ¡vamos a jugar al jardín!

LOS GRERK

—A Glug le encanta que le lancen palitos —rechinó Pummice mientras metía la punta de un par de tentáculos en una cerradura y abría la puerta que daba al jardín de atrás—. En el cobertizo hay un montón, Nelly. Coge los que quieras.

Nelly le acarició la cabeza a Glug y acompañó a Pummice y a Scroot por el pasillo hacia la puerta principal.

—¡Cuidado con el pegamonstrumento! —exclamó Nelly al ver que los Grerk se acercaban peligrosamente al cubo morado.

—Oh, tranquila. Ya se habrá secado —chirrió Pummice.

Nelly miró dentro del cubo. La pasta viscosa de color verde guisante se había transformado en un sólido bloque.

«¡Increíble!», pensó. «Tengo que echar un poco de esto en los cereales de Asti».

—Volveremos a las ocho, Nelly —rechinaron Pummice y Scroot desde la puerta, agitando todos sus tentáculos a modo de despedida—. ¡No te olvides: estufado de mocodrilo a las siete!

—No lo olvidaré, prometido —dijo Nelly, agitando la mano para decirles adiós.

Los Grerk se alejaron por el caminito del jardín delantero y cerraron la verja tras ellos.

—Bueno, y ahora... ¿cómo voy a entretener yo a un querro durante dos

horas? —murmuró Nelly, algo preo-
cupada.

Al darse la vuelta se topó con Glug,
que no paraba de botar, ansioso.

Las uñas de sus seis patas repique-
teaban contra el suelo como piezas de
dominó revolviéndose sobre una mesa.

—Está bien, Glug —dijo Nelly con
una gran sonrisa—. ¿Dónde están
esos palitos?

CAPÍTULO 6

El jardín de atrás de los Grerk se parecía mucho al de Nelly... si no fuera por los cráteres que se habían formado allá donde a Glug le había dado por ponerse a excavar.

En algunas zonas, el césped parecía más bien un campo recién bombardeado, aunque en otras partes crecían un montón de flores.

Nelly cruzó el jardín, dejó atrás seis dientes de león en flor y se dirigió a la puerta del cobertizo de madera de los Grerk.

Fue fácil entrar.

Solo tuvo que correr un pestillo.

Nelly se asomó con precaución, no fuera a encontrarse con alguna sorpresa.

Y la sorpresa fue que los palitos... ¡de palitos no tenían nada!

Eran palotes, ramas, prácticamente troncos de árboles, unas cosas enormes y pesadísimas fabricadas por una monstruoempresa llamada *Horrojuguetes, S. A.,* y estaban apilados en perfecto orden en una esquina del cobertizo.

Nelly cogió aire, rodeó uno de ellos con los dos brazos, dio un gruñido, después soltó un gemido y tiró con todas sus fuerzas.

LOS GRERK

Tras ella, las cuatro colas de Glug se movían frenéticamente. El querro estaba encantado.

El «palito» pesaba una tonelada y media, y cuando Nelly intentó levantarlo y ponérselo al hombro, resoplando y cada vez más colorada, le pareció tan grande como un poste de la luz.

A Glug se le salían los ojos de la emoción, y enseguida empezó a botar sobre sus seis patitas de araña, como si fuera un yoyó.

Nelly salió del cobertizo andando hacia atrás. Acababa de descubrir que era mucho más fácil arrastrar aquel armatoste que llevarlo a cuestas.

Ya sobre el césped, se preparó como si fuese una levantadora de pesas: cara de esfuerzo, postura en cuclillas y palmas de las manos sobre el tronco, lo más alejadas posible la una de la otra.

Glug seguía brincando como loco, con sus dos lenguas naranjas colgando, esperando ansioso a que Nelly le lanzara el «palito».

Nelly lo miró como pidiendo disculpas y dejó caer el tronco justo a sus pies, como un peso muerto.

—Cógelo —le dijo al querro, casi sin aliento.

Glug se quedó parado. No entendía nada. Este era un juego distinto al que estaba acostumbrado. Ladeó la cabeza, volvió a botar como un yoyó dos o tres veces y, al final, soltó un

aullido de lobo y echó a correr directo hacia el palo.

Clavó sus colmillos en él y empezó a agitar la cabeza de un lado a otro tan deprisa que sus dos lenguas naranjas parecían una sola.

En un abrir y cerrar de ojos, entre gruñidos babeantes, Glug dejó el tronco convertido en serrín.

Nelly se quedó de piedra al ver aquello. ¿Qué podrían hacer con ella semejantes colmillos si al querro le entraba hambre antes de tiempo?

Giró la muñeca y miró el reloj.

Las 18:45.

—Solo falta un cuarto de hora para el estofado de mocodrilo... —suspiró, algo más tranquila—. ¡Buen querrito, Glug! ¡Querrito guapo! —dijo dándole una palmadita en la cabeza.

Glug se puso a revolcarse entre el serrín, aunque enseguida ladeó la cabeza y miró hacia el cobertizo. Ahora entendía el juego y quería repetir.

Nelly se agachó a su altura y le rodeó el cuello, agotada.

—Lo siento, Glug. Estoy molida. Juguemos a otra cosa, ¿vale?

El querro empezó a dar vueltas a su alrededor mientras ella se devanaba los sesos pensando en cómo entretenerlo un ratito más.

«¡Ya lo tengo!», se dijo de pronto. «¡Yo mando cosas, y que Glug las haga! Si es un querro de competición, tiene que ser bueno obedeciendo órdenes, ¿no?».

Nelly se puso muy tiesa, frunció el ceño y señaló claramente el suelo con su recién elegido «dedo de las órdenes».

—¡Siéntate! —le mandó al querro—. ¡He dicho que te sientes!

Pero Glug se limitó a lamerle el dedo de las órdenes con sus dos lenguas y a botar sobre sus seis patitas de araña.

Nelly retiró el dedo a toda prisa y se lo pasó bajo el brazo para quitarse las babas.

—¡Rueda! ¡Rueda por el suelo, Glug! —exclamó, y esta vez utilizó la «mano de las órdenes», con los cinco dedos.

El querro desplegó al instante sus lenguas naranjas, dispuesto a darle otro lametón, pero en esta ocasión Nelly fue lo bastante rápida como para escapar de sus babas.

Puso la mano sobre la cabeza de Glug y volvió a repetir la orden mientras hacía una serie de gestos imitando el movimiento de rodar como una croqueta.

Glug se la quedó mirando con mucho interés... y luego se levantó de un salto dispuesto a premiarla con otro lametón.

Nelly se apartó. Aquello no funcionaba. Para nada.

Se rascó la cabeza.

Si «siéntate» no había funcionado y «rueda» tampoco, estaba práctica-

70

mente segura de que «levanta la pata» sería una pérdida de tiempo total. Y esas eran las únicas órdenes perrunas que conocía.

Rastreó todo el jardín con la mirada y al final se detuvo en el cobertizo. Por allí no había ninguna pelota para lanzarle a Glug, así que quizá debería intentarlo con otro «palito». Aunque, por otro lado, quizá no.

La sola idea de tener que levantar otro armatoste de aquellos le daba agujetas.

Nelly miró a Glug y volvió a rascarse la cabeza.

Los Grerk habían dicho que Glug era un «Peonza de Oro», y eso solo podía significar una de estas dos cosas: o bien el premio en los concursos era una peonza... (se imaginó a Glug con una peonza dorada colgando del cuello como si fuera una medalla), o bien...

CAPÍTULO 7

Nelly decidió arriesgarse.

—¡Peonza! —gritó mientras hacía girar en el aire su dedo de las órdenes.

Para su sorpresa, la respuesta de Glug no se hizo esperar. Al momento se sentó a los pies de Nelly y la miró con ese brillo en los ojos típico de los perros (y, por lo visto, también de los querros) de competición.

Con las lenguas colgando y la orden de Nelly aún resonando en sus oídos, Glug hizo girar su cabeza dibujando un círculo completo, 360 grados, primero en un sentido y luego en otro.

Nelly se quedó boquiabierta. ¡Aquello era lo último que podía imaginarse!

—Buen querro... —susurró, arrodillándose y dejando que Glug le babease toda la cara—. ¡Querrito listo!

Emocionado, Glug obsequió a Nelly con unas cuantas peonzas más de propina.

—Y ahora, ¡vamos por tu premio! —le sonrió Nelly, señalando en dirección a la cocina con su dedo de las órdenes—. Vamos, Glug. ¡Estofado de mocodrilo, ñam-ñam!

Glug aulló como un lobo, se levantó de un salto y empezó a menear sus cuatro colas a la vez, loco de contento.

LOS GREFK

«Parece que le encanta el estofado de mocodrilo», pensó Nelly, y cruzó el jardín a toda prisa mientras Glug jugueteaba a mordisquearle los talones con sus dientes afilados como cuchillos.

De camino a la cocina, Glug la adelantó para esperarla junto a su comedero, con la vista fija en la encimera, sin pestañear siquiera.

Nelly cogió el abrelatas, lo puso en el borde de la lata y, al ritmo de cada vuelta que daba, la cabeza de Glug hacía la peonza.

«¡Sí, está clarísimo que le encanta el estofado de mocodrilo!», sonrió mientras esquivaba los hilillos de baba que le caían al querro al oler la comida.

75

Levantó la tapa de la lata y olisqueó con curiosidad su contenido.

Atufaba a una mezcla de pies apestosos y huevos podridos.

Leyó lo que ponía en la etiqueta:

El estofado de mocodrilo
EL QUERRO FELIZ
contiene trozos de mocodrilo
de primera calidad
procedentes de los pantanos
más pestilentes, aliñados
con gelatina de monstrupiente
de cascabel.
EL QUERRO FELIZ,
la elección de los campeones.

Un producto con denominación de origen.
Consumir antes de septiembre del 3004.

Nelly se tapó la nariz, se agachó para coger el comedero de Glug y volcó la lata dentro.

76

LOS GREHK

Su contenido cayó como una avalancha de huevas de rana.

Nelly puso cara de asco, dejó el comedero en el suelo y dio un paso atrás.

El lazo de la cabeza de Glug subía y bajaba a toda velocidad, y sus colas no dejaban de menearse mientras se zampaba el estofado hasta no dejar ni rastro de él.

Antes de que Nelly pudiera decir «abrelatas», el comedero ya estaba vacío y el querro jugaba a empujarlo por el suelo de la cocina con sus dos lenguas, cada una en una dirección distinta.

Por si acaso, Nelly se subió a la encimera, no fueran a antojársele sus pantorrillas de postre.

Después de cinco babeantes minutos, las dos lenguas de Glug acabaron cansándose del comedero vacío y el querro salió trotando al jardín.

Desde la ventana de la cocina, Nelly observó cómo Glug olfateaba el tronco de una enorme encina, daba tres vueltas a su alrededor y por fin levantaba cinco de sus seis patas. No una, ni dos..., sino cinco patas a la vez, ¡y sin perder el equilibrio!

Nelly lo miró asombrada y también con un poco de vergüenza. Después de todo, Glug estaba a punto de hacer algo muy privado y ahí estaba ella, cotilleando por la ventana de la cocina.

Miró hacia otro lado, pero enseguida le pudo la curiosidad.

¿Cuántos chorritos de pis haría Glug? ¿Uno, dos, siete, veinticinco?

Volvió a mirar hacia el tronco del árbol, pero antes de que pudiera resolver el enigma, el sonido del timbre la hizo volverse.

Nelly miró hacia el pasillo. ¿Serían los Grerk, que habrían vuelto antes de lo previsto?

niñera de monstruos

Tras un momento de duda, no tuvo más remedio que dejar a Glug y sus chorritos para ir a ver quién llamaba. Se secó las manos en el jersey y salió corriendo hacia la entrada.

Cuando pegó el ojo a la mirilla, allí no había ningún Grerk, sino una ancianita de aspecto delicado con falda gris, camisa blanca y una encantadora sonrisa.

Llevaba una cestita de mimbre colgada del brazo izquierdo, y en la mano derecha sujetaba un *sobre* a rayas amarillas y negras.

Parecía completamente inofensiva, así que Nelly abrió la puerta, aunque dejó la cadena puesta.

—Hola —saludó la mujer—. Siento molestar, pero estoy recaudando dinero para la Sociedad de Prevención de la Crueldad contra las Avispas (SPCA). A principios de semana dejé un *sobre* como este en su buzón...

Nelly miró el *sobre* que la mujer agitaba justo delante de su nariz.

—Lo siento, señora, pero es que yo no vivo aquí —le explicó—. Solo estoy haciendo de canguro.

La mujer puso cara de desilusión.

Nelly miró su cestita y vio que dentro solo había un sobre.

Era todo lo que la pobre anciana había conseguido recaudar hasta el momento.

De pronto, a Nelly se le iluminó la cara.

—Espere un momento —dijo—. Creo que ya sé dónde han dejado su sobre los Grerk. ¡Estoy segura de haberlo visto en el salón, sobre la repisa de la chimenea!

A la mujer se le puso una sonrisa de oreja a oreja.

LOS GRERK

—¡Voy por él ahora mismo! —dijo Nelly.

Dejó a la mujer en la puerta y corrió por el pasillo dejando atrás el cubo morado y los papeles pintados peludos hasta llegar al salón.

«¡A los Grerk les deben de encantar las avispas!», pensó al coger el sobre de la SPCA y notar el peso de un montón de monedas.

—¡Lo he encontrado! —exclamó mientras se abría paso entre los muebles forrados con papel de plata, las latas de pintura de lunares y los libros con hojas viscosas—. Estaba en la repisa de...

Nelly se calló en seco.

Al otro lado de la puerta no había ni rastro de la señora.

—¿Dónde se habrá metido? —preguntó confusa en voz alta mientras miraba de un lado a otro en busca de alguna señal de la mujer.

La respuesta le llegó desde la altura de los tobillos.

El sonido de un gemido lastimero hizo que Nelly bajara la vista hacia el camino de entrada, y ahí, en el suelo, tumbada boca arriba, estaba la anciana, y su cesta de mimbre, colgando de un rosal.

Nelly se la quedó mirando, horrorizada, y ahogó un grito. Sobre la camisa blanca de la mujer había seis huellas embarradas de un querro de buen tamaño.

LOS GREEK

¡Glug se había escapado!

—¡Por ahí! ¡Se ha ido por ahí! —dijo la señora medio atontada, señalando hacia la calle.

Nelly salió de la casa de un salto, sorteó el cuerpo desparramado de la mujer y corrió hacia la verja de entrada.

Miró a derecha e izquierda, desesperada, pero ni rastro de Glug.

Con una horrorosa sensación de malestar, volvió tristemente sobre sus pasos y ayudó a la ancianita a levantarse.

—Glug solo estaba jugando —le explicó—. En realidad es un pedazo de pan.

La señora tiró su cesta de mimbre en la papelera más cercana y se fue a su casa tambaleándose.

—¿Qué he hecho? —gritó Nelly, horrorizada, y se sentó hecha polvo en el peldaño de la entrada.

Aunque había puesto la cadena, estaba claro que Glug se había escapado por la rendija de la puerta de entrada mientras ella iba a buscar el sobre. ¿Quién se iba a imaginar que los querros son como de goma?

—Ha sido por mi culpa... —gimió Nelly—. ¿Qué voy a hacer ahora?

CAPÍTULO 8

ejarse llevar por el pánico, eso fue lo que hizo Nelly.

Dejarse llevar por el pánico y correr arriba y abajo por toda la calle Dulce agitando las manos y llamando a grito pelado:

—¡GLUG, GLUG, GLUUUUUUG!

La gente se volvía y la miraba con cara rara.

No había ni rastro de Glug por ninguna parte.

El querro de pedigrí exquisito, el pura raza Peonza de Oro que iba a participar al día siguiente en un campeonato con su collar y su lazo nuevos, había desaparecido.

Aquello era un desastre.

Nelly volvió al número 55 y se derrumbó en el suelo frente al muro del jardín.

Miró el reloj. Eran las siete y veinte. Los Grerk estarían de vuelta en cuarenta minutos. ¿Cómo iba a conseguir que Glug volviera a tiempo? Necesitaba ayuda, pero no podía pedírsela a sus padres. No iban a entender nada sobre querros con cabeza giratoria. Y, por supuesto, tampoco podía confiar en su gemela Asti.

LOS GRERK

Nelly volvió dentro de la casa y sacó su móvil del bolsillo del pantalón.

No estaba todo perdido aún. Llamaría a Gritt y a Lump, sus monstruosos amigos de los números 42 y 93. Si ellos acudían en su ayuda, aún quedaba esperanza.

Gritt y Lump no tardaron mucho en llegar. En cuanto oyeron el lío en el que estaba metida Nelly, las puertas de los números 42 y 93 de la calle Dulce se abrieron a la vez.

Lump fue el primero en tropezar con el cubo morado lleno de pega-monstrumento y, segundos después, Gritt apareció con gran estruendo por el pasillo del número 55.

Encontraron a Nelly en la cocina, completamente histérica.

—He buscado por todas partes —gimió.

Gritt acarició a Nelly con sus tres patas peludas.

—No te preocupes —le dijo—. Glug tiene que estar en algún sitio. Seguro que lo encontraremos.

LOS GRERK

—Tengo una idea —la voz de Lump sonaba como si fuese un sorbido mezclado con un ruido de ventosa—. ¿Por qué no abrimos un par de latas de estofado de mocodrilo? Seguro que Glug las huele a diez calles de distancia. ¡Si con eso no logramos que vuelva, no lo conseguiremos con nada!

Nelly sabía distinguir una buena idea en cuanto la oía. ¡Y esta lo era! De hecho, era aún mejor que una buena idea, ¡era una idea genial!

—¿Dónde guardan los Grerk la comida del querro? —preguntó Gritt.

El dedo de las órdenes de Nelly señaló rápidamente hacia un armario de la cocina.

Gritt lo abrió y pasó su roja pata peluda por el estante de arriba. Con

su único ojo, que estaba en el extremo de una antena, hizo de periscopio por lo alto del armario y confirmó lo peor...

No quedaba ni pizca de estofado de mocodrilo. Nelly había abierto la última lata.

—¡Lo había olvidado! —se lamentó—: Los Grerk dijeron que tenían que salir a buscar comida de querro. Un lazo, un collar y comida de querro, eso es lo que iban a comprar. ¿Y ahora qué hacemos?

Lump y Gritt empezaron a abrir todos los armarios de la cocina, pero no encontraron nada que por su olor jugara ni remotamente en la misma liga que el estofado de mocodrilo.

—No tenemos más remedio que salir a buscar a Glug —dijo Lump—.

LOS GRERK

Yo iré por los números impares. Tú busca en los pares, Gritt. Nelly, tú quédate aquí por si vuelve.

Nelly se quedó dando vueltas por la cocina mientras sus dos monstruosos amigos salían pitando en busca de Glug.

Volvió a mirar el reloj. Ya eran las siete y media. El tiempo pasaba volando. Treinta minutos más y los Grerk volverían a casa con un lazo y un collar nuevos para un querro que no aparecía por ninguna parte.

Lo único que Nelly podía hacer era esperar. Y tener esperanzas.

Desde la ventana de la cocina, miró el jardín. Pensó en el juego del «palito»

y se acordó de aquellas dos lenguas naranjas. En ese momento habría dado lo que fuera por que Glug la volviese a babear de pies a cabeza.

—Acaba de comer, así que pasará un buen rato hasta que tenga hambre. Y a lo mejor ni siquiera así vuelve... —suspiró angustiada mientras fregaba el comedero del querro.

Justo cuando lo estaba dejando en el escurreplatos, escuchó el tintinear del cubo morado, el furioso repiqueteo de unas garras sobre el suelo y el estruendo que produjo la mesa de encolar al volcarse. Los rollos de papel peludo salieron volando por todos lados y un monstruo de seis patas apareció en la cocina corriendo a toda pastilla, pasó entre las piernas de Nelly y se escondió en el armario de debajo del fregadero.

¡Glug había vuelto!

Casi no le había dado tiempo ni a pestañear cuando Nelly volvió a escuchar el ruido del cubo morado, esta vez acompañado del traqueteo de las enormes patas peludas y los tentáculos con ventosas de Gritt y Lump.

—¡Ha vuelto! —exclamó Nelly, emocionada—. ¡Glug ha vuelto a casa!

—Ya lo sabemos —dijo Gritt—. Lo vimos saltando las vallas de las otras casas cuando venía de camino.

—¿Dónde se ha metido? —preguntó Lump casi sin aliento.

Nelly se agachó a la altura del fregadero.

El querro estaba muerto de miedo, con los cuatro rabos entre las patas.

—¡Oh, se ha hecho una heridita en el morro! —se preocupó Nelly.

Gritt y Lump se acercaron para valorar los daños.

—Es solo un rasguño —dijo Gritt.

—Dirás un minirrasguño —matizó Lump.

—¿Quién te ha hecho eso, Glug? —le preguntó Nelly con voz cariñosa—. Tranquilo, no pasa nada. Ya puedes salir. Ya estás en tu casita. Tus amos volverán enseguida y te traerán un lazo y un collar nuevos para que los estrenes mañana en el campeonato.

—Iré a cerrar la puerta, no sea que intente escaparse otra vez —anunció Gritt.

—Yo pondré en orden el pasillo y la entrada —añadió Lump.

—Buena idea —dijo Nelly, y *se* quedó en la cocina, intentando convencer a Glug de que *saliese* de debajo del fregadero.

Cuando Lump y Gritt volvieron, *se* encontraron a Nelly con las manos en la cabeza.

Glug estaba sentado *sobre* las baldosas de la cocina, rascándose por todas partes con *sus* seis patas. Todo *su* pelaje estaba en movimiento, como si estuviera vivo...

¡Glug estaba lleno de pulgas!

CAPÍTULO 9

—¡Madre mía! —exclamó Gritt—. ¡Glug ha estado olisqueando al crucho del número 252!

—¿Qué es un crucho? —preguntó Nelly, angustiada.

—Es como un chucho, pero más mezclado —le explicó Lump.

Nelly no había visto unas pulgas como aquellas en toda su vida. Eran del tamaño de conguitos, con púas como de erizo, saltaban como pelotitas superelásticas... ¡y había cientos y cientos!

Miró el reloj, desesperada.

—¡Solo nos quedan doce minutos para librarnos de ellas! —gritó.

—Si hay algo que odien las pulgas, ¡es el jabón! —dijo Gritt a la vez que cogía a Glug entre sus brazos rojos peludos y lo llevaba corriendo al baño.

Nelly y Lump los siguieron rápidamente.

Nelly vació un enorme bidón de gel en la bañera más grande que había visto jamás, y Lump abrió los grifos y puso el tapón.

Mientras Gritt esperaba a que la bañera se llenase, Glug le plantó un lametazo cariñoso en cada una de sus peludas mejillas rojas.

—¡Le gustas! —sonrió Nelly.

—Vamos, no hay tiempo para tonterías —dijo Gritt, y metió a Glug en el oloroso baño de espuma.

El resultado fue increíble. Las pulgas salían volando como auténticas balas. Volaban del cuerpo peludo de Glug directas hacia el techo y las paredes del baño.

—¡Ha funcionado, Gritt! ¡Ha funcionado, Lump! En cuanto las pulgas notan el jabón, ¡saltan! —se entusiasmó Nelly.

Gritt sonrió y sacó a Glug de la bañera, limpio de pulgas.

—¡Oh, no! ¡Mirad! —exclamó Nelly—. ¡Están volviendo!

Era cierto. En el instante en que Glug salió de la bañera, las pulgas volvieron a pegarse a su cuerpo.

—¡Mételo otra vez en la bañera! —gritó Lump.

Gritt obedeció y las pulgas salieron volando al instante.

—¡Sácalo! —gritó Nelly.

Al momento, las pulgas volvieron a adueñarse de su cuerpo.

—¡Mételo otra vez!

—¡Sácalo!

—¡Mételo!

—¡Sácalo!

Era inútil. Dentro de la bañera todo iba bien, pero en cuanto salía, Glug se

LOS GRERK

convertía en un imán irresistible para las pulgas.

—¿Y si lo llevamos al jardín? —propuso Lump—. ¡Podemos lavarlo fuera, con champú y una manguera!

Gritt bajó las escaleras con Glug y todas sus pulgas a cuestas. Nelly y Lump lo seguían a todo correr.

Gritt dejó al querro sobre el césped mientras Lump, con sus cuatro tentáculos, le echaba champú, lo enjabonaba, le apuntaba con la manguera y lo aclaraba.

Otra vez las pulgas salieron volando de su cuerpo peludo, solo que en esta ocasión se refugiaron en los árboles y arbustos que había alrededor.

Lo malo fue que, igual que antes, en cuanto Glug se sacudió el jabón, las pulgas volvieron a invadirlo.

Gritt meneó la cabeza y gruñó.

Lump cerró sus cuatro ojos e hizo ¡POP! con sus ventosas.

LOS GRERK

Pero Nelly dio un grito de alegría.

—¡Rápido-rápido-rápido! —exclamó—. ¡Tengo una idea! Gritt, lleva a Glug al salón. ¡Vamos a hacer de decoradores!

Gritt y Lump no preguntaron. No había tiempo para explicaciones.

Nelly pasó corriendo por la cocina y cogió un bote de lavavajillas por el camino.

—Necesitamos un cubo. El morado no nos sirve. Hay que encontrar otro, ¡cuanto más grande, mejor!

Gritt le pasó el querro a Lump, salió corriendo al jardín de atrás y volvió con un cubo de basura vacío bajo el brazo.

—¡Perfecto! —dijo Nelly mientras arrastraba los muebles forrados con papel de plata hacia el centro del salón.

Miró el reloj. ¡Solo quedaban seis minutos y medio para que volvieran los Grerk!

—Tenemos que mezclar un montón de pegamonstrumento para empapelar. ¡Rápido!

Lump se hizo cargo al momento.

Volvió a pasarle el querro a Gritt y con un tentáculo abrió seis paquetes de pegamonstrumento, con otro los echó en el cubo de basura, con otro añadió agua y con otro revolvió la mezcla hasta lograr una sustancia viscosa de color verde guisante.

LOS GRERK

«Por más tentáculos que uno tenga, nunca *son* demasiados», pensó Nelly, y le pasó cuatro brochas de encolar a Lump, que empezó a embadurnar las paredes de pegamonstrumento a toda velocidad.

Al cabo de unos minutos, Gritt lo relevó, y para ello tuvo que pasarle a Glug.

Cuando Lump y Gritt se hubieron turnado varias veces, decidieron que ya era hora de dejar al querro en el suelo y ponerse a trabajar de verdad.

Entre los tres se pusieron manos a la obra, nueve manos en total (en realidad, dos manos, tres patas y cuatro tentáculos).

—¡Quedan cuatro minutos! —alertó Nelly.

Las paredes se cubrieron rápidamente del viscoso mejunje verde.

Lump miró con sus cuatro ojos el trabajo de Gritt y apuntó con aire perfeccionista:

—Te has dejado un poquito sin embadurnar por ahí.

—¡Da igual! —exclamó Nelly, apuntando a Glug con el bote de lavavajillas.

Lo apretó con todas sus fuerzas y un chorro de detergente con frescor duradero de monstrulima-monstrulimón se desparramó por el pelaje del querro.

Una vez más, las pulgas salieron disparadas hacia el techo y las paredes, solo que en esta ocasión se quedaron allí, pegadas en el sitio,

¡y todo gracias al pegamonstrumento de secado rápido!

—¡Aún no hemos acabado! —exclamó Nelly, pasándoles a sus amigos las latas de pintura amarillo limón con lunares negros—. ¡A pintar el techo y las paredes! ¡Rápido, rápido!

En un momento dieron una capa de pintura amarilla y salpicaron de lunares negros todas las paredes y el techo. Esta vez Gritt tuvo mucho cuidado de no dejarse ni «un poquito sin embadurnar». La crítica le había dolido, pero se consoló pensando que era lógico que Lump, con sus cuatro tentáculos, tuviera ventaja sobre él y sus tres patas.

Mientras Lump y Gritt se encargaban de colocar el papel pintado, Nelly se puso a secar el pelaje de Glug con un secador de pelo para que quedara como un auténtico querro de competición.

No sabía por qué motivo Glug había vuelto a casa, pero estaba encantada de que lo hubiera hecho. Volvió a agitar el secador frente a su lazo y se agachó a admirar el resultado. Perfecto. Parecía un auténtico campeón de campeones. Excepto por aquella pequeña marca en el morro.

Pero aún tenía arreglo.

—Por favor, ¿me dejas la lata de pintura un momento, Gritt? —le pidió Nelly.

—No me habré dejado un poquito sin embadurnar, ¿verdad? —preguntó él, preocupado.

LOS GRERK

Nelly se echó a reír y negó con la cabeza.

—¡Tú no, pero yo sí!

Con mucho cuidado, metió un dedo en la lata y lo posó en medio de un círculo negro de pintura.

Entonces, con mucha delicadeza, aplicó el dedo sobre el morro del querro, justo en el lugar del rasguño.

—Perfecto. ¡Has quedado como nuevo, Glug!

—¡Misión cumplida! —soltó Gritt con aire triunfal—. ¿Quieres que limpiemos las brochas?

—¡No hay tiempo! —exclamó Nelly—. ¡Más vale que salgáis por atrás y desaparezcáis antes de que vuelvan los Grerk!

Eran las ocho menos un minuto.

—Eso está hecho, Nelly —dijo Lump con un sonoro ventosazo.

—¡Cuidado con el cubo, y gracias por vuestra ayuda!

Lump y Gritt salieron tan deprisa como habían entrado.

Nelly se dejó caer sobre la funda de papel de plata de un sofá y, al momento, Glug hizo lo mismo, con sus dos lenguas colgando.

Nelly resopló, dejó caer los hombros y se dedicó a mirar la nueva decoración que lucían las paredes y el techo del salón de los Grerk.

—Espero que les guste —dijo mordisqueándose el labio, hecha un manojo de nervios.

LOS GRERK

Cuando los Grerk llegaron a casa, dijeron que no les gustaba... ¡Les encantaba!

—Pensé que aquí pegaría algo como con púas que diera sensación de movimiento —dijo Nelly señalándoles la extraña textura del techo y las paredes.

—¡Qué original! ¡Qué extraordinario! ¡Qué creatividad, Nelly! —chirrió Pummice—. Nos has dejado impresionadísimos.

Scroot miró un poco más de cerca:

—¿Me engañan mis ojos, o esas manchitas amarillas y negras se están moviendo de verdad?

—Bueno, sí, la pintura hace ese efecto —dijo Nelly tragando saliva.

—¡Y le has lavado el pelo a Glug! ¡Qué amable! —rechinó Pummice—. ¡Ya está listo para la competición de mañana! ¡No hacía falta que te molestaras!

—Oh, sí que hacía falta, créanme —sonrió Nelly.

Y se quedó unos minutos más en el número 55 para ver a Glug con su nuevo collar brillante y su nuevo lazo dorado.

Por fin, Nelly se despidió de los Grerk y se alejó por la calle Dulce en dirección a su casa.

—¡ERES UN GENIO DE LA DECO-RACIÓN, NELLY! —chirriaron desde la puerta Pummice y Scroot mientras agitaban sus tentáculos, entusiasmados.

LOS GRERK

Nelly *se* dio la vuelta y *les* devolvió *el* saludo.

—¡ASÍ SOY YO! —dijo entre risas, alzando una lata de pintura amarilla con lunares negros—. ¡Gracias por la pintura! ¡Enseguida redecoraré mi habitación!

—¡De nada! —rechinaron los dos Grerk.

Nelly soltó un suspiro de alivio y continuó andando hacia su casa.

«¡Bufff, por un pelo!», pensó.

CAPÍTULO 10

ada vez que Nelly volvía de sus locas y apasionantes aventuras como niñera de monstruos, sentía como si acabara de bajarse de una montaña rusa.

Las paredes, los muebles, las voces de su familia, el sonido de la tele..., todo lo que había en el número 119 era tan tranquilo, reconfortante y normal, que incluso después de la aventura más divertida y *babosa*, para Nelly siempre era un placer volver a casa.

Esa noche, además, le esperaba su *pizza* favorita. ¿Qué se encontraría al llegar? ¿Una corteza fina? ¿Una masa bien gordita?

Lo que se encontró fue el caos.

Asti se había vuelto loca, sin motivo aparente.

Estaba histérica, fuera de control, pataleaba y meneaba los brazos como solo ella sabía hacerlo.

—¡LO VI! —gritaba—. ¡LO VI CON MIS PROPIOS OJOS!

Sus padres intentaban calmarla con un trozo de *pizza* hawaiana con extra de piña. Pero cuanto más insistían en que se lo comiera, más se enfadaba ella.

LOS GRERK

—¡SALTÓ POR ENCIMA DE LA VALLA! ¡POR EL SETO DE LOS VECINOS! ¡ERA ENORME! ¡ESPANTOSO!

Nelly dejó su pizza picante en el plato y escuchó atentamente lo que decía Asti en pleno berrinche. Después de todo, su hermana no solía contar cosas interesantes muy a menudo.

Presintiendo que estaba ante una aliada en potencia, Asti le contó el motivo de su frustración:

—Seguro que tú sabes qué era, Nelly. ¡Uno de esos repugnantes amigos tuyos! Tenía por lo menos diez patas, y era tan grande como un rinoceronte —exageró.

Nelly miró a su madre.

Su madre miró a su padre.

Y los tres miraron el trozo de *pizza* hawaiana.

—¡OS DIGO QUE ESTABA AHÍ FUERA, EN EL JARDÍN, CERCA DE LA JAULA DEL CONEJO! —gritó Asti—. ¡TENÍA DOS LENGUAS NARANJAS Y LO MENOS DIEZ PATAS, Y PEGÓ LA CARA A LA JAULA...! Y... Y... ¡Y LLE-VABA UN LAZO AZUL EN LA CABEZA!

Nelly volvió a mirar *su pizza* picante. Era de masa gordita.

—¡NELLY, TÚ TIENES QUE SABER QUÉ ERA! ¡SEGURO!

Nelly le hincó el diente a la *pizza* y meneó la cabeza muy despacio.

—¿Estás segura de que no era un tejón? —le preguntó a *su* hermana, como quien no quiere la cosa.

LOS GRERK

—¿UN TEJÓN? —chilló Asti—. ¡LOS TEJONES NO SALTAN VALLAS! ¡LOS TEJONES NO AÚLLAN COMO UNA MANADA DE LOBOS!

—¿Y un zorro? —sugirió amablemente Nelly.

Asti terminó de explotar, dio un puñetazo a la mesa que hizo volar su trozo de *pizza* hawaiana y subió a su cuarto pisando fuerte las escaleras.

Su padre recogió el trozo de *pizza* de Asti y añadió algunos trozos de piña a su *pizza* boloñesa.

—Estará cansada —comentó Nelly.

Su madre meneó la cabeza, desconcertada, y acabó preguntándole:

—Bueno, ¿qué tal con los Grerk? ¿Te ha ido bien, cariño?

—Sí, muy bien, gracias —respondió Nelly, pensativa.

Más tarde, antes de marcharse a su habitación a escribir en su monstruoso cuaderno secreto de niñera de monstruos, Nelly se ofreció a llevar las cajas vacías de *pizza* al contenedor de cartón.

A la vuelta, se paró a hablar con un amigo.

—Hola, precioso —susurró—. ¿No tienes nada que contarme?

Bola de Nieve dejó un momento su hoja de repollo, saltó por la jaula y apretó su naricita rosa contra los barrotes.

—¿Por casualidad no te habrás encontrado a un querro llamado Glug, verdad? ¿Y por casualidad no le habrás dado un mordisquito en el morro, verdad? ¿Y por casualidad no serás tú el motivo por el que Glug volvió corriendo a casa, verdad, *Bola de Nieve*?

El conejo dejó caer las orejas hacia un lado y miró a lo lejos a través de los barrotes con aire indiferente.

—¡Te debo una, *Bola de Nieve!* —susurró Nelly con una gran sonrisa.

¡Aquella había sido una de sus monstruaventuras más geniales!

índice